DREAMS AND SHADOWS

DREAMS AND SHADOWS

C. Robert Cargill

HARPER Voyager
An Imprint of HarperCollinsPublishers

A hardcover edition of this book was published in 2013 by Harper Voyager, an imprint of HarperCollins Publishers.

FIRST HARPER VOYAGER PAPERBACK EDITION PUBLISHED IN 2013.

Book design by Paula Russell Szafranski

Images courtesy of Shutterstock © 2012

Library of Congress Cataloging-in-Publication Data has been applied for.

ISBN 978-0-06-219043-7

13 14 15 16 17 OV/RRD 10 9 8 7 6 5 4 3 2 1

For Jessica,

she is everything

ACKNOWLEDGMENTS

The circumstances of this book getting from my hands into yours would not have come about without the efforts and support of a number of incredible people to whom I owe debts I feel I can never truly repay. They are wonderful people, one and all, and I hope, over the years, to find some way to settle our balance.

For Harry Knowles, who tossed me blindly into the sea to let me sink or swim, who often tossed me to the wolves to toughen me up, and who tossed me a rope when I needed it most. For Brian Keene, who asked me why I wasn't doing this and told me that I could.

For all my readers over the years, everyone who has ever sought out my articles, written a letter or tweeted a tweet, for good or for ill (but mostly for the good). For all the editors over the years, too numerous to name, who hired me, poached me, or all around coached me. And for every person who ever fired me from a job or drove me to quit, reminding me what I really wanted to do.

For Paul Gandersman for all the coffee and for helping me find the book's pacing; Ari Marmell for all the coffee and for helping me find the book's structure; Jason Murphy for the scotch and helping me find the courage; Patricia Knowles for slapping Harry every now and again and letting me know I was on the right track; Luke Mullen for being the guy you can call for a favor no matter what the hour and no doubt will at some point help me bury a body. Their early notes all proved invaluable.

For the trickster Diana Gill, who Mr. Miyagi'd me into writing a better book than she found, and the entire team at Voyager: Shawn Nicholls, Dana Trombley, Will Hinton, Adam Johnson, Jessie Edwards, and Pam Spengler-Jaffee. For Simon Spanton, whose enthusiasm proved to be a beacon on the darker, harder nights. For Peter McGuigan, a rock star of an agent who once showed me more swagger in two weeks than I've seen out of most people in a lifetime, Stephanie Abou, and the outstanding team at Foundry. For my manager, David McIlvain, whose advice always clears the static, and to his confidant, Mac Dewey, who was an early believer.

For Scott Derrickson, my writing partner, my friend, and the guy who held the door open for me. He read this before anyone else, made suggestions before anyone else, and believed in this before anyone else. And I am all the better for it. We also make movies.

And for Jessica, who loves her writer, whose writer loves her more than breath, and who loved this story so much she demanded I write it down. She met a boy, she made him a man, and she never let him give up. For all that, this book is truly hers, because without her, none of the people listed above would have ever seen it. And neither would you.

And for the tireless efforts of Deputy So-and-So of the local police department, without whose research this book wouldn't be possible.

DREAMS AND SHADOWS

BOOK ONE

CHAPTER ONE

THE BEAST THAT ABSCONDS
IN THE NIGHT

Once upon a time, there were two people who fell very much in love. They met in a high school library, peeking over tenth-grade French books, his eyes sneaking up from a rather dense untranslated passage, hers waiting perched behind a pair of horn-rimmed glasses. He was a sucker for horn-rimmed glasses. Hearts thundered. Breaths shortened. Stomachs swarmed with butterflies. She smiled and his world stopped.

He stammered, he sputtered, trying to smile back, failing in a train wreck of lips sneering back over teeth. And when his head slumped forward into his book, she giggled, for she knew that he was hers.

From the first words they spoke, they rarely spent a silent moment together. Each shared a passion for conversation—one that drove most around them mad—and it was never hard for them to find something to talk about. Their first date led from a movie theater to the Dairy Queen, on to a slow walk home, talking at length about every aspect of the film—from Ewan the dreamy Scottish actor to the scene in which someone dove into a toilet. He reached down, took her by the hand, each finger tingling as they brushed against her milky white teenage skin. Their gazes locked, tingles spreading from their fingertips, across their hands, up the backs of their necks, down their spines, ending at a curl in their toes.

That's when he felt it. His fingers intertwined with hers; he could feel her trembling like a scared kitten. While he'd noticed it earlier, he hadn't really thought much of it, thinking that she was just cold, a frail leaf shaking in the breeze of the ICE-COLD AIR-CONDITIONING advertised in block letters on the outside wall of the single-screen theater. No. She was nervous; she was scared of screwing this up. And he smiled, for he knew that she was his.

It was a perfect first kiss. He pulled her tight, kissing her as deeply and passionately as he knew how. Years later they would both laugh at the two stupid kids trying their first hand at necking, but in that moment—in each other's arms—it was bliss. Over time they'd get it. And years later on a hot, humid day in April, they stood before a courtyard full of their family and friends, formally announcing to the world, "Till death do us part." And they meant it. Every word.

And with that he took her into his arms, kissing her as deeply and as passionately as he knew how. This time he got it right. Then the preacher announced them to the world. Jared and Tiffany Thatcher.

While they had never lived very far out in the sticks, neither expected to end up downtown in a condominium high-rise built for aspiring yuppies and college kids with rich parents—on the seventeenth floor, with a view that looked out over the lake, onto the southern, hipper part of town. It was expensive, especially with a baby on the way, but worth it. They were buying into the cliché, becoming a bedtime story for little girls, proof that dreams do, in fact, come true, that someday *your prince will come,* and everything else that goes with that.

They didn't mind being a cliché or a bedtime story. Not one bit.

It was a Sunday on which their first and only child was born. He was strong, healthy, and had all the right numbers of fingers and toes. "A perfect specimen of the Thatcher genes," as Jared put it. They had excelled at making a perfect baby; his name, on the other hand, had proved to be a bit of a hang-up. They'd beaten themselves silly trying to think of something clever, something charming, something that perfectly expressed the love they shared. But nothing came. And as the nurse approached them with the birth certificate, they sat huddled together with their beautiful, swaddling-wrapped baby boy, Jared waving her off, asking for a few minutes more.

"Can you believe it?" he asked his wife. "How did we get here?"

They gazed in wonder at their son, lost in memories of that first kiss. That night. That movie. And it hit them. "Ewan," they both said at once. Their eyes locked, Jared taking his wife into his arms, kissing her as deeply and passionately as he knew how. It was perfect. It said everything. *Ewan.* The boy who would change their lives forever.

Ewan Thatcher never cried, he never wailed, he only cooed. And depending on the tone, pitch, and warble, Tiffany knew whether he was hungry, needed changing, or just wanted to be held. He loved to be held, and Tiffany never wanted to put him down. "You're gonna spoil that kid," Jared would say, trying to hide his beaming smile. "No one gets to spend more time in your arms than me."

"You're the spoiled one," Tiffany snarked back playfully. "You had your time. It's his turn now."

It was an uncommonly beautiful evening the night that Tiffany would last set eyes upon her son. All the windows in the house were open, a slight breeze brushing in past the curtains, tickling the skin with butterfly kisses. She thought nothing of the open windows; they were on the seventeenth floor and Ewan could barely roll over by himself.

Tiffany had just put Ewan back down after a late feeding, humming an off-key tune to coax him back to sleep.

And if she were listening, rather than humming, she would have heard the faint, distant sound of skittering claws across polished concrete.

Just outside her window, clinging to the underside of the balcony, was a writhing mass of brown, bulbous flesh—a silently snarling beast with a misshapen head and an uncommonly large brow resting above tiny, jaundiced, bloodshot eyes. Its balding head gripped slight patches of graying hair, wisps desperately combed over concealing the wrinkled flesh beneath. Muscles bulged out in odd places, beset by dripping flab.

Its giant monkey-like arms gripped the edge of the balcony as it writhed in agony at the tuneless sound escaping betwixt Tiffany's lips.

For Dithers, a Bendith Y Mamau, Tiffany's song was the last screeching wail of a strangled animal; the dismal, shrill sound of a pack of harpies swooping down upon their prey. She meant well, but that didn't stop him wincing painfully at each mis-struck note. Dithers flailed against the wall, praying the veil wouldn't fail him and leave him exposed so high up. He held firm, thankful that he was dangling above another balcony and wouldn't have far to fall were she to begin slaughtering a song he actually knew.

He'd heard bad singers in his life, but this mother hadn't a chord in her throat that could strike so much as a single note, let alone string together a melody. She deserved what she had coming to her; she deserved it for what she was doing to music. Reaching back, Dithers checked the squirming leather sack dangling from a strap slung over his shoulder. All he needed was for that suckling beast to return to her bed so he could perform the single most important task of his life.

In his cradle, Ewan drifted into an infant's slumber, the notes of his mother's tune drifting in and out of his formless dreams. Tiffany smiled, knowing she had a good two or three hours more before he would gurgle and coo again. She lingered for a moment, marveling at the wonder in the crib. Her hand stroked the top of his head and he fussed—just a little—before settling back. Her song ended, and she retreated swiftly back to bed, stepping lightly so her footsteps wouldn't wake him.

Dithers breathed deep, squinched tight his eyes, saying a silent prayer. In one fluid motion, he swung back, kicking off the bottom of the balcony, slinging himself around—up and over the bars—before landing graceful as a cat. He glanced around—no one to see him, not so much as a pigeon or an angel this high up tonight. He'd have liked to smile, but the job wasn't over, too much still to go wrong.

Focus. Eyes on the crib.

He darted in through the open door, brushing past the gossamer curtains, giving a cursory glance to ensure he wasn't seen. *No one must know. No one.* But the building was new, its otherworldly inhabitants yet to properly stake their claim to the nooks and crannies of every dark corner. All the better. He didn't want a fight. He just wanted to grab the kid and go. With the kick of his foot, he was perched upon the crib's railing. He took a brief moment—nothing more than an instant—to think about what he was doing, running over the checklist one more time.

Then he reached into his sack with one hand, scooping up baby Ewan with the other.

In one rehearsed motion, he swapped the contents of his bag for the child in the crib. Then he was off, vaulting over the balcony, soaring blindly out into the night below without pausing to admire his own handiwork.

Dithers sailed seventeen stories down, his outstretched arm catching the trunk of a tree, swinging him, spiraling around, leaving a candy-cane scratch in the bark. His feet had barely touched the ground before he tore off into a full run, making his way behind a building, out into the darkness. In the sack behind him, enjoying the bumpy ride in a cushioned bag, a groggy Ewan smiled and cooed.

He would never see his mother again.

Seventeen stories up, the curtains still rustled. Beyond them, in the crib, a child looking remarkably like Ewan lay in identical pajamas. Spattered with vomit and feces, reeking of the thick smell of swamp rot, the child fussed, uncomfortable on the cozy mattress. There wasn't the slightest hint of glamour in the air, not a bit of mountain laurel on the breeze. It was about as awful and antiseptic a place as he'd ever been. And so he began to scream.

Tiffany shot up out of bed as if it were on fire, tearing away the covers, running full speed toward the baby's room. *Something was wrong. Very wrong.* For a baby who never made a noise louder than a cough to wail like that, it had to be a matter of life and death. She careened around the corner, stockinged feet slipping on the hardwood floor, arms flailing like a windmill to keep her balance, as she slid to a stop next to Ewan's crib. The changeling shrieked and it cried and it screamed its little head off, the sound pushing in on her inner ear as if she were twenty feet underwater.

Reaching in to pick up her child, she stopped, her hands hovering above the baby. *This isn't right,* she thought. "What's wrong, sweetie?" she asked. "Tell Mommy what you need." But the changeling continued its hellish squeal. Tiffany peered closer, her eyes trying to make out its features in the dark as she reached in, once again attempting to pick up her child.

Then the smell hit her, a rotting, fetid stench like week-old garbage littered with animal corpses, left to sweat in the humid Texas heat. She shuddered, covering her nose with the back of her hand to keep from gagging.

Looking again, she caught a glimpse of a single, sharp tooth. *Is he teething? Already?* Cautiously, she stuck a finger in his mouth, running it along bleeding gums. The little fiend bit down, sinking a single, jagged, cavity-ridden tooth into his new mother's flesh.

She yanked back her hand, yelping, sticking the bloody finger in her mouth. The screaming stopped and the changeling opened his eyes, gazing upon Tiffany for the first time.

She could see the creature's yellow, catlike eyes—black slits where the pupils should be—glowing in the dark of his crib. And she screamed, terrified of the monster staring back at her. The changeling smiled and—hearing the nourishing fright in his mother's voice—let out a soothed coo.

Tiffany couldn't explain it; she couldn't find the words. Every time she opened her mouth, the story falling out seemed implausible, unbelievable even to her. With the baby wailing in the other room, Jared stared at his wife with a look she'd never seen before. He'd been in the room, examined Ewan a dozen times himself. The baby was fine. Clearly upset, but fine. There were no jagged teeth. No glowing yellow eyes. There was no monster in that crib. But something *was* wrong.

"It wasn't a dream," she said bitterly. "I know what I saw."

He reassured her, putting a sympathetic, worried hand on her arm. "I know you do, baby. I believe you." But he didn't.

"I want to take him to the doctor," she demanded.

"We'll take him. But . . ."

"But don't tell him what I told you?"

"I didn't say that," said Jared.

"You didn't have to."

THE PEDIATRICIAN HAD kind eyes when she burst into tears in front of him. Of course, having only met her a few times before, he had no idea how out of character her hysterics were. And when she finally felt at ease enough to let her secret out, he remained unflappable, even smiling a little. He'd heard all this before; it was never good and rarely ended well.

"Ewan is fine, Mrs. Thatcher. He's a perfectly healthy baby boy." He looked over at the changeling who lay perfectly still, smiling, growing evermore content with his mother's rapidly mounting anxiety.

"I don't understand," she said, trembling. "When I brought him in he was screaming his head off. He'd been screaming for eight hours straight. He's not all right."

"Ma'am, look at him. Whatever was wrong seems to have passed. What's happening is completely normal. It happens all the time. The stress of a new child . . ."

"I know what I saw," she snapped. The doctor didn't flinch.

"I know. I believe you. Which is why I'd like to prescribe something."

Tiffany relaxed for a moment, allowing herself to believe that someone finally understood—but that confidence was eroded when the doctor called Jared into the office to join them. *Postpartum*. That wasn't the scary word. *Postpartum* was fine. *Psychosis* was the word that almost broke her.

The first day was by far the easiest. Tiffany took her medication, spent the day cradling the baby, sitting in the handcrafted rocking chair bought for her by her proud in-laws. The gentle creak of the chair on the floor was a kind reassurance of better times.

Creak. Creak.

The baby was quiet all day. Not a peep. Jared wanted to say something, but he thought better of it. At least Tiffany was at peace, and completely bombed out of her mind on some lithium derivative that cost nearly a day's pay.

Every so often she would examine the baby. No fangs. Blue eyes. Tiny, adorable fingers with a faultless collection of diminutive fingernails. Perfect.

But as dusk set in, the baby *changed*. His brow bent out of shape, bulging a little to one side. A lingering smell wafted in on the breeze. And as the sun crept below the horizon, the baby squinted his yellow eyes.

Tiffany jumped, dropping the changeling square on its head, and the wailing returned. Jared ran into the room, saw his son crying on the floor, his wife standing contemptuously over their child. He froze. Tiffany looked up at him, pointing a crooked finger at the abomination on the floor. "That's not my baby!" she cried. "That's *not* my baby!"

Each day became progressively worse. Soon she couldn't go anywhere near the baby, not to feed him, not to touch him, not to so much as look at him. The crying only worsened, so bad Tiffany eventually retreated into her bedroom, spending hours at a time with a pillow clutched over her head, though it never entirely drowned out the sound. The howls became whispers and soon the whispers carried instructions.

She couldn't talk to Jared anymore. *What was she going to say?* She couldn't tell him what the baby wanted her to do; the creature was becoming something far worse than a mere imposter. There was only one thing that would satisfy it, one thing that would stop its wailing.

She wanted to beat it with a brick, to crush its tiny skull to pieces, wringing the life out of its monstrous little neck, to toss it off her seventeenth-story balcony and watch it sail down into the tree line below. Oh, she dreamed of many dark and devious things in the dead of her sleepless nights—such foul atrocities she dare not speak them aloud lest she lose Jared along with her remaining sanity. The drugs helped a little—kept her fuzzy, unable to hurt her baby—but they couldn't keep out the whispers.

After a week and a half without taking so much as a few steps out the door, the fridge was bare, the cupboards gathering dust. They needed groceries. Jared sat beside his wife, put a hand on her shoulder and asked her if she would be okay. Surprisingly, she sat up, threw her arms around him, kissing him square on the mouth. And for the first time in over a week she smiled. Then she kissed him again, as deeply and passionately as she knew how.

"I'm feeling much better, actually," she assured him. "Really. Go. Just don't be long."

Jared felt as if a fifty-pound weight had been lifted from his life and he strode happily off to the store. And as he returned home and unlocked the door, he heard the familiar creaking of Tiffany in her rocking chair. Normalcy at last. The door swung open, and inside, on the couch, sat the baby, cooing and smiling, happy as ever.

Creak. Creak. Creak. An overturned chair. *Creak.* Horn-rimmed glasses upturned and cracked on the floor. *Creak.* A trickle of blood at the side of her mouth. *Creak.* Images. Flashes. Not enough time to process. There she swung, the most beautiful woman in the world, a rough, blister-dealing rope wrapped around her delicate neck, and tied to a beam above her. *Creak.*

Slender toes three feet off the ground. *Creak*. Lifeless eyes still open, begging for respite.

Creak. Jared fell to the ground beneath his wife. Reaching up, tears already streaming down his cheeks, he gently stroked her foot. *Creak*. He grabbed hold, steadying her, and as he looked over at his son, wondering what he was going to do without her, he caught a glimpse of a wicked smile and tapering eyes. The changeling giggled mischievously. With that, the sun buried its head behind the hills and there was the unmistakable sight of yellow and the shadow of a single jagged tooth.

At once Jared knew what his son had done. He knew what Tiffany had done. Most important, he knew what he had to do.

He rose to his feet, walked over, scooping the changeling into his arms, then methodically made his way down sixteen flights of stairs—the shrieking creature howling the whole way down. Both of them knew how this was going to play out. Jared lived but a block from the lake and he took his time, thinking only of Tiffany—not of the way he'd left her, swinging from the rafters, but the way she'd looked when he first saw her over that French book. He remembered her the way she had looked on that walk. The way she looked at their wedding. The way she looked when they first held Baby Ewan in their arms.

He remembered all the ways he saw her, including the time he saw her last, as he performed his slow and dastardly procession.

The block was quieter than usual, with no one so much as jogging or walking their dog. As he approached the darkening water, he paused, looking down at the child in his arms, but the creature's howls reassured him of his decision. He leaned down to the water's edge, right along a concrete slab that led to a steep, immediate drop-off into the lake, and plunged the changeling underwater. The shrieking stopped, a still quiet filling the coming night. Jared looked down, catching glimpse of something lurking beneath the surface of the water. A shadow drifting slowly toward him.

He peered closer. *Tiffany.* She looked up, slowly rising to the surface, her arms outstretched, hair drifting in the current. But as she approached, her hair darkened, her skin grew pale, her eyes became black orbs swimming lifeless in their sockets. Before he knew what he was looking at, two watery arms took him by the lapels, pulling him headlong into its depths. He struggled, fighting, but could not reach the surface.

Two arms grappled him tightly, a woman holding firm upon his back, swimming them both ever deeper.

Jared was in the cold grip of the depths, his lungs swollen with mossy, alkaline lake water, gasping for a single breath.

The changeling floated helplessly a few feet beneath the surface. A second woman appeared, kicking like a dolphin, flinging herself out of the gloom toward the child above her. She grabbed the changeling, swimming him back to the surface, out into the night air.

"He's ours now," the woman whispered into Jared's ear, her voice audible, without so much as a gurgle. Then came the blackness, hollow, crashing, choking. And with that, Jared Thatcher drowned, sinking slowly to the bottom of the lake.

Above, the pale woman emerged from the water, the changeling still shrieking in her arms, its tormented yowl shattering the stillness. "There, there," she soothed, stroking his grotesque head while her eyes scanned the shoreline for any sign of witnesses. She smiled. "You're home, child. You're home." The screaming stopped and the changeling cooed, smiling up at his new mother. He *was* home. Home for good. And he hungered no more.

CHAPTER TWO

ON THE BENDITH Y MAMAU AND THE CHANGELINGS THEY LEAVE BEHIND

An excerpt by Dr. Thaddeus Ray, Ph.D., from his book *A Chronicle of the Dreamfolk*

The Bendith Y Mamau can smell love, as if it were a tangible thing. They also detest it, for they do not understand it. While they are known to feel familial attachment, the Bendith Y Mamau cannot reproduce, thus they do not mate and never have the need for anything resembling love. It doesn't help that they are amongst God's ugliest creatures. However, that is not to say that they do not possess beauty of some sort.

The Bendith Y Mamau are the world's greatest musicians. They cannot sing a note, their baritone voices more akin to a walrus's bellow than anything else, but with an instrument in their hands they can weave some of the most sensuous, melodic music ever heard. It is music so complex, with such extraordinarily complicated structures, that it transcends normal composition and plays at notes as yet unknown to mortal men outside of the Aboriginal songlines of Australia. Each note contains the very essence of magic and weaves powerful spells that hold sway over emotion and memory. It is this music that fairy communities often use to hold captives, without need of chain or tether, which of course leads to the Bendith Y Mamau's primary function in any fairy community.

Pronounced "ben-dith uh mo-may," a Welsh phrase meaning "mother's blessing," they are the chief child thieves of any fairy court, and the first to whom a community will turn when they desire fresh infants. Each community has its own differing needs, but a thriving, healthy court will often call upon their Bendith Y Mamau to tend to the acquisition of living mortals. Their strength, speed, and agility make them incredible hunters, while their oafish nature gives them a single-minded purpose and focus not found among the more thoughtful races of the fae.

Many myths persist that the Bendith Y Mamau leave behind their own misshapen children, but this simply isn't the case. Each Bendith Y Mamau is born sterile, the result of the unholy mating of fairy and goblin. What brings fairies and goblins together in such a manner is still a secret known only to the fairies and goblins who have participated in such a distasteful procreation, but it is thus far the only known way to produce one.

The children they leave behind during abductions are changelings, the stillborn infant children of unsuccessful fairy unions. When the conditions are not adequate for proper reproduction, whether it be that the child is born out of season or the mother finds herself in a corrupt place ill-suited for childbirth, it is possible for the pregnancy to self-terminate. In such a case, the stillborn child has a chance of becoming a changeling. If the mother feels a sufficient amount of grief or sheds too many tears upon the corpse, the baby may simply come alive, its energies beginning to feed upon the pain and agony of its mother. Changelings are quite dangerous to anyone responsible for birthing one and must be disposed of as quickly as possible.

However, no fairy mothers, no matter how unseelie, will abandon the product of their wombs to the wilderness. Instead these mothers turn to the Bendith Y Mamau, tasking them with disposing of the changeling and returning with a child that they may raise as their own. Fairies, of course, prefer infant children, but Bendith have been known from time to time to dimwittedly return with a child old enough to speak.

A changeling need only glimpse its predecessor for but a fleeting second as they are being switched to take on its likeness. At that point, imprinting ties the changeling developmentally to the original child. To all but its new mother, the changeling will appear in vision, sound, and action as if it were the child it replaced. Something may seem off or weird about it, but rarely will anyone suspect that this is a doppelganger of any kind. A mother, on the other hand, always knows the difference. By the light of day she has only a feeling, but once the sun has fallen and night overtakes the earth, the changeling's true nature is revealed. It is that sudden revelation, and the fear it brings, that allows the creature to feed so easily.

A changeling exists solely by feeding off the physical, mental, and emotional pain of its mother. As long as there is agony, torment, or anguish it will be able to nourish itself. But if a mother remains calm, the child begins to starve and then to wail. It will scream, fuss, and throw fits in hopes of driving its mother half to madness. A mother worried about her true birth child or one already suffering from some bout of depression is best suited to feed such a creature, but any suffering mother will do. Unable to digest real food, a changeling may bite at its mother's breasts or vomit up anything force-fed to it, adding further confusion and worry. Most changelings left in the charge of human parents find themselves smothered, drowned, or exorcised, on the rare occasions when they aren't just abandoned to die alone.

Adult changelings are incredibly rare, as they are very tricky beings to raise; their need for nourishment is only indefinitely sated by the sacrifice of its new mother to a sudden, violent death. The amount of energy released by such a death, especially one at the behest of the changeling, seems to be the only thing capable of keeping such a child alive until it is old enough to consciously torment other victims.

Changelings possess the ability to change their appearance at will, shrouding themselves in glamour to masquerade as someone they've met at least once before, or revealing their true selves to someone other than their mothers. Their natural state appears to be one of twisted mockery of the person they originally replaced. A fully grown changeling will look like an uglier, physically inferior version of their initial counterpart at the same age. Their personalities remain their own, however, and changelings grow up as maladjusted, unusually cruel, hateful creatures who long for nothing more than to make others suffer.

Finally, changelings appear to have some form of eidetic or photographic memory. From the moment they awaken in the body of a stillborn infant, every memory is theirs to keep. It is not uncommon for adult changelings to speak at length about their childhood mothers and lament the fairy mother who first cast them away. Most scholars believe this to be the primary source of the changelings hate and taste for suffering, the psyche's embodiment of a child who so loved its mother that it returned from death, only to be turned away and replaced by another, better child.

CHAPTER THREE

THE BOY COLBY'S
CHANCE ENCOUNTER

Colby Stevens was nothing special. Neither unattractive nor unlikable, he lived a life that had gone relatively unnoticed by even his closest relations. He lacked neither talent nor intelligence—simply opportunity—and it seemed, even at his young age, as if he were destined to live out a life of mediocrity amid the tract-home sprawl into which he was born.

But at the age of eight years and three months, Colby Stevens would make the single most important decision of his life, a choice that would not only forever change *his* life, but alter the destinies of countless others for years to come. He was the most dangerous sort of creature, a wily and precocious child, clever beyond his years, happened upon by the wrong sort of man. But on the eighth year, second month, and twenty-ninth day of that life, he was still a relatively unnoticed burden, seemingly destined for nothing—something which made him a particularly strong candidate for what this stranger had in mind.

Colby had no friends and no prospects to speak of. He was a carrot-topped little boy, a mess of shaggy tresses and freckles, who wanted nothing more than to venture out into the *woods*—an undeveloped plot of land no more than half a mile wide that, to an eight-year-old, gave off the distinct impression of being a forest. Clumps of tangled brush, fallen logs, and the occasional abandoned tire lingered around a copse of trees where Colby imagined all manner of fairy, dragon, and unnamed adventure—rather than the pale stone strip mall everyone else saw waiting in its future.

But today it was a magical forest and Colby couldn't wait to explore its wonders yet again. So he tore down the stairs from his bedroom, his feet slamming the steps. *Thudthudthudthud-thudthudthud.* His hand caught the end of the banister and he swung around, sliding across the hardwood floor in his socks. For a moment he felt as if he were flying.

"What in the happy hell are you doing?!" his mother yelled from the couch. "Can't you see Mommy has a headache?" Colby's head sank low, his ears almost meeting his shoulders. He whispered.

"Sorry, Mommy."

His mother glared at him as he shuffled warily into the living room. She was lying facedown on the couch, her bathrobe tied loosely around her. Sylvia Stevens wasn't an old woman, but she carried herself that way, always ill in the morning, groaning as she moved. At twenty-seven she felt as if she'd seen it all. Married early, kid soon after. She hated every minute of it, and it showed in the premature crow's-feet growing around her young eyes. She reached over for her glass and pulled it to her lips without looking. Dry as a bone. She sighed deeply, frustrated by this latest tragedy, reaching for the orange juice she had at the ready.

"And where are you tearing off to this morning?" she asked, barely paying attention.

"Mommy, it's two o'clock."

"That may be," she said, pouring half a glass of juice, "but where are you going?"

"Out to play in the woods."

"All right. Do you have your watch?"

Colby smiled proudly, as if he'd just handed his mother a report card lined with straight A's. He stuck his arm all the way out, showing her his watch—a gaudy piece of molded plastic crap made in Taiwan, painted to look like a cartoon character from a long-since-canceled television show. He'd gotten it by way of a fast-food kid's meal and considered it his proudest possession. After all, Mommy always looked to see if he had it on. That meant it *must* be special. She smiled, nodded, and put down the orange juice.

"Okay, now I don't want you home till after five, you hear me? Mommy needs her quiet time alone." Sylvia picked up the bottle of vodka next to the juice, filling the other half of the glass with it. Colby nodded. "Now you be careful out there. I don't want you coming home early bleeding from your head, okay? Be safe."

"I know, Mommy. I'll be good."

"You run along now. Mommy needs her shower."

Colby spun on his heel and took off running for the front door. "Bye, Mommy," he yelled without looking back. The door opened, slammed behind him, and that was it; he was tearing off toward the woods, making his way fleetly down the street. He passed the large wooden ROAD CLOSED sign that kept cars from turning onto the dirt road, bisecting the woods into two distinctly different patches, and stopped.

Colby looked back at his house just in time to see a car pulling into the driveway. A well-dressed man in a finely tailored suit stepped out, slowly loosening his tie. There was a spring in his step—an urgency in the way that he walked—as if he couldn't wait for what was behind that door. He knocked, looking both ways as he did. The door opened immediately. Sylvia leaned out, also looked both ways, then pulled him inside by his jacket, the door slamming behind them. Without so much as a thought, Colby turned back to the woods.

There is no place in the universe quite like the mind of an eight-year-old boy. Describing a boy at play to someone who has never been a little boy at play is nigh impossible. One can detail each motion and encounter, but it doesn't make a lick of sense to anyone but the boy. It's as if some bored ethereal being is fiddling with the remote control to his imagination, clicking channel after channel without finding anything to capture his interest for very long. One moment he's aboard a pirate ship, firing cannons at a dragon off the starboard bow before being boarded by Darth Vader and his team of ninja-trained Jedi assassins. And only the boy, Spider-Man, and a trireme full of Vikings will be able to hold them off long enough for Billy the Kid to disarm the bomb that's going to blow up his school. All while Darth Vader is holding the prettiest girl in class hostage. And just in case things get a bit out of hand, there are do-overs.

It's kind of like that, only breathless and without spaces between each word. At one hundred miles per hour.

And that was exactly the sort of play Colby was engaged in as he made his way from tree to tree, a stick in hand, fighting off a pack of ravaging elves and wicked old men, led by a one-handed, shape-changing monster. Colby pointed to the sky, commanding a flight of hawkmen to descend upon the elves to buy them enough time for the cavalry to arrive. He swung his sword and cast spells, fighting off all manner of creatures.

Colby spun, a whirling dervish in jeans shorts and a polo shirt, and struck a deathblow to whatever creature was in his head at the time. Instead of whistling through empty air, the stick stopped midstroke, striking with a dull thud across the very real silk-sash-covered belly of a large, ominous figure—one who had not been standing there a moment before. Colby's eyes shot wide. He was in trouble.

The stranger looked down, his hands resting on his hips, unsure of what to make of the unintentional strike.

He was tall. Not grown-up tall. Abnormally tall. Seven feet of solid muscle upon which rested a jaw carved from concrete, chiseled with scars. His hair, long, black, and as silken as the robes he wore, was pulled back into a ponytail high atop the back of his head. A brightly colored sash looped his waist, a number of ornamental baubles, bells, and buttons completing the garish, almost cartoonish, outfit. The man looked down at the stick still resting on his stomach—which Colby was too frightened to even consider removing—growling softly.

"Hmmmm," he murmured.

Colby froze in place. "Um . . . uh . . . I'm sorry. I'm real sorry. I . . . uh."

The man smiled, shifting to good humor in the blink of an eye. "No need to apologize," he said, bowing. "There was no harm done. In truth, I should be the one apologizing to you. A thousand pardons to you, sir, for I should not have appeared so unexpectedly." He spoke boldly, with the lofty confidence of an actor on the stage, his voice large and resonant, almost echoing off the neighboring trees without seeming to carry very far at all. He possessed an eloquence to which Colby was un-accustomed, one where even the smallest, simplest words and gestures carried weight.

"I'm sorry," said Colby, the man's reply sounding more to him like his mother's sarcasm than an honest apology.

"No," boomed the man, shaking his head. "I am the one who is sorry. I am Yashar. What is your wish?"

Colby had no idea what to make of the strange man, but found him intriguing. At first he thought he might be some sort of pirate, but now that he'd said the word *wish* he was beginning to reevaluate him. "My mommy says I shouldn't talk to strangers," he said. "She says that bad men like little boys with red hair and blue eyes, but I told her that my hair wasn't very red and she said it didn't matter how red it was, just that it was red. Is that true?"

"There are men that like many things. I am not one of them."

"You don't like small redheaded boys?"

The man bellowed a laugh, honestly amused. "No, I am not a man."

"Well, you're still a stranger and I can't talk to you."

"But I told you my name. I am Yashar."

Colby crossed his arms. "It doesn't work that way."

"Well, how do I become anything but a stranger if you won't talk to me?" asked Yashar.

"I guess Mommy or Daddy would have to introduce us."

"What if I told you I wasn't a man, but a djinn?"

"Like the card game?" asked Colby.

Yashar leaned in close, as if to whisper a carefully guarded secret. "No, like a genie." He smiled big and broad with all the reassuring boldness he could muster.

Colby eyed him skeptically, folding his arms. "If you're a genie, where's your lamp?"

Yashar cocked an eyebrow at Colby, displeased but not altogether surprised. He dropped every last bit of pretense. "Look, kid, if I had a nickel for every time I was asked that—"

"You'd be rich," Colby said, interrupting. "My daddy says

that. Well, if you're really a genie, prove it. Don't I get three wishes?"

Yashar turned his head, playing coy for the moment. "Not exactly."

"I knew you weren't really a genie."

"You watch too much television," said Yashar. "That three wishes and lamp garbage, well, it doesn't work that way. It never worked that way."

"Well, how does it work then?" asked Colby with wide, inquisitive eyes.

"Oh, I see: one minute I'm a stranger and you can't talk to me, but when you find out that you might get something out of it you're all ears. I don't know if you're the right child after all." Yashar turned as if he was about to walk away. *One, two, thr—*

"Right child for what?" asked Colby.

"For remembering me."

"I'll remember you! Promise!"

Yashar nodded. "Well, we'll need a little test. Meet me back here at the same time tomorrow. If you remember, you just might be the right child."

Colby lifted the plastic face on his watch, checking the time. It read 3:45. "What'll I get?"

"Whatever you want, my boy," Yashar said with a laugh. "Whatever you want." He spun around, his robes a kaleidoscopic torrent becoming a colorful smear, before vanishing altogether, his sash fluttering alone on the wind, finally folding into nothing. Where he'd been, he was no longer, and left no trace behind to prove otherwise. But his voice whispered into Colby's left ear, gently carried by a breeze over his shoulder. "Tell no one. Not a soul."

Colby stared, dumbstruck, at the empty spot where Yashar once stood. He couldn't believe it, he could have anything he wanted. *Anything at all.* Yashar had said so. This was all so exciting. He turned, forgetting about everything else, and sprinted back home. He ducked, dove and wove about trees, thinking about all the treasures he might ask for. *Would he get only one wish? Is that what he meant? Or could he have anything and everything?* Oh, he hoped he meant anything. Anything at all. Anything and everything. There was just so much to ask for.

Arriving at the ROAD CLOSED sign, Colby stopped dead in his tracks. The man's car was still in the driveway. Colby's watch read 3:47. *Crap.* He wished that the man would hurry up, finish helping Mommy with her headache and leave so he could go home. But he wouldn't get his wish until tomorrow, and the more he thought about it, the more he realized that this would be a rather silly and wasted wish. He would wait, no matter how long an eternity that hour and thirteen minutes might be.

He would wait, because when Mommy said five o'clock, she meant it.

CHAPTER FOUR

THE TEN THOUSAND BOTTLES OF THE FISHMONGER'S DAUGHTER

Translated from fragments unearthed midway through the twentieth century, "The Ten Thousand Bottles of the Fishmonger's Daughter" appears to have, at one time, been collected as one of Scheherazade's many tales presented in Burton's *The Book of a Thousand Nights and a Night*. However, at some point it fell into disuse and doesn't appear in any complete subsequent copies. Some scholars argue that this is simply a local tale added by an unscrupulous scribe meaning to include his own work in such a respected manuscript, a common practice of the time and one of the problems Gutenberg sought to eradicate with the invention of his printing press. Others argue that it is a lost folktale that became unfashionable, failing to espouse the beliefs of Islam, as many *Nights* tales do. Perhaps the best argument against its inclusion as a true *Nights* story is that it does not portray the sultan in a good light, something contrary to Scheherazade's ultimate goal—that of appeasing her murderous sultan husband. It is included here for the sake of completeness and should not be considered in actuality to belong directly in *Nights*.

Excerpt from *Timm's Lost Tales: The Arabian Fables* by Stephen Timm

Once upon a time there lived a very selfish djinn. While he was one of the most powerful and clever of his kind, he had become infatuated with the lifestyle of man. He would seek out men of this world and grant them wishes, be it great wealth, power, or a multitude of women, and in return he would ask them one simple favor: to make a wish that in no way benefited them directly. These men would often think of wondrous, selfless ideals—feeding the poor, sheltering the homeless, curing the sick. But all the while the djinn had been seeding them with notions that he was in some way trapped or poor or suffering. To each man he told a different tale and often each man—hoping to further gain his favor—would grant the djinn some creature comfort with his spare wish. In this way the djinn amassed such wealth that it began to rival the sultan's own. This estate afforded him a great many wives, all of whom he loved very much, each spoiled and pleasured in a way no other harem was ever spoiled. This djinn had a good life, one he felt he had earned many times over.

But in this very same kingdom, at this very same time, lived a very selfish sultan. Though the most powerful and respected man of his day, he had grown comfortable with his status and with all of his worldly things. And when he heard about the growing wealth of the djinn, the sultan grew nervous. Soon this djinn's wealth would eclipse his own and he might one day claim himself to be sultan, ruler of all he surveyed. As far as the sultan was concerned, this djinn was one wish away from stealing everything that was rightfully the sultan's—all of which was bequeathed to him by Allah upon his birth. And as no djinn was going to take away a birthright gifted by Allah, the sultan summoned together his wisest viziers to hatch a plan to put this djinn squarely in his place.

For days the viziers talked it over and could come to no agreement. Some thought they should put the djinn's women to the sword and burn his estate. Others, fearing reprisal, thought they should only *threaten* to put his women to the sword and burn his estate. Still others thought the sultan should absorb the lands and estate as his own, by the will of Allah. But none of these options truly protected the sultan and his kingdom from possible reprisal—for while the sultan's army was mighty, djinn were numerous and there was no telling how many would come to the aid of one of their own.

It was the sultan's wisest vizier, a man whose name is no longer known to us, who sat silent for three days and three nights, letting the other men talk themselves hoarse before speaking up. And when he did, there was not a voice left in the room to contradict him. "You waste your time with talk of force and threats," he said, condemning his fellow advisors. "If you wish to best a man, whether in warfare or in guile, you do not confront his strength. You play upon his weakness." And with that he laid out his plans to humiliate the djinn and leave him no longer a threat to the sultan. But the vizier demanded a price from the king—albeit a small one—for it is said that a djinn can sense desire in the heart of a man and it was essential to the plan that the vizier be given a reward.

He asked, humbly, for the hand in marriage of the mute virginal daughter of a fishmonger, said to be the most beautiful girl in all the kingdom. The sultan himself had considered adding her as one of his many wives—for what man does not want a silent wife, especially one so beautiful? But this request he granted to his vizier, for the vizier's cunning was legendary and the sultan wanted never to find himself on the wrong side of it.

The next evening the djinn's residence was visited by a poor, traveling beggar. The djinn welcomed him in and offered him food. The beggar thanked him and gladly partook of the meal offered him. "You have quite a nice estate," said the man. The djinn smiled, for he was proud of the home he had created. "It's not as nice as the sultan's palace, but it is a fine estate." The djinn smiled a bit less.

"How is your stew?" the djinn asked of the beggar.

"Oh, fine, sir. Fine. It is an excellent meal. It reminds me of the time I dined with a foreign head of state. He had the most magnificent cooks. They cooked a goat the likes of which you have never tasted, roasted to perfection with the finest of imported herbs."

The djinn looked at the beggar suspiciously. "How is it that a beggar like you has dined with kings and visited the sultan?"

"Oh, sir. I do not wish to burden you with my tale."

"Oh, but you must," insisted the djinn.

"Many summers ago the man sitting humbly before you was vizier to the sultan himself." The djinn looked upon the man now with great interest. "But the sultan, he is a wicked and most selfish ruler. I served him for many years and asked only one thing of him, the hand of a beautiful girl in a nearby village. But the sultan, once he set eyes upon the girl, decided that he himself must marry her and deprive her of her most cherished innocence. When I dared to speak up, he cast me out—sparing my life for the years of service I had offered him—stripping me of my title and wealth. I have lived upon the kindness of strangers ever since. Oh, if only there was a way to correct these ills!"

Touched by this tale of woe, but even more so enraged by the selfishness of a man higher in station than he, the djinn decided he would help this man. He could sense the longing for the young maiden in the man's heart and thus revealed his true self to the man. Awestruck by the golden form of the djinn before him, the man fell to his knees as the voice of the djinn boomed through the marble halls. "Sir, this night I will give you the chance to avenge yourself and right these wrongs!"

"Do you swear it?" the beggar asked.

"I do," swore the djinn. "I will grant you three wishes. The first two are for you. The third must benefit someone other than yourself. Do you promise to do this?"

"Oh yes. Yes I do."

"Then what is your first wish?"

"I wish for the sultan to grant me the hand of the woman I desire most."

The djinn nodded his head, clapped his hands, and made it so.

"What is your second wish?"

"That no matter what, you do not in any way harm the sultan or his viziers for what they have done, nor may you rob them of anything rightfully theirs without their knowledge."

"Why not?" asked the djinn, puzzled by this request.

"Because if I let harm come to these men, it would make me no better a man than they."

The djinn smiled and nodded approvingly. Truly this was

a man of character. He nodded his head, clapped his hands twice, and made it so. "And your third wish?"

"That all of your possessions, your estate, and your wives be immediately bequeathed to the sultan."

The djinn was immediately shamed. He had been tricked. In a rage, he drew back his arm to strike the man but could not, for this was a vizier of the sultan's and he could not harm him for what he had done; the djinn knew that now. It was only then that he truly understood what he had done.

"You swore an oath, djinn. Grant me my third wish."

A tear came to the eye of the djinn. His estate, all of his possessions, and the wives he had loved so much; in a moment, they would all belong to the sultan. Sadly he nodded his head, clapped three times, and made it so.

"Now, I order you out of the sultan's estate, djinn." The vizier smiled, ordered the servants to tend to the residence in his absence, and returned to the sultan to claim his bride.

Shamefully the djinn walked out of the sultan's estate and for three days and three nights continued without stopping, trying to get as far away from his old life as possible. When he could walk no more, he found a nice inviting branch in a large fig tree and fell into a deep sleep.

The next morning a young farmer was collecting figs from his trees when he accidentally stumbled upon the djinn. Startled by the disturbance, the djinn awoke angrily, lost his balance, and fell from the tree. The man dropped immediately to his knees and begged the djinn's forgiveness. It was then that the djinn looked around and, seeing himself surrounded by fields of fig trees, realized he had mistaken the farmer's orchard for simple woodland. He begged the farmer's forgiveness, but the farmer would not hear of it.

"This is your tree now," the farmer implored. "You have chosen it."

"But it is your tree, in your orchard."

"I have many trees in this orchard. This one is now yours for as long as you want it. Please forgive my awakening you. Is there any way I could repay this offense?"

It was then that the djinn noticed just how hungry he was. "Some food would be nice, if you can spare it." The farmer nodded to this request. "But do not salt it or you will have offended me tenfold." The farmer left and returned an hour later with a bowl of the day's stew. The djinn sat beside the tree and hungrily devoured his meal. He motioned for the farmer to sit beside him. "Thank you for your kindness. You have given me food when I was hungry and a tree when I possessed nothing else in the world. How can I repay your kindness?"

"All I ask is that you spare me your wrath," pleaded the farmer.

"I have no wrath for you, young man," said the djinn.

"Then I have all I need."

"But what is it that you *want*? What is it that you *wish*?"

"Wish?" The farmer blushed. "There is a girl in a nearby village who I care very much for."

"And you wish that she loved you?" the djinn asked.

"No," said the farmer. "She already loves me. But her father has promised her to another man."

"Then you wish she was promised to you instead?"

"Yes," the farmer replied.

"What else would you wish for?"

"I wish she could speak so I could know what she was thinking at all times."

"She cannot speak?"

"No. Not since birth."

"What then would be your third wish?"

"Third wish?" he asked. "What else could a man wish

for? A home, a wife, and land is all a man needs. The rest he must earn for himself, or else it has no value."

"No value?" the djinn asked, surprised.

"No. Gold a man hasn't earned is just something shiny on a pile that means nothing to him. We are not the sum of worthless piles. Our worth is the work that went into them."

The djinn smiled, impressed by the wise farmer. "What is your first wish?"

"I wish the fishmonger's daughter was promised to me."

The djinn nodded his head, clapped his hands, and made it so. "What is your second wish?"

"I wish the fishmonger's daughter could speak."

The djinn nodded his head, clapped his hands twice, and made it so. "Not only is she the loveliest woman in all the land, but now she has the sweetest voice as well. What is your third wish?"

"I wish happiness upon all those you visit equal to what you are about to bring me."

At this the djinn paused. "What?" he asked.

"You have done so much for me just now. My only wish left is that you may continue to gift others with a fate as wondrous as mine."

At this the djinn smiled, nodded, and clapped his hands three times, making it so.

At that very moment, miles away, the vizier grew very angry, for he knew what the djinn had done and he swore the djinn would pay. Furious, he called together the rest of the viziers and the kingdom's wisest wizards and together they pored over tablet and text looking for a final solution to the djinn problem.

That next morning the fishmonger rode up to the farmer's home with his daughter in tow. Unsurprised, the farmer met him out in front. "It is the strangest thing," said the fishmonger. "Last night my daughter came to me and with the voice of a dozen nightingales said, 'Father, I love a man and I wish to marry him.' And a voice so sweet cannot be denied, especially when she told me that she loved a man as well regarded and noble as you. So I come to you with dowry in hand asking if you would marry my daughter and make me the proudest father in all the land."

The farmer smiled, nodded, and promised the fishmonger that he would love his daughter with all his heart. And so the two were quickly married and lived happily upon figs and fish for the remainder of their lives.

But the vizier was furious. After weeks of combing through scripture and scroll he still could not find a way to kill a djinn outright. He did however find two fragments of dark script that detailed two very important points. The first was that each djinn is only as old as memory and that they die when no one can remember their name. The second was a method of trapping them in a vessel where they could be stored and kept forever. Separate, these notions were dangerous to the djinn, but together they proved to be the path to their undoing.

At once the vizier commissioned the artisans of the kingdom to cast bottles and lamps constructed of the finest, carefully chosen materials. Then he ordered his riders to pay a visit to the fig farmer and his new bride. The riders returned by morning, bearing the freshly cut heads of the newlyweds. Commissioned then to ride in all directions, the riders sought out djinn wherever they could be found. Each rider was given a dozen bottles and lamps and was told they dared not return until each vessel was filled.

The vizier's revenge was not swift. It was slow and deliberate. Word did not spread quickly enough and, within a year, ten thousand bottles returned filled with djinn. But not a one was the djinn he was looking for. Each bottle was stored in a vault that was then buried twenty feet beneath the sand. Robbed of both his prize and his bride, the vizier took solace in his hollow victory.

This victory was short lived, however, for the djinn were numerous—more numerous than ten thousand—and did not take the news of their imprisoned brethren without insult. While the magic of the bottles prevented the few remaining djinn from opening or even finding them, the riders who carried them were not so tight with their secrets—especially after they had run out of bottles. It took turning only a few of the riders inside out before their tongues loosened and the djinn were able to discern the villain behind these wicked oubliettes.

The vizier awoke from a night of bad dreams to find himself alone in a desolate wasteland, far from his kingdom. There he wandered for three days before the sun and sand drove him to near madness. Just before he succumbed completely, the djinn set wild dogs upon him, which tore him limb from limb to slake their own thirst with his blood. After that, his bloodline was forever cursed, with his family condemned to strangling their newborn children until not a single relation remained. Lastly, the djinn struck the vizier's name from the record of time, some say banishing its syllables from the tongues of men altogether.

The djinn then laid waste to the entire kingdom, made barren all of the surrounding lands, and razed the sultan's palace to dust. The selfish djinn, the cause of this swift and terrible war, joined the mass exodus and departed—morose, quiet, and heavy with shame. He was never heard from again.

CHAPTER FIVE

COLBY STEVENS'S BIG DAY

No manner of exhaustion can keep a child asleep much later than six a.m. on Christmas Day. Colby awoke at 4:35. Today he was promised anything he wanted. Anything in the world. And while it would be nice to say that Colby had pondered, even for a moment, the starving children in Africa, the plight of those ravaged by disease the world over, or even the homeless guy who slept off a twelve-pack of the cheap stuff on the corner behind the convenience store—he did not. Colby thought about toys. Lots and lots of toys.

Having assembled every catalog or advertisement left lying around his house, Colby had attacked the most expensive and extravagant toys pictured with a black Magic Marker, circling them with gleeful abandon, knowing full well that each was most likely not to make the cut. This was, after all, his chance to ask for the *one perfect thing*—that bright, shiny indulgence that would make him the envy of everyone around him. His mind reeled as he began to ponder gadgets of the strangest kind—toys achieving almost Seussian levels of combinations—the best of the best melded with electronic gadgets; televisions and games systems embedded with compartments for light sabers and a fold-out pool table. His ability to fathom the ludicrous almost exceeded his desire for something truly spectacular.

He'd begun his search the afternoon before, continuing it under the cover of darkness and blankets—a San Francisco penlight his father had given him serving him well until the battery coughed and died. Then he was up again after a short rest, far before the sun, ready to attack the problem once more with the dedication of a scholar trying to solve the riddles of antiquity.

So, hours later, when his eagerness could swell no more, he dressed to meet his new best friend. He pulled on his crispest slacks and the white button-down shirt he wore every time his grandmother took him to church so they could pray for his mother and some woman named Jezebel. He combed his wet hair to one side with a nice wide part a few inches above his ear. Then the icing on the cake—his Christmas clip-on tie and the whitest socks he could find. He looked perfect. Absolutely perfect.

Thudthudthudthudthudthud. Down the stairs and around the banister, into a perfect slide toward the door. *Home free.*

Sylvia's voice broke the morning's perfection. "Just where do you think you're going this early, young man?" her voice cracked from the other room.

"Out to play in the woods."

"Come here and let me have a look at you," she demanded.

Colby poked his head around the wall, peering into the living room. His mother lay on the couch, almost as if she hadn't moved a muscle from the day before. She blearily eyed him up and down. "Uh-uh. No way. Get back upstairs and change. You are not wearing your church clothes out in those woods. You'll come back filthy. Get upstairs right this instant and don't leave this house until I see you dressed right. You got that?"

"Okay, Mommy," he sighed. Defeated, Colby returned up the stairs, the slow, deliberate thumping of his feet going off like firecrackers in a coffee can inside Sylvia's head. She growled wearily, but he was too far away to hear it. Moments later he returned, this time dressed far more conservatively: jeans, a T-shirt, and his tennis shoes. Sylvia nodded her approval, reaching out with the last threads of motherly affection she could muster for the day, fussing with his clothes.

"Okay. That's better. Whatever possessed you to dress up in your Sunday best? Some little girl got you dolled up like that?" Colby didn't know how to answer, so he stammered a little, flanked with a pause on both sides. "Well, don't let her break your heart, dear. Someone will always break your heart."

"Okay, Mommy," he said reluctantly.

"Now, you go out and be good. Where's your watch?"

Colby smiled brightly, his arm sticking all the way out.

Sylvia nodded. "All right. Remember, back after five, but not after six."

"Okay," he said, smiling. Then out the door, around the corner, and off into the magical kingdom beyond the ROAD CLOSED sign. *Crap, 10:53. Four hours.*

The hours passed at a glacial pace, as if each second were made almost twice as long by the anticipation, and as Colby entered the final stretch toward three forty-five, his stomach tightened up, his bladder tingling—a nervous, almost sick feeling filling it—while his feet tapped uncontrollably. He spent the last seven minutes staring intently at his watch, each minute seeming longer than the one before it. As the final four changed into a five, he shot to his feet, looking around with wild, excited eyes. But there was nothing to see. No one slipping out of the bushes or from behind a tree. He waited a bit more. "Hello?" he called out. "Yashar?"

Nothing.

3:47.

"What a gyp!"

"You learn that from television too?" asked Yashar, stepping out, smiling, from behind the tree Colby had just spent an hour slumped against.

"You came!"

"But of course. And you remembered. Quite the punctual one as well. Right on time."

Colby smiled. "Mommy says always be on time. You're not going to break my heart, are you?"

"Pardon me?" asked Yashar.

"Well, before I left my house, Mommy said someone will always break your heart."

"Yeah, Mom's a keeper."

"I love her," said Colby proudly.

Yashar looked down at Colby with a mix of sadness and admiration. "And that's why I chose you."

"So, do I get my wish?" he blurted out.

"My, you get to the point quickly." Yashar laughed. "Just a little small talk then BAM! Right to the point. I bet you'd make a good businessman."

"My daddy's a businessman. He sells computers. He travels a lot and isn't around, but he's real neat. He brings me stuff from all over the place. I've got snow globes and T-shirts and post-cards. Would you like to see them?"

"No, thank you," Yashar politely declined. "I've probably

been everywhere your father has and snow globes just don't look quite as pretty as the real thing."

"Yeah, but did you know that it snows at the Alamo?"

"Yes, but not nearly often enough to warrant a snow globe."

"Well, I've got a whole lot of cool stuff. You could come over and play sometime."

"Why don't we play out here?"

"What would we play out here?"

"Anything you wish," said Yashar in a lyrical manner, as if he'd uttered the phrase a thousand times before. He even managed to gaily swoosh his arm through the air, as if conjuring happiness with it as he spoke.

"Oooh! When do I get my wish?"

"Such impatience."

"Yeah, yeah. I know. Patience is a virtue. You adults always say that. But how do I know you're a real genie? You don't even have a bottle."

"Quit it with the bottle stuff, kid. It's insulting."

"What?" asked Colby, confused.

Yashar collected himself after slipping out of character. "It hurts my feelings."

"Why?"

"Let me tell you a story." Yashar looked around and saw a fallen log, moss covered but solid enough to support their weight. He took a seat atop it and patted the spot beside him. Colby hopped up on the log next to him, listening intently.

"There once was an evil man," he began.

"Was he a wizard?" asked Colby.

"No, he was a vizier."

"What's that?"

"He's the king's most trusted advisor. If the king has a question or a command, the vizier tells him whether it's a good idea or not. Sometimes the vizier tells the king what he should do, but he does so in a way that makes the king think it was his own idea."

"So they're bad men?"

"Some of them, but most were wise and benevolent. This one, however, was bad, an evil, wicked man. He was jealous because of something I did. You see, there was this man, and he was a good man; he worked hard and did everything to the best of his ability. All he desired was for the most beautiful woman in the kingdom to be his wife. Now this wasn't all bad because she actually loved him too—very much so—but this vizier, he wanted her as well and not for so noble a cause as love."

"What did he want her for?"

Yashar paused for a moment. "So that people could look at him and say, 'He must be a great man to have such a beautiful wife.' "

"Oh. I thought he wanted her for sex," said Colby, disappointed.

Yashar glared at Colby. "Where did you learn of such things?"

"A kid in my class named Ruben. Once, when we were in his basement, he showed me some of his daddy's magazines and they had women with no clothes on and Ruben said that it was so you could have sex with them. But I didn't like the pictures, I swear!"

"Do you want to hear my story or not?" asked Yashar.

Colby nodded excitedly, his head bobbing like a woodpecker against an invisible tree.

"All right then. I made it so this beautiful woman would marry the good man instead of the evil vizier. That made the vizier very angry and he commanded many wizards—"

"Cool! I knew there would be wizards in here somewhere! Wizards are always in the good stories."

"Well, this isn't a very *good* story."

"Then why are you telling it?"

"Because it has a point."

"Like a fable?"

"Exactly," said Yashar. "Except that this one is true. And very sad."

"Oh. What happened?"

"Well, the vizier was so angry at what I'd done, he commanded his wizards to weave a spell that would trap us djinn in bottles."

"Like on TV?"

"Worse! In the stories, the djinn could stay in the bottle for ten thousand years and be okay as long as someone eventually found and opened the bottle. But the truth is, if everybody forgets about us, we fade away."

"But everyone knows about genies."

"Yes, but not each individual genie. If everyone forgets about me, Yashar, or all the people who remember me die, then I die too. My essence fades away into the sunset."

"So a lot of genies died?"

"Almost all of them. They used to say that there were as many djinn as there were grains of sand. Now they number less than the trees in this field."

"And it's all your fault?"

Yashar grimaced at Colby, not that it was an unfair question. "Yes."

"Well, I won't forget you. Promise."

"That's what I'm counting on, Colby. That's what I'm counting on. You are very much the kind of child I was looking for."

"What kind is that?" asked Colby.

"The kind not afraid to dream. The kind not in a hurry to grow up."

"Why would I want to grow up? Grown-ups are sad and have headaches and some of them smell funny."

Yashar smiled. "Would you like to play knights of the round table?"

"How do you play that?"

"Well, I give you a sword and then summon a mean and nasty dragon and you kill it for your king."

Colby brightened. "Would I get to save any pretty girls?"

"Colby, you're eight."

"Yeah, but girls are real cute."

"You woo women with that sort of talk?"

"No. Usually I call them names and they let me chase them around." Colby thought for a moment. "Yashar, what's sex like?"

Yashar smiled. "A lot like chasing girls around the schoolyard. Except you have to call them sweet names instead. You ready to do this or would you rather stand around gabbing all day?"

"No, no, no. I wanna play knights."

"So let it be done."

CHAPTER SIX

DJINN AROUND THE CORNER

An excerpt by Dr. Thaddeus Ray, Ph.D., from
his book *A Chronicle of the Dreamfolk*

There are few supernatural creatures so misunderstood
and underrepresented in modern myth as the djinn. Like
many other popular supernatural creatures (namely angels,
demons, and fairies) it is not so much a specific *type* of creature as it is a *class* of creatures. Not all djinn are the same.
In fact, there seem to be as many different types and kinds
of djinn in the world as there are types of fairies, but no one
has ever taken the time or care to catalog them. Some have
postulated that djinn are simply another type of fairy, while

others still believe that they are angels cast out of Heaven, many of whom serve the evil Shaitan (pronounced Satan) who turned his back on God by refusing to serve man. What is known for sure is that each djinn varies wildly from the next, each possessing only a certain specific set of traits that they all share.

Djinn (both the singular and the plural of the word, only rarely dialectally pluralized as jnoun) possess free will and are not, like other supernatural creatures, entirely bound by region, diet, or behavior. They are much like us in that respect. There is no single habitat in which you can expect to find them, or one thing you can expect to find them doing. Unburdened individuals, each one finds his own purpose, worship, or enjoyment on his own terms.

However, there is one thing they cannot do: break an oath of any kind. Once a djinn promises, swears, or even implies that he is promising, he is compelled by every fiber of his being to uphold that promise, even at the expense of his own life. Of course, nothing prevents a crafty djinn from finding and exploiting any loopholes in said oath. Most stories involving djinn tend to focus upon this aspect of oath bending, but in practice it appears to be fairly uncommon.

All djinn love the heat and they love to sleep. No one knows why and the djinn never speak of it, but they have been known to sleep in the desert for years on end if undisturbed. Djinn also love to eat, but suffer physical pain and illness at the slightest touch of salt, and serving one salty foods is a surefire way to earn his ire. Steel and iron similarly repulse djinn, but don't seem to affect them like the fey. Despite these weaknesses, djinn are creatures of energy, bound by their own laws, and they cannot be killed in a conventional manner. The only known way for one to die is for them to fade away when completely forgotten.

Djinn feed off memory—they are inexplicably bound to it. As long as someone remembers them specifically as an individual (and most important, as a djinn) they live. But if everyone who knows them dies, they begin to starve and will perish within a fortnight—their energy dissipates into the atmosphere, creating one of the most spectacular sunsets you will ever have the privilege to see. This means that as long as he keeps himself out of trouble, a djinn can theoretically live forever. But while they are impossible to kill outright, they may be imprisoned and are often bound by those who wish to possess their power for their own.

At one time the djinn were quite numerous and scoured the earth in search of pleasure, adventure, or spiritual truth. It wasn't uncommon for someone's home to be "haunted" by a djinn, the basis of numerous superstitions. For example, not stepping on the threshold of a house originates from cases of people tripping over and awakening sleeping djinn that had passed out in their doorways.

The word *djinn* evolved from the word *janna,* meaning "to conceal" or "to hide," as every djinn can turn invisible at will. Each also has at his disposal a bevy of other abilities. Some can change shape, often taking animal form or a human appearance, though some appear with cloven hooves or the feet of a camel when doing so. Oddly, any attempt to transform into the shape of a beautiful woman will leave the djinn with sideways eyes that run from forehead to cheek. Other djinn can fly; pass through walls; or are possessed of great, inhuman strength. However, the most powerful djinn are those that master the ability to grant wishes.

Wish-granting djinn are actually a very rare and truly powerful lot, able to completely alter the fortunes and fates of men. Even then, they cannot just alter reality of their own free will. A djinn may only summon a wish from the mind of someone else, usually a mortal, and only when certain conditions are met. First, a djinn must bind himself to that mortal, swearing to grant one or more wishes. Second, the mortal must speak that wish aloud. Finally, the djinn must consent and then grant the wish. However, at this point they can make any modifications they want, including tacking on any conditions (how, when, and where, etc.) that were not initially specified in the wish, within the confines of the original oath.

The chief limiting factor of these wishes is that djinn cannot change the past, only the present. Even the future is truly out of their grasp, save for the passing on of blessings or the laying down of curses, both of which seem to obey rules of their own. Otherwise, these djinn can make changes as small as the ownership or manufacture of items to as large as convincing the world of a truth that never before existed—such as the identity of a nation's ruler. Powerful (and power-hungry) men have long sought djinn for this reason, and many djinn have gone into hiding as a result.

To find a djinn in this day and age is indeed a boon, though woe to the fellow a djinn finds first. One can never know what they truly intend.

CHAPTER SEVEN

THE BOY COLBY MAKES HIS CHOICE

Fairies are real?!" Colby shrieked at the top of his lungs. "Cool!" His face lit up at the mere thought. Despite meeting an actual djinn and getting offered the chance to make a wish, Colby hadn't bothered to ask himself one very important question: *If djinn were real, what else was out there?* But now that very thought weighed heavily on his mind.

"Real?" Yashar answered coyly. "Well, that depends entirely on how you look at it."

"What else is real?"

"Many things are real. Trees are real, people are real . . ."

"No, what other *cool* things are real?"

"Cool is a relative term, Colby. But I assume you are asking about what you might call . . . supernatural?" Colby looked puzzled. He didn't know that word. "Well, you know fairies are real and you know the djinn are real."

"Genies."

"Yes, genies. But angels are also real, wizards . . ."

"Ghosts?"

"That's where things get a little murky. But yes. In a sense."

"Dragons?"

"No."

"Monsters?"

Yashar paused. He nodded slowly, lost in thought, as if remembering something terrible. His gaze was at once both fatherly and frightening. "Colby," he said. "Monsters are real. Very real. But they're not just creatures. Monsters are everywhere. They're people, they're nightmares. They're jealous viziers. They are the things that we harbor within ourselves. If you remember one thing, even above remembering me, remember that there is not a monster dreamt that hasn't walked once within the soul of a man."

Yashar leaned in closer, poking a single stern finger into Colby's chest. "One day there may be a monster here. One with the teeth of a shark, the strength of a lion, and the cruelty only a man can bring to bear."

Relaxing his gaze, he leaned back and smiled. "But do monsters of flesh and blood and bone exist? Monsters with wings and gaping jaws that can swallow children whole; that smell of rotting garbage and belch out sounds so foul they make your very knees shake? Do they exist?" He playfully poked Colby in the ribs, tickling him. "Oh yes, Colby. They exist. They very much exist."

"Cool! I wanna see 'em. Not just the monsters, but everything. Fairies, angels, wizards. I wanna see 'em all. That's my wish."

Yashar laughed. "What?"

"That's my wish. I wish I could see everything suprana . . . tral . . ."

Yashar became instantly serious. "Supernatural?"

"Supernatural," Colby proudly belted out. "I wish you would show me everything supernatural."

"No," said Yashar. "That's very dangerous. I forbid it."

"But that's my wish. You'll protect me, right? I wish you'd show me and protect me. That's my wish."

"You don't want anything else?" asked Yashar, pausing a moment so Colby could answer. "A utility belt?" He spoke with a hint of desperation. "A bicycle? A girlfriend?"

"Nope. That's my wish. And you promised anything I wanted. And genies always keep their promises, right?"

Yashar's heart broke: he *had* promised. No matter how badly he knew it would turn out for Colby, he had to see it through. He knew that this wasn't the worst mistake he'd ever made, but he was beginning to worry that it might come close. Sighing deeply, he shook his head. *Well, this is new.*

"So that's it, then? Your wish? You're sure you don't want anything else? *Anything* else?"

"Nope. I want to see everything."

"Then your wish is my command," the djinn said sadly.

Colby smiled. Yashar did not. Leaning in, Yashar placed a single hand on Colby's forehead, pinning back the boy's eyelids with his thumb and forefinger so he couldn't blink. Then he spit lightly into each eye.

Colby yelped. "Hey!" he protested, wriggling away.

"Wipe your eyes and see the world anew," said Yashar.

Colby opened his eyes but saw nothing different. There were no fairies flitting about, no angels perched in the branches of trees, just Yashar looking down gravely upon him.

"Enjoy it now, kid," he said. "I don't think you'll be smiling in the morning. Come on, you've got some packing to do."

UPSTAIRS, IN COLBY'S bedroom, Yashar gazed at the various pennants and posters adorning the wall, clearly placed there by a father wishing his son would grow up liking the same things he did. Nothing on the walls spoke of Colby at all—excepting perhaps that his parents didn't really know him that well. Colby tiptoed across the creaky wooden floor, trying not to disturb his mother, still asleep on the couch in the living room below. Yashar took a few steps, pacing toward the window. "Shhh," Colby warned. "Mommy said not to be back until five, and if she wakes up there's gonna be trouble."

Yashar looked back over his shoulder at Colby. "Half a bottle of Stoli in her stomach says she doesn't wake up until *seven thirty*."

Colby nodded. "Okay, but if she wakes up, you do the talking."

Yashar secretly smiled. At least the kid had style. Sure, it probably came from too much television and an overactive imagination—but at least he was interesting. Colby sifted through his things, overstuffing a backpack with trinkets and toys. All manner of books, electronic games, and stuffed animals poked out of the sides in some peculiar form of non-Euclidian geometry, preventing the zipper from moving, let alone properly zipping up.

Yashar shook his head and decided to bring a quick end to this madness. "Leave it."

"What?" asked Colby, terrified.

"Leave it all."

Colby looked up at the djinn—his eyes as big as saucers—as if he'd just been commanded to kill a puppy with a blunt knife. "But . . . but these are my toys."

"You won't need them. Not where we're going."

"We won't need toys?"

Yashar shook his head. "Not on an adventure, no. And anything you do need, I'll get you."

"So I can't take anything?"

"No," Yashar said sternly. Closing his eyes, he took a deep breath: *He's only eight.* "One toy, only one. Which is your favorite?"

"That's easy," said Colby. He walked over to his nightstand, taking from it a battered, worn, one-eyed mess of a teddy bear, its fur matted and dirty, but its sewn-on smile intact, peeking out like a ray of distilled childhood through the grime and sweat of eight years of abuse. "Mr. Bearston. He's my favorite."

"Well, you can take Mr. Bearston with you. Put him in your backpack and let's go."

"I think I'll carry him for a while." Colby set down Mr. Bearston, upturned the backpack, shaking it until every last bit of its contents spilled out onto his bed. Then he zipped up the pack, slung it over his shoulder, picked up Mr. Bearston by a single paw, and held out his other hand for Yashar to take. "Ready."

"Say good-bye to your home, Colby. Next time you see it, you will be a very different person." Yashar meant that, but it wasn't true. For he had no way of knowing that Colby would look around one last time, say good-bye to all his toys; take off his gaudy, colorful watch and leave it on the nightstand on the way out; walk quietly down the stairs, kiss his mother on the brow; and tiptoe out the door only to never, ever return. But that's exactly what would happen. Colby, like Ewan before him, had no idea that this would be the last time he'd ever see home.

And the two walked off into the evening—Colby holding Mr. Bearston in one hand and Yashar's meaty palm in the other—toward adventure.

CHAPTER EIGHT

THE VEIL BETWEEN TWO WORLDS

An essay by Dr. Thaddeus Ray, Ph.D., from
his book *The Everything You Cannot See*

Between the realm of the natural world and that of the
supernatural is a veil, a thin gossamer web that muddles the
vision of mortal man and keeps him from seeing what is going
on all around him. It is a sort of one-way mirror, an energy
that allows the beings of the other side to peer in and prey
upon the ever-replicating resource that is man while simultaneously preventing man from really knowing what stalks him
from the other side. Not everything beyond this veil is harm-
ful. Most creatures are indifferent and care no more about us

than you care about the squirrels living in the tree across the street. Yet they remain sheltered, far from prying eyes despite often being steps, if not inches, away.

Whether blessed with the ability to sense certain energies or touched by a madness that ignores the veil altogether, some people are immune to the ethereal strands that separate *us* from *them.* Those who can see are often diagnosed with schizophrenia or some form of psychosis, though it isn't clear which comes first: the perception of the supernatural or a psychological break. Perhaps some people are just so far gone that they accept the existence of things everyone else subconsciously filters out. Maybe the sight of such things shatters the fragile human mind, for once you've accepted the existence of that which is *clearly not there,* nothing is impossible.

Anyone with an open mind can peer beyond, if even only for a moment. When your guard is down and the energies on the other side are strong, it is possible to almost see the other side. Moreover, certain substances, such as plants, mushrooms, and synthetic hallucinogens, have been known to weaken the mind's grip on reality and allow a greater chance of seeing something beyond. While not a sure thing, it has been known to help enough that certain beings from the other side enjoy taking advantage of those under the influence.

Furthermore, it is possible for the beings of the other side to cross into our world, to appear in a manner that allows our minds to perceive them either as they are or as they wish us to believe them to be. Still others choose to enchant their victims with their own energy, like fairies and their glamour, to usher mortal men into their own nightmarish, quixotic realm. Fairies themselves have been known to steal away children in the night, bathe them in the glamour of a virginal spring-fed lake, and keep them living beyond the veil until they are old enough to know better.

No one is quite sure why the veil exists, whether it is a by-product of the energies that make up supernatural beings, or an actual barrier put in place that one day might be broken through and overcome. Perhaps it is for our own good. Man fears what he does not understand, and everything else he first subverts, then controls or, ultimately, destroys.

CHAPTER NINE

THE BOY EWAN
PREPARES THE HUNT

The nearly seven years since Ewan Thatcher had been abducted were not particularly kind to him. The ward of Dithers the Bendith Y Mamau, he was not what anyone in their right mind would consider *cared for*. Thin, gaunt, and covered head to toe in boyish dirt, he was slightly malnourished, rarely cleaned, and relegated to a cot of hay on a cold, chalky stone floor at night.

Despite this, Ewan—still as quiet and complaint free as ever—managed to find something worthwhile in everything about his life. Today, for example, was the day that Dithers was taking him along on a hunt. It would be a great day—Ewan knew it in his heart. There was no breeze to give away his scent and it was still early enough in the season that the Texas sun had yet to choke the air with hundred-degree heat. Ewan crouched silently in tall grass, crawling on all fours, so close to the ground that his deer-skin tunic was the only thing separating flesh from soil.

Dithers's head poked through the grass behind him—the Bendith clearly much better at hiding than Ewan. He sniffed the air. Crawling up beside Ewan, he gestured deliberately. Two bunny-eared fingers atop his head. A hopping fist. A finger across the mouth. Two fingers to the eyes. A point to a nearby tree. *Rabbit.*

Ewan nodded.

BANG!

A sound clattered over the hill, echoing through the woods. Ewan looked up.

Bang! Sputtersputtersputtercough.

They listened intently, hoping the wind would carry a sound or two. Dithers perked up. *Crushed gravel and a few mechanical ticks.* A devilish smile crept slowly across his lips, revealing a twisted row of teeth overgrown with yellow plaque and specks of rotting animal flesh. Ewan's eyes grew wide with excitement. The sound was unmistakable now.

"Campers?" Ewan asked excitedly.

Dithers nodded, bringing a stiff, shushing finger to his mouth. "Campers," he whispered. He paused for a second, trying to plan through his unbridled exhilaration. *Think, think, think. What to do? Who to tell?* "Quick!" he said. "Get on my back."

Ewan sprang to his feet, bolting to Dithers, who in turn threw his arm around Ewan's waist, slinging him over his back like a sack. Wrapping his arms tightly around the Bendith's thick, burly neck, Ewan held on for dear life. The Bendith lunged forward like a firing rocket, bounding off rocks and fallen logs, staying airborne as long as possible. His clawed hands grasped branches, swinging them ever higher, racing upward, until the two soared limb to limb some twenty-five feet above the ground.

There it was, along an old, abandoned back road in the distance: an ancient, avocado green Volkswagen Thing. This boxy, angular, postwar convertible monstrosity puttered along with its top down, a pair of scantily dressed, tattooed twenty-somethings arching their backs over the folded-down canvas roof, sunning themselves as their male companions sat smoking up front. The car overflowed with camping gear and there was no doubt where they were headed. Campers called it Devil's Whisper Rock. The local fae had another name for it.

The Great Stage.

This was the Hill Country, thick with trees, dense with brush. It was still a mostly untamed wild yet to see any real development. The land was almost virginal, rich with energy. Much of that energy settled and flowed through a valley between two large hills, collecting into something of an ephemeral river—a bubbling stream of magic pooling at a rocky outcropping where the veil was thin. On moon-soaked nights, appearing before mortals was easier there than any other place in the region. Stories, passed down from person to person, evolved over time into modern legend about the things you could see and hear at Devil's Whisper Rock—sometimes in the hushed tones of someone afraid to be taken as crazy, other times in the boisterous drunken chorus of someone shouting, "You'll never believe what I saw once!"

It was a night much like tonight . . . most of those stories began. More often than not, the stories were just fragments of dreams the teller would swear were real. But then, there were the other times.

Times like tonight. Dithers would see to that.

His smile grew wide enough to swallow Ewan whole. He came to an abrupt stop atop a hulking branch that looked out over the valley. "You smell that, boy?"

Ewan sniffed the air, smelling nothing but Dithers's sweltering, rotten breath. He shook his head, despite being out of Dithers's line of sight. "No."

"You'll catch wind of it soon enough. It's strong stuff. Pungent." Dithers sniffed at the subtle wafts of smoke on the breeze.

"What is it?" asked Ewan.

"It's the smell of a weak mind. Slow. Lethargic. Easy to spook. It makes it easier to see us."

"Why would we want them to see us? I thought we were supposed to stay hiding. Me more than anyone else."

"Normally, yes. You more than anyone else. But not tonight. Tonight we hunt." Dithers paused, thinking for a moment. "Here's what I want you to do. I want you to run along and collect a few of my friends. Do you think you can do that?"

"Uh-huh!" Ewan spat out eagerly.

Dithers slid down the trunk slowly.

"Okay," said Dithers over his shoulder, the poetry of his words becoming melody and the melody of his words becoming magic. "Four friends I task you to bring to me, and four friends you shall find. Tarry not, speak not a word, and every order you must mind. First race on through the meadow, then over the limestone hills, to fetch for me my closest friend, the Buber, Nibbling Nils. Tell to him the details, then quickly on your way, for three more friends you are sure to fetch before the end of day. Then on down the foothill, and over through the yard, and fetch for me my other friend, Aufhocker Eberhard. Then on to Dragana, that dancing girl you like, and tell to her that her favorite song she shall dance again tonight. But not all my friends you've found just yet, for there is one last still, find for me the elusive one, the Shadow we call Bill. And once all four you've told at last what we shall do tonight, the six of us will have our fun and hunt by the moonlight." Dithers smiled and nodded, looking back at Ewan. The magic was clearly seeping in; he could tell by the look in Ewan's eyes. "Now, who are you gonna bring me?"

Ewan gazed upward, searching for the names. "Nibbling Nils, Bill the Shadow, Dragana, and Eberhard."

"And if you see anyone else?"

"Keep running."

"Right. And if anyone asks you a question, what do you tell them?"

"Nothing."

"Good. Now, go get 'em, boy."

Ewan hopped off Dithers's back, tearing off on his quest. He knew the way; he'd been to the haunts of all four so many times he could run it blindfolded. Dithers hadn't a single doubt in his mind about Ewan getting back in time. He was a good kid, hungry to prove himself. But now it was Dithers's time to shine; he needed to stalk this new prey, keeping any other fairies away until nightfall. Tonight he was going to prove his worth to his friends; tonight would be a fine hunt. *Tonight.*

TONIGHT THEY WERE *hunting campers! And Dithers trusted him enough for a special mission all his own.* This was the most exciting thing ever to happen to Ewan. He wasn't going to screw it up. Not one bit.

Well-worn animal trails honeycombed the forest, all of which he knew like a good cabbie knows side streets. The problem wasn't how to get to the four haunts he was assigned—it was how to get there without crossing the haunts of others. Some were frightening, others charming. A few were even fairly tricksy. The one he was most afraid of running across, however, was the Old Man. The Old Man was ancient; the Old Man was wise; and worst of all, the Old Man loved humiliating others. There was nothing the Old Man would love more than to ruin the hunt. Ewan could not let that happen. So he could not go anywhere near the Old Man's hunting grounds.

Stupid Old Man. He was going to ruin everything.

Okay, stop thinking about him, Ewan thought. He knew better than to focus his thoughts on a spirit as powerful as that. Some spirits can be summoned just by saying their names aloud, others just by thinking about them. He huffed and puffed his way up the hill, rounding the top, almost running smack into someone. *OH CRAP! The Old Man!* Ewan was cooked. He just knew it.

The Old Man smiled down at him, a mischievous expression on his wrinkled face. His skin was a coppery brown; his hair was long, knotted, and jet black, streaked with stray grays; and despite his apparent age, his muscles were firm and taut. He wore a deerskin tunic much like the one Ewan was wearing— only adorned with more fur and soiled from years of outdoor living. "Hello, Ewan. Don't worry, I'm not going to give away your secret."

"What secret?"

The Old Man raised an arm and wryly pointed a stiff finger past the hill. "I believe you'll find Nils over in that direction." He smiled shrewdly, then folded in upon himself, transforming into a coyote. A foot taller than the average coyote, its salt-and-pepper mane was thick, full, and glistened when struck by the sun. Trotting off, he disappeared behind a tree, never to emerge from the other side.

Ewan couldn't wait until he was old enough to learn that trick.

Nibbling Nils. Ewan regained focus and once again took to the trails, eager to find himself the crotchety old Buber before the crotchety old Buber found him instead.

CHAPTER TEN

THE YOUNG CHANGELING
KNOCKS

Nixie Knocks the Changeling was born in the rain under a starless black sky. The moment he opened his eyes he saw her. *His mother. Caitlin.* She was beautiful, her eyes big and brown, her hair henna red. The very first thing he could remember was the patter of raindrops on his face. The rain was cold but her tears were warm; that's how he could tell the difference. After three days of sobbing over her stillborn child, rocking and cradling him, praying for him to stir, he'd awakened. He looked up for the first time and saw her, his hunger hollow and angry, crying out for his mother to feed him. He loved her so much it hurt; he loved her so much he fought his way to the land of the living. And when she quickly bared her breast to suckle him, he bit down with all of his might.

She screamed. It was then that Caitlin knew exactly what he was. And she hated him; she hated him with every fiber of her being. Knocks knew hatred's flavor better than anyone. He could eat pain, he could live indefinitely on fear, but he couldn't eat hate. His stomach couldn't take it.

She threw him to the ground, screaming, "Aodhan!"

It was then that Knocks first met his father. Tall, muscular, handsome. He rushed to his wife's side, placing a caring hand on her delicate exposed shoulder. "What is it, my love?"

She pointed at Knocks, refusing to look at him. "Fetch the Bendith."

"But, Caitlin . . ."

"Fetch him," she demanded with a choked sob. "That is not your son."

Knocks writhed on the ground, drinking his mother's pain. It was the only thing she would ever give him.

Dithers wasted no time. He took one look, nodded knowingly, and threw him over his shoulder. "What should I bring you?" he asked Caitlin.

"Bring me a son. One strong and noble and deserving. One worthy of Sidhe parents."

Dithers nodded silently, carrying Knocks off into the night. But as he made his way to the edge of the forest, he found it blocked by a massive stone of a man: Meinrad the Limestone King, Green Man and Leshii of the Balcones Canyonlands.

Possessing no skin or flesh, he was head to toe tan and yellow limestone instead, beset with flecks of gray and clear quartz, sprouting green flowering bushes where a man's beard and hair might be. He stood seven feet tall, but walked with a crook in his back from years of his weathered stone settling in. His eyes and mouth were recesses in the rock, his nose a knobby pecan branch with green budding leaves growing into the bush of his beard. Meinrad shook his head, wagging a protesting finger. "Where are you going?" he asked.

"To fetch Caitlin a new child," said Dithers.

"That is not Caitlin's child. Her child was poisoned by its mother's vanity and died in her womb. This is a changeling. This child belongs to the court. It belongs to the Limestone Kingdom. And you know what must be done with it."

Dithers shook his head. "I don't know, King."

"It is time you did your duty for the court, as many Bendith have done before you. You must fetch us a child. A child we can raise as *one of our own*. Do you understand?"

Dithers nodded.

"You know what is being asked of you?"

"I do."

"And you know what will happen if you fail?"

Dithers gulped silently. "Yes."

"No one must know. No one."

Nixies don't write. They've never had a need for it. So when the other fairies heard them speak of the changeling—*Nox,* meaning "night," named for the night he first came to the nixies—they heard it as *Knocks*. The changeling, who knew not the difference, wouldn't protest until he was far older. Sometimes names just happen. Such was the case of Nixie Knocks the Changeling.

"Mama, I'm hungry," said Knocks, all of four years old.

"I know, baby," said Laila. "Mama's gonna get dinner for you."

"But I'm hungry."

"Mama knows. Stay here and don't let anyone see you."

Laila was the eldest of four sisters. And while her younger

siblings Annalise, Elke, and Rebekka had all agreed to adopt Knocks as a group, Laila was the only one he called Mama. To him they were all his mothers, but there was only one *Mama*. And Laila took that honor very seriously. So it was she who took charge of his feeding. While he wasn't hungry often, Knocks was a handful when he was. Downright dangerous even.

Nixies don't look like ordinary women. Their skin is a pallid green, smooth and scaly, their smiles lined with razor-sharp, needle teeth with which they feed upon fresh fish. Instead of legs they have large, powerful tails that pound them through the water at incredible speeds. And much like Knocks, they possess the ability to shroud themselves in glamour and walk amongst the city dwellers unnoticed.

Laila stepped away from the tall grass along the shore, putting a stiff finger against her lips to remind Knocks to keep quiet and hidden, then slipped silently into the water. Her skin grew pale, then rosy, her hair shimmering a golden blond; her breasts swelled, stiff nipples poking out through the thin pink fabric of her bathing suit. Her eyes grew large, her lashes long. She smiled big and bright, treading water in the lake just beside a biking trail, lying in wait.

Within moments a biker happened upon her. He was fit, tattooed, straddling an expensive, showy mountain bike. Skidding to a stop by the water, he looked out, giving her a flirty smile. "Swimming alone?"

"Unfortunately," said Laila with a hint of disappointment.

"Boyfriend a no-show?"

"No," she giggled. "I don't have one. My friends. They canceled."

"That's a bummer. A pretty girl like you shouldn't have to swim alone. I'd join you, but I don't have a suit."

Laila smiled. She reached back with a single hand, undoing

the tie on her bikini top and flicking it off in one fluid motion.
Without missing a beat, she shimmied out of her bottoms, toss-
ing the wadded-up suit onto the shore with a wet *SLOP*. "There.
Now neither do I."

The biker managed a single kiss and a hand swept up the
inside of her thigh before he found himself drowning beneath
the waves. Knocks crouched on shore, his hands balled into
white-knuckled fists, savoring the agony of each gasp for air.
The man thrashed beneath the surface. He was strong and a
good swimmer, but Laila was stronger.

The fear. The pain. The desperation. Knocks's hunger began
to subside.

When the man had finally given up and the lake was allowed
to claim him, Laila secured his body to the bottom with a tangle
of lakeweed and swam back to shore. She stood over Knocks,
dripping wet and smiling, stroking his cheek. "There, there. Is
that better?"

Knocks nodded.

"Good. Now, let's get his wallet and go shopping. Mama
wants a new dress."

BY THE TIME he turned six, the nixies realized that they
could no longer keep their adopted son around the lake. Stories cropped up about a ghostly child lingering around the spots
where people had drowned. Other tales whispered of an ethereal, disembodied giggle heard as grown men flailed for their
lives. And while the authorities never took any of these claims
seriously, the nixies had noticed an uptick in interlopers searching for the Ghost Child of Ladybird Lake; that was attention
they could no longer ignore. So by a vote of three to one the
nixies decided to leave Knocks in the Limestone Kingdom—
which was where he now resided. Laila, the only sister to vote

against abandoning him, followed him out to the court, raising him among the fae of the Hill Country.

And he hated it there.

The Limestone Kingdom was far from the hustle and bustle of the big city; far from the traffic snarls, the hulking stone buildings, the excess of weekend nights. There were no shootings, no stabbings, no drunken date rapes. No homeless lay suffering on the corner, no despondent teens slit their wrists over self-centered teenage crushes. No children were beaten, abused, or humiliated in any way. There was almost no one around at all. You could walk for miles before seeing a living, breathing human being—and even then all they wanted was to live quietly, as far away from the beautiful chaos of the big city as possible.

There wasn't a drop of delicious dread anywhere to be found. It was like living in a world without oxygen, and Knocks was desperate for a single breath of misery. He knew what drowning felt like; he knew better than almost anybody. And that's what this was. They were slowly drowning him in a lake of emptiness.

His only respite was his nightly swim with Laila. Together they lay there—floating in the middle of a spring-fed lake—staring up at a field of stars so vast it strained the eye. When those stars reflected off the lake's crystal sheen, it was like floating deep in the murky void of space—stars everywhere, swallowing them whole, an inky, airless vacuum with only Laila's comfort staving off suffocation. Only the thin ring of trees surrounding the horizon served in any way to dissolve the illusion.

"Mama, I saw them today," he said one night.

"Saw who, sweetie?"

"Aodhan and Caitlin. My parents."

"You can't be sure it was them."

Knocks furrowed his brow, giving his mother a stern look, as if she should know better. "It was them." She stroked his head, nodding, acknowledging her mistake. "I hate them. I hate them so much."

"Oh, honey, you shouldn't hate them."

"They threw me out like the trash and asked for *him* instead."

"You know the rule. We don't talk about him."

"But, Mama—"

"But nothing," she said, squeezing him tight. "You are not *him*. You are Knocks. And if those self-centered prats hadn't tried to trade you in, I would never have gotten the son I always wanted."

"I still hate him."

"You have to control that, Knocks. We don't survive by letting our instincts take over. We only survive by being smart. He's not smart like you. He has his own cross to bear. You remember that. One day you'll look back and be thankful that you're not him."

"Okay, Mama."

"Don't *okay, Mama* me. You say *yes, ma'am*."

"Yes, ma'am."

"That's better. We should be heading in. The sun's coming up." The two swam to the edge of the lake, making their way to shore. In the breaking rays of the morning light he looked down, glimpsing his own reflection. Though it was clearly him, all he saw was a bent, broken picture of Ewan. His eyes were mismatched, one clearly larger than the other; one of them tilted forty-five degrees to the side. His hair grew out in patches, the same brown color as Ewan's, but shaggy and worn, split ends fraying over spots of scabby, balding skin. The front of his skull was larger, with a bulbous, elliptical tumor of flesh growing out of the side. Both ears were ragged and tattered, chewed up, gnawed down like a cat that had been in too many fights. Worst of all were his teeth—crooked, rotten, and worn—the incisors tilted at a forty-five-degree angle opposite his eyes, creating a discordant symmetry.

Perfect, special little Ewan. With his perfect tangle of brown hair and his perfectly aligned eyes and his perfect, perfect, perfect smile. Knocks simmered quietly, but Laila glowed, putting a loving hand on his shoulder.

"See what I mean? You're so handsome. You don't look anything like him."

AT FIRST HE thought little about his appearance; after all, his mothers had always held him close, stroking his hair, telling him how beautiful he was. But the fairies of the court of the Limestone Kingdom were very different creatures. From far off, they offered a wave or a smile, shouting a stout, "Ho, Ewan," before getting close enough to realize their mistake. For a moment Knocks would drink in their heady confusion, the stomach-turning angst generated by the changeling's visage. But as revulsion gave way to pity, his hatred for these creatures only grew.

He was nothing to pity; he was not a monster. And if only he had been born to Laila rather than the hollow, loveless womb of that stuck-up Sidhe, he would never know what any of this was like. Instead, he lived near a walking reflection of what his life could have, *should have,* been. Any other court in the world, and his life would have been different. But Laila wanted to be close to her sisters. And for that he almost detested her too.

THE SUN WAS already high in the sky. It was perfect out, and no matter how many times his mother told him, he couldn't stay away. Knocks couldn't help himself. He skulked near the pair as they hunted rabbits out on the outer fringes of the kingdom. And when he heard them talk of the night's plans, he giggled silently, giddy at the prospect. Ewan would be given the chance to prove himself in front of a pack of watching adults. Knocks could not let an opening like that pass without incident.

It would be glorious. He would humiliate him, lay in wait for just the right moment to spring a trap that would prove once and for all that while Ewan was the prettier, Knocks was by far the craftier, the more dedicated, the most worthy of celebration. Ewan might be the shining star of the day, but the night belonged to Knocks. And as he thought about his chance, a familiar fire sparked, smoldered, and finally blazed within his belly. Tonight he would satisfy that blaze; tonight Knocks would feel the last of the lingering pity that belittled him in front of the others. *Tonight.*

There was only one way it could be any better.

Mallaidh.

CHAPTER ELEVEN

COURTING YOUNG MALLAIDH

At eight years of age, Mallaidh (pronounced Molly), had endeared herself to the whole of the fairy court through her hoydenish charm and unearthly grace. Her eyes were pools of childhood; the golden wisps of her hair were ever in motion, always caught in some light breeze, even when there was no wind, glinting, even when there was no sun; and she had a way of wrinkling her nose just so as to make the freckles across the bridge of it dance. She was delightful. Were she not preceded by her own mother, the title of "fairest of them all" would have been hers.

Not that she cared; had she concerned herself with such

things, she would not have been half as captivating. Instead she had this way about her that never included attending to her own looks or fashion; rather, she appeared desperately in love with whomever and whatever she was with at the time. Her moods were infectious. Blithe and untamed, she was a free spirit, untethered from routine or convention. Hers was an essence that pined for adventure and longed for a life sprinkled with magic.

A life like her mother's.

Cassidy Crane (a surname she'd picked up in the hole-in-the-wall bars of the Austin club scene) was something of a legend. A slender, raven-haired punk-rock goddess, she was a demure boot-wearing, butt-kicking beauty with specially inked tattoos that, if you looked closely enough, you could watch move and change color with her mood. She didn't tolerate lovesick fools and was always at the hip of the brightest and the best up-and-coming talent. Artists, musicians, and writers all found time with Cassidy—if they had the gift. But it wasn't until her steadiest beau—an incredibly talented actor—overdosed and died in her arms that she secured her immortality: Mallaidh. That name was the last thing Cassidy left her daughter before vanishing back into the ether of the rock scene.

When Cassidy walked the foothills and trails of the Limestone Kingdom, she ruled the roost—so when she left the swaddling-wrapped Mallaidh at the foot of Meinrad's cave, it was thought by all that her daughter would follow in her footsteps. Thus far, she had. Mallaidh was the highlight of the hills, the glowing talk of whomever she graced with her time.

And to Nixie Knocks the Changeling, she was the center of the very universe.

Mallaidh was neither unusually cruel nor given to any sort of boorishness, so whenever Knocks came around to call there was no reason to be unduly rude. She flirted; it was in her nature. Her eyes grew big and brown and she smiled in a way that dislodged his stomach from its moorings, sinking it a solid foot. He had no choice but to fall madly, deeply in love with her. Though she did not return his affection, she did enjoy the attention, and she devoured it when—time and again—he would pay her a visit in the vain hope that she might see him differently once and for all. Times like today.

"Hello, Mallaidh," he said, his eyes making indirect contact while his foot nervously drew semicircles in the dirt. His arm was concealed poorly behind him, fresh-picked, dying wildflowers clutched hopefully in his grimy little fingers. He was eager, nervous, unsure of himself. As far as Mallaidh knew, this was his natural state. His upturned cockeye blinked, entirely independent of the other, and Mallaidh tried to pretend that seeing that didn't bother her so much.

"Hello, Knocks," she said sweetly, her voice almost cooing. Her mood was particularly bright today, mirroring the radiant skies and the soft, billowing clouds that drifted dreamily in the distance. "What's the haps?"

"The . . . haps?" he asked, confused.

"Oh, did I say that wrong?" She leaned in flirtatiously, trying coyly to play it off. "You used to live in Austin. That's what they say there, right? *What's the haps?*"

"I don't know. I . . . I've never heard that before."

"Oh, how silly of me," she said, recovering for both of them. "I must have gotten it wrong. You know people better than I do."

"No, I . . . I . . . ," he stammered.

"Don't be modest. You're smart. Don't let anyone tell you different."

He scuffed the ground harder, not yet consciously realizing that he'd drawn a heart in the dirt. "So, Mallaidh."

"Yes?"

"What are you doing tonight?"

"I don't know yet," she said, curiously. "Why?"

Knocks leaned in close, almost uncomfortably close. The next part he whispered. "I have a secret."

"Ooooh." She loved secrets. "What is it?" she whispered in the covert tenor of a secret agent.

Knocks smiled and looked both ways. "There's a hunt tonight."

"There is?" she asked excitedly. "Why haven't I heard about it?"

"Because it's a secret. Only a few of the forest bogeys know."

Mallaidh grimaced playfully, watching the young boy trying to present himself as a man. "Since when are *you* a forest bogey?" she asked.

"W . . . we . . . w . . . well . . . ," he stuttered "I'm not. But I heard them. And I'm gonna go take part."

"Oh," she said, disappointed—a young belle offered a chance to a dance to which she was clearly not really invited. "Well, I'm too young for a hunt. And I'm afraid there's nothing for me to do." She was clearly losing interest in the conversation. "Look, I—"

"Oh, well, Ewan and I are—"

"Ewan's going to be there?" she interrupted. Her eyes lit up as if someone had set off fireworks behind him.

Knocks's eyes narrowed into angry slits. He strained for normalcy, his eyelids fighting to stay open against the weight of his jealousy. Through gritted teeth he spoke, very slowly. "Yes. Ewan will be there."

"And I can go with you?" she asked, clapping excitedly, bouncing.

Knocks paused for a second. "Yes. Of course you can come with me," he said, smiling broadly. His plaque-encrusted, yellow teeth sprouted as randomly from his gray gums as trees did from the ground, his sickening grin turning Mallaidh's stomach. She muscled through it, betraying nary a second of her discomfort.

"Where should I meet you?" she asked.

Knocks answered in a sour staccato he tried disguising as mere theater. "The Great Stage. Sunset. Come alone."

Mallaidh smiled, touching Knocks lightly on the arm, above his elbow. "Oh, I'm so excited," she said. "I can't wait! See you tonight." She winked before slipping immediately back into the forest.

Little did he know it wasn't his demeanor or appearance that so spoiled his chances. To Mallaidh, a changeling was just another fairy—a revolting and misanthropic fairy to be sure, but a fairy nonetheless. And that simply wouldn't do. Not for a Leanan Sidhe. Fairies were prone to long, meandering lives, their life force like an artisan's candle, meant to burn long and slow. But mortals, they burned out quick and flashy, like puddles of gasoline. They were exciting, fresh, always on the precipice of death. And for a Leanan Sidhe, only the company of a mortal would truly do.

It was the life her mother had led, which meant that it was good enough for Mallaidh as well. But try telling that to a changeling.

Knocks inhaled deeply, the air still perfumed with her breath, notes of lilacs mixed with peaches in sweet cream. He looked on, smiling, dumbstruck at the touch, for a moment forgetting the rotting flowers wilting behind him in his grasp.

He stared agape into the woods behind her, the lingering smile slowly sinking as reality once again set in. The flowers burned in his grasp, a stinging reminder of his humiliation. Reaching back with his other hand, he grabbed hold, mindlessly twisting until the heads of the flowers popped off and the stems were a green, ragged tangle of carnage staining his hands a mossy olive. There was much work to do.

CHAPTER TWELVE

THE SAD AND RATHER LONELY
END OF ABRAHAM COLLINS

Abraham Collins was not cool, and he knew it, and no measure of tattoos, concert tickets, or hipster duds could change that fact. He'd tried. Instead, he came across as a dried-up imposter, one pocket protector and a scientific calculator away from cliché. To make matters worse, he wasn't sharp enough to be accepted amongst the intellectual elite of the company nerds either. He was the sort of fellow you would expect to find at home on any given night of the week, surrounded by costly looking, designer-at-a-discount furnishings, slumped on the couch watching television, wondering why he couldn't find himself a girl. Any girl.

So when his coworker and only close friend, Dallas Wise, invited him to fly wingman on a weekend camping trip with two secretly tattooed twenty-somethings from the secretarial pool, he jumped at the chance. It wasn't until they rolled up in their beat-up, ugly-as-sin military green Volkswagen Thing that Abraham realized what this really meant.

Dallas had laid claim to Stacy in advance, leaving Abraham with Carly, a slender, lithe vixen, all tan and teeth in a bikini top and jeans skirt. Way out of his league. He knew it, and when she looked up from her purse and they made eye contact for the first time, she knew it as well.

By the time they were settled by the campfire, everyone had a good, clean buzz going and the air hummed, backlit by the pinks and purples of the setting Texas sun. Dallas and Stacy cuddled by the fire's edge, each with a beer in hand and a comfortable smile dangling on the tips of their numb expressions. Abe nervously shifted atop a chalky rock, trying to think of some clever way to get close to Carly as she grew ever more oblivious.

Dallas reached into his pocket, pulling from it a small, loose Baggie filled with dried mushrooms. Each had a long stalk with an oblong cap, speckled brown and white at one end with a deep blue bruising at the base, fading as it trailed up the shaft. They evoked thoughts of Lewis Carroll caterpillars and smoldering hookahs, and the excited eyes of everyone around the fire glistening with anticipation. The girls eyed each other—Stacy proud of her date, Carly impressed that he had actually come through.

"Just a couple caps for me," said Carly. "I'm a lightweight."

"Me too," nodded Stacy. "Any more than five or six caps and I'll be over the moon all night."

Dallas plucked a few mushrooms out of the bag and fed them to Stacy one by one, their eyes locked in a flirty stare as she eagerly gobbled each cap. After the fifth cap, Dallas grabbed a small handful for himself then tossed the Baggie to Carly. He popped the entire handful into his mouth, chewed a little, swallowing hard, hastily trying to muscle past the taste. Carly picked up the bag, plucking a few choice caps for herself, and politely passed the bag to Abe.

Abe stared longingly at Carly, who gave him only a cursory glance as she handed it over. He'd lost her. There wasn't much time left to grab her attention before they rode the wave and crested into the night. The last thing he wanted was to be humping the leg of a girl more interested in staring at the stars than slipping into a tent with him. He needed her attention. And fast.

"Five caps," he blurted out without thinking. "That's it?" Everyone looked up at him. He smiled bravely, leaning his head back, pouring the remainder of the bag's contents straight down his throat, shaking every last cap, stalk, and broken bit into his waiting maw. He chomped furiously, the dried mushrooms turning into a thick, disgusting wad of paste in his mouth. It was like chewing raw dough. He couldn't swallow; he tried. His gag reflex fought back, but he forced it down in one painful lump, his stomach shuddering at its arrival.

Dallas snorted out a chuckle. Carly buried her face in her hands. Abraham smiled through the queasiness, trying to disguise his amateur-hour mistake as something more masculine than it was.

Dallas recognized the strained look in Abe's eyes. "Hey, Abe," he said.

"Yeah?" Abe mustered, still trying to hold down the mushroom loaf swelling in the pit of his gut.

"Why don't you go grab some firewood before your dose kicks in? That way we won't have to go out later."

Abe smiled. "Yeah. That sounds good. Ladies, if you'll excuse me." He stood up, casually disappearing into the brush, eager to put distance between himself and the camp to vomit properly out of earshot. His mouth was already watering, a purge wasn't far off. *Damnit, damnit, damnit. Carly can't hear this.* Churning, his roiling stomach began to bloat; at any moment he would lose it. Farther and farther he shuffled into the woods, finally letting loose with a furious heave.

Wiping his mouth clean of slop with his sleeve, he looked around for stray branches for the fire. He didn't want to spend too much time away. After all, within the hour everyone would be feeling good, and he wanted very much to be sitting next to Carly when they did. So he loaded his arms with as much wood as possible, turned around, and returned to camp.

Only, he couldn't remember from which direction he had staggered. *Oh, damnit.* He knew he wasn't that far, but the trees all looked the same. *What the hell am I doing in the woods?*

He wandered, night slowly creeping in over the forest. Trees menaced the horizon, shadows crept hungrily behind him. This was a bad idea, a truly, spectacularly bad idea, and as the few minutes' journey stretched into what seemed like an hour, Abraham Collins was sure this was how he was going to spend his weekend: wandering aimlessly through the woods while his best friend scored. And that's when he saw the campfire.

Abe staggered back into camp, dropping the armload of wood into a pile, wiping the cold sweat from his brow. His head was pounding, his stomach steadily expanding with gas. While the fire was still roaring in the center of camp, no one was sitting around it. "Guys? Dallas?" he called out. There was a rustling to his left, coming from one of the tents, then a giggle and a *SSSHHHH.* The tent unzipped and Dallas partially emerged from the small separation it created, giving the weird impression that there was nothing left of him but a disembodied, floating head.

"Hey," Dallas whispered. "Did you get the wood?"

"Yeah," said Abe.

"Good. Good." Dallas fumbled for words, watching them rattle around behind his eyes before realizing he would never catch any of them. Instead, he gave Abe a telling look.

"Where's Carly?"

"Dude . . . ," Dallas began.

"Where is she?" Abraham asked once again, this time with a slightly more powerful intonation.

"Dude," Dallas repeated, "you blew it." Abraham's jaw went slack. "You had your shot, Bro-ham. Come on," he whispered, quieter still, "I've got both of them in here. And you saw them. I can't pass this up."

"I don't . . . I don't believe you."

"No, seriously. They're both—"

"No, no. I believe *that*. I just. I can't believe . . ."

"Look, dude. What can I say?"

"Nothing. Just, just don't say anything. I'll just sit out here all night. Alone."

"Yeah, about that." Dallas gave him a concerned but pleading look. "Can you do me a solid and not hang out by the tent? I mean, it would be kind of creepy, you know?"

Abe tried to speak up, his mind sifting through the hundred or so things he would like to say were he to man up. Then he sighed and did what he always did: he slunk away, envied his best friend for what he knew was going on, and dreamed of a day when it might be him in that tent. As he walked away, he stepped on a large twig. The *SNAP* echoed, bouncing around the camp. He looked around, startled, realizing what was going on.

Great, he thought to himself. *Now the stuff kicks in.* He listened for a moment to the fire, the crackling pops and snaps like an orchestra of Black Cats set off in a soda can. Abraham was sweating, cold, and had a headache beginning to crescendo.

Now the auditory hallucinations were settling in, meaning he was just moments from finding out how badly the mushrooms were going to hit him. Looking up, he saw the moon, big and bright in the sky, and decided that if he was going to trip his balls off, he might as well find a good spot for staring at the stars while he did.

It didn't take long to find a large, almost comfortable limestone boulder resting cautiously on the edge of a steep cliff overlooking a lush, serene valley. Moonlight dripped over it like pooling blood. Colors were sharper than before, flickering—almost shimmering—ghost trees waking from their daylight slumber, stepping out of their stumps to walk and sway amongst the living. Abraham stared at the ghost trees wondering if they hungered, if they had any desire to scare anyone, or if, as ghosts, they simply wanted to feel the slightest touch of sunlight again. As Abraham stared at the ghost trees' sultry moon dance, he felt time slowing to a crawl, the whirling spin of the world reduced to a slow-motion stutter as he fell out of the time stream entirely, able to look in at the captured moment, waiting, paused for him, beyond the thin veil of reality.

Yes. The mushrooms had finally kicked in.

If he wasn't going to get laid tonight, he might as well have the trip of a lifetime. So once again he raised his eyes and took in the splendor of the moon. Larger and larger it loomed, until it could come no closer and it too began to shimmer, shake, and finally lose the tension that held it together. Slowly the moon melted before his eyes, first with small, single droplets forming on its craggy surface before streaking, then in waves as entire patches buckled and ran down the front of the sky, vanishing. Shocked at the sudden loss of the moon, the stars took photos, winking in and out as they captured pictures of the strange turn of events.

With the moon gone, the stars had a full-blown freak-out,

each spiraling through the night on a panicked carousel, screaming, wailing for help before several thousand of them collided,
exploding in the center, together forming a brand-new moon
so the earth would no longer be so alone. Everyone needed a
partner. Everything needed a friend. Nothing in the universe
wanted to be found sitting alone on a rock in the middle of
nowhere wondering why they weren't allowed in the tent. Everyone should be allowed in the tent. After all, that's all the world
was: one big tent for us all to fuck in. But not Abe. Abe wasn't
allowed in that tent either. No, Abe was destined to spend the
rest of his life outside that tent, outside of time, outside of himself, looking back in at a moment when he would be left alone
forever.

Dallas, Carly, and Stacy hadn't taken this many mushrooms.
They wouldn't be able to step out of time like this. So they
would stay at the camp, trapped inside the thin walls of reality, unable to see what Abe saw. And that made him even more
alone. Alone.

Alone.

Psst. Over here.

"What," mumbled Abe. Or at least he thought he mumbled
what. Did he? Had he really said anything? He tried again.
"What?" That time it worked. The word came out. Or did it?
"What," he repeated again. Or maybe he hadn't repeated it at all.

Come here.

Okay. That wasn't really a voice. That was all in his head. He
wasn't really hearing anything.

"Come here, silly."

Abraham looked up, saw a shadow in the tree line behind
him. The voice sounded familiar. Feminine. Sexy. Carly.

"Carly?" he asked in a shouted whisper. "Is that you?"

"Yeah, sweetie. It is."

"How did you get out of time?"

"What?"

"Time. How did you escape it? You didn't take as many shrooms as I did."

She giggled. "Time isn't all that hard to get away from. Like you."

Abraham tried to spin around on his rock. It wasn't working. His head merely flopped back and forth on his neck. "What do you mean?"

"You wouldn't know *hard to get* if it walked up and hit you with a brick."

"Hard to . . . hard to get?"

"Yeah."

"You were playing hard to get?" he asked.

"Yeah."

"You're good."

"You've got to be," she said with a wry smile.

"Why'd you wait so long?"

"I wanted to make sure you weren't a creep."

"Oh. Am I a creep?"

"No, but your friend is. Do you know what he wanted me to do?"

He thought for a moment about the dozens of stories Dallas had told him, about all the things he'd gotten women to do. "Probably." It wasn't hard to imagine how he'd chased Carly off. "I can guess, I mean."

"Well, do you have any ideas about what *you* could get me to do?"

Abe giggled a little. "I could think of something, I suppose."

"Well then, what are you still doing on that rock?"

"I can't really move."

"Yes, you can."

"No, I mean, I've become one with it or something."

"No, you haven't. I'm not coming over there. You'll have to

come over here. So summon the strength of the earth or the ancients or whatever you have to do, but get your ass off that rock and over here. I want to show you something."

That got Abe's attention. He sat up, the energy of the universe flowing through him, the stars and wind against his back, and he levitated from the rock as if willed to do so by a powerful force. There was an electric pulse on the night air and he could feel it now. It originated deep inside the pit of his gut, tethered to the shadowy, naked form of Carly, hidden just behind the bushes. He was drawn to her. It was meant to be. There he floated above the ground, his legs no longer responding to what his brain was telling them, his torso drifting, barely supported by them. *Wait, was he drifting or was he walking?* He couldn't tell anymore.

His floating stopped a few feet from her, his center of gravity shifting as he wobbled atop a pair of rubbery legs. The pulse was stronger standing next to her, the dull hum of the world originating from where she was standing, as if Carly herself was the center of the universe. *Was she,* he wondered, *the center of the universe?* He didn't know. There was a lot he didn't know; he was beginning to realize that. The universe was a vast expanse, far greater than he could ever conceive, and he had seen but a fraction of an inch of it. Tears started to form in the corners of his eyes as he finally understood what the universe was trying to tell him.

"Those were really good mushrooms, weren't they?" she asked.

"Yeah," Abe snapped back. For an instant, he wished his mouth could match the poetry in his mind. That his mouth worked at all astonished him.

"Will you dance with me?"

He smiled and giggled oafishly. "Yeah."

"Dance with me," she cooed. She shimmered, as if she were made of gemstones, and as she swayed, the moonlight glimmered off her curves. Her eyes locked with his, her sway becoming a writhe. Then the writhe became a swagger and she took slow, sensual steps toward him. A twirl, a wave, a beckon. She was dancing now, fully invested in the throes of a lurid seduction. *"Dance with me."*

He wasn't going to blow it this time. Abe began to dance. There was no rhythm to his movement, no fluidity, no poetry. The moves he made were absurd; a prancing duck amid elegant swans fared better at attracting a mate. Carly smiled; the dance was enough. Every molecule in his body exploded, awash in tingling arousal, doused in a transcendent, enlightened glow. This moment, this moment right here, was the very best twenty or so seconds of Abraham Collins's life.

It was then that Abraham Collins realized that not only was he dancing rather poorly, but that he could not stop dancing poorly—or stop dancing at all. Something else had taken him over, thrusting his legs in the air before slamming them back down on sharp stones and prickly burr patches. And as he tried to gaze down to see the state of his feet, he realized something odd: he couldn't look down. It was only then he noticed that Carly didn't look like Carly at all.

The drugs weren't wearing off, but he was beginning to see through them. This wasn't Carly; this wasn't anyone resembling Carly. Sure, she was lithe and beautiful, but it wasn't her.

No, this girl was different. A waifishly thin goddess with a ballerina's body and a virginal face pristine with innocence; she shone in the moonlight like a ghostly angel, wisps of magic misting off her as she moved. Her movements blurred, blending together—a liberal mix of her speed, the shadows, and the psilocybin coursing through his veins. He couldn't take his eyes off her, not for a moment. Not even to look at where he was danc-ing. The fog of the high was lifting ever so slowly, but for some reason he was no longer in control of his own feet.

"Do you love me?" she whispered.

"Yes," he answered without thinking. He wasn't sure why.

"Will you love me forever?"

"Yes," he answered again without hesitation. "I will love you as long as forever and more."

"Then I will see you at the bottom."

It was then and only then that Abe saw that his feet were no longer touching the ground. He was floating—the earth a hundred feet below. He hadn't flown or ascended in any way; rather he had danced past the rock he had once reclined upon and found his way over the cliff. Abraham was falling, his ve-locity far outracing the slow speed at which he could take it all in. In his head, it might have taken an hour to hit the ground. But to the watching fairies, the moon and the stars still swirling around it, it took but seconds for Abraham Collins to plummet to the rocks below, and even less time for his legs to fracture and splinter beneath him as he impacted with the force of a speeding truck.

It would have been best had he blacked out, had he not felt every painful snap and shattering bone. Unfortunately, even at the end of his life, Abraham Collins couldn't catch a break.

CHAPTER THIRTEEN

ON THE PSYCHOLOGY
OF FOREST BOGIES

An excerpt by Dr. Thaddeus Ray, Ph.D., from
his book *A Chronicle of the Dreamfolk*

The chief problem in dealing with forest bogies is their complete and total lack of self-awareness. While they are unconsciously driven to certain behavior, they may not understand why, or even desire the outcome they will inevitably achieve. This is the unfortunate conundrum of many bogies' existence. Not everything that causes harm sets out with that intent. Sometimes their motives are far more profound or lofty.

This is not meant in any way as a defense of the bogey.

While not all of them are innately and intentionally evil, many are. Take for example the Buber. A Buber is a vicious, mean-spirited, shape-changing beast (often appearing in the guise of an old woman or an elderly man with a long gray beard) without an ounce of humanity anywhere in its hideous form. It will kiss a sleeping human being and consume its life force before slipping into its body and possessing it. Once it has consumed every last ounce of a person and done all the evil it can, it leaves behind the empty, lifeless husk with white, colorless eyes the only sign of possession. Bubers are dedicated purely to evil.

On the other hand, by all accounts Aufhockers are friendly, mischievous spirits known for their proclivity for jumping aback a person and riding them like a horse. In centuries past, many pixies and sprites were known to jump astride horses in the middle of the night and ride them to a lather, returning them before dawn exhausted and useless for the next day. This was not done with malice as much as it was done in the name of good humor. There was no permanent damage, as a tired horse could always rest. Such is the thinking of the Aufhocker. Rather than riding horses, they jump on the backs of travelers and ride them into the forest. Much like pixies and sprites, they find the stunt funny, intended only to scare the traveler, riding them until they are exhausted and cannot take another step. What the Aufhocker does not consciously realize, however, is that they are driven to ride these people to their deaths.

It is why one should never trust a bogey, even a well-intentioned one. Like a wild dog, it might look approachable, but if you get too close its nature kicks in. These creatures must be avoided and their tactics understood. If you run across a maiden in the woods and she asks you to dance, she's a bogey. Perhaps she might offer you gold or some manner of payment to dance, lie, or otherwise find yourself occupied with her, but the end result will always be the same.

Or take for example the infamous Erl King (or the Elf King's Daughter, from whom the tales of the Erl King arose) who will strike you ill for rejecting him. Damned if you dance, damned if you don't. In this case there is nothing one can do. Thus it is wisest to ignore any and all travelers while wandering through the woods. There is a good chance they mean you harm.

It would seem that these creatures feel emotion only to serve an end: to feed. Like a human being feels a rumble in its stomach to alert him to the need for food, a forest spirit feels love, jealousy, or anger. In this way they are both drawn to their food and possess the means to lure it to its doom. It is entirely feasible that a nixie truly loves the men she lures to watery graves, hoping and believing that they will live forever beneath the waves. Though one must never mistake this emotion for true feeling, nor believe you might be the exception to the rule. The soils of many forests are littered with the bones of people who thought the same.

CHAPTER FOURTEEN

THE VEIL RISES ON
THE GREAT STAGE

Ewan and Dithers hovered over the small boulder, careful not to step in any of the blood pooling at its base. Abraham Collins lay sprawled across it, his back broken, legs shattered, savage fragments of bone tearing out through flesh. His legs twitched and jerked, still dancing, jagged bone sawing away at muscle and skin.

Dithers looked down with pity. *This was no longer sporting.* Abraham Collins looked up from his rock, broken almost in two, reaching for Ewan, his eyes bleary with blood.

"Angel?" Abraham wheezed out in between coughs. Ewan took one deliberate step backward, leaving Abraham's hand pawing desperately at the space between them. Dithers and Ewan exchanged looks.

Dragana the Veela peered over the side of the cliff, one hundred feet above them, her heart as broken and mangled as Abraham's body below. She flung herself over the side, dancing slowly down along the cliff face, each elegant foot kicking off stray rocks and ledges, toes perfectly pointed as she stepped. Drifting to the ground, she rushed up, put a gentle hand on Abraham's chest, watching as blood seeped—occasionally spurting—through gashes punctured by splintered ribs. She looked away, dramatically. "Why did you have to leave me?" she whispered, her voice cracking with tears.

Dithers motioned to Ewan and then pointed at Abraham. "You know what you have to do."

"What?" asked Ewan, not actually sure what he had to do.

"Like I showed you, like you would a rabbit," said Dithers. He paused, waiting for Ewan to catch on. "It's not kind to let them suffer like this."

Ewan nodded.

"I can't watch this," said Dragana. She took a step back toward Abraham, cradled his cheeks in her hands, and kissed him deeply on the mouth. Then she pulled away, wiping a smear of blood across her lips with the back of her hand. Dragana turned away, facing the night.

Ewan wobbled Abe's blood-soaked head in his hands like a large pumpkin, looking to Dithers for approval. He rocked it back and forth just a little to get the motion right, as if he were testing a hammer or perfecting a golf swing. Then, in one swift motion, Ewan snapped Abraham's neck. The sound was quick and slight, barely even noticeable. Dragana flinched anyway.

And with that, the twitching dance ended and the blood gurgled no more.

Ewan smiled cautiously. "Was that right?"

Dithers smiled back, reaching over, ruffling Ewan's hair like a proud father. "That was exactly right. Come on, there are still three more."

Dragana wept quietly, turning back to mourn her lover, clasping his hand to her breast. Dithers and Ewan together walked away from the corpse. Ewan leaned in close, whispering ever so quietly. "If she loves them so much, why does she do that?"

Dithers put a hand on Ewan's shoulder and shook his head. "Because she doesn't know any better."

ELSEWHERE IN THE forest, Dallas's disembodied head once again poked out from the front of the canvas tent. "Did you girls hear that?" he asked of the pair hastily dressing behind him. The girls both nodded.

"Yeah," said Carly. "Your creepy, high as hell little friend probably just walked off the side of a cliff or something."

"I'm serious," said Dallas. "If that was Abe, he could really be hurt."

Stacy grimaced. "Well, why don't you go check it out?"

Dallas shook his head. "I'm not going out there alone."

"Yeah," Stacy nodded. "You really are."

"It's dark and I'm tripping balls."

Carly handed him a camping lantern from her pack—crisp, new, fresh out of the plastic, having never seen a day of use. "You better be careful then."

"Yeah," Stacy giggled. "Don't walk off any cliffs there, stud."

"Yeah." Dallas looked down at the lantern, fumbling with it for a second, trying to figure out just how to get it switched on, then, finally working it out, turned it all the way up. His head was fuzzy. Everything was hazy, out of focus. The light was *sooooo beautiful*. Colors he'd never seen before scintillated within the bulb, casting wicked shadows across the faces of the two beautiful women huddled before him. Their eyes twinkled in the light, catching the stray, brilliant rays and reflecting them back like—

SNAP! Stacy snapped her fingers inches away from Dallas's nose. "Focus," she said firmly, waving her hand in front of his face.

Dallas shook off the wandering, distracted feeling and remembered for a moment that his friend was somewhere out there in the dark. Standing to a crouch, he scooted out through the front flap of the tent, staggering off into the woods looking for Abe. "And bring back a pizza!" shouted Carly jokingly.

"Yeah! Pepperoni!" Stacy giggled. Carly laughed along with her. Then, not wanting to look at the creepy, misty darkness outside the tent any longer, Stacy hurriedly zipped the front flap back up.

"These guys are losers," whispered Carly sharply, beneath her breath.

"Shut up." Stacy smiled. "Dallas is cute."

"Yeah, but his friend is a *night-mare*."

"I know. But you still owe me for the cabin. I got stuck with your brother all week. You can deal with a creepy little dork leering at you for two days."

DISCOMBOBULATED FROM A head full of high, Dallas stumbled through bramble patches, his footfalls heavy and uneven; his senses disconnecting further and further from reality. *Where am I going?* he mumbled incoherently. He had no idea where Abe had wandered off to and it was dawning on him that sometime between entering the tent and hearing Abe's cry, a thick, dewy fog had set in. It swirled through the dim wood, rivers of elegant mist pouring down the sides of knobby mounds like swift, wispy waterfalls, spilling a thick pea-soup miasmic sea across mossy earth, ankle high and impenetrable by the naked eye. The air was thick with the humid nighttime sweat of Texas spring, tendrils of misty haze reaching up waist high, swallowing entire sections of the forest whole.

This was a very, very bad idea, thought Dallas, now sure that his friend had taken a nasty spill off the side of some cliff. "ABE!" he bellowed. "AAAAAAAABRAHAAAAAAAAм!" There was no reply—not from crickets or cicadas, or Abe in distress. Then Dallas felt it. Despite the heat, there was something about the air that held the cold, damp chill of death upon it. It wasn't a smell, it was a feeling, a creeping doom; a bleak, barren, soulless hollow that the light of the moon couldn't pierce.

All the light had fallen away from the world, with only the fog illuminated now. Even the stars struggled against the black, managing only the slightest pinpricks of twinkles through a gloom that was both everywhere and nowhere at once. It wasn't the dark of night; it was the tenebrous shadow of bad omens. Dallas had done a lot of things to score a night with a girl like Stacy in the past, and he would easily have done a lot more to score a night with both Stacy and Carly at the same time. But suddenly, ingesting hallucinogenic mushrooms and stumbling through *the middle of fucking nowhere* didn't seem worth it.

He'd been walking for at least ten minutes, his legs growing heavy, his head wobbling a bit on his neck. It was time to turn around; he'd done his part for Abe. He spun on his heel, gazing across nebulous fog, only to see the flicker of a campfire and the tent not fifty paces away. *What? But I . . . ?* "Shit." He hadn't been out there ten minutes. He hadn't been out there five. Time was fucking with him. And no matter how little he cared for Abe's predicament compared to his own, there was no way the girls would let him back in the tent so soon after leaving. So he turned back into the night, calling out to Abe once more.

The girls each drifted off into a deep sleep. Carly slipped immediately into a colorful dream fueled by afterglow, laced with Dallas's musky scent. Stacy wasn't so lucky; she sank into a grim, dusky void, vacant of restful peace. There was something dark and lonely here, something unnatural. She wasn't alone in her dreamless sleep, unsure what it was that loitered in the empty black of her subconscious, leering at her thoughts, sifting through her memories with filthy, perverted fingers.

Perched above her, in plain view, stooped a skeleton of a man, an ancient, drooling Methuselah, with hollow, sunken sockets surrounding lifeless black orbs; an unfettered beard speckled with wood chips and slivers of cedar; and a flare of wild, untamed white hair exploding out of his skull like a dying dandelion. *Nibbling Nils. The Buber.*

Stacy was a feast of shame, brimming with insecurity, lashed together with frayed strands of delusion. Nibbling Nils ran his slobbering tongue over his shriveled, cracking lips. He stroked Stacy's cheek with a bony hand, pinching both sides of her face, forming a gaping pucker. Then he leaned in, kissed her deeply, his enthusiastic tongue flitting around the inside of her mouth. She tasted like an unripened raspberry, a bitter, tart fruit laced with regret but full of promise.

Delicious. Her soul flooded into him like a geyser, an eruption of despair and self-loathing, salted with empty bliss and drunken diversion. He cringed a bit at the taste of her childhood—far too sweet for his liking—but the broth upon which a thousand of her disappointments were stewed.

Everything that was Stacy Long faded away, swallowed hard into the belly of a dirty old man. He would soon drink her dry, hollow her out, slide in and wear her into the night like a silk dress. But there were still several years of staggering mediocrity to finish gulping down, and he was in no hurry.

ELSEWHERE, DALLAS CONTINUED blindly through the woods, calling for Abe. It was pitch black and the misting fog had developed a personality all its own, at times sweeping up like a storm surge, silently herding him farther off the trails. Slowly but surely, Dallas was getting lost. It seemed now as if finding camp was going to be as impossible as finding Abe. He tried convincing himself that nothing had happened—that Abe was sleeping off his mistakes under a tree somewhere, dreaming of all the things he was never going to do with Carly—but the mushrooms were getting the best of him and panic was setting in.

Scratch! PAIN. Dallas glanced down at his arm with a wince. He'd somehow walked into the sharp end of a jagged branch, his pink exposed flesh flooding with a shock of crimson. He cupped it with his hand, trying to stanch the flow.

He swore repeatedly. He cursed the tree; he cursed himself; he even cursed the way the fog began to turn scarlet as blood dripped, swirling into it, splashing into the thick, frothy roil before diffusing into the surrounding mist. The fog ran red with blood, pinkening into a soft blush before vanishing into the black. *Wait, that's not right.*

Dallas didn't care whether this was the drugs or not. He'd had enough. He turned without thinking, running blindly into the night, his legs pumping furiously, managing to make it a full fifty feet before a looping root reached out of the earth, took hold of his ankle, and twisted it, slamming him face-first into the rocky soil. Gasping, he tried to catch his breath, but it had been knocked clean out of him and sat swirling in the impenetrable fog beside him. Then he reached out, trying to grab hold of it. His lungs wheezed to life.

That's when he heard the scuffing sound of footsteps through brush. Then the tinkling notes of a soft voice whimpering in the evening air. "Dallas?" Stacy called out. "Dallas, where are you?"

"I'm here," he coughed out, trying to form wheezes into words. "Here."

"Dallas?"

"Here!" This time the word came out, all the way out. Dallas pushed himself to his knees, rising to his feet, careful of the ankle that was throbbing too much to merely be twisted. He didn't want to look at it; he didn't want to know. "Stacy?"

Stacy made her way carefully through the soupy darkness. There was something strange about the way she walked, as if she were uncomfortable with her own feet and measured every stride, but Dallas was only just beginning to notice it as she took her final few steps toward him. Then he looked into her eyes, saw only milky white orbs, the irises cloudy, drained of color. She had no expression, showed no emotion, a bag of flesh held steady by the hooks and pulleys of an invisible puppeteer.

"Stacy?"

Without a word, Stacy slashed his throat with her camping knife. His severed windpipe gurgled his surprise as he reached out futilely in self-defense. She thrust the knife violently into him, stabbing each individual organ alphabetically, one by one and twice for the lungs. Dallas twitched with a sickened spasm, his body convulsing, the last seconds of life clinging desperately to remain behind in this world. He reached out, lost two fingers; he swung with an open paw, lost three more. Stacy's strength was unnatural and Dallas never landed a single blow for himself before tumbling to the ground to bleed out in the thick fog.

The trees rustled. "He was mine," a voice called from the dark.

"I got him first," said Stacy, her voice raspy and cold.

Bill the Shadow stepped out from behind a thick tree. He was an inky blot of a man, a tattered black coat and weathered fedora the only details that weren't too fuzzy to see. Except for his eyes. There was no missing his eyes. He drew a deep drag off a cigarette, its bright orange cherry searing the dark surrounding his featureless face. "Oh. I see."

Then, with a wave of his hand the trees descended upon Stacy, their branches like talons and teeth, anxious to sink into her waiting flesh. Stacy recoiled, but the forest was far quicker.

The branches first tore the clothes from her body then the skin from her naked flesh; they continued to swing with an angry rage, rending chunk after bloody chunk, tossing each aside while hungrily clawing at the prize beneath. They reached in together in a gnarled wooden unison, dug deep into what remained of Stacy's body and in one terrible motion tore it apart in an explosion of muck, bile, and bone. Where a woman once stood, now only Nibbling Nils remained. "Fuck . . . you," he said.

"I'd say we're even, old man," said Bill the Shadow. "Let's not make this a bigger deal than it has to be." He narrowed his eyes.

Nils backed down. He didn't want Bill's wrath any more than Bill really wanted his. "Yeah. Whatever. Fuck it."

Bill smiled. "Kind of fun though, wasn't it?"

Nils curled the corner of his lips into a slobbering sneer—the closest thing he could manage to a smile. "Yeah. It really was."

"Come on, let's go watch the Aufhocker."

CARLY JERKED AWAKE, surprised by something that wasn't there. She hadn't heard anything, couldn't see anything, and apparently Dallas and Stacy had slunk off for another tryst. She thought for a moment of the two off in the dark, passionately wrestling, clawing at each other, and she sighed deeply, left with no other option but the loser. But even he wasn't around. Carly Ginero was a crestfallen second place, her role that of booby prize to an unworthy, unwanted suitor. She really hated Stacy sometimes.

SNAP! A twig cracked outside the tent. She didn't think,

didn't stop for a moment to wonder if it was an animal or an intruder; she got up, storming out of the tent, angry that she had been left alone. Calling out into the night, she barked: "Now just where the hell have *you* been?" She trailed off, her eyes losing focus gazing out into the eerie silence. No one. No one at all. She looked around, uneasy, wondering who or what might be lurking in the woods just outside the dwindling firelight.

She saw the rustle of movement, heard another twig crack. Her head whipped around and there, just beyond the bushes, stood the creepiest, most emaciated little boy she'd ever seen. He stared back at her through the dark, his eyes hollow, empty. Her heart sank into her stomach and she froze in place. Then, with the flutter of eyelashes and the slight twitch of eyebrows, the little boy turned and ran into the woods, daring her to chase him.

That's when the thing leapt from the dark, grappling her from behind. "Run," breathed a husky voice into her ear with air so hot it singed her hair. Carly sprinted, immediately hitting her full stride. Her bare feet tore over broken ground, rocks digging in, scraping the skin from her heels. She ran harder than she'd ever run in her life. There was nothing but fear now, a terrible anxiety that this was how she would meet her end—alone and screaming in the dark underbrush.

Eberhard rode astride her back—all three goblinoid feet of him—a snaggletoothed smile resting beneath his crooked hook nose that showed no malice at all. Only amusement. He hooted and hollered, his grip firm, his stance that of a prize-winning jockey. "Run, my little pretty, run!" he cackled. "Run until your feet fall off."

The forest thundered with the steady, drumlike pounding of her heart. *BA-DUM! BA-DUM! BA-DUM! BA-DUM!* So great was the pounding that they couldn't hear the rustling leaves, snapping twigs, or even the crackling branches below them as

Carly's delicate feet were nibbled apart piece by piece by a ravenous forest. Nor did they hear the distant rumble of thunder, or see the stars engulfed by dark black clouds backlit by distant fires. And by the time the rumble had become an unbridled roar, it was too late.

Eberhard and Carly looked up to see a dark rider atop a shadowy mound of matted fur emerging from the wood in front of them. In its hand it carried a monstrous ax—the blade alone half the size of a grown man—and by the time either realized they were in danger, the ax swung, cleaving Carly into two perfectly bisected pieces, then followed through, taking the Aufhocker in two pieces with her.

Carly stopped running, each leg still shuffling forward a bit more before both of her halves fell in opposite directions, the wet, gelatinous slop of her innards spilling out upon the earth the last sound she would ever make. And were the countryside not echoing with the deep, brutal thunder of Hell, someone might have noted the lonely sadness and what it had to say about her troubled, meandering, unfulfilled life. But Carly Ginero—the daughter of an autoworker and a nurse, who had dreamed up to the last moments of her life of becoming a princess—would not be the last sad story to come to an end that night. Nor would her end be the most spectacular. In death, much as in life, she would prove to be an unnoticed footnote amid a much larger story—not even a close second in her bid to be noteworthy—for tonight was another woman's big night, and that woman had waited seven long years in Hell to get it.

CHAPTER FIFTEEN

THE WILD HUNT

An excerpt by Dr. Thaddeus Ray, Ph.D., from
his book *A Chronicle of the Dreamfolk*

There are few sounds in this world more terrifying than
the thunderous onset of a Wild Hunt. These dark, murderous,
black riders arrive foretold only by the tumultuous cacophony
of their steeds coming from miles off, the strike of each hoof
uniting into a deafening roar that can set a man's ears to ring-
ing from a quarter mile away. It is the sound of the damned
that some say are the echoes of Hell, reminding the riders
that their stay in our world is short. They are also a beastly
warning of a calamity to come; gifted with terrible visions,
the riders are seers of unfortunate futures.

Hearing the strikes of the hooves and the howls and horns of the riders means one shall experience the coming disasters firsthand. *Seeing* the riders, however, means almost certain death.

No one knows when the first hunt took place, though history is rife with their tales. Antiquity tells us stories of mounted mobs sweeping through the desert atop black steeds whose nostrils billowed smoke and whose hooves sparked fires in the brush as they rolled across villages, slaughtering dozens before vanishing, never to be seen or heard from again.

The earliest historically recorded appearance comes to us from the *Peterborough Chronicle*—the copy of the *Anglo-Saxon Chronicle* so named for the monastery at Peterborough in which it was kept. The *Anglo-Saxon Chronicle*, a literary record of the events of the day—updated yearly—had this to say about the 1127 appointment and arrival of Henry of Poitou as the new abbot of Peterborough:

"Let no one think strange the truth that we declare, for it was well-known throughout the entire country that as soon as he arrived there—that is, on the Sunday on which one sings, *'Exurge, quare obdormis, Domine?'* immediately thereafter many men saw and heard many huntsmen hunting. These hunters were black and big and ugly, and all their dogs were black and ugly, with wide eyes, and they rode on black horses and black goats. This was seen in the deer park itself in the town of Peterborough and in all the woods between Peterborough and Stamford. And the monks heard the horns blowing, which they blew at night. Reliable witnesses observed them at night. They said it seemed to them there might well have been twenty to thirty blowing horns. This was seen and heard from the time he came here, all that Lent up to Easter. This was his arrival. Of his departure we cannot yet speak. May God provide!"

No record exists of what calamity this portent meant to foretell, whether one of the great losses in the Crusades or some local treachery that history has wiped clean, but the description is unmistakable. Throughout record these riders have made their presence known and run down the wicked, the sinful, and the unbaptized, the lawbreakers, heretics, and purveyors of immorality that have offended the master of the hunt.

This head huntsman only seems to command the hunt for scant periods of history. Sometimes the same mad huntsman is reported for decades whilst others are seen only once. The rhyme or reason behind how a man becomes head of such a pack is unknown. What is known, however, is that whoever leads the Wild Hunt has mastery of his hounds and fellow riders. The wickedness of such a display seems entirely to rest upon the cruelty of his command. On some occasions, like the Peterborough incidents, the hunt seems to leave little or no carnage behind. Other, more bloodthirsty rides, however, show no mercy to even the most venial of sinners.

Some, but not all, accounts of these rides include mentions of hounds. These range in description from the terrifying Black Dogs, roughly the size of a calf, spoken of in English folklore, to the nearly indescribable hellhounds yelping incomprehensible gibberish amid sharp barks. Most accounts, however, seem to describe the Barguest (or barghest), a massive shaggy hound with powerful jaws that can tear limbs clean off, and teeth sharp enough to rend flesh instantly from bone. These hounds emit the pungent stink of brimstone, their eyes burn like coals, and they possess the ability to vanish in a flash of hellfire. Daring to cross paths in front of a Barguest can cause a wound to mysteriously appear that will fester, blister, and refuse to heal. Their most notable quality, however, is their howl, which is reserved for the nights on which someone of great importance is to die. Unlike the banshee, this person need not hear the howl, for it is not for them. It is for everyone else, a signal that someone great or powerful among them is that very night trapped in the clutches of Hell.

There is no known ward or protection against the Wild Hunt. It must simply run its course. If ill fate so has it that you find yourself hearing the roar of their hooves: find shelter, crouch low, and pray they do not notice you. An open field, the forest, or anywhere without nearby shelter is the last place you want to be when the hunt is called—for those hooves and horns may be the last thing you hear, and will certainly be the last thing you see.

CHAPTER SIXTEEN

THE THUNDEROUS HOOVES
OF TIFFANY THATCHER

Tiffany Thatcher had spent seven years with a rope around her neck, her heart heavy with regret, her feet charred black from the fires burning beneath her. She had but from the tolling of the witching hour to the ticking of its last, lingering seconds to find her prey and strike it down.

The Devil granted few reprieves; why he had chosen her she had no clue, but if it meant an hour off the noose she would take it without question—especially if it meant bringing that *thing* back with her. There wasn't a moment she didn't relive that night, not a second spared from the rope burn and the tears. But in Hell, she did more than choke, she spun lazily in front of a window, watching her husband drown over and over again beneath the lake's waves as she burned.

And Jared's murderer was here, dripping wet, wandering through the woods. Tiffany could smell the lake water on her; could smell the blood and tattered flesh beneath her fingernails; could smell the stain of her sins. Tonight she would drag that creature back to Hell with her, tearing apart anyone else that got in her way.

With her rode a morbid procession of a dozen maddened spirits, each somehow wronged, desperate to stave off the pits of Hell for even the smallest slivers of eternity. Together they rode, galloping through the hills of the material world atop mastiff-size goats as black as a starless night, looking for souls to take their place. The sound, deafening though it was, proved a comforting relief from the endless wails, moans, and screams that accompanied every painful, waking moment of the hereafter. This sounded like adventure; it sounded like life again. And though revenge was at the heart of their crusade, it was the exhilaration of the ride, the thrill of feeling alive again, that made it worth the extra suffering they would endure if they didn't each return, soul in hand.

The gates of Hell were open and the Wild Hunt was called. They had a message for the world, and if the world was wise, it would listen.

The beautiful woman that was once Tiffany Thatcher was no more. All of her delicate loveliness had been drained, leaving a pale, ghoulish husk, her hair slicked down with years of sweat and grease. What strode atop that hellish steed was not the mother who had once cradled her cooing child, but a gaunt, cadaverous nightmare with sores oozing ochre puss and a beastly snarl that barked out orders to the braying hounds chasing behind her. Evil. Tiffany Thatcher was the very picture of evil. And she would have her revenge, even if she had to wipe the landscape clean with hellfire to do it.

So she led her charge and sounded her horns, setting the forest alight with the strike of her goat's ebony hooves. Tiffany Thatcher was the master of the hunt, and tonight the hunt would take no prisoners.

ACROSS THE FOREST, mere miles away, two young fairies bounded through the brush, traveling swiftly toward the Wild Hunt rather than away.

"Hurry up," Mallaidh anxiously called behind her. "We're going to miss it."

"I don't think they've started yet," Knocks reassured her. "Besides, a good hunt takes all night. That's what they say."

"I know, I know. But I don't want to miss it. I've never been on a hunt before. What do you think Ewan will be doing?"

Knocks stopped in his tracks and grumbled abrasively under his breath. Mallaidh, already outpacing him, didn't stop, nor did she look back. He hastily started again, trying to keep stride. "Probably nothing."

"What do you mean nothing?" she sang, as if to contradict him.

"Well, it's his first hunt. He's probably just watching. Maybe he'll be a decoy for Eberhard or something, but I doubt he'll get a chance to do anything. It's not as if he's really one of us, you know."

Mallaidh stopped and turned around, putting two delicate hands on her hips. "I *know* that. That's what makes him special."

Finally able to catch up, Knocks walked up to her and stopped, standing almost nose to nose with her. "What? *Not* being able to do anything special makes him special?"

Mallaidh thought about that for a second, then shook her

head. "No. That he was chosen to be one of us makes him special!"

"Aw, phooey." Knocks waved both of his hands, dismissing her outright.

Mallaidh giggled. "Phooey? You sound like an old woman sometimes."

Knocks scowled. "Shut up."

Mallaidh, unsure if he was joking, smiled big, melting Knocks down to his basest elements. "No, you shut up," she said. She reached out, touching him on the shoulder, then gave him a playful shove. Even at her young age she understood her gifts. Knocks had no immunity to her wiles; he had to look away, his ill-hanging cheek-flesh blushing a purplish red. "Come on," she said. "We're missing it."

"Wait." Knocks looked up. "Do you hear that?"

"The thunderstorm?" she asked.

"Yeah."

"For the last few minutes or so, yeah. What about it?"

"I don't know," he said. "It doesn't sound right."

"Well, come on. Let's see for ourselves." Mallaidh reached out and took Knocks by the hand. He smiled, as if somehow his life had been made complete, and the two ran off into the dark woods toward the distant sound of thunder. "Knocks?" she asked.

"Yeah?"

"What's a decoy?"

THE SOUND HAD grown deafening. The riders were sweeping through the valley, their charge seemingly unstoppable. Dithers bounded through the woods, Ewan thrown over his shoulder. He was fast and agile, but not fast enough to outrun unholy steeds; he had to stay high, out of sight. At first he traveled over branch and bush until he found a densely packed spot of brushwood where they could hide, shrouded on the upper limb of one of its tallest trees. There they looked out over the dark valley, the moon now hidden behind a plume of black clouds. Without the moonlight there was little to see. Orange embers drifted slowly to the earth like an ashen rainstorm, and the movements of the riders could be tracked as distant streaks lit by the glow of the fires set by their goats' hooves.

"Dithers, what are those clouds?" asked Ewan, his voice cracking and buried beneath ten minutes of pants-wetting fear.

"Ewan, behind those clouds is Hell. Those clouds are there to keep us from seeing how awful it is."

"But why is Hell here?"

"Because the Devil has unfinished business here on earth."

"Is he coming for us?"

"No, no," Dithers reassured him. "There's no reason for the Devil to come for you. He's here for someone else."

"A fairy?"

"Maybe."

"If he's not coming for us, then why are we hiding?"

"Because he'll take whoever gets in his way. And tonight, we're in his way."

"Like Eberhard?"

Dithers shared a pained, grieving look with Ewan. "Yeah. Exactly like Eberhard."

"I liked Eberhard."

"I liked him too." Dithers looked off into the distance and said a silent prayer for the Aufhocker, hoping quietly that Eberhard wouldn't suffer so terribly in Hell.

THE RIDERS MADE an end run up one side of the hill and down the other, three of them sweeping in, rejoining Tiffany Thatcher on the way back down. One of them, a particularly large, wicked-looking specter, rode by her side. His tangled hair was pulled back into a topknot, and slung over his shoulder he hefted a gargantuan, blood-spattered ax that had already split a person in half this night. Behind him he dragged two shrieking souls, their tormented screams barely audible over the galloping hooves beside them. Tiffany could see their sins. The diminutive fairy was covered in a layer of grime inches thick, with untold amounts of blood on his hands, and the girl, while no murderer, was also no saint; these were clean kills. They would pay the toll.

But time was running short. She whooped and cried, then lifted a horn to her lips. The call went out with a shrill twitter—riders dispersing in every direction without missing a stride; her only remaining companions two bounding hounds, their glowing eyes burning bright enough to silhouette their massive skulls.

And that's when she caught wind of her prey.

It did not flee. Rather, it was headed right for her. And it wasn't alone. *No, there was something else . . . familiar. A second prize. A bonus to accompany her vengeance.* Had all the parts of her that understood joy not burnt out long ago, she might have felt elated. She pressed her buck harder, her hands firmly gripping its hooked razor-sharp horns, riding it pitilessly into the night, a trail of cinders fluttering in their wake.

FEAR WAS NOT a feeling to which Nibbling Nils was particularly accustomed. While he was familiar enough with its taste and the tickle it caused in the back of his throat while probing through the thoughts and dreams of a good meal, it was something he had never himself experienced. Anger. Bitterness. Loathing. These were the emotions he was used to feeling, not fear. So when he found himself running through the woods on all fours, sprinting across broken limestone trails, vaulting over boulders to gain precious seconds on the time between himself and the three shadowy, brimstone-reeking riders behind him, he was understandably pissed. But being scared came as something of a surprise.

Other fae in the valley feared Nils; he was the stuff of nightmares, a draconian master of fright—not some rabbit to be chased down by dogs in a field. This was not how Bubers met their end. And yet, there behind him trailed a pack of slavering hellhounds, their jaws dangling midgrowl, smoldering craters left in the wake of their footfalls. As the three riders drove their hounds, so too did the hounds drive Nils and, for the very first time in his life, he was afraid.

No matter how hard he ran, they kept pace. No matter how inaccessible the terrain, they managed their way over it. No matter what he did, they would have him—or so it seemed. But he had one last trick up his sleeve, one last chance at making it through the hour. He was cornered, running out of ground to cover, headed dead on toward a cliff face. Nils was betting that no matter how fast they could gallop, they probably weren't especially good climbers.

But *he* was.

It was a harrowing dash, with logs, boulders, and all manner of shrub in his way, but through thorn and thistle, past pond and pecan tree, Nibbling Nils made it to the last few steps before a massive limestone escarpment. Without even casting an eye back to see how close the riders had gotten, he shot up the rock face, grasping for handholds, propelling himself up the side. It took only seconds to skitter up the fifty-some-odd feet, and as he gave one last kick, he lunged upward in an arc, over the edge of the cliff, landing squarely on his feet.

Much to his surprise and almost immediate alarm, he was not alone. He had managed to land almost perfectly beside Dragana, who stood there weeping, her eyes welling with tears. Together they peered over the side, watching as the riders and hounds sat patiently below, staring back at them. Nils extended his middle finger their way, smiled a crooked grin, then sneered at Dragana. "What the fuck's your problem?"

She looked up over her shoulder, nodding into the forest behind her. They were not alone. Three more riders perched atop their flickering midnight steeds, leaning casually forward, each goat's fur ruffling in the wind. They gave one another knowing looks, then let their skeletal, rotting jaws flap loose an infernal scream before heaving forth, blades held high.

Nils's expression fell. "Aw, hell," he muttered. He looked over the cliff once more, seeing that the riders below hadn't moved. Dragana took his hand in hers and wiped away a stream of tears with the other.

Nils reluctantly accepted her hand, giving her a weak smile. "Well. That's that, I guess."

THE WORD PASSED quietly through Dithers's lips like air leaking from a balloon. "Shit." Below, the rider blazed by without missing a step, its ax slicing through the core of the tree as easily as it would flesh. Flame licked the trunk, showering the ground with a spray of smoldering splinters. There was only time for instinct now. Dithers grabbed Ewan, slung him onto his back once more, and then flung himself off the limb toward the earth below. He grasped at passing branches, slowing his descent, but still cratered down with a concussive thud, knocking the wind out of Ewan.

Dithers bounded forward. The riders were on to him almost immediately, but Dithers launched himself a good twenty feet into the air, flying once again branch to branch, far out of the riders' reach, matching their speed when not occasionally gaining ground.

Ewan held on tight, gasping for air as he tried to recover from the hard landing. His stomach hurt, but as he finally managed to force his lungs back into action, the pain subsided, air rushed back in. He looked around, seeing only a blur of foliage and the occasional flicker of flame. "Dithers," he asked, "what's happening?"

"The Wild Hunt," said Dithers.

"I thought you said they weren't coming for us."

Dithers paused. "I was wrong," he said. Ewan tightened his embrace; it was the only thing he could think to do.

WHUMP! The blackened arrow struck Dithers in the chest with the force of a clenched fist. It was a full inch thick, carved from hellish black wood, tipped with forged pieces of jagged nightmares. He doubled over in midair, flailing backward, frantically grasping for a branch to regain his momentum. Ewan lost his grip, tumbling to the ground while Dithers slammed into the trunk of an oncoming tree, folding to a stop over a large limb. Ewan scrambled to his feet, running into the thick brush. Hoping to hide while Dithers collected himself, he dove headlong into a bramble patch.

He looked up, saw Dithers dangling from the tree with an arrow driven all the way through his chest, the searing tip flickering a blue-green flame out a hole in his back. Dithers twitched a bit. Ewan closed his eyes tight, clenching his fists, rocking gently back and forth, unsure of what to do.

"WHAT'S THAT SOUND?" shrieked Mallaidh.

Knocks quivered in place, too frightened to move. "I . . . I don't know." What at first had sounded like distant thunder now nearly deafened them. It was clear that, though they could not see it, something was tearing through the forest around them, kicking up a terrible fuss. The earth trembled like a pounding kettle-drum, the whole world falling apart just beyond the trees.

Then from out of the woods sprang a grim shape, dripping wet, its teeth bared, green skin slick with algae.

"Mama!" he shouted, recognizing her. She threw her arms around Knocks.

Laila the nixie looked down at the little boy in her arms. "Oh, child, I'm so happy to see you."

Knocks looked up. "Mama, what are you doing here?"

"Child, this is the Wild Hunt. These things will kill you. What are you doing out here?" Knocks stammered for a moment. He knew he wasn't supposed to be out. More important, he knew he shouldn't be anywhere near the scene of a hunt. He was in trouble. Big trouble.

"Mama, I—"

"He was with me," interrupted Mallaidh, the full brunt of her charms brought to bear for Knocks's sake. "I wanted to see the hunt."

Laila looked askance at her adopted son's escort. "You're as much trouble as your mother, you know that? You could have gotten my boy killed."

Mallaidh shook her head. "No. We were just—"

"You were just leaving," interrupted Laila. "You will not seduce my boy with your wicked ways, slut. Get out of my sight." Laila stroked Knocks's bulbous, balding head with one hand, pointing away fiercely with the other.

Mallaidh stood there, humiliated, her eyes narrow and bitter. Her ears rang with the sound of thunder, no longer able to tell where it was coming from. She had no sense of the rider galloping straight at her. Laila stared wide-eyed at the form riding up behind the young fairy, stood up, her son gripped tightly in her arms, and took off into a full run. Knocks reached back over his mother's shoulder, trying to grab Mallaidh—despite her distance—screaming at the top of his lungs, "Mallaidh!"

Mallaidh turned around, only then spying the looming rider about to trample her. She shrieked, but just a little, a slight, scared yip escaping her delicate mouth as she completely seized up in fear. Something slammed into her from the side, tackling her to the ground mere inches from passing hooves. She looked up, the ground exploding around her, to find the kind eyes of the boy who had just saved her life.

Knocks watched helplessly as Ewan emerged from the darkness of a nearby bramble patch to save Mallaidh, Ewan standing in the place where he should have been. Even as scared as he was, he felt his stewing hatred of Ewan simmering stronger still.

Back in the grove, Ewan and Mallaidh gripped each other as firmly as they could, the sound of hooves growing closer by the second. The rider trotted slowly up behind them, its goat bleating, grunting against the reins, the goat wanting little more than to stomp these creatures underfoot. Flanking it on each side sat drooling, snarling, muscular piles of awfulness—hounds beset with razor-sharp fangs and shaggy fur matted with blood and ichor.

The children looked up at the mount and its rider, the beast's nostrils choking the air with sulfur. The rider leaned over, its face emerging from shadow into the dim light. Pale, sickly, rotting from the inside out, Tiffany Thatcher looked nothing like she had the last time they had met; the only mercy in this moment was that Ewan had no idea he was looking upon his own mother.

Tiffany had trouble finding words. She could feel the minutes ticking away, her time on earth drawing to a close. She had a toll to pay; this was not it. Her eyes darkened and she cast a single finger at Mallaidh. "She will be the death of you!" she spat at Ewan. "She and her kind will kill you to spare their own. I have seen it!"

Shuddering, Ewan looked up, shaking his head. "Go away!"

His mother looked down at him, feeling only the slightest, fleeting pangs of motherhood. Then she nodded. "You'll die for her," she growled bitterly. She tugged at the reins, urging her steed into the woods. With a sharp whistle she called off both her hounds. Mallaidh and Ewan looked on as the creatures bounded into the forest after her, leaving them alone.

"You saved me," whispered Mallaidh into his ear.

Ewan released her, and jumped to his feet, brushing himself off nervously. "No, I . . . I'm sorry . . . I mean . . . I . . . was on the other side of the bushes." He hadn't realized in the moment how tightly he'd held her or, more important, how tightly she'd held him back. In the most ladylike fashion possible, she too rose to her feet, took Ewan by the hand, kissing him gently on the cheek.

"My hero," she said softly. Then she looked down at her small hand held in his and quietly begged, "Don't let go. Don't ever let go."

"I won't," he said.

"I know."

TIFFANY ENTERED THE small clearing where the two stood, slowing her lurching beast. Her hounds hurdled over hedges, flanking her quarry, preventing their escape.

It had been nearly seven years but Knocks recognized the demon on horseback. The face of his first adopted mother was something he could never purge. She was dead, of that he was certain. He'd watched her tie the rope around her neck, cheered her on as she wobbled, toppling the chair beneath her. From the looks of it, she too had not forgotten their time together.

"Knocks," whispered Laila into her son's ear, "I'm going to put you down and I want you to run as fast as you can. Can you do that for Mommy?"

"No, Mama," he whimpered back. "I can't."

"Yes. Yes you can. And you will," she said sternly. "Mama has something she has to do." Slowly, she put Knocks down on the ground, giving him a shove. But he was only able to take a few steps before the two hellhounds brayed a deep bellow that stopped him in his tracks. He wasn't going anywhere. Laila took a few steps, putting herself squarely between Tiffany and Knocks.

Tiffany Thatcher sat atop her uneasy beast, her eyes steeled upon Laila. Laila, naked, dripping with mossy lake water, didn't let her nakedness or stature disadvantage her. She held firm, unwilling to give up an inch of ground.

Tiffany's goat paced back and forth, its powerful muscles impatient to charge—ready to surge forward and run this creature down. It bleated once more, sounding its restlessness. But Tiffany Thatcher stayed her mount. Cold and unrelenting she stared at Laila, then opened her mouth, letting out a shrill shriek in some pained language spoken only in the deepest, darkest parts of Hell. The trill formed words that came out in a deathly warble sounding eerily like a chorus played backward.

"He was not yours to take."

Laila looked around, a little confused. "He was not yours to begin with," she replied.

"No!" Tiffany shouted, her anger whipping up a hot wind that rustled the trees and kicked up a cloud of dry dust. "He. Was not. Yours. To take." The goat was having a hard time keeping itself in check. With a jerk of the reins and a firm hand on its horns, Tiffany dug spiked barbs into the fiend, managing to stay it a bit longer. "He was mine," she hissed.

"I didn't take your son. I only took what was left for the lake. Your quarrel is *not* with me. And it is *not* with my boy."

"No, you took him! You took him and you drowned him! And you kept his soul! He was mine!"

"Your son isn't dead. He's . . ." Laila fell silent, her heart breaking. Tiffany Thatcher had not pierced the veil of Hell and ridden across time itself to kill the doppelganger that had driven her to suicide. This wasn't about that at all. This was about Laila and the man she had drowned beneath the waves of Ladybird Lake half a dozen or so years ago. Until then, Laila was ready to die—she had something to die for, *something* that actually meant *something*. But this wasn't sacrifice; this was revenge. Laila wasn't going to die for her son; she was going to die for her sins. For her nature. And that wasn't a very good reason at all to die.

"I loved him. I love him still," said Tiffany of her husband. With that, she let loose her hellbeast and rode it full bore into the waiting nixie, whose eyes stayed locked upon Tiffany's.

This fate was unavoidable. The only thing Laila had left in this world was one last lesson to offer her son. She turned, looking at Knocks—who cowered crying behind her—and mouthed "I love you." Then she turned back to see the smoldering blackness of her own death.

The huge infernal goat ran her down like a cardboard placard, its hooves tearing off limbs as it passed over her. Knocks leapt to his feet, screaming at the top of his lungs, "Mama!" He stopped in his place, his arm outstretched, as if he were capable of stopping time in its tracks. But the goat still lunged, dragging limp pieces of his mother along with it, meat smeared and tangled in its long black fur.

Tiffany reared the creature around, passing within inches of Knocks, and wheeled about again, trotting back toward him. She stopped, looking squarely at the boy while holding Laila's agonized soul firmly by the scruff of her neck.

Tiffany's lip snarled back across jagged teeth—sharpened and fractured from trying to gnaw her way out of Hell. Her eyes went black and what little color had remained in her skin vanished entirely. She raised her arm, pointing a crooked finger at the abomination below her. "That's not my baby," she howled on the wind. "That's *not* my baby!" Kicking its sides, Tiffany urged her lurching steed forward once more, its hulking muscles surging toward the changeling. But as its shoe touched the dirt with its step, the hoof disintegrated into ash, like the end of a lit cigarette. The immolation swept up its leg to the torso, and in that fraction of a second, both goat and rider were consumed, exploding into a cloud of cinders. Her hour was up.

Ash and embers drifted slowly to the ground, the remnants of Tiffany Thatcher coating Knocks in a fine layer of gray and black. Not entirely sure what to make of what had just happened, he staggered in a daze over to where his mother last stood, but she was gone, every last bit of her dragged off by the Wild Hunt.

Mallaidh and Ewan emerged hand in hand from the wood, scraped and shaken, but no worse for the wear. Knocks looked up, seething. Mallaidh abruptly let go of Ewan and ran to Knocks. She put a hand on his shoulder to comfort him, but he struck it off, shaking his head.

He looked over at Ewan. "You. You did this! This is your fault!"

Ewan had no idea what he was talking about. While Knocks possessed a memory seven years long and perfect in every detail, Ewan had no idea who that horsewoman was, what she meant, or why she had killed Knocks's mom. But Knocks knew all too well, and he hated Ewan for it.

"Nuh-uh!" denied Ewan. "It's not *my* fault."

"I hate you!" screamed Knocks, tears streaming down his cheeks.

Mallaidh tried once more to comfort him. "Knocks, Ewan had nothing to do with this."

"Yes, he did!" he shouted. "Yes he did! Yes he did! Yes he did!" He looked directly at Ewan. "I hate you!" he screamed again. Then his passion cooled and his eyes grew cold. "*I will see you dead.*" He straightened, stiff as a board, storming off into the forest. For a moment his choked sobs were the only reminder of his presence, but soon even they vanished.

DITHERS AWOKE TO a ghostly quiet, a searing pain in his chest. He shook the cobwebs from his head, wondering just how it was that he came to find himself draped over a creaking limb in the middle of the night. Then at once it all came screaming back to him. *THE WILD HUNT!*

He scanned the ground frantically for any signs of his young ward. If he returned to court without Ewan, they would have his hide. One job, he had but one job to do: protect that little boy from harm. But now he'd lost him, given him up to a pack of unruly hellspawn that had no doubt carried him back to the very pits of Hell.

He sniffed the air. The brimstone was gone. Gone too were the clouds that had obscured the moon, the entire valley awash in bright blue hues. While the scattered remnants of fallen trees and smoldering hoofprints remained, there were few other signs that the hunt had even taken place. The arrow that had pierced his chest had vanished, its flaming tip having cauterized the wound into a painful burn. The valley was empty, quiet, abandoned even by the dead.

Dithers dropped down from the tree. He looked up, held his breath, and waited. *They're gonna kill me.*

The bushes burst apart, Ewan springing from them in a full run. Dithers threw his arms open wide, his crooked mouth splayed ear to ear with a glowing, thunderstruck grin. "Don't you ever run off like that again," he chided, swinging Ewan around.

"But I had to. You dropped me."

Dithers paused for a moment, still holding the boy a foot off the ground, trying to recall what had happened. "I did, didn't I?" he asked, the memories fading back into place. "I'm sorry. I'll never do that again. Where did you run off to?"

Mallaidh emerged from the woods behind them. "To get her." Ewan pointed.

Dithers smiled coyly now. "I see. You had to save the pretty girl, didn't you?"

Ewan looked away, embarrassed. "Nooooo."

"Yes he did," said Mallaidh. "He saved me quite well." Ewan shrugged, words failing him.

Dithers's grin slowly drooped. "And the others?" he asked. "Did anyone else make it?"

"Nixie Knocks did," Ewan replied. "I didn't see anyone else."

Dithers set Ewan down and let out a shrill whistle. "ANYONE OUT THERE?" he called into the night. "*ANYONE?*"

For a moment there was no reply, until . . .

"Well, shit." Emerging from the dark seeped the misty form of Bill the Shadow. "That was a nightmare." He gazed over at Dithers, looking him up and down, then tipped his hat. "You look a little banged up, old buddy. How you holding up?"

"I'll be fine," muttered Dithers. "Hurts like a thousand needles stabbing me all at once, but I'll live. You see what happened to anyone else?"

Bill nodded sadly, reaching up, removing his hat, holding it politely over his chest. "Dragana and Nils."

Dithers swallowed hard, shaking his head, his eyes glazing over with the hint of tears. "They were good friends."

"As good as one can find in the Limestone Kingdom," agreed Bill.

"Well," said Dithers, "I guess we should collect Nixie Knocks and head back to the court."

"Bah!" cursed Bill. "Let that creepy little shit run back to his precious *mama* in the lake. Let *her* deal with him."

Mallaidh spoke up sadly. "His mom got killed. The horse lady got her."

"You saw it?!" asked Dithers. Both children nodded slowly. Then Dithers looked at Bill. "What did they want? Did you hear anything?"

Bill shook his head, but Mallaidh nodded eagerly. Ewan looked at her as if to tell her to stop, but it was too late. Mallaidh spoke up, sounding a little hurt, trying to make sense of the words coming out of her own mouth. "She said I was going to kill Ewan." Bill and Dithers traded confused looks. "She said she saw me kill Ewan."

Bill shook his head, spitting in the dirt. "Aw, hell. Now we've got to talk to Meinrad."

"We were going to have to talk to him anyway," said Dithers.

"Yeah, but now it's messy." Bill motioned to Ewan. "This could have been about him."

"We don't know *what* this was about."

"No," he said, peering out from beneath the shadowy brim of his hat. "But I could hazard a guess."

Dithers looked cheerlessly at the children, then back up at Bill. "Let's get them home."

IT WAS ALMOST dawn before they arrived back at camp, the sun reaching up to pluck the stars one by one from the night sky, its glorious pink crown peeking over the horizon, the muggy morning dew drenching everything as if it had rained all night. Ewan wanted nothing more than to drink a saucer of milk and fall into bed. Dithers, on the other hand, had a long day ahead of him. He walked Ewan back to their cave, a small alcove set in a limestone rock face, sheltered by a large hackberry tree. On the stone floor, offset into a dug-out burrow, lay straw swept into the shape of a crude mattress. Next to it was a fresh saucer of milk, left by pixies sometime during the night.

Dithers pointed to the makeshift bed. "Go ahead and drink up your breakfast, then get some sleep."

"Okay." Ewan got on his knees by the bed, picking up the solid, stoneware saucer in both hands, and lapped up the milk, careful not to spill a single drop; he was told never to spill a drop.

Then, after guzzling down the entire bowl, licking it clean, he set the saucer down, collapsed on his straw pile, pulling a brown rag of a blanket up to his neck. "Dithers?"

"Yes?"

"Did we do bad tonight?"

"No. Why would you say that?"

"Well, Hell came up to punish us for the bad things we were doing to those people."

"No, no, no," said Dithers, waving his arms frantically, dismissing the thought entirely. "Hell came up for a very different reason."

"What reason?"

"I don't know. That's what we're going to figure out."

"They weren't mad because I killed that guy?"

"Ahhhh. So that's what this is about." Dithers bent down on one knee, putting both hands on Ewan's shoulders. "What you did was gentle, Ewan. That boy was suffering."

"But I killed him like a rabbit."

"Yes, but he was already dying. You just killed him before the pain got any worse."

"But that means Dragana killed him."

"Well, yes. She did. That is what she does . . ." Dithers looked away, mourning for a moment. "Did, I mean."

"But why did she kill people? Isn't that wrong?"

"No," Dithers said, shaking his head. "People are food."

Ewan's eyes grew wide and he sat up, propping himself on his elbows. "People are food? But I'm a people!"

"No, Ewan. You're a special peop . . . person. You're not like them."

"Why not?"

"Because you were chosen to be a fairy, like me. Do you drink fairy milk?"

Ewan looked over at the bowl as if it should be obvious. "Yeah."

"And do you play with the other fairy children?"

"Yes."

"Then you are mostly fairy. And one day, very soon, your journey will be complete and we will celebrate under a full moon and make you one of the court forever."

"Will I have to kill people?"

Dithers laughed. "No. You'll be a special sort of fairy."

"What kind is that?"

"One with a very important destiny." He smiled, pointing a knowing finger at the young boy. "Every fairy has a job, a reason for being. We all serve a purpose. Some fairies are rulers, like the Limestone King; other fairies are hunters, like redcaps or nixies; some fairies dance; some fairies, like me, make beautiful music for all of their friends. Each one of us has something to contribute, something we are called on to do. And sometimes that involves killing things."

"But isn't that wrong?"

"No. It's wrong to kill *each other*. But every fairy has its own special way of feeding, and sometimes that involves the life force of people." Ewan looked at Dithers skeptically. "Tell me this, Ewan. Would you have felt bad for that rabbit, had you gotten a chance to kill it for dinner?"

"No," he said, looking guiltily down into his lap.

"Why not?"

"It was going to be dinner."

"Well, that's all people are to some fairies. Dinner."

Ewan looked up, tears welling in his eyes. "But no fairies will eat me, will they?"

Dithers laughed again. "Nope. I won't let them. That's my job. Meinrad gave that job to me almost seven years ago and I haven't let him down yet."

"Is that your job? Taking care of me?"

"You bet. And I'm good at it, don't you think?"

Ewan smiled, nodding, wiping his eyes dry with his sleeve. "Very."

"Well then, give me a hug." Ewan wrapped his arms around the Bendith's neck, Dithers squeezing back. "Get some sleep."

Dithers stood up and stepped outside. He gazed into the distance at the sun cresting over the hills.

"Meinrad wants a word," said a familiar voice from over his shoulder. He looked back. *Coyote.* The old trickster stood there staring at him, sullen, with mournful eyes as Dithers's heart sank into his stomach; the only thing worse than Coyote smiling at you was when Coyote *wasn't* smiling at you.

"Shit."

"I wouldn't worry too much," said Coyote. "You'll be fine. As long as you told someone about taking the *Tithe Child* on a hunt before you left."

Though it seemed impossible, Dithers's expression fell even further and he buried his face in his hands.

Coyote smiled. "Like I said, I wouldn't worry. I knew."

Dithers looked up at him. "How did . . . ?"

Coyote cocked his head back toward Dithers's cave. "Ran into your boy yesterday. And no one can keep anything from me that I don't want them to." He patted Dithers on his meaty shoulder. "Come on. Let's go get you out of trouble."

The two walked off together out of the camp, into the woods.

"So what do you think they were trying to tell us?" asked Dithers. "Do you think it's about the tithing?"

Coyote smiled. "For your sake, my friend, let's hope not."

CHAPTER SEVENTEEN

THE DEVIL'S DUE

An excerpt by Dr. Thaddeus Ray, Ph.D., from
his book *A Chronicle of the Dreamfolk*

There are few things in this world more insidious than the
notion of tithing the Devil. Certainly there are more violent
acts and more stomach-turning deeds to be found among the
habits of the fae, but none are so deliberately thought out or
so cruelly and coldly enacted as that of the Tithe.

While many tales exist of its origin, most point to a deal
struck by the fae sometime before the Common Era. Popular
tales insist that fairies once had incredibly brief life spans,
most never living long enough to see their teen years. They
left behind no art, no literature, and no tangible mark on the

world at all. Generation after generation of fairy were born of this world, lived, and then died in it, while the world went on mostly unaware that they were ever here. They tried desperately to find a way to live longer, with no success, until the Devil himself offered them a deal.

If they were willing to sacrifice one of their own once every seven years during the darkest part of the night on the darkest night of the year, he would grant them extraordinarily long lives that would dwarf even those experienced by human beings. They would be seemingly immortal, outlasting entire generations of men. That sacrifice was called the Tithe.

They accepted. The fairies drew lots every seven years and one unlucky fairy would accept his or her fate. Soon after that, when their extended lives carried them into their forties or fifties, they began selecting the fairy who was the eldest among them and ended its life for the sake of them all. If, however, they did not select a fairy on the night and hour that the Devil demanded, he would himself come and take one of his own choosing—usually the purest among them.

But as the years wore on and the fae discovered the sheer length of their near immortality, they began to relish it. They wondered why they should have to eventually give up their lives for a deal made ages ago by fairies no longer around. It is believed that it was the Tuatha De Danann who first attempted the practice of child tithing and that it was this shame that forced them beneath the hills from which they would later claim their name: *Sidhe*. What *is* known is that the first Tithe Child sealed the bargain forever and that, unbeknownst to the descendants of the first dealmakers, the Devil had included a clause stating that if ever a being not born of fae blood was offered up, fairies would spend eternity out of time, loosed from its stream. Thus fairyland, and fairy time with it, was born.

While there are a number of tales that dispute various aspects of the story, what is certain are the rules and how they are presently meted out. Children are taken as infants, often replaced by changelings to disguise the kidnapping, and brought to live amongst the fairies. There they are raised on fairy milk and food handled only by the fairies themselves. This has two effects. The first is that over time the magic of the fae seeps into the essence of the child and allows them, if they so choose, to become a fairy when they are old enough— usually about nine or ten. The second is that consuming fairy food prevents them from ever leaving without the consent of the head of the court (usually a king).

The ritual changing of a child into a fairy is often carried out on the same night as the Tithe. The reasons for this are unclear and are said to vary from court to court. Regardless, once the child is a fairy, they are sacrificed, their soul offered up to the Devil.

As each court is liable for its own tithing, fairies tend to group together geographically in as large a group as possible to limit both their responsibility as well as their odds of being selected if the tithing does not go as planned. This is the core principle behind any governing fae body and the reason so many fairies of different type and disposition will allow themselves to be ruled by a single figure or council. Fairies that go it alone quickly find themselves collected and dragged unwillingly to Hell.

Children raised for this purpose are rarely aware of their role in the community and often believe that they will live out long lives among the fairies they are raised with. It is only in the last moments of their lives that they are afforded a glimpse into the true hearts and intentions of the fairy court they serve.

CHAPTER EIGHTEEN

THE BOY COLBY ARRIVES

Colby Stevens and his friend Yashar had walked untold miles to get to where they were now, the city several weeks behind them. And while occasionally tedious, with hardly anything of interest in sight, the promise of what was just within their reach excited Colby more with each passing step. Yashar had been true to his word: he had at the ready unending supplies of sunblock, refreshments, and delicacies of all kind. Were they not walking almost every moment of the day, it would have been a vacation. But they *were* walking.

They found themselves trekking through an abandoned stretch of state highway—a more than generous description given its patches of broken asphalt, its fading white dashes, and the overgrown brush along both sides that thickened straight-away into a dense tree line. It was the very definition of middle-of-nowhere Texas, a relatively uninhabited area of the world full of beauty, wildlife, and a complete lack of recognizable civiliza-tion. The road was driven enough to be clear of branches and debris, but not so often that they saw a passing car more than once or twice an hour.

"Mommy says my daddy is a fairy," said Colby, from out of the blue.

"What?" asked a blindsided Yashar. '

"My mommy says Daddy's a fairy. It's why he goes on so many business trips without her."

Yashar nodded. "I don't think that's what she meant." He laughed a little.

"What do you mean?"

"I mean . . ." *Sigh.* "She probably meant . . . because he flies around. Like a fairy."

"Oh." Colby paused, mulling over that little piece of infor-mation. "So fairies fly?"

"Some do."

"Not all of them?"

"No. Pixies and will-o'-the-wisps fly all the time. Some crea-tures float. But most walk around like us."

"But then why would Mommy think that Daddy flies like a fairy?"

"Because people have forgotten more about fairies than they actually remember. They think of them as cute, fun little crea-tures like Tinkerbell; they've forgotten all the bad things they can do, the evil that some of them are capable of."

"Evil? You mean bad things? But I thought we were going to see *fairies*. Fairies don't do bad things."

"Oh, I'm afraid they can and do. That's what I'm telling

you. Not all fairies are good creatures; they will do you harm quicker than you can say their name. Some will lead you astray in the night, while others will swallow you whole and spit out your bones. They are masters of disguise, whether concealed in the wood or dressed as a hapless beggar. You might have met dozens of them over your life and never known it. Beautiful women, handsome men, unwashed bikers, and stray dogs: I've seen fairies assume all shapes and sizes to get what they want."

"So they're bad?" asked Colby, now a little scared.

"Not all of them. Only the unseelie ones." Yashar leaned in a bit while maintaining his pace. "*Unseelie* means 'bad fairies.' " Then he smiled. "Some, on the other hand, want nothing more than to do good in this world—to shower you with attention and gifts of food or love or hard work. They are sometimes pleasant little creatures of daylight and daffodils, brimming with goodwill, wishes, and a desire to leave the world a little more magical than they found it. We call those seelie."

"How can you tell the difference?"

"You just have to *know* the difference. Fairies are like people, they each have a job, a purpose in life, and after a while you just figure out which are which. Some you can tell right away. Others are much sneakier."

"Oh. Do you know the difference?" asked Colby.

Yashar smiled reassuringly. "I do."

"How?"

"Years of practice."

"So you'll teach me how to tell the difference?"

"I will," said Yashar.

"How are we gonna find them?"

Yashar pointed along the side of the road. "You see these trees and the growth surrounding them?"

Colby nodded.

"Well, if you keep your eyes sharp, you'll notice every so

often a small break in the woods upon which not a living thing grows on the ground. Those paths are walled in on both sides by lilies and lilacs, bluebonnets and sunflowers. They start and they stop, with no rhyme or reason, as if someone began walking on them from out of nowhere then disappeared back into the nowhere. Those are called fairy paths, and they are roads that will take you to the fairies. There is a magic to them, and when you learn to read the ambient magic in the world, you will learn to feel and hear them as well as they can be seen. A fairy path is the first sign that they are near; small dips in the universe that bridge our world to theirs."

"They live on another planet?"

"No. They live on ours. But they live in a place normal people can't see, in the nooks and crannies of the mind, in the places most people wouldn't think to look."

"But you know where to look, right?"

Yashar nodded. "And so do you."

"I do?" asked Colby.

"I gave you the sight to see them and the instinct to know where to look. You'll see what I mean soon enough. I can hear the tinkling of such a trail close by."

Colby exploded like a popcorn kernel in a hot oiled pan. "We're almost there?"

"We are," said Yashar.

"We're gonna see fairies?!"

"We are."

"How much longer?"

"Moments."

"IcantwaitIcantwaitIcantwait."

"You can wait."

"I can't wait."

"You're going to have to. We still have a small bit of walking to do. But I can feel them close."

"How do you feel them?"

Yashar stopped, turned to Colby, and then took a knee. He put both hands on Colby's shoulders. "Calm down for a second."

"I'll try."

"Take a deep breath." Colby breathed in an overexaggerated breath of air, exhaling loudly. "Now again." Colby breathed in again. "Do you feel that?"

"Feel what?" asked Colby, a little unsure of what he was looking for.

"That tickle. Over to your left."

Colby thought deeply, his mind wandering over every muscle in the left side of his body. He shook his head. "No."

"It feels like a little tug, as if a string is pulling a small part of you in another direction."

Colby calmly thought, his eyes growing wide. "YES! It feels like . . . like . . ."

"Something is over there behind the trees, right?"

"YES!"

"That's your senses telling us something is near. Your mind has been awakened to the world most people don't know exist. Soon you'll be able to distinguish between the tickle of *something* and the tickle of *something specific*."

"Like what?"

"Like the difference between someone you know and something you don't."

"Do you know what we're feeling right now?" asked Colby.

"What you're feeling is a fairy path. But when we follow that path, we'll find some fairies."

"Cool!"

"Yes, very."

The two turned back to the road, Colby exuberant, a whirling tempest of warm sunshine. Soon they took the last few steps toward the path, the tugging leading them off the pavement, into the brush, the highway disappearing into the thick foliage behind them.

The path felt alive, an electric trail of tingling sensations, rippling like waves lapping against the shore. Sweet aromas hung in the air—milkweed mixed with lavender—teasing Colby's nostrils as he made his way deeper and deeper into the trees. The tree line became a forest, its canopy brooding darkly above them, dimming the harsh sun into a soft, warm glow.

The path continued deep into the wood, winding erratically, as if it had been carved out by drunken pixies chasing a confused cat. It wove through small grottos, past fields filled with tall grass and thick knobby trees. Colby bounded from patch to patch, always ahead of Yashar, his eyes glued to the ground around his feet. He could have walked within fifty feet of an elephant to one side and missed it entirely, but not missed a nickel halfway covered in dirt if it was anywhere on the path.

He had no idea what lay around each corner or bend—whether it be a pixie or a nixie, a spriggan or a sprite. Yashar had mentioned them all, and while the tales often went in one ear and out the other, fragments of them remained; there were a lot of things he expected to see around each turn and tree, but the last thing he anticipated coming across was a little boy no older than he. But that was exactly what he found.

It was two in the afternoon on a rather warm and delightful Tuesday—nestled perfectly in the bosom of spring—that the boy Colby and the boy Ewan first set eyes on each other. There was no preamble to their meeting, no warning or alarm. Both boys darted around a tree, stopping dead in their tracks, their eyes locking immediately.

"You can't see me," Ewan stated.

"Yes I can," replied Colby, very much able to see the boy standing right in front of him.

"No you can't. I'm invisible."

Colby shook his head. "Not to me, you're not."

"Oh yes I am. I'm a fairy and you're just a boy. You're not supposed to see me."

"You're no fairy," said Colby.

"I'm mostly fairy," said Ewan. "That's all that matters."

"What's a *Mostly* Fairy?" asked Colby.

"It means I'm almost a fairy, so I'm still partly boy."

"Well, I'm all boy."

"I know," said Ewan.

"How do you know that?"

"Because Dithers taught me the difference between all the fairies and you don't look like any of them. You just look like a boy."

"What's a Dithers?"

"He's the fairy that takes care of me."

"Wow! You have a fairy?!"

"Yeah. He feeds me and takes me out to hunt and stuff."

"I have a djinn," said Colby proudly.

"What's a djinn?" asked Ewan.

"You know," said Colby, "the smokey guys from lamps. They grant wishes." Ewan shook his head, sure that this boy was now making things up. "Haven't you ever heard of Aladdin?"

Again Ewan shook his head. "No."

"Or Ali Baba and the forty thieves?"

"No."

"Don't you know anything?"

"YES!" said Ewan, putting his hands firmly on his hips. "I know lots of stuff!"

"Like what?"

"Like where the pixies live, and what a Buber is and where to find Bill the Shadow and why you should never dance with a fairy when they ask you to."

"But you've never seen *Aladdin*?" asked Colby.

"No."

"Well, you don't know anything then."

Both grimaced for a moment. "I'm Ewan," said one boy to the other.

Colby extended a hand. "My name's Colby." Ewan stared him down, distrusting the outstretched arm. "Don't you know how to shake hands?"

"No."

Colby stamped his foot, exaggeratedly throwing out his arms. "Gah! You don't know anything!"

"What do we have here?" called Yashar from behind Colby. Colby turned to look at Yashar, shaking his head.

"I found a boy who doesn't know anything."

Yashar sauntered up the path. "Did you now?" At first he wasn't sure what to make of Ewan. Thin, dirty, relatively unkempt, the boy appeared to be entirely feral. But as he peered closer, he could see the hints of glamour flickering off him, shimmering, sparkling beneath the surface. This boy lived among the fairies and was probably a stolen child adopted by some lovesick mother. Protective though they were of their charges, Yashar could find no reason the two boys couldn't talk—especially since the young Ewan was most likely a member of the very court they were visiting.

"His name is Ewan and he's never seen *Aladdin*," explained Colby.

"And how would he, living out here in fairy country?"

"Well . . ."

"Well, what? I'm sure there are a number of things this young man can tell us. Can't you?"

Ewan nodded. "I think so."

"For example, I'm sure you could tell us if Meinrad is still the king of the Limestone Court."

"He is!" Ewan spat out excitedly.

"And I'm sure you also could tell us how far we are from the center of camp."

Ewan turned around and pointed. "Back that way and over three hills!"

"And who is your mommy?"

"I don't have a mommy," said Ewan. "I have a Bendith."

"A Bendith Y Mamau?" asked Yashar, intrigued.

"Uh-huh! His name is Dithers and I love him a lot."

"I'm sure you do," said Yashar, nodding. "And where is Dithers?"

"He's back at our camp. He has to plan a funeral for some of his friends."

"Oh, I'm sorry to hear that."

"Yeah, he hasn't said anything, but his best friends got killed last night and I think he's sad. He seems very worried."

The death of a fairy was a rare occurrence; the death of many was no accident. "How did they die?" asked Yashar.

"They got caught by the Wild Hunt," said Ewan.

"Are you sure?"

Ewan nodded sadly. "Yeah, I saw it."

Yashar allowed only a hint of surprise to show. "You saw the Wild Hunt?"

"Uh-huh."

"What's a Wild Hunt?" asked Colby.

"Don't you know *anything*?" snarked Ewan.

"At least I've seen *Aladdin*!"

"All right, stop it, you two," interrupted Yashar. "Who was the huntmaster? Do you know?"

"Some lady. I don't know who she was."

"Well, why don't you take us back to meet your Bendith?"

"Okay!" Ewan turned, running excitedly back toward camp. "Come on!" he called back with a wave.

Colby turned to Yashar. "What's a Bendith?"

"A child thief."

"Really?"

"Yes," said Yashar.

"So they stole that little boy and are turning him into a fairy?"

"Yes. Colby, listen to me very carefully. Remember what I told you about fairy food?"

Colby repeated the instructions in a monotone voice, as if he'd been forced to say them a hundred times. "Don't eat or drink anything a fairy offers you, no matter how good it looks, or you'll be stuck with the fairies forever."

"That's right. And you mustn't forget that you're walking into fairy time; things will not all happen as they seem. Time does not adhere to fairies the same way it does to you or me; it slips and slides off them like a duck shedding water. Sometimes fairy time is slow time; a day in fairy time is a week in our world. But a week could also be nothing more than a day. Such is the riddle of glamour. Remember that. Now, go catch up with your friend. I'll be right behind you."

Colby smiled, pretending to understand more than a single word he'd just heard, and ran off to catch up with Ewan.

"I still don't think you should be able to see me," said Ewan, disappointed. "I've been working real hard at not being seen."

Colby nodded. "Well, I'm special. I made a wish."

"A wish for what?"

"A wish to be able to see things I normally wouldn't see, like fairies, angels, and stuff."

"That's not fair!" said Ewan.

"What do you mean that's not fair?" asked Colby.

"Some of us try real hard to be invisible. But you just get to see us."

"Yeah, but that's all I can do. I can't turn invisible or anything."

"Oh." Ewan pondered that for a moment. "Well, that might be fair."

"What else can you do?"

"Nothing yet, but I'll be able to do other stuff one day."

"So you're gonna be a fairy?"

"Yeah, after my becoming."

"What's a becoming?" asked Colby.

"It's a special day where I stop being a boy and start being a fairy all the time."

"Oh, I want a becoming too! How can I be a fairy?"

"It's real hard. You have to spend years learning and drinking lots and lots of fairy milk."

"Oh," said Colby. "I'm not supposed to eat or drink anything the fairies give me. You can't ever leave if you do."

"Why would you want to leave?" asked Ewan.

"What do you mean?"

"Why would you want to leave? There's nothing out there but people and they're just cattle."

"There's more than people," said Colby.

"What else is there?"

"Well, there are lots of things. Yashar has told me about angels and ghosts and monsters and wizards and . . . um . . . there is other stuff, I think. Do you have TV out here?"

"What's TV?" asked Ewan.

"You don't have TV? Do you have video games?"

"No, what's that?"

"Oh, well, we have TV and video games too. That's a pretty good reason to want to leave. It's pretty neat. It's a box that they tell stories on, and a video game is where you get to control the story and jump over things and shoot stuff and stuff."

"Shoot?"

"You know, with a gun?" asked Colby. He made a pair of

fist pistols and pretended to open fire at Ewan. "Bang, bang," he shouted, but Ewan, completely unfamiliar with the concept, had no idea what to make of it; he merely shook his head. Colby stared at him, his eyes wide and jaw slack. "Man, you really don't know anyth . . ."

Colby trailed off midsentence, walking abruptly into a sudden fog of drunkenness. His entire body felt warm, fuzzy, his head swimming in a numbing sea. Everything was hazy, dreamlike, colors exploding into starbursts, revealing layer upon layer, dancing in perpetual motion, as if each shade were a drop in a kaleidoscopic ocean.

Colby's depth perception shifted radically; approaching an object seemed to flatten or deform it, causing the very strange sensation that the world had been bent out of shape then returned to its original form as best as the bender knew how— leaving millions of tiny creases and imperfections that Colby now noticed for the first time. He floated; while his feet still touched the ground, he felt buoyant, drifting through an ocean of ecstatic elation. Everything was muffled, as if he were twenty feet underwater, his body tingling, tickled by a thousand fish while he was down there.

For minutes he stood still, stuck in a thousand-yard stare, gazing into a chimerical world he'd long daydreamed about. The trees were the same; the ground was the same; the air was the same. And yet, it was all very different. The same color, but different; the same texture, but different; the same world, but different. Colby stood on the edge of forever and let the sensation wash over him—not just buzzed, but thoroughly drunk off it.

Such was fairy time, and he was swept entirely into its flow.

"Come on. What are you waiting for?" asked Ewan of his new friend.

Colby grinned, dazed, staring dumbstruck into the woods. He looked up at Ewan, trying to shake off the euphoria, but it wouldn't pass. He would be swimming in this feeling for a while. "Sorry," he said. "I'm coming." Together they continued up the hill, each step fighting a current rolling steadily against them, as if they were metal men walking through a magnetic field. The trees buzzed with static, like a thousand cicadas screaming.

They walked for what seemed like forever. Time was irrelevant now. A day was just the shifting of the sun in the sky, nothing more. Everything began to make sense. The interconnectivity of every living thing was transparent, obvious—even if Colby didn't know what any of those words meant. He got it now. The universe was a magical, beautiful place; bristling with energy, full of life, overflowing with joy.

Up the hill. Down the other side. Fields of flowers rippled in the wind, exploding with smells. Tinkling notes of fairy music wafted in on the afternoon. There was so much to take in and so little ability to process it all that Colby didn't notice as pixies began to flutter about, closing in, circling the boys. There were four in all, each six inches high, beautiful, shimmering in glamour.

"A boy!" exclaimed Caja, the smallest and shrillest of the four.

"Indeed, a boy! A boy!" echoed Broennen, the prettiest of the lot.

"Oh, it's not that big a deal," said Melwyn, shrugging apathetically and narrowing her eyes at the interloper.

Only the fourth pixie, Talwyn, showed any reservation at all. She hovered ten feet away, flitting back and forth from behind a large oak, catching only glimpses of the young boy, assembling them together to form a complete picture in her head. Once she saw her sisters swarming the boy, flying as close as a span to him without a single reflexive swat to strike them down, she peered around the tree and took a good, long look, folding her arms and narrowing her eyes. "I don't trust him," she said, pronouncing judgment. "He shouldn't be able to see us."

"That's what I said!" exclaimed Ewan, happy someone was finally agreeing with him.

Colby looked around, smiling nervously. "What are these things?" he asked.

"Field pixies." Ewan smiled.

"Oh, you're ceiling fairies!" said Colby.

Ewan leaned over, whispering. "Seelie," he said under his breath.

Colby whispered back. "That's what I said. Ceiling."

Ewan tried again, still trying not to let the pixies hear. "No," he said "SEE-LEE. Seelie. No *ling*. See-lee."

"Oh, seelie," Colby whispered back.

"Yes. Seelie," said Caja with both hands on her hips, floating inches from his head. She cocked her head disapprovingly, wondering whether it was a good idea to have a new boy around at all. This one seemed rather thick. "Who *are* you, anyway?"

"I'm Colby."

Caja looked at her sisters.

"Go on! Go on!" they said in unison. Each fluttered about, trading places, never flying in one spot for more than three seconds at a time.

Caja nodded. "And what do you do?"

"What do you mean?" asked Colby.

"What do you do? What are you? What is your reason for being?" she asked, as if he was simply too stupid to understand.

"I'm a kid," he answered.

Unimpressed, she pressed on. "And?"

"And I can see things," he continued.

"See things?" she pressed further.

"That other people can't."

"OH!" she exclaimed. "Well, that's *quite* special! And how did you come by that?"

"A djinn spit in my eyes," he answered.

The four fairies hovered in place, bewildered, their wings still beating furiously, their limp jaws dangling open. "Ew," said Talwyn. "Gross."

"Ew, I know, right?" agreed Broennen.

"I don't think we should let him pass," said Melwyn. "All in favor?" Four tiny hands shot into the air at once. It was unanimous.

Ewan looked worried, troubled that he might not be able to bring his new friend to camp. Then he smiled, leaning over, whispering something into Colby's ear. Colby furrowed his brow, shaking his head. "Uh-uh."

"Do it," urged Ewan.

Colby continued his exaggerated head shake. "No way. You do it."

"I can't," said Ewan.

"What are you two up to?" asked Caja.

"I'm not doing that in front of girls," said Colby.

"If you don't, you'll never get to the village. They won't let you."

Caja glowered, wary of Ewan's scheming. "Ewan?"

Colby hung his head, sighing deeply. Then he stripped off his shirt, turning it inside out, and put it back on. The pixies' eyes grew wide with shock and for a moment it seemed as if the entire wood had gone silent.

Talwyn covered her mouth, pointing. "His shirt! It's . . . it's . . ."

"It's inside out!" cried Broennen. The pixies burst into fits of laughter. Each spiraled out of control, careening, flailing about the forest, chortling with churlish, uncontrollable laughter. They spun, flitting; wheeling about the wood as if dangled on the end of a string whirled above the heads of the boys. "It's inside out!" Broennen repeated. "Inside out!"

"How silly! How silly he is!" cried Melwyn.

Ewan grabbed Colby by the arm. "Quick! Let's go." Colby nodded and the two ran off together up the next hill. They sprinted as fast as they could, their little legs carrying them up and over the hilltop, then down toward the small valley dip below. Behind them they could still hear the wild laughter of the pixies, a sound seemingly chasing them, driving them like stampeding cattle down the slope. "Don't look back!" yelled Ewan to his new friend "And whatever you do, don't turn your shirt back right side out!"

"Okay!" yelled Colby, falling behind. Colby wasn't nearly as athletic as Ewan, who gracefully darted over rocks, weaving in and out of trees. He kept up as best he could, but the sharp pain of a cramp through the side of his stomach soon brought him to a stop. Overwhelmed, Colby, with a single arm, propped himself against a tree, wheezing, trying to work through the discomfort.

Ewan looked back over his shoulder, saw that he had lost Colby, and, without slowing down, swung around on a tree trunk to backtrack.

"Oh my god, oh my god, oh my god," Colby panted. "Who were those girls?"

Ewan stopped in place, not even winded. "Those were the pixie sisters. Talwyn, Melwyn, Caja, and Broennen."

"They were mean!"

"I think they were just playing."

Colby looked up, confused. "So why did we run?"

Ewan smiled. "Because they are nasty pranksters, and I didn't want to see what they had in mind for . . ." Slowly, Ewan's smile drooped as he trailed off. "Uh-oh."

Colby soon shared Ewan's worried expression. "What do you mean, uh-oh?"

"Don't look behind you."

Colby turned around. Behind him, not five feet from where he was standing, stood a brown pony, ornately saddled, staring right into Colby's eyes. Its mane was braided in places, long red plaits running down through nicely combed hair. This was no wild horse, but rather someone's kept beast, wandering in the woods alone. The pony threw its head back, motioning to its saddle.

Colby smiled broadly, his eyes flung wide. "A pony!" Reaching with an outstretched arm, Colby attempted to stroke the pony's mane.

"No!" shouted Ewan. "Don't! It's a trick!" Colby recoiled, now wary of the pony, taking two slow steps backward. "I told you not to look behind you."

"Sorry," said Colby.

The pony tossed its head furiously and whinnied, stamping its feet in the dirt. Suddenly it began to shudder, like a dog shaking off water, shrinking, as if it were casting itself off into thin air. Horsehair became skin, the saddle a belt, the mane a shock of hair atop a human head. This was no pony; it was a little girl.

She looked all of thirteen, face freckled from ear to ear, with long hair—redder and deeper than Colby's—and two long braids running down to her waist amid a sea of tresses. Her hands were balled into angry fists resting on her hips and she scowled long and hard at Ewan. "How dare you, sir," she spat. "That was a right old trick I had goin', an' you had no place takin' it from me."

Ewan shook his head. "He's my friend. I found him. And if anyone is going to tricks him, it is going to be me." He grinned wide at Colby. "I choose *not* to tricks him."

From deep within the forest came the dull, muted thud of a gallop—another pony, equal in size to the first. It ran, its hooves kicking up dust as it tore full bore toward the three children. Its saddle was as ornate as the first, but this pony appeared more powerful, much less done up. Rounding a large oak, it set eyes on the children and, without missing a stride, shook and went from pony to boy, his bare feet still carrying him straight toward them.

He came to a full stop, inches away from what could only be his sister. They stood shoulder to shoulder, his face as freckled as hers, his hair as deep a red. "Crap. Did I miss it?"

"Nah," replied his sister, sighing deeply. "Ewan spoilt it but good."

"Ewan!" whined the boy. "We were just gonna take the chil' fer a li'l ride."

Ewan shook his head. "Sorry. No ride today. I'm taking him to camp. He brought a djinn."

"What's a djinn?" asked both children excitedly, their eyes wide and curious.

"I have no idea," he answered. "But he sounds important." Ewan then turned to Colby. "This is my friend Colby. He's just a boy." Then he smiled, motioning to the two puckish rascals standing before them. "This is Acadia and Otis. They're Lutins. You gotta be careful with them or they'll run you all around and wear you out. Then they'll dump you in a pond or something."

Acadia smirked mischievously. "Not always."

"Yeah," Otis said, smiling. "We jus' did that ta *you*."

Acadia looked at her brother, then, without saying a word, the two brightened up a little more. "So, now that we're not tricksin' you or nothing," she said, "you be wantin' a ride to camp?"

Colby nodded excitedly and looked at Ewan. Ewan shook his head disapprovingly. "Have you learned nothing?"

Colby cast his eyes to the ground, scuffing the dirt. "We'll walk. Thanks."

The two grimaced back at the boys, looked at each other, and turned away, transforming themselves back into ponies. Together they galloped off, back into the woods.

"You have to be careful out here, Colby," said Ewan. "Seelie or not, some of these fairies are very tricksy."

"You mean tricky?"

"Tricksy. Trust me. That's how you're supposed to say it." Ewan pointed up the hill. "Come on. We're almost there."

The two once again traipsed through the vibrant wood, the echoes of galloping hooves and distant laughter adding a heartbeat to the twittering trill of life all around them. The scents were stronger here, the wildflowers delivering delirious intoxication, hints of jasmine and honeysuckle tickling notes of mountain laurel. Meanwhile, time continued to waver, patches of moments sprinting ahead of them as the trees wobbled and oscillated in a fast-forward stop-motion flutter before their boughs and leaves slowed down, waving again at more appropriate speeds. Clouds burst and dissipated above them. Temporality held no sway here. They were two soap bubbles circling time's drain, sometimes spinning very quickly—about to be sucked down into the darkness—before being flung back out to orbit slowly for a while longer on the outer edge again.

As they approached the very top of the hill, a shadow flickered beside a tree, as if it were somehow outside of time, slipping in and out of the peculiarity that held them both so tightly. Ewan looked nervously at Colby. "Oh no," he whispered. "It's the Old Man."

"Who's the old man?" asked Colby.

"Only the tricksiest of them all."

Coyote laughed, his smile as bright and as untrustworthy as ever. "Don't fill the boy's head with tales about me. Let him find out for himself." The two boys fidgeted in place, staring at Coyote, both spooked—Colby because he didn't know what to expect, Ewan because he did. Coyote grinned broadly at them, his copper skin cracking with weathered smile lines and crow's-feet. "And just who might you be, young man?"

"I'm Colby Stevens, sir."

"Colby Stevens, huh? Never heard of you." He shook his head and looked at the ground, seemingly tsking under his breath, all the while hiding a playful smirk. Then with a glimmer in his eye he looked up and said, "But I think I might just know who you are. Come on, let's show you around."

From the haze of mist and trees emerged Yashar, having stayed just close enough to keep an eye on Colby, but far enough away to not seem like it. He grinned, tickled by what he'd seen.

Coyote waved at Yashar. "Is this yours?" he asked of Colby.

"Yes, sir. He's my djinn."

Coyote looked Yashar up and down, stroking his chin. "Do we know each other, stranger?"

"*Of* one another, yes." Yashar smiled. "You're the trickster, Coyote."

Coyote's smile grew impossibly wide, considering how broadly he'd been smiling before. "And that would make you the Cursed One."

Yashar nodded, unfazed by the nickname. "Yashar," he said, offering his hand in friendship.

"Coyote." The two shook hands. "Come, let me show you both around camp." Coyote walked away, rather abruptly leaving the three behind.

Yashar, walking along beside them, motioned with a hurried flap of his hand for the boys to follow. He looked down at Colby. "So, did you learn anything on your walk?"

Colby nodded excitedly. "Yeah, it turns out Ewan knows stuff after all!"

"Really? So he's not as dumb as you thought?"

"No! Well, he still hasn't seen *Aladdin* and doesn't know what a video game is, but I can teach him that."

"Can you?" asked Yashar.

"Yeah, but only if he keeps teaching me how to defeat fairies."

"I can teach you that!" Ewan beamed.

Colby nodded with a smile. "Cool."

CHAPTER NINETEEN

Coyote the Trickster
and the Lake Bird

An excerpt from *Twelve Dozen
Trickster Tales,* by Randolph Wagner

Once, Coyote found himself walking through the forest, singing at the top of his lungs. Coyote could not sing a lick, but that didn't stop him from belting out tuneless note after tuneless note. He sang from dawn until dusk with nary a complaint from the other woodland creatures, mostly because no one wanted to tempt Coyote into making a meal out of them. But as he walked through the woods that day, he came across a fantastic mountain, covered base to tip in pine trees, upon which rested a beautiful, mirrorlike lake so calm you could see in it the reflection of miles around.

But as Coyote made his way up that mountain, singing as he often did, he began to hear a few precious notes of the most wonderful singing he'd ever heard in his life. The melody of this song was comprised of two different singers, chirping tweets together in harmony to create such beautiful songs that Coyote demanded to know their origin. So he made his way up the mountain, past the lake and toward a rather large tree upon which sat the singers: Blue Jay and Cardinal.

Both were large birds, stout and proud, with fancy plumage and well-cared-for feathers. Each sang such lovely songs that Coyote found himself struck noteless, unable to concentrate while listening. When the two finished singing, Coyote broke into applause.

"What wonderful music!" Coyote exclaimed. "However do you sing so well?"

"Practice," said Blue Jay.

"Noble birth," said Cardinal.

"Oh yes," agreed Blue Jay. "You have to be born with it too."

"Well, I'm quite the singer myself," proclaimed Coyote. "I have sung since the beginning of time and never has a creature complained."

"We would love to hear you," said Blue Jay.

"Oh, yes, we certainly would," said Cardinal.

So Coyote began to sing in yips and howls that hurt the delicately trained ears of the two birds. They flapped their wings to cover the sound, but the notes were too powerful and sharp. When Coyote finished his song, both birds fell out of the tree laughing. Never had they heard such terrible singing. Together they rolled on the ground, slapping themselves with their wings over how funny Coyote looked and sounded.

"That is the worst singing I have ever heard," said Cardinal.

"Yes," agreed Blue Jay. "I would rather listen to Frog and Raven sing all night than listen to you for another moment."

"Well, perhaps you could teach me to sing, then," said Coyote.

"Oh no," laughed Blue Jay. "You could no more teach a rock to dance than teach a coyote to sing!"

"Oh, well," said Coyote, shrugging, "I guess I'll just go ask Lake Bird instead. He's a much better singer anyway."

The two birds stopped laughing and looked up at Coyote. "What is a Lake Bird?"

"Oh, I wouldn't worry about it if I were you. Please, go back to singing. The forest sounds empty without you."

Both birds jumped to their feet. "No," said Blue Jay. "Tell us. What is a Lake Bird?"

"Yes," said Cardinal. "Tell us!"

Coyote leaned in close to the two birds. "Well, he is a most accomplished singer, so good that no one can quite hit the same notes. He lives in the lake, beneath the surface, and will attack anyone who gazes upon him the moment he sees them. He will at first look surprised, but then will charge unless you charge him first."

"Well, I've never heard his singing," said Cardinal.

"Nor have I," said Blue Jay.

"He does not sing so loudly, as he does not wish to offend any of the other creatures by hurting their feelings." Coyote shrugged at the birds. "If *I* wanted to be known as the best singer on the mountain, I would first have to kill Lake Bird."

"Well, *I* am the best singer on the mountain," said Blue Jay. And he flew off to kill Lake Bird.

Blue Jay flew to the lake and landed on a nearby tree branch. He looked around but did not see Lake Bird anywhere. "That filthy Coyote is lying to me," he said. But he decided to fly over the lake to see if Lake Bird was actually living *in* the lake. As he flew over the lake, he saw his own reflection. His reflection looked surprised, and Blue Jay, remembering what Coyote had said, instantly charged at the bird in the lake.

Blue Jay splashed into the water and drowned.

Back up the mountain Coyote waited with Cardinal. After a while, Cardinal began to worry about Blue Jay but did not trust Coyote. "I don't think I should go to that lake," he said.

"Of course not," said Coyote. "I'm sure Blue Jay will be back soon."

"No," said Cardinal. "Something has happened. I'm sure of it."

"Well, if something happened to Blue Jay, you definitely shouldn't go down to that lake."

"Why not?" asked Cardinal.

"Blue Jay might not have been as good a singer as you, but I think he would be better in a fight. If he could not kill Lake Bird, then I certainly wouldn't recommend that you try to."

Cardinal did not trust Coyote, so if Coyote wanted him to stay with him, he must have had a reason. So Cardinal flew away to check on Blue Jay. He landed on a tree near the lake and looked around, but saw neither Blue Jay nor the Lake Bird. So he decided to fly over the lake to see if he could see Lake Bird below the surface.

Then Cardinal saw his own reflection, which, like Coyote had said, looked surprised. So Cardinal dove at the Lake Bird, splashed into the water, and, unable to swim, also drowned.

After hearing the second splash, Coyote made his way down to the lake, fished out both birds and cooked them over a roaring fire. They tasted even better than they sang, and that is how Coyote became the best singer on the mountain.

CHAPTER TWENTY

THE FIVE STONE COUNCIL

Night had fallen. After dinner, both Ewan and Colby retired to the floor of Dithers's limestone cave, Yashar having conjured up the boys a sleeping bag each and a stack of comic books to be read with a small penlight.

The adults, however, had more pressing concerns.

Coyote had spent the entirety of his night getting to know the interlopers, knowing full well what was to come. So when the trees moaned out their message in the wind and the bugs buzzed and hummed just a bit out of tune, he knew that by moonrise he'd best find himself at the Five Stone Circle waiting for Meinrad—if Meinrad wasn't there first. So leaving Yashar to the hospitality of the nocturnal fae, Coyote made his way to the circle to discover that he was, in fact, the last to arrive.

Five gray slate stones stuck out of the ground, forming a thirty-foot circle, at the center of which rested a large, flat-topped, limestone boulder covered in garlands and flowers. At the foot of each of four of the five stones stood an elder, bound there by ceremonial purpose. At the center-most stone stood Meinrad, the Limestone King, who nodded silently to Coyote, motioning to the fifth and final stone. Coyote solemnly took his place.

"The moon is above the horizon," said King Ruadhri, head of the local Sidhe mound. "You are cutting it awfully close, old friend." Dressed entirely in silk robes and adorned with tasteful jewelry, his graying hair spilling in a sleek train down his back, festooned with fresh flowers, and framed with a silver crown, Ruadhri was the very model of regal elfin beauty.

"It still sits on the edge of the world," said Coyote. "Almost late and right on time would seem to mean the same thing."

Ruadhri frowned. "It would seem that way."

Meinrad gazed around at the elders, stone groaning against stone with the slow turn of his head. "The council knows why they've been gathered. I would like now to know what it thinks."

"I think he looks delicious," growled Schafer the redcap. "He'll cook up well for breakfast." Schafer was a squat and portly redcap standing immediately to Coyote's right; never had there been a more unpleasant, rotten, dastardly cudgel of a creature in all the days of the court than he. Dressed head to toe in soiled, loose-fitting garments, he wore a scraggly beard that unfurled almost to the ground from his massive overbite, dangling just above cast-iron boots that were rusting slightly around the rivets. His long, gangly fingers, which ended in sharp, yellowing, talonlike claws, gripped tightly a massive iron pike. The only portion of him that appeared ever to see care was his meticulously dyed red woollen cap. Still dripping from a bath in this morning's freshest carcass, the hat seeped bloody tears down the side of his red-stained cheek, tinting his beard a reddish-brown before it trickled into gray and finally white on its way down toward his knees.

Meinrad nodded, shaking a wise old finger at the redcap. "Ah, but what of his companion—a djinn whose tale I'm certain you are all in some way familiar? What might he think of his ward's blood freshening your cap?"

Schafer folded his arms, glaring at Meinrad with a stare that could curdle milk at twenty paces. "He can deal with me directly."

Rhiamon the Gwyllion, the voice of the dark things, laughed. An aged, decrepit crone, this once beautiful maiden had a single gnarled goat horn growing out of the side of her head, curling back into a twice-completed spiral. Though crooked and hunched, a certain grace still shone through years of wrinkles and liver spots hidden only by flowing, ash-colored, gossamer dresses woven from wisps of smoke. "He could evaporate you with a thought were his ward to wish it."

"It's not like I'm going to announce it first," said Schafer.

King Ruadhri shook his head in contempt. "I cannot believe we are discussing this as if it were even a possibility."

Schafer spat on the ground. "Do you have a better idea, sparkles?"

Meinrad's voice boomed, "You will show respect to the council or you will find yourself off it, redcap."

"My apologies, my lord," said Schafer, enjoying how far he'd managed to get before castigation.

"Can we not just say what we are all thinking?" asked Ruadhri.

Rhiamon reached up, scratching the base of her single horn. "That the arrival of the boy Colby and the visit by the Wild Hunt last night are somehow linked?"

"Yes," Ruadhri said. "Without a doubt this is what we were warned of. The boy brings with him trouble and that trouble is most likely *cursed*."

"Which is why we should kill him," said Schafer.

Rhiamon shook her head. "I'm not so sure that is the solution."

Meinrad nodded. "Better we banish him now rather than risk the anger of his companion."

"Well, if we can't kill him . . . ," agreed Schafer, waving off the end of his answer with a firm flick of his wrist.

King Ruadhri nodded. "Schafer and I are oddly in agreement." He turned his gaze to Coyote. "What say you? You've been surprisingly quiet."

"I don't like it when he's quiet," said Schafer. "It makes me think he's up to something."

"I can speak up if you like," said Coyote, beaming.

"I like it even less when you speak. Then I *know* you're up to something."

"I think you have this backward but far be it from me to argue. Banish him if you must." The faces of the council fell all at once. There were two places one never wanted to find themselves with Coyote: agreeing with him and disagreeing with him.

Ruadhri's face fell firmly into the palm of his hand. "I know I'm going to regret this, but what exactly do you mean?"

Coyote motioned to Ruadhri as if to say *I'm glad you asked.* "Prophecy, in my experience, has never been hints of what *might* happen; it is warnings of what *will be.* Banish this boy now, and you might be paving the road to your own destruction. Of course, ignore him and you risk the same thing. Even more troubling is that this boy and his guardian, though arriving at the opportune time that they did, never saw the Wild Hunt. Only Dithers and the younglings did. Everyone else who saw it is now dead. So who was the warning really meant for? Those of us here on the council? Or the boy upon whom our court will so soon rely?" He paused. "It was *his* mother, after all, who came."

The council stood silent. The air was still. The night felt hollow, devoid of answers. Schafer was the first to speak up. "I hate you so much," he growled.

"This doesn't change anything," said Ruadhri. "If it does not concern the boy, then there shouldn't be anything keeping us from turning him away."

Coyote shook his head. "No, there isn't." Everyone stared blankly at him. "I told you there was no reason for me to argue. You merely have it backward. Unless"—his smile crooked to one side—"the very act of me speaking up is what brings about the hunt's future."

Schafer crossed his arms, pacing back and forth in place, his eyes trained upon Coyote. He swore softly through gritted teeth.

Coyote bowed politely. "My work here is done. So if there's nothing else, I'll take my leave."

Schafer spit in the dirt. "Trickster, if you're up to something . . ."

Coyote stopped smiling and the very air around the court grew cold. "Redcap. When will you ever learn? I'm *always* up to something."

CAITLIN SLIPPED OUT of her dress and into her nightgown in a single, fluid motion. Her eyes were heavy, the lure of her bed too great to stay up any longer. Aodhan followed closely behind her. Crawling beneath the covers, the two lovers wove their bodies together.

Above them, perched silently in the rafters of their underground dwelling, crouched Knocks, a white knit cap clutched tightly in one hand and a small, wicked dagger held in the other. He peered down at his parents from the dark.

"I saw him today," said Caitlin.

"Who, my love?" asked Aodhan.

"Our son."

"How was he?"

"He looked good," she said. "Strong. Healthy. It makes me so angry."

He squeezed her tighter. "I know."

"Why can't he live here? Where he belongs? With us."

Knocks loosened his grip on the knife, his jaw and eyes widening at the admission.

"I know. I know. But Meinrad was very specific. He could not have been clearer. He's not ours."

"But he should be. We asked for him. I told Dithers: bring me a son. And he went out and got our son. And he brought him back to the court. And Meinrad took him away."

"It's for the best."

"I just miss our baby boy, Ewan, so much."

"We'll have one of our own one day. A proper one. I promise."

Knocks gritted his teeth and tightened his grip on the knife.

EWAN AND COLBY each lay passed out in their sleeping bags, a cluster of half-open comic books sprawled between them, lit by a slowly dying penlight. Each was deep asleep, so much so that Coyote almost dared not wake them. But he knew what was coming, and there was only one thing left to do. He reached down and shook Ewan awake by the shoulder, then—as Ewan groggily yawned and rubbed his bleary eyes—did the same for Colby. Both, for a moment, felt as if they were still in some dream.

"Sorry to wake you," said Coyote. "But I'm afraid something has happened."

Both boys yawned simultaneously. "What?" asked Colby.

"The Five Stone Council has ruled that you must leave the kingdom by sunrise."

"What?" exclaimed Ewan loudly.

"Sssshhhh . . . ," shushed Coyote, speaking softly. "Not so loud that the whole camp will hear you. We haven't much time. If you two boys want to play, now is the last chance you will get." The boys looked anxiously at each other. "I don't know when you two will be able to see each other again, but for the time being, you have only a few hours before the sun comes up."

Ewan and Colby shared confused glances. "But why does he have to leave?" asked Ewan.

"Because little boys have no place in the Limestone Kingdom," said Coyote.

Ewan frowned. "But *I'm* a little boy."

"You've not been *just a little boy* for some time now."

"But I don't want him to go."

"Then enjoy the time you have left."

"What will we do?" asked Colby.

Coyote smiled broadly. "I'm sure you'll think of something."

Ewan shot up. "Come on," he said. "I've got some things I want to show you."

"Wait." Colby jumped to his feet. He picked up Mr. Bearston from under the cover of the sleeping bag and propped him up against the wall. "Watch our stuff," he commanded the bear. Then the boys ran off into the dark together.

ELSEWHERE, IN A moon-bathed clearing outside of camp, a pack of redcaps seven strong gathered together and pulled their caps tightly down upon their heads. Each wore iron boots and held aloft a freshly sharpened pike. They grinned sickly smiles out of mangled mouths, some stroking their beards while others beat their chests. While Otto, Reinhardt, Karl, Axel, Dietrich, and Heinrich were almost indistinguishable from one another in the daylight, at night they were identical. Together they were a huddled mass clawing at the night, hungry for the flesh of the two boys wandering through the woods unattended.

There was a giddy eagerness in the air. Schafer looked out at his rabble, smiling. "I have a treat for you," he said. "Not only will you dye your caps red in the blood of a boy tonight, but we've got a friend joining us this evening." The redcaps could smell him before he stepped into the light. Everyone knew the scent at first whiff, the unmistakable combination of lake water, shit, and piss. It was Knocks. In his hand he held a dripping-red woollen cap.

One of the Redcaps chortled. "What, you dip that in a dead deer, boy?" The redcaps laughed.

Knocks stared coldly from behind the cap and held up a small blade, still wet from kill. "No. My birth parents."

"Any of you have a problem with that?" asked Schafer. Only silent shaken heads bobbled in the dark.

Knocks wiped the blade on his cap. He looked around bitterly. "I lost my mother last night. My *real* mother. I have no people. Will you let me kill with you tonight?"

The redcaps grunted, raising their pikes, howling in unison. *Yes.*

"Thank you," he said. He put the cap atop his head, pulling it down tightly, covering his ears. Once again, the redcaps cheered.

Schafer spat. "I can't come with you and you know why. But you know what to do." He narrowed his eyes and pointed a single, bony finger at the pack. "Bring 'em back in pieces."

CHAPTER TWENTY-ONE

Days Like a Passing Shadow

Though the woods were dark, the bright moon provided just enough pale blue light for the boys to see where they were going. Colby and Ewan walked briskly, each anxious about the few remaining hours before being separated indefinitely. They were deep within the forest, but Ewan knew the way by heart.

"So what do you think it'll be like?" asked Colby of Ewan.

"What *what* will be like?"

"You know, being a fairy."

"I don't know," said Ewan. "Dithers says it will be like being a big boy, that I'll have big-boy responsibilities and will have a very important job that will be explained to me one day."

"Wow, that sounds cool."

"Yeah, I don't even know what kind of fairy I'll get to be."

"What do you mean?"

"Well, I'm going to turn into a fairy."

"Yeah?"

"Nobody told me what kind I'll become. You don't get to choose."

"Oh," said Colby. He sounded disappointed, as if turning into a fairy wasn't as cool as he'd initially thought. "What would you like to be?"

"Well, I wouldn't mind being a Bendith. Dithers is great and I'd love to be able to run that fast and swing from trees. I also really like music and he plays the most beautiful music in the whole world."

"He does?"

"Oh yeah. When he plays, fairies come from miles around and dance all night. There was one fairy—her name was Dragana—she was real pretty. She used to dance all the time. But she died."

"How'd she die?"

"Wild Hunt got her."

"What's a Wild Hunt?"

"It's a bunch of people on really mean goats who hate fairies and kill them and then drag them to Hell. One of them told me I was gonna die. She was real scary."

The two shared a moment of quiet as they walked, Ewan suddenly sad, Colby unsure of what to say about it. "What else would you want to be?" asked Colby, trying to steer the conversation back on course.

"Oh, a Sidhe I guess," said Ewan.

"What's a Sidhe?"

"They're really pretty fairies in nice clothes. They talk really funny and use a lot of big words, but there's this girl and she's kind of a Sidhe."

"How can you be *kind of* a Sidhe?"

"Well, there are different kinds. I don't know the difference, though."

"Oh," said Colby.

"Whatever it is, I hope I'm not a redcap."

"What's a redcap?"

"They're these really ugly old dwarves with knives for fingers and metal boots; yellow, ugly teeth; and wet, red, magic hats."

"Wet hats?"

"Yeah, they're red because they have to dip them in blood. If their hat ever dries out, they die. So they have to keep killing things. Sometimes it's just deer or rabbits, but they're always looking for people because apparently people blood dries slower than animal blood. But if you can steal the hat off their head, you take their strength with it. They're really mean and smelly and stupid."

"Yeah, they sound mean. I hope you're not one of those," said Colby.

"Excuse me?" came a voice from the woods. There was a rustling in the bushes and footsteps on uneven ground. The boys' faces whitened with panic and they looked at each other, trying to figure out what to do. Then from the bushes she sprang, tackling Ewan to the ground. Ewan shrieked. He looked up into the eyes of the little girl pinning him, realizing that he knew them well. "*There's this girl?*" Mallaidh asked coyly.

"Uh, no," he answered nervously. He looked to the side, trying to avoid eye contact.

Ewan tried to sit up, but Mallaidh gently pushed him back down into the dirt. She stood up, dusting herself off, giving Colby an interested look. "And you must be the *boy* I've heard so much about."

Colby licked his hand, just like he'd seen on television, and tried to slick his hair back over his ear. Instead, he managed to part his hair in a terrible cowlick. Unaware of his appearance, he continued with his suave, mature older man routine. "The name's Colby."

Mallaidh giggled. *Boys were silly.* "I'm Mallaidh."

"What are you doing out here?" asked Ewan, picking himself up off the ground.

"Following you," she answered matter-of-factly.

"Oh," said Ewan. He could not for the life of him figure out why she wanted to tag along.

"Where are you going?" she asked.

"The Great Stage."

Mallaidh's jaw went slack. "Are you mad?"

"No," said Ewan, shaking his head. "I've been there before, you know."

"Yeah, but not this way you haven't!" Mallaidh pointed ahead of them into the dark woods.

"What's wrong with this way?" asked Ewan.

"Yeah," repeated Colby "What's wrong with this way?"

"This path takes you deep into the heart of the woods, where Black Annie's cabin is!"

Ewan looked dismayed—almost embarrassed. A sheepish grin crept slowly across his face, trying to stay hidden, but stepping foolishly into the open with the upturned corners of his lips.

Colby cocked his head to one side and then turned to look at Ewan. "Who's Black Annie?"

"Only the meanest, scariest, foulest creature in all the Limestone Kingdom," Mallaidh announced. "She'll snatch you away in the night and skin you alive. Then she'll drape your skin outside over a tree branch until it dries to leather and then she'll wear it as a belt so she can keep you close to her forever! She'll scatter your bones so you'll never be at rest, and before she's done she'll eat everything else left of you. And this path takes you right through her hunting grounds."

"I've never seen her," said Ewan to Colby, as if to suggest that she might not exist.

Mallaidh corrected him. "That's because Dithers never lets you out at night where the forest bogies can feed on you," she said. Then she crossed her arms, turning her head away, giving him a withering sideways glance.

"Oh," he said. "Maybe this way wasn't such a good idea."

"I don't know," said Colby. "I kind of want to see Black Annie. She sounds sca-ree." He drew out the last syllable as if selling the others on how much fun it is to be scared. They weren't buying it.

Mallaidh shook her head definitively. "We're not going."

"You don't have to come with us," said Ewan.

"Yeah," Colby agreed. "We didn't invite you anyway."

Mallaidh huffed, shooting the boys an icy stare. *What do you mean you didn't invite me anyway?* Both boys took one noticeable step back. Ewan had never seen the intimidating Mallaidh before; it was clear she was not to be trifled with.

"Okay, okay," he said. "We won't go to the Great Stage."

"Then what do we do now?" asked Colby.

"Now we find something else to do," said Mallaidh. "Do you know any people games?"

"Duh! Of course I know people games," said Colby, rolling his eyes. *Stupid girls.*

"Oooh! What can you teach us?" asked Ewan.

Colby shrugged. "Do you know how to play tag?"

"What's tag?" asked Mallaidh and Ewan in unison.

"Jinx!" shouted Colby. Both children stared at him, dumbfounded.

"I don't get it," said Mallaidh.

Colby looked at her as if she was speaking Russian. "Get what?"

"You just shout *jinx*?" she asked.

"Nooooo!" said Colby with mock exasperation. "You said the same thing at the same time and I was the first person to say jinx, so you owe me a Coke."

"That's a stupid game," said Mallaidh. "Why's it called tag?"

"That's not tag!"

"Well, what's *tag*?" she asked.

"Tag is where I touch one of you." He walked over to Ewan and tapped him on his shoulder "And say *'you're it'* and then you're it."

"What's *it*?" asked Ewan.

"It is the person who has to *tag* someone else."

"So we just stand here touching each other?" asked Mallaidh, not sure where the fun in this game was.

"No, you're supposed to run and chase each other. You're not supposed to make it easy to get caught."

"Ooooooooooh!" said both Ewan and Mallaidh together.

"Jinx!" said Colby.

"I don't understand that game," said Ewan.

"Neither do I," said Mallaidh.

"All right," nodded Colby, "one game at a time." He pointed to Ewan. "You're it."

Colby took off running. Ewan looked at Mallaidh and straightaway made for her. Mallaidh arched her back to dodge Ewan's incoming hand—his swiping paw passing inches above her shoulder—and then she too took off running into the night. Ewan smiled; he liked this game. He knew that Mallaidh knew the woods quite well and that over uneven ground he had an advantage over Colby, so he scanned the ground for tracks, discovering the direction in which Colby'd run.

"Uuuuhn!" came Colby's voice through the dark, followed immediately by a thud and the scuffing of a sliding body on soil. He'd tripped, most likely over the loop of a tree root or a dug-in chunk of limestone. *This game was too easy,* thought Ewan.

But as he rounded a tree, to where Colby should have been scrambling to his feet, he instead saw him sprawled out on his back. Knocks sat squarely on his chest with a large piece of stone held aloft in both hands over his own head—ready to crush Colby's skull in a single swing. Ewan—with only a second to react—charged Knocks with a flying tackle to the side of his head. Already unbalanced by the rock, the rush sent Knocks reeling into the dirt. Ewan grabbed Colby by the arm, helping him to his feet. "Come on," he said forcefully. "We need to go!"

Then, a soft grumble came from the dark of the woods, a guttural growl that started out low, then became a bestial bellow that sounded the arrival of the redcaps. First there came glowing eyes in the dark, like embers flickering up from a dying flame; then shadows; then the glint of metal in the moonlight; then chaos. Shrieking redcaps stormed out of the woods, their pikes held high and their slobbering mouths gaping wide.

The hunt was on.

The children ran.

"Craaaaaaap!" yelled Colby, his little legs carrying him as fast as they could.

"Redcaps!" yelled Ewan. "Mallaidh!"

ELSEWHERE, YASHAR AND Dithers stumbled back to camp together, both a little heady from a few too many bottles of wine. Dithers strummed his lute, drunk enough that singing seemed more than appropriate, but not so inebriated as to hamper his skill. Yashar smiled, remembering for the first time in decades why he used to spend so much time with the fairies. The fire was warm, the company warmer, and the night was becoming a blur of fuzzy cartwheeling stars.

But as they walked up to Dithers's cave, two things sobered them instantly. First, the boys were no longer asleep in their beds—nor anywhere to be seen, for that matter. Second, Coyote sat cross-legged between where the two boys should be, worry painted convincingly on his face.

"Where are they?" demanded Yashar.

Coyote pointed out into the night. "The boys are out in the wildwood."

"Why aren't they here, asleep?"

"They wanted to spend some time together before you and the boy were banished at sunrise." Coyote raised an eyebrow as if asking *you didn't know that?*

Yashar looked at Dithers. "Why are we being banished?"

Dithers shrugged, his malformed head bobbing with confusion. "This is the first I've heard of it."

"The council," said Coyote, "felt that the boy was somehow a threat to the Tithe Child."

"The Tithe Child? You didn't mention that you had a . . . ," began Yashar. Then he realized what he was saying. "Oh." He looked squarely at Dithers. *"You've got to be kidding me."*

Dithers looked back at Yashar unapologetically. "If you know what that is, then you know that I couldn't say anything."

Yashar nodded. "I know," he said. He looked out into the night. "Let's go get them before this gets any worse."

COLBY AND EWAN sprinted as fast as they could, the forest behind them a wall of rustling bushes, as if the trees themselves were stampeding.

"We can't outrun them," said Ewan breathlessly.

"Yes, we can," huffed Colby. "Keep running."

"No. They're faster. You can never outrun a redcap."

"Then how do we kill 'em?" asked Colby.

"We don't," said Ewan, as if that was the stupidest question he'd ever heard. He looked back over his shoulder and saw Colby falling a little behind. "Run faster!"

"Then how do we *stop* them?"

Ewan shook his head. "The only thing that stops a redcap is scripture."

"What's a scripture?"

"I don't know."

Mallaidh called out from the woods, running as fast as she could to keep up with the boys. Her breathing was fine, and she spoke as effortlessly as if she were sipping tea instead of running. "It's holy words. From a book."

Redcaps emerged from the darkness in front of them. The patter of footsteps continued behind them. They were surrounded. The children stopped, looking around for any way out of the ambush, but they were surrounded.

"What kind of book?" asked Colby.

"What?" asked Mallaidh.

"What kind of book is a scripture?"

"Like a Bible or a Torah," she said.

"So, words from the Bible?" asked Colby, as if that were too simple an answer.

"Yes," she said, concerned more with the swarming redcaps than answering his stupid questions.

The redcaps clacked their talons together in unison. *Clack. Clack. Clack. Clack.*

"Oh," said Colby, the redcaps slowly closing in. Then he spoke quietly to himself for a second, catching his breath as he did. "Bow down. Lightning. What . . . I, uh . . ." He tried desperately to find something deep within him—to dig out a memory, dust it off, and read it aloud. And then, like water bursting through a dam, it came. "Lord, bow down thy heavens and descend. Touch the mountains and they shall smoke."

He spoke confidently, from memory, as if reciting from a page. "Send forth lightning and thou shalt scatter them. Shoot out thy arrows, and thou shalt trouble them. Put forth thy hand from on high, take me out, and deliver me from many waters:

from the hand of strange children . . . something something . . ."

The redcaps recoiled in horror. They grabbed their ears to block out the sound, but their clawed hands only dug deep into their flesh, and, unable to muffle the verse, instead tore out chunks of their own faces. Each fell writhing to the ground, suffering from terrible seizures. But as Colby came to the end of what he could remember, the pain subsided and they looked up, raging, ready to tear him limb from bloody limb. Colby came to attention and began again from the beginning.

"Lord, bow down thy heavens and descend. Touch the mountains and they shall smoke. Send forth lightning, and thou shalt scatter them. Shoot out thy arrows, and thou shalt trouble them. Put forth thy hand from on high, take me out, and deliver me from many waters. From the hand of strange children!"

He was yelling now, driving the redcaps backward as they scrambled away from the sound, iron boots kicking divots in the earth as they fled. "Lord! Bow down thy heavens and descend! Touch the mountains and they shall smoke! Send forth lightning! And thou shalt scatter them! Shoot out thy arrows! And thou shalt trouble them! Put forth thy hand from on high! Take me out! And deliver me from many waters! From the hand of strange children!"

The redcaps could not bear it any longer. Their insides were boiling, bubbling up, forming blisters on the surface of their skin. A few of them tore out their own beards, tangles of wiry, white hair coming out—root and all—with bloody patches of skin, meat dangling off the ends. Others pounded their skulls with clenched fists, trying to dull one pain by replacing it with another. One by one, they each stumbled back to their feet and ran away, screaming to block out the sound; any longer in the presence of these words and they would incinerate in place, leaving only a pile of ashes in their iron boots. Better to flee in terror than meet a fiery end.

Dietrich stayed the longest, kneeling stoically before a now screaming Colby, defiantly waiting for him to stumble over the scripture, turn to run away, or finally run out of breath. But he didn't. Colby stood firm in his resolve, repeating the verses over and over again like a broken record, the words beginning to lose meaning, the repetition becoming a blur of syllables.

Dietrich stood up on wobbly legs, teetering like a dying dandelion waving in the wind, ready to burst in the face of a single strong gust. His skin was bubbling, his blisters popping, the sores were oozing pus. He snarled a low, dull, angry growl against the pain; he was a dog on a taut leash, pulling, tugging, waiting rabidly for that leash to snap. There was nothing he wanted more than to kill Colby where he stood, but even he had his limits.

His eyes swollen with blood, his face dripping, he screamed at the top of his lungs and turned to run, joining his friends in their flight. Colby was left standing alone, his friends staring at him, amazed by what they'd just seen.

"Wow!" screamed Ewan. "That was . . . that was . . ."

"That was incredible, Colby," finished Mallaidh. She walked over and kissed him on the cheek. "Our hero."

"Hey!" protested Ewan.

"Oh shut up." She shrugged, furrowing her brow and frowning at Ewan playfully. "You'll always be *my* hero."

"Well, I—"

Then from out of the woods it leapt, a quick, brutal shadow pouncing upon Ewan. Steel glinted in one hand as the other grabbed him by the collar, throwing him to the ground.

"Ewan!" screamed Mallaidh.

It was Knocks. He quickly mounted Ewan and swung the knife down. Ewan flinched, pulling his shoulder away just in time for the blade to sink into the earth beside him. Bucking, Ewan tried to break free, but Knocks was stronger.

Knocks brought the knife up again.

"You killed my mother!" he screamed.

Then he crumpled from the blow of a quick kick to the back of the head, tumbling forward into the dirt.

"You get off of him!" shouted Colby.

Colby kicked him again. Knocks gripped his knife tightly but Colby slammed his foot down hard on his hand, crushing it. The changeling screamed. Then it was Colby who mounted Knocks, pounding him in the face.

"You! Will! Not! Hurt! My! Friend!"

Colby was a beast unleashed, wailing, a relentless fury on the small boy beneath him. Blood poured out of Knocks's nose, his crooked eye beginning to swell shut.

A large hand reached in, grabbing Colby by the scruff of the neck and hoisting him up. Colby, still in a rage, swung furiously at the air in front of him.

"Colby," said Yashar. No answer. "Colby," he said again. "Colby!"

Colby swung his last, futile punch, dangling two feet in the air, grimacing at Yashar, still spinning in his grip. Yashar glared back at Colby. Slowly the look of defiance eroded, Colby shrinking away from Yashar's withering stare. "I'm sorry," he mewled. Then he pointed an accusatory finger at Knocks. "He hurt Ewan."

Knocks leapt to his feet, leaving the knife behind, wordlessly vanishing into the woods.

Colby reached after him, yelling, "Hey!"

"Leave him," said Yashar. "We have greater concerns than him." Yashar set Colby back down on the ground. "I don't know what you were thinking."

"I told you. He was trying to kill Ewan."

"No, I mean what you two were thinking leaving camp."

Colby's eyes welled up with fearful tears. "I . . . I . . . I just wanted to play with Ewan before I had to go."

"And who told you that you had to go?" Colby looked past Yashar at Coyote, who was standing in just enough moonlight to be seen. Yashar made a slight quarter turn, looking back over his shoulder.

Coyote nodded. "The council doesn't want him interfering with the Tithe Child. Who else would they send?"

Yashar shrugged. He knew better than to bother trusting Coyote.

"What's a Tithe Child?" asked Colby

"I am," said Ewan. "It's what they call me when they think I'm not around."

Yashar shot a troubled glance at Coyote, who only smiled in return. This was going from bad to worse. "We have to go," said Yashar with a hint of urgency.

"But I don't wanna go!" Colby whined.

"We *have* to go."

"But I don't wanna!"

"Colby. Stop being so childish."

"But I am a child!"

"Be a big boy," Yashar scolded. "I need you to be a big boy for me. Can you do that?"

Colby began to cry. He didn't want to leave his new friend. He took Ewan's hand in his and held it. "I wanna stay. I'll eat some fairy food and then they have to let me stay."

"Colby!" Yashar got down on one knee, putting both hands on his shoulders, looking him directly in the eye. "We are not welcome here and bad things are about to happen if we stay. We have been asked to leave and they are being very polite right now. But if we are still here after the sun comes up, there will be a very different attitude to our presence. Do you understand?"

"But I wanna stay with Ewan," he said, his eyes swollen and overflowing with tears. "He saved my life from evil Ewan and the redcaps."

"Do you want another wish?" asked Yashar plainly.

"What?" asked Colby, wiping tears away from his cheeks with the back of his hand. He snorted a crying hiccup, a snot bubble erupting out of one of his nostrils.

"If you come with me now, you can have another wish. Any wish you want as long as it doesn't involve staying here." Yashar was getting desperate. He wasn't exaggerating; he was terrified of what would happen if the council were to unleash the unseelie fairies upon them both.

"Really?" asked Colby. "*Another* wish?"

"Yes, really," said Yashar.

"Anything?"

Yashar narrowed his eyes. "Anything but staying here or taking Ewan with us, yes."

"Promise?"

Yashar hesitated, but he was running out of time. "Yes. I promise."

"I need to get my things," said Colby. Without a word Yashar reached into his robes, pulling from them Colby's backpack. He gave Colby a telling look. *It was time to leave.* "Okay," he said. With that, he turned to Ewan, put out his hand, and said, "It was nice meeting you." Ewan looked down at his hand, still unsure of what to do with it. Colby awkwardly turned the outstretched hand into a wave, saying, "We'll work on that next time."

Ewan nodded with a confused grin. "Will you come back to visit me?"

"Yeah!" said Colby. "Of course I will." Colby leaned forward to hug Ewan. This Ewan understood, throwing his arms around him in return. Their embrace was firm, as if they were sealing some pact of brotherhood.

"Good, because I've never had a human friend before."

Colby thought about that for a moment. "Neither have I."

"Next time I'll take you out to the Great Stage and we'll have a hunt together."

"Cool!" Colby said, unsure of exactly what that meant. "I can't wait." He wiped the last of the tears from his cheeks. He needed to be a big boy in front of his friend.

Yashar put his hand on Colby's shoulder. "It's time."

"Bye, Ewan."

"Bye, Colby."

Together, Colby and Yashar turned and began their long walk out of the Limestone Kingdom. At this, Coyote grinned, sliding slowly backward, vanishing into the trees. Only Ewan and Mallaidh remained in the woods. Together they watched as Colby and Yashar walked briskly away.

"Be sure to come back, Colby," shouted Ewan, waving an arm in the air. "Come play with us!"

"Yeah, Colby," said Mallaidh. "Come back!"

Colby turned around and shouted. "Bye, guys!"

"Bye, Colby!" the two shouted simultaneously.

Neither was sure of what to say or do next. So Mallaidh did the only logical thing. She leaned in, kissed Ewan on the cheek, and said, "You're it," then sprinted off into a field of tall grass glistening in a mix of morning dew and moonlight.

Ewan hesitated for a second, looked longingly into the distance at his departing friend, then turned and ran into the grass, tickling the field with the patter of young feet and giggles.

CHAPTER TWENTY-TWO

THE DAMNING OF
COLBY STEVENS

Yashar and Colby walked in relative silence. Every once in a while Colby spoke up, Yashar immediately shushing him, knowing full well that they were still subject to the prying eyes and ears of Meinrad. Afraid of the questions Colby might ask, he thought it best to wait until they were fully out of the wildwood to open up. But as soon as they crossed the threshold and Colby's senses returned to normal, Yashar looked down, putting a hand on Colby's shoulder, and let out a relaxed sigh.

"That wasn't okay, what you did," he said.

Colby stared sheepishly at Yashar. "Which part?"

"All of it. But mostly the part where you beat the crap out of that kid."

"But he—"

"*But he* nothing. You lost your temper. Remember the talk we had about monsters?"

"The ones inside of us?"

"Yes," said Yashar, tapping Colby on the chest. "The monsters in here. That was your monster. And I never want to see it again."

"I'm sorry."

Yashar smiled. "It's all right. As long as you're *really* sorry."

"I am! I am!"

"Good. Now, where ever did you learn that Bible verse?"

"Sunday school," answered Colby. "They made us memorize one, so I picked the cool one where God makes volcanoes and the weird kids throw lightning and arrows at people."

Yashar laughed. "That you did." He shook his head and smiled. "You are an amazing child, you know that, Colby Stevens?"

Colby smiled proudly. "You think I'm more special than a Tithe Child?"

Yashar's smile fell. He dreaded what was coming next.

"Yashar, what's a tithe?"

He sighed deeply. *This was going to be a long day.*

Yashar sat upon a fallen log, its trunk large and round, its wood not yet rotten. He patted a spot beside him in a familiar fashion, inviting Colby up onto the log. "Some things in this world are truly awful," he began. He then explained the nature of the tithe.

Colby listened to Yashar's story, trying to memorize the history of it before the searing realization burned away any sense of childish wonder. "Are they going to kill Ewan?"

Yashar nodded, unable to answer. He swallowed hard.

"NO!"

"Yes, I'm afraid so."

"No! No! *No!*" Colby screamed, jumping off the log, stomping the dirt in an angry circle. "We have to go back!"

"No, that's out of the question."

"We *have* to *go back*! I won't let him die."

"I'm afraid that's what he was raised for, Colby. It is his purpose."

"They can sacrifice someone else! They can have one of those smelly redcaps. They can take any of them they want, but not Ewan. He saved my life. He's going to be a good fairy. Not a bad one. He said so."

"Colby."

"He said so! He said he's going to become a fairy and have a big-boy responsibility. That means he can't die! I have to be able to go see him. He promised. We're going to hunt together."

"No. You're not."

"Yes I am!" The tears had returned, his swollen eyes bursting forth tears even stronger and more forcefully than before. His cheeks were growing redder by the second, his nose slowly pouring a snot mustache onto his face. He was bitter. He was heartbroken. He was confused. But worst of all, he still had one wish remaining. "We have to save Ewan."

"We can't. I am forbidden to interfere."

"I wish we could save Ewan."

"It doesn't work that way, Colby. I don't have that kind of power."

"You're a djinn."

"Yes, I am. And as such, my power only comes from what people wish of me. You can wish me to save Ewan all you want, but fairy magics and pacts prevent me from doing so. They are equally as powerful as I—perhaps even more so—when there are this many of them. I am but one; they are many. They would kill me. They would kill us both."

"Then I'll do it."

"Colby, you can't."

"Yes I can. I will just go and get him."

"Colby they will *kill* you. Do you understand that? These are not nice creatures. They can be kind and gentle and fun when they want to be, but this is about their survival. And there is nothing in this world that will lie down and die for another creature. They will fight you, and you have no defense against them."

"I would if I were a wizard," said Colby pointedly.

"Yes," Yashar laughed. "But you are not a wizard."

"You can make me a wizard." The cold logic in Colby's voice was ominous. Frightening. He wasn't kidding.

"No, I won't," protested Yashar. "That's out of the question."

"Yes, you will. You promised."

"I did no such thing. I never promised to make you a wizard."

"*Anything but stay here,*" Colby repeated. "I asked if you promised and you said anything I wished for as long as it didn't involve staying here or taking Ewan with us."

"But that's what you're asking. To take Ewan with us."

"But that's not what I'm wishing for. I'm wishing for you to make me a wizard."

"I can't just make you a wizard."

Colby bravely wiped tears away from his cheeks. "I wish I were a wizard."

"No."

Colby shook his head, his eyes steely in their resolve. He would not budge. "*I wish. I were. A wizard,*" he said sharply. "*You promised.*"

Yashar attempted to protest, but found that he could not. He knew this was a bad idea; he knew that life would never be the same for Colby Stevens after this moment. But there was nothing he could do; it was out of his hands now. He *had* promised. "You're sure this is what you want?"

Colby nodded. He had never been more certain of anything in his life.

Yashar stood up from the log and knelt beside Colby. He placed a single, meaty hand on Colby's forehead, palming his skull like a basketball, whispering incantations in ancient languages. He leaned in close, putting his mouth next to Colby's ear, and began to explain the secrets of the universe. In that moment, everything that was young and still innocent about the boy Colby Stevens was drained away, replaced by a newfound confidence and understanding. Colby creased his brow, listening closely, not understanding every word.

"Really?" asked Colby "That's all it takes to be a wizard?"

Yashar nodded. "More or less, yes."

"That's easy!"

"It's easy when you wish for it, when you believe in it already. But grown men have destroyed themselves trying to grasp what you understand now. Try not to kill yourself."

"Let's go get him."

Yashar shook his head. "No."

"I'm going to get him."

"I believe you, and I'll be with you when you do it, but first things first. How are you going to convince him to come with you?"

Colby shrugged. "I'll tell him they're going to kill him."

"And what makes you think he'll believe you?"

"Uh . . . ," Colby stammered for a second. "Because we're friends."

"Isn't Dithers his friend? Isn't Mallaidh?"

Colby hadn't thought of that. All this power and he didn't know the answer to a simple question.

"I can make him come with us."

"Magic doesn't work that way. It cannot force the unwilling to do what they do not wish to do, not without robbing them of who they are. Besides, Ewan can't just leave. He's eaten fairy food. They have to release him; he can't just walk away."

"Then what do we do? How do we save him?"

"If we're going to do this, we have to let him know exactly what they intend to do. So we have to wait. We wait for the darkest part of the darkest night of the year and we let them show him their intentions. Then you can get yourself killed for your friend."

Colby smiled. "That's a good plan. But I won't get killed. Promise."

CHAPTER TWENTY-THREE

The Darkest Hour of the Darkest Night of the Year

The procession was long and beautiful, lit by an unearthly glow, as if each participant had been bathed in distilled moonlight. Everyone was there, from the foulest of the unseelie to the proudest of the high court; it was the one night every seven years when a truce forbade a single drop of blood being spilled from anyone but the *volunteer*. Meinrad led the parade, the flowers in his beard in full bloom, the leaves of his branches adorned in merry garlands. Behind him walked Ewan and Dithers, both proud and smiling, each for different reasons. Dithers had done his duty and raised his boy well, and he celebrated by leading the procession with a melody played on a crudely carved wooden flute. Ewan, on the other hand, was to finally become a fairy.

Behind them walked the Sidhe—with Mallaidh in tow. Led by King Ruardhi and Queen Muirne, they were dressed in luxurious silken finery, colored eggshell and rose, with their hair impeccably groomed, pinned up with fabulously constructed laurel. Farther back were the pixies, followed by the wood wives and the salgfraulein—each in their modest, yet lovely, gowns, very middle class to the Sidhe's upper crust—and bringing up the rear were the redcaps, accompanied by their honorary mascot Knocks. In between them all was a smattering of fairies from all over the court. Bill the Shadow and the Lutin twins; Juri the Metsik; Black Annie of the Plateau and her white-cap-wearing feline servant the Yech; Billy Brown Man; Djovic the Forgetful Maiden; Heartbreaker Bryce the Gan Caenack; Ambroas, Arzhur, and Kireg, the Korrigans; Beatriz the La Llorona; Coyote the Manitou. All manner of creature had arrived for the occasion—from the trolls that lived farther up in the hills to the skittering dark things that dwelled in the aquifers below.

The mood was somber, the dirge they sang lovely. It was a sight so serene that it could not be mistaken for anything other than a funeral. The Devil never left behind any traces of a body, not the slightest drop of blood. This was their one chance to mourn his victim. And so they walked, together, for the last time, and sang—though not all in their midst understood why.

Knocks scuffed the dirt as he walked, seething over the lavish event thrown in Ewan's honor. Mallaidh, on the other hand, did her best to keep her composure, fighting off the urge to go fleetly skipping, her heart aflutter with the thought of Ewan finally becoming one of them; after today, they would be together forever.

The procession marched slowly along the fairy trails, the night getting darker and darker around them until the stars shone like spotlights amid the inky black and the train at last came to a stop at the Five Stone Circle. The stone altar in the center was adorned entirely in heather and bluebonnets, an ornate ceremonial knife delicately balancing atop it by its point.

Meinrad turned with a stony groan and faced the procession. The singing stopped. "Bring me the last of the milk!" he bellowed, the very night shaking with his voice. Talwyn, the field pixie, fluttered forward, a small stone cup of fairy milk teetering in her arms. Reaching down, Meinrad took it from her and held it up for all to see. With that, Talwyn bowed, retreating back to her sisters. Meinrad continued.

"Several years ago, the night brought us young Ewan. We raised him as our own. And tonight, he will become one of us and take his place, to do his duty for us all." He motioned to Ewan. "Ewan."

Ewan glanced up at Dithers, who looked down upon him, sadly nodding. Trying to keep from smiling—as he could tell how reverently everyone else was taking this moment—Ewan stepped forward, taking the stone cup in hand. Then he drank deeply of it, upturning the cup, making sure he swallowed every last drop. His whole body tingled; he could feel the magic taking over. Meinrad then took the cup and, taking Ewan by the hand, led him up the path to the altar, King Ruadhri following closely behind.

Meinrad picked Ewan up by the armpits, setting him gently atop the altar. "There's only one last thing."

"I'm ready," said Ewan.

"Lie back."

King Ruadhri stepped forward, picking up the knife. Meinrad stepped away as the assembled fairies fanned out to get a better look.

"King Ruadhri?" whispered Ewan.

"Yes?"

"Will I get to choose what kind of fairy I get to be? Nobody ever told me."

Ruadhri closed his eyes. "Yes. After this one last thing. Now, close your eyes."

"Okay," said Ewan. "I want to be a Sidhe."

Ruadhri raised the knife above his head and whispered a small prayer, begging for forgiveness.

"I DIDN'T THINK there would be so many of them," said Colby, his knees shaking, the lump in his throat swelling as he spoke. "What happens if they won't let Ewan go?"

Yashar narrowed his gaze and steadied himself. "Then we most likely won't live long enough to see Ewan dead."

The two crouched silently in the woods, shrouded in magicks Colby barely understood.

"I don't think I can fight that many of them, Yashar."

"You can't."

"I could if I were a stronger wizard," he hinted.

"It's not about power. It's about how many of them you can focus on at once. And no man can focus on them all. Not even with a wish."

"So what do we do?"

"Pray they don't all come at us at once."

"Yashar, are you scared?"

"Terrified."

"Do you have a plan?"

"Yeah. Stand behind *you*."

Colby's eyes slowly widened, the color draining from his face. "You're not gonna protect me?"

Yashar shook his head. "Not this time. This time you're the one who has to protect *me*."

Colby swallowed hard, nodding, and put on his big-boy face. "Let's do this." He had never been more scared in his life.

KNOCKS WATCHED BITTERLY from his place among the red-caps, gritting his teeth, balling his tiny hands into fists, his knuckles white and knobby. Schafer the redcap leaned in close, whispering something into his ear. At once the child's expression changed; he looked as if he had won some sort of lottery, some prize he'd never known existed. He would have clapped, but he knew better. Once more Schafer leaned over him and whispered, Knocks trying to pretend that he wasn't the happiest little boy in the whole world. The knife couldn't descend soon enough now.

Ruadhri took a deep breath and began to speak in an ancient, all but forgotten tongue, offering the boy to the Devil.

"Don't kill him!" cried a voice from the woods. Gasps and murmurs drifted through the crowd.

"Kill him . . . ?" muttered a few of the children, their eyes peering into the dark, heads turning and necks craning to identify the voice. Colby emerged from the dark of the woods, his arms folded, his face fixed with a determined scowl. Behind him stood Yashar, looking both cautious and concerned.

The children turned, looking to the adults. It was as if a grenade had gone off in their midst. Eyes became saucers, expressions tightened, jaws grew slack with horrified surprise. The old, however, showed no shock at all, only disdain. The hour drew close; the Devil would soon be upon them.

Knocks stood stone-faced, muttering beneath his breath, "Kill him. Just hurry up and kill him."

Meinrad's voice boomed once more, this time at Colby. "Child, these affairs are not yours to meddle in. You will not be *asked* to leave again."

"Let him go," demanded Colby.

Ewan leaned forward, propping himself up on his elbows. "What are you doing? I'm about to become a fairy!"

"No, you're not," said Colby. "They're going to kill you and give your soul to the Devil."

"Noooo," said Ewan, shaking his head. *That was just silly.* He looked around at the somber expressions staring back at him. He looked down at the altar he lay upon. He looked up at the dagger, poised above him. And for the first time, he soberly saw everyone around him for what they were, though he didn't want to believe it. "I'm not going to be a fairy?"

King Ruadhri refused to open his eyes, only shaking his head. "You're as much of a fairy as you're ever going to be."

"That's enough!" shouted Schafer, pushing his way through the crowd. He looked around at his fellow fairies, dozens in number, wondering why no one dared step forward to tear this kid apart. "Hey, genie. Take your whelp and get the hell out of here before I tear his arms off and beat you both to death with them."

Yashar shrugged, shaking his head. "This isn't me. It's his battle, his choice. You need to talk to *him*."

Schafer pounded a fist into his palm. "You need to take control of him before I do."

"Try it," said Colby.

Schafer laughed, staring the kid down. "I'm gonna enjoy this," he spat, his withered tongue flitting over his swollen lip as a punctuation mark to his threat.

He stepped forward, striding boldly toward Colby, cracking his knuckles, popping his neck to each side.

There was a moment of quiet broken only by the sound of Schafer's iron boots crunching on the gravel beneath them. *Crunch. Crunch. Crunch.*

Colby clenched his fists nervously, looking over his shoulder at Yashar.

Yashar stared back blankly.

Colby turned back to Schafer, who was steps away now. "I

don't think you're going to enjoy this at all," he said, his voice cracking.

He raised an outstretched arm and closed his eyes, feeling the pulsing hum of the universe around him. With a thought, he reorganized the mass before him, taking one form of energy and converting it into another with the ease of drawing a single breath.

The redcap didn't have the chance to scream, the energy holding him together folding in upon itself as everything that was Schafer simply ceased to be. His shell abandoned him, collapsing into nothingness, his remaining essence becoming rose petals and daffodils. He burst with an audible *puff,* flower petals floating gently to the ground, their sweet scent wafting out into the night air.

Within seconds the only evidence that Schafer had existed at all was a slight odor and a carpet of scattered flowers in the dirt.

He was gone, the gaping jaws of his friends the only eulogy to his death.

Meinrad gazed upon the floral remains, and then cast his eyes up to an unfazed Yashar. "What have you done?"

Yashar shook his head. "I granted his wish." There was no irony to his tenor, only sadness. "He just wanted to stop you from killing his friend."

With shameful eyes, Meinrad looked at Colby, understanding. He motioned to the altar. "Let the boy go."

"What?!" shouted one of the redcaps. "Are you out of your mind?!"

Meinrad shook his head, his gaze on the ground. "We are not unusually cruel creatures, Colby. You have to understand that."

"He doesn't have to understand anything," another redcap protested.

Meinrad disagreed. "He must, or we will live out this night

again sometime in the future. I doubt it will end so peacefully next time."

"Peace, my ass!" shouted the first redcap. "There will be no peace!"

The pack surged forward, untethered by their rage. They snarled and heaved, launching themselves across the grotto.

Fairies jumped out of their way. The ones who didn't were pushed to the ground by angry, clawed hands.

Pikes swung high in the air.

Colby closed his eyes, took a deep breath.

"No!" boomed the Limestone King. With a single outstretched hand, Meinrad raised the earth from the ground, limestone shards as large as a willow tree trunk punching through, kicking debris skyward.

The redcaps slammed headfirst into them.

Colby lost his concentration, his eyes wide with disbelief.

Meinrad raised an angry fist and pointed a stern finger. "Back away. Now."

The redcaps, leaderless and still punch-drunk from their hit, scrambled to their feet, sheepishly falling back into the crowd.

The limestone receded back into the earth with a grinding rumble.

Meinrad looked over at King Ruadhri—who still stood over Ewan, knife clutched unwavering in his hand. "Let. Him. Up."

Without making eye contact, Ruadhri lowered the knife and motioned for Ewan to hop off the altar.

Colby and Meinrad stared at each other, each waiting to see what the other would do next.

The only sound in the night was that of shuffling feet nervously shifting weight from one foot to the other. The entirety of the court looked on, holding their breath.

Meinrad nodded, knowingly. He spoke up, no longer any peace or shame in his voice. It was quite clear who was in charge.

"Colby Stevens, take your friend and leave this place. The borders of the Limestone Kingdom are open to you no longer. That goes for you as well, Yashar."

Yashar nodded, a glint of regret in the wilt of his lip. "I figured as much."

"I imagine at this point there are few kingdoms left in which you can show your face."

"Not many, but I get by."

"You truly are as cursed as they say."

Yashar nodded. He didn't disagree. "Ewan, Colby. Come on. We're leaving."

Colby looked around the stone circle at the fairies, terrified one might change its mind. But no one dared to lift a finger; no one gave pursuit. They only stared, a mixture of melancholy and loss washing over them. No one liked what was happening; no one liked what would come next. For the moment they wanted only for these boys to leave.

Ewan made a slow march through the crowd, fairies stepping out of his way as he approached—each refusing to make eye contact, equally angry and ashamed. They liked him, they always had; but now all the work they'd put into raising him had gone to waste. *It was all so unfair.*

Then he passed Mallaidh. She looked at him, eyes filled with tears, shaking her head, mouthing wordlessly *"I didn't know."* But he couldn't look at her. She was one of *them.* And *they* wanted him dead. He gritted his teeth, pretending he didn't care.

"No! Noooo!" cried Knocks. "Stop him! We can't let him leave."

"We have to," whispered one of the redcaps. "Or else they'll be sweeping us up off the ground with Schafer."

"No! That's not fair!"

"If life were fair, Knocks," said Meinrad from across the crowd, "we wouldn't have to sacrifice fairies to begin with."

Ewan walked across the grotto to Colby. "Hi, Colby."

"Hey, Ewan. I told you I'd come back."

"Can we go now?" he choked out, fighting off tears.

"Yeah. Let's go."

Ewan turned back to look at the crowd one last time and saw Dithers standing there, eyes cast into the dirt. Slowly Ewan turned back around.

"It's okay to cry, you know," said Yashar. The dam broke, and Ewan began to sob, his whole world having come to an end. Colby took Ewan's hand in his and the two walked off into the night together. "I'm sorry," said Yashar to the fairies, then he too disappeared from view into the gloom of the forest.

Back in the circle, Meinrad took a deep breath.

"We have to go after them," said one of the Sidhe.

"Yeah," echoed one of the redcaps.

"No," said Meinrad. He shook his hung head slowly, rock scraping against stone. "We do not raise children to put to the knife because we delight in their bloodshed; we do so that they might take our place. How many of us need to be sacrificed tonight to protect that replacement? So much as one death in its defense negates the worth of the entire endeavor. We suffered that death. We have gambled and lost. Let us now cut our losses and get to the true matter at hand. Who amongst us shall meet the Devil so that the rest of us may live long and prosperous lives?"

For a moment there was silence. There would be no volunteers.

"Give him the boy!" shouted someone from the crowd.

"The boy is gone," said King Ruadhri.

"No," said someone else. "The *other* boy! The changeling!"

Once again, the crowd fell silent; then came its roar.

It was too perfect. Knocks had taken Ewan's place before, he could take his place again; no one would miss him, not a soul. Only the redcaps showed any reservation, trading curious glances, wondering whether they were willing to sacrifice their new mascot. After all, *better him than one of them.*

Knocks stood expressionless before their jeers and calls for his execution. Inside he felt a rage greater than any he'd ever known, but at the same time he drew power from the intense emotional suffering surrounding him. This crowd was terror stricken and they were letting their emotions get the best of them. It was in this moment that Knocks first glimpsed his destiny, when he first knew where his true talents lay. He looked over at Meinrad. "No."

The roar of the crowd dulled to mere murmurs.

"I don't believe you'll be allowed a choice in the matter," said Ruadhri. "You are an abomination, a slap to the face of this court. And now you have a chance to do your duty."

"How long have you been doing this?" asked Knocks.

"Longer than we would like to admit," answered Meinrad.

"Are there rules?"

Ruadhri and Meinrad exchanged glances. The crowd looked around. Then all eyes fell upon Dithers. "Yes, there are, actually," said Meinrad.

It was as Knocks suspected. He looked at Meinrad. "You yourself said that I was poisoned by my mother's vanity. A Sidhe's vanity. Why punish me for the sin of my parents?" Then he looked at Dithers. "I didn't lose Ewan." He raised an arm and pointed an outstretched finger. "He did."

"No!" cried Dithers. "I didn't lose him!"

"Yes, you did," said Knocks.

"No! You all stood here! You all saw! We all let him go! We all failed!"

"It was the agreement. You swore to protect the child or take his place. I was there. In your arms when you did it. It is time to uphold that oath."

Everyone looked at Meinrad. Meinrad closed his eyes, solemnly nodding. "The boy speaks the truth."

"No! Noooooo!" Dithers tried to run, but the fairies around him closed ranks, boxing him in.

For a moment he considered leaping into the trees, but imagined the whole of the court hunting him through the woods, running him down only to throw him atop the altar anyway. He knew his life was forfeit; that was the deal. And as the hands reached in and took hold of him, he struggled and flailed, but only so much as his instincts would allow.

Deep down, he knew that this was the only way it was going to end.

Knocks smiled. He could taste the fear, not only in Dithers but in every other fairy around him. They saw what he had just done. Not only had he eluded death, but he had done so after they had demanded it. If there was one thing they all knew about changelings, it was that they could never forget. More than any other, this night would haunt them. They all knew it. And Knocks savored the rich flavor of that.

He watched, satisfied, as the fairies threw Dithers atop the altar and King Ruadhri approached with the knife. All was once again silent, save for Dithers's struggling grunts.

Then a laugh rang out in the night—a single, cackling bellow of a bray, the likes of which only one creature in the world could make. *Coyote.*

He stood hunched over, wheezing, gasping for breath between loud guffaws and hysterical hollers. Coyote straightened up, trying very hard to get the words out. "Prophecy," he said between laughs, "always has a way of working itself out in the end." He shook his head, looking directly at Dithers. "*This* is what the hunt was telling you." Then he turned around, still laughing, and walked off in fits, following the boys and the djinn into the wildwood, calling out behind him, "This is what the hunt was telling *all of you*."

Dithers knew now that this was true. He looked out into the crowd, and despite the dozens gathered together, he saw only one: the fractured, deformed, spitting image of the boy he had cared so deeply for—morbidly smiling back at him. *Enjoying it all*. He looked up, saw the glint of a raised knife, and let out a howl that shattered the night.

COLBY AND EWAN jumped, startled by the sound, the distant screech like a drowning cat in a burlap sack, clawing at the last few seconds of air. They kept walking, pretending they couldn't hear it.

"They've made their decision," said Yashar grimly.

The boys still walked hand in hand, heartbroken. "Colby?" asked Ewan. "Why did they want to kill me?"

"They have to sacrifice a fairy or the Devil will take one of them. So they made you a fairy to save themselves."

"So I'm a fairy now? For real?" he asked.

Colby looked up at Yashar for the answer. Yashar nodded. "Yes. For now."

"Oh," said Ewan, sadly. "I thought it would be . . . different."

CHAPTER TWENTY-FOUR

THE LAST MINUTES
OF CHILDHOOD

It was after dark and the only light was a nearby flickering streetlamp that buzzed like a bug zapper every time it went out. Yashar, Colby, and Ewan stood on the steps of the children's shelter, Ewan dressed like a Dickensian urchin, a note from an imaginary mother pinned to his clothes. The details were cruel, involving all manner of drugs and abuse, but the story was necessary in case Ewan ever slipped up and mentioned monsters or fairies or his time in the woods; child psychiatrists were fond of metaphor and archetypes.

"Why can't I come with you?" asked Ewan.

Yashar looked coldly at Colby and nodded. Colby nodded back. "Yashar says where we're going, you won't be welcome."

"Because I'm a fairy?"

"Yeah."

"What about you?"

"They're not so picky about wizards."

"Oh." Ewan frowned. "I've never been alone before."

"I know, but I'll come back and visit you every chance I get."

Ewan looked down at the ground, scuffing his feet. Colby looked at Yashar, neither knowing what to say. Then Colby smiled. "You won't be alone." He stripped off his backpack, unzipping the flap, and pulled out Mr. Bearston. The bear was even more of a mess now than when it had first gone on the journey—dirty, frayed, and a bit worn down. But there was a look in his remaining eye, as if he'd seen something. Something wonderful. Something frightening. Something to believe in. At least, that's how Mr. Bearston looked to Colby. He didn't need him anymore; Ewan did.

Colby looked down at the bear in his arms, speaking plainly to it. "You have a very important job to do, Mr. Bearston. Our friend Ewan needs you to watch out for him. Can you do that for me?" With a single hand he made the bear nod. "Very good, sir. Go to work." He handed the bear to Ewan, who took it in both arms with an immediate hug. "He'll look after you now."

"Thank you." Ewan stepped forward, throwing his arms around Colby's neck, Mr. Bearston still dangling from one hand.

"You'll come back for me?"

"I always do."

"Bye, Colby."

"Good-bye, Ewan."

With that, Colby pulled away, nodded to Yashar, and gave a quick wave before walking off. Ewan stood sadly on the steps, watching his friend disappear around the building. Then he turned and made his own way into the shelter, ready to tell the lie that Yashar had prepared for him.

"So will he remember *anything*?" asked Colby.

"Only music," said Yashar.

"Why music?"

"No one knows."

"Will he remember me?"

"If you keep your promise to visit him, though he probably won't remember where you met."

"Oh," said Colby, letting out a deep sigh.

"You will keep your promise, won't you?" asked Yashar.

"Of course I will!" he said excitedly. "Ewan and I will be best friends forever."

"I know you will. You're a good friend."

The two walked in silence for a moment. Then Colby spoke up again. "Yashar?"

"Yes?"

"Are we going home now?"

"Why would we go home, Colby? You haven't seen everything yet."

"Oh," he said. "Do I have to?"

Yashar nodded as if there was no debate. "It was your wish," he said, "and you made me promise. So yes."

"Would you hold my hand?"

"The whole way," said Yashar. "The whole way."

Yashar took Colby's hand in his, and the two walked into the night, away from the first of their many adventures together. And while they did, in fact, go on many more adventures—taking them to many other great and terrible places—this was not where this adventure truly ended for Colby Stevens; for just as all little boys must grow bigger, so too must their problems.

BOOK TWO

CHAPTER TWENTY-FIVE

UNDERSTANDING THE NATURE
OF THE SUPERNATURAL

An essay by Dr. Thaddeus Ray, Ph.D., from
his book *The Everything You Cannot See*

All matter is energy. To fully understand the supernatural creature, you must first fully grasp this simple, scientific principle. Every component of the universe is composed of the same basic building blocks. Take apart a person, a tree, a drop of water, and a ray of sunlight and you will find many of the same parts. The differences between them are derived from how they are assembled and how fast they vibrate. Simple concept, complex execution. The same is true with the world of preternatural beings and events.

When scientists sit down to calculate the mass of the universe, their math always comes up with giant holes, empty voids where other numbers should be. So there become required elements that must exist to match their theories. They conjure concepts like dark matter, dark energy, and a dozen other names and phrases yet uncoined. While some might ascribe the error to the theory itself, there is another possibility: that there is a form of currently immeasurable mass or energy out there—a particle or particles that obey their own laws and react in their own, distinct ways to every other particle in the universe. Particles we have no way of detecting or measuring. I call one such particle, and the energy it creates, *dreamstuff.*

Dreamstuff is the essence of consciousness, the particle of soul. Everything self-aware contains some amount of it. Like any form of energy or mass, it obeys its own rules and can be found in varying degrees throughout the universe. Here on earth it collects and flows in concentrated amounts through what are most commonly referred to as ley lines. Like any free-flowing substance, it often collects in small pools, tributaries, and even lake-size offshoots where it may swirl about indefinitely before it is either absorbed by other elements or returned to the flow. That is not to say that there isn't dreamstuff all around you even as you read this, but that the concentrations are nowhere near that of ley line intersection points or a pooled collection.

It is thought that the unborn absorb this energy throughout their mother's pregnancy and on through early childhood until they've collected enough to achieve self-awareness, assembling a soul of their own. At some undetermined point before their birth, they accumulate enough to be able to exist free of the womb, but not quite enough to retain memories. Most theories point to a person's first memory as the moment they achieved true awareness and completed their soul. Those who study this process refer to this variant energy as *soul-stuff*. Thus we mortal creatures are a combination of standard matter and dreamstuff. Just as there are manifestations of matter that contain no consciousness, like rocks, trees, and the lower forms, could it not also be that there are manifestations that are none *but* consciousness?

So what is a supernatural being? It is a being comprised almost *entirely* of dreamstuff. Simply put, it is what happens when dreamstuff collects into a form, much like humans are comprised almost entirely of water. Each creature is created by the governing principles under which this form of energy and matter operates.

As dreamstuff collects in an area, that area begins to take on properties governed by the sentient inhabitants of the region. If they are a peaceful, nature-loving population, the odds are good that the dreamstuff will enhance the natural beauty of the area and produce creatures that are as playful, helpful, and as delightful as the locals, ultimately enhancing those emotions in the population and thus feeding off that particular brand of dreamstuff. If, however, they are fearful, warlike, or particularly bloodthirsty, the odds are they will find themselves surrounded by monsters that prey upon those very emotions.

The stronger the concentration of dreamstuff, the more readily creatures can be pulled from it. Particularly rich regions can bring into being a creature from a single nightmare, its traits the product of a single man's imagination, while starved or blighted areas might require the belief of an entire population to produce a single, weak being. Either way, the powers, abilities, and weaknesses of any such creature lie wholly within the belief in those traits. For example, stories of inside-out clothing warding off certain fairies aren't so much *that* fairy's aversion to the practice as much as a specific *population's* aversion, which is then acquired by the spirit in question. However, sometimes only those who believe that wearing their clothing in such a fashion would ward them off actually do so. Things get exponentially trickier when taking into account that these beings possess psyches of their own (one might argue that they are actually nothing *but* psyche) and their own belief of such things might be able to affect their own form and traits, thus explaining the differing levels of potential manifestation among the more intelligent species.

Just as all flesh must consume flesh, food to live, all beings of dreamstuff must similarly feed upon dreamstuff. Helpful fairies such as brownies or the Heinzelmännchen of Germany appear to feed upon the goodwill and joy of those they help, consuming the positive energy and converting it into the dreamstuff they need. Some feed in a passive way, while others, like the Leanan Sidhe, act more directly to siphon the energy they need to live. Likewise, those creatures that prey upon fear and agony must work in some way to generate those emotions if they cannot find a place populated by those already experiencing them. Particularly clever or lucky creatures often make homes in places where the suffering they feed upon is readily generated, like hospitals, prisons, or (history permitting) death camps.

Primitive creatures, like vampires or the Black Annis, must consume the energy directly from flesh or blood. Lacking the ability to simply feed off ambient energy, they often have to take every drop of blood or consume a body down to the bones to get enough nourishment to last them until their next meal, which tends to be far more often than those creatures operating at higher levels, thus putting them at far greater risk of discovery. These beasts often find themselves destroyed by careful mortals or, sometimes, other supernatural creatures looking to draw as little attention to themselves as possible.

All supernatural creatures are formed in belief. They are shaped by it, they are compelled by it, and they will be forever bound to it. Without belief they would not exist. Once a man not only understands this immutable fact, but embraces it, he will find that all supernatural creatures are but an extension of his own will. The biggest danger to a creature living beyond the veil isn't being forgotten, rather, it is being discovered by the man who has somehow stumbled upon this rather unfortunate natural law. This makes man a very dangerous species to tangle with, and history is filled with encounters between such witchcraft or wizardry against local supernatural populations, to the detriment of both parties.

Magic and miracles are but the psyche's manipulation of ambient dreamstuff and the exertion of will upon it to change one thing into another. When a thousand people traipse up a hill that they consider to be a holy place (in fact a dreamstuff-rich environment), and their holy symbols become transmuted from one substance into another (like plastic into gold), just as they believed it would, is it the will of some greater being? Or does their combined sense of will projected upon the surrounding energies cause the transmutation, just as applying fire in just the right manner to a substance can change it from one thing into another?

Men who fully understand these principles, armed with both belief and understanding and backed up by a sufficient amount of ambient dreamstuff, we call magicians, wizards, warlocks, witches, or holy men. The practices of these people, as varied in their rituals and results as are supernatural creatures themselves, are simple concepts with complex execution. Once you grasp that, there is no manner of manipulation that will ever be truly foreign to you and no creature you cannot understand on a basic level.

Of course, this knowledge makes these things no less dangerous, any more than understanding the inner workings of a lion will protect you from the grip of its jaws. Rather, you have endangered yourself just for daring to understand them. There are things that go bump in the night, and many of them prefer to be known as no more than that.

Be wary, be vigilant. For few of us practitioners die of natural causes, and most of us die young.

CHAPTER TWENTY-SIX

THE YOUNG MAN
COLBY STEVENS

There was no such thing as destiny, and no such thing as prophecy; there was only matter slamming into other matter like two toy trucks in the hands of a child. There was no rhyme or reason, no grand scheme to it all—just shiny new things rapidly becoming broken, battered, and old by comparison. Since childhood, Colby Stevens had convinced himself that Yashar had chosen him *for a reason*. That he had made his wishes *for a reason*. That he had saved Ewan from the clutches of Hell *for a reason*. But it was now apparent to him that nothing actually happens *for a reason*. Shit just happens, and there wasn't a reason for *any of it*.

By the age of twenty-two most people think they've seen the world, convinced they've lived a lifetime already, having been gifted some arcane knowledge to impart. But by twenty-two Colby *had* seen the world. He did have knowledge to impart. But there was no one to tell, no one who would believe him.

Colby Stevens was a broken man, a shiny toy battered beyond recognition, whose spark had long since faded and whose new-toy smell had given way to the dank sweat of fear. He was no longer the wide-eyed child keen to see it all. Rather, he was particularly eager to crawl into the hole he had found for himself to hide, hoping never to see anything new again. Nothing would have felt luckier than the doldrums of normalcy—a quiet hobby, a wife, a street without angels perched upon ledges or fading ghosts wandering in and out of his sight.

But Colby Stevens was not a lucky man. Not at all. Not even a little bit.

It's not that there wasn't any light in the world; Colby had seen plenty of light, plenty of goodness. But that was just one side of the coin. The dark of the world was so black that it was blinding, the crushing, lingering weight of everything that was wrong coalesced into creatures he dared not name aloud. *They* were what drove Colby into hiding; *they* were what made life so unbearable. And the creatures, the memory, *the knowledge* could not be gotten rid of, no matter how hard he wished. Some sins even a djinn could not wipe clean. Such was the lesson of his first wish.

Even the dark things seem shiny and new the first time around.

Once again, Colby had few friends and no prospects to speak of. He was a carrot-topped, scrawny excuse for a young man—a tangled mop of greasy red hair atop a gangly, frail, freckled frame that drooped and bowed when he walked. Puberty had been cruel. His eyes were sunken—deep, dark circles pooling beneath them—and his nose seemed a tad too cartoonish to be real. Had he often smiled, he might be laughable, but smiling was something he did rarely these days. Despite his comical appearance, his dour expression and grim countenance kept him from looking either goofy or creepy—leaving him merely awkward and gawky.

He was twitchy. Nervous. He looked around constantly, staring long and hard at the empty spaces in the room. There was an off-putting way about how he would stare over people's shoulders when he talked to them, as if there was something looming behind them that they could not see. When he walked down the street, he muttered and mumbled to himself. This strangeness was not lost on those around him, and thus he rarely found himself with company.

At the age of twenty-two, Colby Stevens was a man who knew too much; who had seen too much; who understood too much. But no one would think that to look at him. Especially not when serving as the stock boy and acquisitions clerk for one Harold Puckett.

Puckett's Stacks was not the sort of bookshop one happened upon; it was the sort of bookshop for which one looked deliberately. One of the few walk-down shops in all of the Austin metropolitan area, no sign announced its presence or map marked its location. You had to know it existed and know someone who knew how to find it, for once you were there it was likely to have exactly the sort of book you were looking for. First editions, rare editions, self-published masterpieces, scribbled notebooks of famed madmen, books of math, books of magic; this was where you found such things. And Colby Stevens had become Mr. Puckett's prime acquisitions man.

How Colby came about applying was still something of a mystery to Harold Puckett. He'd simply turned up one day, announcing that he was there to fill the position. "I hear you need some help," he'd said, a smile on his face and his hair neatly combed—the one occasion on which Harold would see him looking so professional.

Harold nodded, only moments before having muttered to himself how much he needed some help around the shop. He'd never placed an ad or mentioned to a single soul his need or desire for an apprentice, but there Colby was, fully aware of it, ready to start that very afternoon. Such was his relationship with Colby Stevens: he wanted something, and Colby anticipated his request. It was the sort of relationship one never questioned openly for fear it might one day vanish, so Puckett went along with it, and paid Colby a healthy wage—a wage Colby earned several times over with his nose for rare finds and his ability to sell the most unknown work to a customer who'd never known how badly he or she had always wanted it.

That was Colby's real gift. While one could spend all day discussing the distinctive way in which he carried himself or how uncomfortable one felt around him, his strengths were unmistakable. He possessed an uncanny insight into human nature that bordered on mind reading. Of course, Colby couldn't read minds, but sometimes he acted as though he could, which unsettled even those who knew him well. There were few things that surprised him and he always knew when someone was behind him, even when they were creeping up to catch him unawares. Colby Stevens was a strange, mysterious man. And Harold Puckett felt that this made him right at home in his bookshop.

"Excuse me, sir," said a patron to Harold Puckett. "I'm looking for something a bit . . . exotic."

"You mean like erotic?" asked Harold. He wasn't kidding. The man was shifty, squirrely, speaking a few hairs under the volume you would normally ask such a question. That was the sort of man looking for antique porn.

"No, no, no," said the man nervously. "I'm looking for something . . . occult."

"Ah," said Harold, understanding. "Did you have a particular title or author in mind?"

"Do you have any Grady?"

"Grady? Hmmm." He thumbed his beard for a moment. "I think I ran across a couple of his somewhere. I sure don't remember selling any recently. Let me check." Harold leaned over the counter, looking past the stacks. As if summoned, Colby rounded a corner, arms overflowing with weathered old tomes. He craned his neck over the pile and made his best *you rang boss* face.

"Yeah, Harry?" Colby asked, anticipating the question.

"You see any Grady lying around the stacks?"

"Hans Grady? Yeah. Over in early American metaphysical." He briefly sized up the customer. "I'll show you where it's at." Colby set down the overwhelming mountain of books and beckoned the customer to join him, making his way back across the store. When the customer was close enough to hear a polite whisper, Colby lowered his voice, speaking with great care and discretion. "Now, I have to ask you, are you a collector or a practitioner?"

The customer anxiously fidgeted. "I really don't see how that's any of your business."

"Well, not meaning to pry, but it's important to know if Grady's really what you're looking for. I mean, if I were a collector, Grady would be an interesting name to have on my shelf. But if I were actually trying to get some use out of the book, well, I'd end up using it to steady my wobbly couch."

The customer coughed nervously. "Really? And why is that?"

Still in hushed tones, Colby spoke, occasionally looking around to ensure relative privacy. "Grady's ideas are all flash and no substance. The rituals he uses are purely for show, and the effects he gained from them, if any, would have come from his natural talent and not his work. His theories are hogwash and his calculations are scrawled twaddle. Now if I were look-ing for something with substance . . ."

"Um, well, I am something of a practitioner, myself," said the customer proudly, trying his hand at modesty.

"Of course you are, and that's certainly nothing to be ashamed of, especially here. What are you looking to do?"

"I don't know. Maybe something . . . tantric?"

"You looking merely to increase *performance*, or are you looking to touch an external or internal consciousness?"

The customer looked him square in the eye. "I want to see beyond."

Colby gave him a knowing look and a stern nod. "I have just the thing for you over here." He reached back without looking, running his fingers along a shelf before plucking a book from it. The volume was heavily worn, its edges dulled by time, the bind-ing a tad loose. "Now this is Donaldson. Not very well known outside certain circles, but excellent nonetheless. Here, open it."

The customer took the book, handling it as if he'd just been handed the Shroud of Turin, examining every scratch and spot of wear as if they contained clues to the book's origin. Opening the cover, he paged through it as Colby leaned over pointing gently at the margins.

"See those notes?" he asked.

"Yes."

"Recognize that handwriting?"

"No, not right offhand. Should I?"

Colby was whispering very quietly now. "Now, Harry would kill me if I told you this, but I believe it's none other than Crowley."

"*Alistair* Crowley?" he asked, slightly louder than Colby.

"Sshh. Yes. There's another sample later in the book that I believe belongs to Arthur Waite, but Harry hasn't been able to get anyone to authenticate it. Now this text predates the Her-metic Order of the Golden Dawn, so . . ."

"You think this is what inspired Crowley?"

"Might be. I promise nothing, except that the book is dead on. Its theories on celestial body alignment and its use in astral travel are the best found anywhere."

"I'll take it," said the customer without hesitation.

"You also might want to check out Donaldson's other works. We've got a few more behind the counter that we secured at a recent estate sale. Ask Harry, up front."

"Thank you," said the customer excitedly. "Thank you very much, sir."

"Don't mention it." Colby winked. "Just be careful with that stuff. There are things over there that don't like visitors." The man smiled in return and made his way back up front.

Harold waited at the front counter, a proud smile on his face. He looked down at the book. "Donaldson, huh?"

"Yes. Your clerk said you might have some more up here?" The man peered eagerly around Harold, hoping to catch a glimpse of another volume.

"Donaldson's a little pricey," said Harold, slowly moving out of the way to allow the man to eye the stacks for himself. "But a few just came in this weekend. I can never keep this guy on the shelf for very long."

"He sounds like he's worth splurging on."

"So I'm told."

Though the man's eyes bulged a bit when Harold handed him the total, he smiled as he wrote the check. He was no longer nervous, but elated. As he handed the check over to Harold and took his books, he glanced around and smiled. "I'll be back."

"We look forward to it," said Harold.

The bell chimed on his way out, leaving Harold and Colby alone in an empty store. Harold smirked. "You know damn well that wasn't Crowley's handwriting."

Colby poked his head from around a bookshelf. "Of course.

It was McGreggor's. But nobody knows who the hell that is—though they should."

"Aren't you the one who thinks Crowley was a cretin?"

"I . . . think those were my words, yes," said Colby, playfully pretending he needed to remember.

"I'd hardly call the man a cretin."

"The man sure knew how to write," said Colby. "That's why he's famous. But he didn't know dick about the other side."

"Well, you just sold the guy a week's sales' worth of books with his name."

Colby nodded, doing the mental math. "Yeah. That sounds about right."

"Speaking of names," said Harold, pointing a finger into the air like an exclamation point. "I've got something for you." He fumbled beneath the battered wooden counter, rooting around and running his fingers up and down the broken spines of books until he managed to come upon just the tome he'd been looking for. Pulling it out, he spun it around, presenting it to Colby faceup. "I found a Ray at an estate auction this weekend, and I know of your fondness for his work."

The book was very simple: a vanity-press printing with no art on the cover and the words *The Everything You Cannot See* by Dr. Thaddeus Ray in a nondescript, no-frills font. It had neither a dust jacket, nor any copy on the back cover. It was the literary equivalent of a brown paper bag. Colby politely took the book from Harold's hands and nodded a thank-you. "I don't know if fondness is the right word."

"Well, every time a Ray comes up for auction, I spy you lingering over it for a few moments longer than the others. And since they're so rare, and this woman clearly had no idea what her husband was dabbling in, I thought I'd get you one. This is his first, I believe."

"Yes. First of four. Only twelve hundred and fifty copies were printed, if I'm not mistaken."

"Well, now this one is yours," said Harold.

"You know how much this would bring at auction? The sale of this would run the shop for months."

"And I'm giving it to you. It wouldn't be much of a gift if it were easy to part with, now would it?"

Colby nodded, smiling weakly, something of an achievement for Harold to have gotten out of him. "Thank you," he said. "This means a lot to me."

"You're welcome. Now get out of here. I'm closing up. Go home." Harold smiled.

THOUGH HE OWNED a car, on days like this Colby biked to work. Austin is a city swimming in trees. In the spring, every neighborhood is swollen with oak and pecan, branches arching over cracked suburban side streets; bushes bursting from the grass, threatening to swallow sidewalks whole. It is a green oasis surrounding a dammed-up river the locals prefer to call a lake. From the air it looks like a city devoured by a creeping green, its buildings like a series of tall, thin, Incan temples, destined to be overrun by jungle, left forgotten, to puzzle future civilizations. Of course, come summer, that shade is the only thing protecting residents from the harsh, bitter scalding of an unforgiving sun and its hundred-degree afternoons, when the green full beard of spring gives way to the brown withered stubble of drought.

It was spring once again: with its early-morning mistings, evening thundershowers, and temperate afternoons; a beautiful patch of green between the depressing yellow-brown of winter and the intolerable yellow-brown of August. This was the time of year Colby loved most. It was still early in the season, when the days could get well into the high seventies, but the nights were a brisk, wintery forty-five. Austin weather was like that this time of year: dysfunctionally bipolar. It was a time of year trapped perfectly between two very different worlds. And Colby Stevens felt a certain kinship with that.

Colby owned a small house on the east side of the city, squarely in the section of town teetering between hipster chic and too poor to live anywhere else. There was nothing special about it, a rather plain, unremarkable house on an ordinary, unexceptional street. He kept it in good repair, paying a neighborhood kid to keep the lawn up so as to not attract unwanted attention. It was a bar code of a property, generic, ordinary, and anonymous. Just as Colby wanted.

Colby opened his front door, breathing in deeply through his nose. There was nothing peculiar. He laid his keys down in the bowl sitting on an entry table just past the foyer, giving a good look around in all the nooks and crannies of the room. Closing his eyes, he concentrated deeply. There was nothing out of place and nothing present that shouldn't be. Finally, he could relax.

He walked over to his bookcase, looked carefully at the shelf third from the top, and ran his fingers along four other copies of *The Everything You Cannot See*. The shelf was comprised almost entirely of books by Dr. Thaddeus Ray, filled in with a few other obscure reference manuals on the occult. Colby parted the four, splitting them right down the middle, sticking this new copy, his fifth, in between them. Then he sighed deeply, his only consolation being that Harold meant well.

"You have plans?" asked a voice from behind. Colby sniffed the air and immediately recognized the familiar scent of brimstone and gazelle musk. *Yashar*. He didn't bother to turn around.

"What did you have in mind?" he asked.

"Drinks," said Yashar. "Lots of them."

Colby nodded. "I think I can squeeze you in."

CHAPTER TWENTY-SEVEN

SECOND STREET PREDATORS

Simon Sparks was an oozing slug of a man poured neatly into a three-piece suit. Well-dressed and impeccably coifed, he was like cheap scotch—just refined enough to seem classy to anyone who didn't know better. Mid-thirties, condo, job in finance, a sleek car that could be started by remote, a band of pale flesh around his left ring finger, and a gold ring tucked neatly into his front-right pocket.

Simon had a theory about women, and if you knew him well enough that he both trusted and wanted to impress you, he would lay it all out. "They're all broken," he would say. "Every last one of them. Oh, it's not their fault. It's not biological either.

I'm no sexist. It's societal. We do it to them; we break them down, bit by bit, year by year. With magazines and commercials and movies starring big-breasted bimbos who can barely get a line out of their mouths before spilling out of their dresses. Women look around them, see a media full of undeniably—and unattainably—beautiful women, and then they look in the mirror and see a collection of flaws too numerous to name." Then he would take a drink. He always drank right there to let it all sink in.

" 'My hips are too big, my ankles too fat, my nose is too long, my lips are too thin, my hair too stringy, my breasts a little lopsided, my nipples are too large or too small or too brown or too pink.' And the worst ones, the very worst offenders of all, are the really, spectacularly beautiful ones. The ones who stop traffic." He would take another drink right here, nodding, smiling, as if he were about to tell you one of life's biggest secrets. "The ones the nice guys are terrified to talk to and who spend all of their time getting battered to pieces by the cocky assholes who do. Those girls are kicked to shit and left hungry for any kind of attention.

"Those are the girls that do the dirtiest stuff. They'll let you do anything to them. They'll drop down and give you twenty and beg you at the top of their lungs to give it to them harder, give it to them deeper, and give it to them in any place you want. As long as you give it to them. And don't leave in the morning before getting their number. Because that's what breaks them. That's what they don't understand. They think that if they were prettier, you'd call them back. That if they had done it right, you would call them back. That if they were only interesting enough, you would call them back. But you won't. You will never call them back. Because pretty as they are, they are not worth the hassle with your wife."

That was Simon Sparks. And Simon Sparks was once again

on the prowl, once more hustling his wares in a walk-up Second Street bar too trendy to be open during normal hours on normal days. He made his way through the club, eyeing only the youngest and leanest of the night's crop. Few paid him much mind; even fewer met his exacting standards. And then he saw her. *Grace.*

She was five feet nine inches of lithe, firm, blond dysfunction. Her confidence was faulty and laid on a bit too thick, but her dress was tight enough to reveal just how flawless she would look naked. Simon eyed her up and down, trying to figure out exactly which of her features bothered her most. *Was it her lips? Her hair? Her thighs?* If he guessed right the first time, he could shave a half hour off winning her over. Women were tricky that way. They wanted to be thought of as beautiful, but they only wanted *you* if you thought they were *almost beautiful.*

"My name's Grace," she said with a cute southern drawl. *Georgia. She was definitely from Georgia.*

"Simon."

"What do you drive, Simon?"

"An A-6. You?"

"Tonight? Hopefully an A-6."

Jackpot. Simon smiled wryly and cocked a brow. "You wanna get out of here?"

"That's not how it works, Simon. First you buy a girl a drink. And *then* you ask her to leave with you."

"What are you drinking?"

"Blue Label. Neat."

Simon stuck a finger in the air without taking his eyes off her. "Bartender! Two Blue Labels!"

"Neat," she said, sliding a hand up his thigh.

"Neat!"

SIMON AWOKE STRAPPED to a rickety chair in a dilapidated warehouse, hands bound together with duct tape, a sweaty sock taped firmly in his mouth. Groggy, he sifted through memories, trying to figure out exactly where he was. He remembered the blonde. *Grace. Grace was her name.* He remembered leaving with her, going to his car and letting her drive. Then he remembered drifting off in his seat, confused. "Oh, don't worry about that," Grace had said. "Those are just the drugs kicking in."

He looked around, frantic. The floors were stained with oil, smooth concrete marred with gouges from heavy machinery. The air was moist and rotten, like old death. And two shadows lingered just outside of the light.

"Look who's awake," said the taller of the two.

Simon immediately began to cry. And to sob. He shook his head, jumping around in his chair, clacking its legs on the cement, screaming through the sock, "MwomwoMWO! Mweee! MWEEEHEHEHEHE!"

The taller of the two stepped into the light. He was a thin, gaunt mutant, balding despite his youth, with hair combed over the scabby, bulbous portions of his head. One of his eyes was cocked to the side, and his teeth were feral—sharp, crusty, and yellowed. *Knocks.*

He smiled. "I'm sorry, Simon. I'm afraid I can't hear you properly beg for your life. Let me help you with that." He walked over and tore the tape from Simon's mouth.

Simon immediately spat out the sock, heaving from the taste. "Please don't kill me!" he shouted.

"Why ever not?"

"Let me go. Please let me go."

"There's no fun in that. Not unless we chase you and run you down. Dietrich!" He waved to the short shadow behind him. From the darkness it came, a malignant, twisted dwarf of a man wearing a sweaty red nightcap on a head two sizes proportionally larger than it should have been. The dwarf dragged a long tire chain that skittered, snaking across the floor.

"Please, God, no!"

Dietrich swung the chain across his legs, splintering his kneecap. Simon cried out.

"Please! Do whatever you want to me. But please, don't hurt my family!"

Knocks and Dietrich stared, dumbfounded, with jaws slack, eyebrows furrowed. "What?"

"I'll get you your money!"

"Money?"

"I told Jorge that I'd get the money and I'll get it."

Eyeing him up and down, Knocks sniffed at the air. "You're not lying, are you?"

"No! Of course not."

"You really are afraid we're going to kill that cold bitch of a wife of yours?"

"Hey! Don't you dare!"

Dietrich whacked his splintered kneecap again, this time shattering it.

"Don't get sanctimonious, douche bag. Why else would you be prowling for southern tail, unless you had somehow convinced yourself you were entitled to it?"

"That's none of your business, you son of a . . ." He stopped himself, trailing off immediately into regret.

"Dietrich, I think perhaps you'll be killing his wife after all."

"No! No! Please. I'll get you your money!" He was sobbing again. "I'll get you your muh-huh-ny."

Knocks smiled and narrowed his eyes, motioning to Dietrich. "Knock him out."

The chain cracked into the back of Simon's skull and the world fell immediately into black.

SIMON AWOKE TO the rising sun, sweat and blood pooling on the fine leather front seat of his car. His head throbbed, his knee screamed. But he was alive. *Thank dear, sweet, merciful Christ, I'm alive!* Through the morning dew glistening on his windows he could make out the cold, drab gray of an empty parking lot. Reaching back, his fingers tickled the gooey slop at the base of his skull. Everything about the night before felt like a fading dream.

He needed to get to a hospital. He could call Mallory from there. It seemed like the best way to keep out of trouble. Wives don't ask too many questions in the ER; they're just happy you're alive.

KNOCKS HADN'T TAKEN pity on the man—he wouldn't know how—but Simon's predicament had given him an idea. What Simon felt in that moment when he imagined his family being beaten to death with a tire chain was deeper and more profound a pain than Knocks had felt in decades. It was a true, heartsick terror that wasn't driven by survival, but rather longing. And love. The dread was palpable. Nuanced. *Delicious.*

When you beat a man to death, the fear subsides the moment you stop hitting him. And after a while, your victim only wants to see it over and done with. Fear fades into acceptance and there's nothing left but to turn the redcaps on him to tear him to pieces and slake their caps. Knocks had spent years feeding this way, luring in sleazebags and horny hipsters with the promise of a tawdry backseat screw, only to beat them down in a dark alley or abandoned warehouse with a couple of his redcap friends. But that only lasted an hour at best.

Fear like that meant regular violence. Too regular. People got wary around that much crime. So Knocks waited only until the last possible moment, when his hunger could take little more. Then he would lash out and feed.

But there was something about having a worm on a hook, writhing and squirming in agony, that appealed to him. He wanted to see just how far this would go. So he let Simon go free with a warning, just to see what would happen. Then, whenever Knocks felt the pangs of hunger, he crept into the bushes around Simon's house, placing a phone call to Simon's home number. After a few seconds of heavy breathing, he hung up. Simon, terrified that would be the night they were coming to kill him, would turn off all the lights and huddle in the dark with his family, slowly losing his grip on everything he loved. Thus terrifying his wife and kids even more than the thought of them dying terrified him. And Knocks consumed every last bit of anxious panic.

He'd discovered the long game. And while police would later fish Simon's headless body out of Ladybird Lake—murdered by his Mexican Mafia creditors—Knocks had already moved on to something even more dastardly. There was no way to truly duplicate a Simon Sparks; he was a lucky break. But one night, while creeping around Simon's house, he'd noticed how deeply tormented Simon was at the thought of his wife leaving him over his behavior. Here was a man who spent evenings after work shacked up in some hotel with boozed-up college girls and strung-out strippers, terror stricken at the notion of his frigid, nagging wife calling it quits. It was counter to everything the guy stood for. But there it was. Love.

And that's when Knocks discovered the true frailty of the human heart. He remembered his own heartbreak from youth, when little Mallaidh the Leanan Sidhe snubbed him for that detestable Tithe Child. As the anger and bitterness welled up within him again, he wondered how hard it would be to string someone along—to create the perfect soul mate for a person, only to slowly unravel them over time, first breaking their heart, then their spirit, then even their will to live.

It turned out to be much easier and more rewarding than he'd imagined.

No longer willing simply to prey upon one-night stands, he turned his sights toward lonely outsiders, the invisibles of society, those souls passing unseen through the world, eking out a meager existence, cloistered at home on a Friday night with a stack of books, a cup of tea, a video game. Finding them would prove simple enough. They were everywhere. Though they felt alone, their population was dense and numerous, found in bookstores or movie theaters or working in the farthest, most isolated corners of large offices.

The trick was to find someone who had a hard time making eye contact. Those were the invisibles who felt they were invisible for a reason. They felt unattractive or unlikable, and they dressed the part, with baggy clothes, face-shadowing glasses, and only passing attention paid to their hair or makeup. Knocks began to spot them in even the most crowded rooms. A quick brush past them and he could feel the tingle of loneliness, the tickle of their yearning to be loved. And that's when he would strike.

LIZZIE ANDERS WAS a mess. In another life she could have been beautiful. But not this one. This was the life in which she cried herself to sleep, still thinking of herself as the ten-year-old girl who had pissed herself in gym class, earning the nickname Pissie, which stuck until graduation. The boys would tease her about being into water sports and the girls, far crueler, would get up and move whenever she sat near them. She'd skipped college and gone into data entry straight out of high school, making it a point to never look up from her computer.

It was a complete shock to her the day Knocks spoke to her on the bus. He was beautiful. Radiant. Pop-star looks and a thousand-watt smile. He said his name was Billy. He'd asked if the seat beside her was taken and never stopped talking after that. She tried to shut him down with silence, but every time she immersed herself in a book or looked out the window, he found something else to talk about.

It was as if he knew her already. Her every interest, her every dream. He was magical. The guy she cried herself to sleep thinking about, knowing that he couldn't be real. Not for her. Not for Pissie Anders. But there he was, and he wouldn't give up.

Their love affair lasted three magnificent weeks. On their second date, they'd made love on the floor of her studio apartment. By their fifth date, they were making love so much she would pass out from exhaustion. By week three, they were planning trips around the world that they would take after their kids graduated.

And then he stopped calling. At first it was three days without seeing him. Then five. At last they'd gone three weeks without speaking until he showed up late one night, reeking of booze, for a quick roll on the floor before passing out and sneaking out before dawn.

When next they spoke, Knocks told her he had met someone else. Someone prettier. Someone better in bed. Someone who didn't urinate frequently out of fear of wetting herself. Someone he could spend the rest of his life with. That night, Knocks waited outside her window as she drew a hot bath and sawed through her wrists with a steak knife. He giggled as she wailed in the tub. Knocks hadn't giggled like that since he was a child watching his mothers drown men in Ladybird Lake. Every moment he didn't call her was a delicacy, but this, this was a feast. Nothing had been this satisfying since Tiffany Thatcher had strung up her rope. And as the life drained out of Lizzie, staining the water a deep, dark red, Knocks knew it would be a long while before he was hungry again, enough time to set up another hearty meal.

Knocks savored the taste of young love gone sour, with its fondness for razor-blade carvings and pill-popping professions of love. Teen hearts shattered the hardest. Allison Jacobs was a brainy girl with a bright future when an equally intelligent poet with a tousle of curly locks came along. She threw herself into the daydream. When it ended, she threw herself under a city bus. Jaclyn Stanton was a pimple-peppered, perpetually silent high school senior dressed head to toe in black, pining for some dark, Gothic mystery. Her Romeo came to her at night, avoiding the sun, enjoying the silence with her. The night he left her, she never saw morning, choosing instead to slit her own throat. Matthew Cash was an engineering student whose love came to him after traded glances at a bookstore. By the end, he'd put a shotgun in his mouth just to hear the sound it would make.

Knocks understood his place in the universe now—his reason for being. He knew why his first two mothers had shunned him; he knew what it was that scared them. They knew what he could become. And while it had taken a long time to get there, all that suffering had only made him better at what he did. It didn't fill the void, it didn't dull the pain—but it was comforting to know that everything he'd been through served a purpose, making him what he was now.

A shark.

Nixie Knocks the Changeling was ever moving, always eating, forevermore lurking as a shadow on the edge of darkness. And there seemed, for a time, to be nothing that could distract him from his single-minded feeding.

THE MAN APPEARED from out of nowhere, emerging from the dark one night to walk beside him. Knocks tried not to make eye contact—at first attempting to stay anonymous—but the man knew good and well who he was. Looking up, Knocks recognized him instantly.

"Hello, Ewan," said Coyote. His skin was as coppery as it ever had been and his hair was as tangled and black as he remembered.

Knocks glared at Coyote, gritting his teeth, spitting out, "I'm Knocks."

"Of course you are," Coyote apologized. "It's dark and I'm used to seeing Ewan out and about at this time of night around here."

Knocks stopped in place. "What?"

"Oh, I thought you two would have run into each other by now, what with him working downtown. He and Colby are both here. Weren't you all friends as kids? I seem to remember something like that." Coyote smiled slyly. "Well, I'm off. Running late and all."

Knocks stood there, dumbfounded, a fourteen-year-old fist slamming into his gut as Coyote once again slunk away into the shadows. It felt something like what Lizzie had felt. Like what Simon had felt. What they all had felt at some point. *Had Ewan been here all along?* he wondered. *Living out his perfect little life?* For a moment, the shark was gone. He was a seven-year-old boy watching his mother trampled to death beneath hellish hooves; watching as the love of his life fell into the arms of another; watching the little boy he was made to look like reap the rewards of the Tithe, only to escape its fate, leaving the crowd howling for *Knocks's* blood. One can never go back to fix the wrongs of their pasts, but they sure as hell can relive them. For a moment, the seven-year-old Knocks stood awash in the painful tides of time.

But with those tides came the shark; and with the shark returned, Knocks knew what he had to do. His anger and pain and confusion and heartache knew only one relief, had only one release.

He had to find and kill Ewan Thatcher.

CHAPTER TWENTY-EIGHT

THE YOUNG MAN
EWAN BRADFORD

The years since he'd left the Limestone Kingdom had not been unusually kind to Ewan Thatcher. Never having known his given surname—as the fairies hadn't used it—the kindly old shelter worker who'd taken him in off the street had named him Ewan Doe. And it wasn't until he found his way to his first foster home that he'd taken the name Bradford.

The Bradfords were sweet enough, a pudgy pair of professional types who had tried for fifteen years to have a child of their own. Barren and cursed, they took in what they called *strays*, making the best of what the system could find them. Parenting, much like conceiving a child, wasn't in their genes. It took less than a year for them to get fed up with Ewan's screaming nightmares, strange behavior, and eccentricities before dumping him back into the system and trying their luck with another. From that point on, Ewan referred to the Bradford line—the point at which a family had kept him for as long as the Bradfords had. Three hundred and twelve days. Only two families since had ever gotten that far, neither getting much further. In the fourteen years since he'd entered the system, he'd been with twenty-two families.

Despite the foster care system having shipped him all over Texas, it was only natural that, when of age, he found his way to the only home he really knew. So on his eighteenth birthday, he packed his stuff, hugged his latest foster mother good-bye, and took the bus to Austin, Texas, where lived his closest friend in the world, the only person who remembered him from *before*: Colby Stevens.

While Colby had mysteriously turned up time and again throughout his life, consistently writing letters that always knew how to find him, he was still something of a mystery to Ewan. Always off on some adventure in a far-off part of the world, it struck Ewan as odd that he felt the need to keep in touch with someone he had known stateside when they were too young to remember even meeting. But Colby was a good friend, always there for him, providing the only real sense of stability in his erratic life.

At the age of twenty-one, Ewan was a mess. Tall, gaunt, and tattooed, he wore both his clothing and his dyed hair shaggy and black, concealing his innate good looks. While he never wore makeup, it was hard to tell without looking closely, his skin so pale and his eyelashes so thick that, coupled with the hair, he seemed to be aspiring to vampire chic. In truth, he embraced the look because with his hair its natural brown, he simply looked ill—like he was missing some essential component of his diet.

The occasional crack about his style from a stranger was much easier to take than smothering concern. *Are you eating right? You look sick. You need more iron in your diet. Or bananas. Potassium is good for that sort of thing.* There was no need for the attention; it was humiliating. He was just naturally pale. So he dressed the part and people left him alone.

His apartment was a third-story, one-bedroom walk-up in a shadier part of town nestled between gas stations, a strip club, a liquor store, and a greasy-spoon diner where Janis Joplin had gotten her start as a singer—paid for by washing dishes and working as a bar back at a downtown club. While he could have made better money elsewhere, he kept the job because it meant occasionally talking the manager into substituting Ewan's band as an opener when acts fell through, netting him almost weekly stage time. The manager—a seedy, overweight, and similarly overconfident hipster who looked surprisingly like a balding, overcooked potato in plaid—would let him play, but not for cash; that way they both got something out of the deal. He got a free act and Ewan got to experience firsthand how piss-poor his band really was.

He had no idea what his band's name meant, but it had sounded cool when it came to him: Limestone Kingdom. They weren't particularly good, but they weren't dreadful either; they were just uninspired. Ewan played guitar, backed up by a pair of brothers he'd found through an ad on a telephone pole: LOOKING FOR LEAD SINGER/GUITARIST TO FRONT BASS AND DRUM DUO. MUST HAVE OWN EQUIPMENT AND SONGS. He wrote most of the music himself, but could never get it right. There was this music lingering just out of reach in the back of his head—something familiar but inaccessible—and that's where he tried to write from. But it came out all wrong. So he assembled the chords the way he thought people would like them, layering them with lyrics about his life, short and poorly lived though it was. It never gelled, but he kept plugging away at it with the hope that one day they'd click and he'd never have to wash dishes again.

He was mediocre, unremarkable, and altogether ordinary, everything he strived every moment to break free of. So when his manager slapped his back with a meaty palm and asked, "Do you think you can get your band here by eight?" he was ready.

"Hell yeah," said Ewan. "They'll be here."

The crowd was thin that night; the cancellation had been the headliner, bumping the opening act into the top spot, leaving Limestone Kingdom to open for the openers. Far from ideal. But it was still a gig and they played their hearts out—which is to say they played as well as they could. Few noticed and fewer cared. Thirty or so people milled around, mostly in groups, nursing beers or doing shots, often checking their watches and phones for the time, wondering how much longer before the next band took the stage.

Only one person in the audience was watching. She was hard to notice at first—sitting in a pool of shadow at the back corner of the club—but the moment Ewan caught a flash of her eyes, she was the only thing he could see. She was transfixed, sipping her drink, watching not the band, but Ewan himself—her eyes unwavering, as if he was the only thing onstage.

Thin and waifish, a stiff breeze could have knocked her over, dragging her several feet. Her eyes were large, brown, and dazzling, set below a high forehead framed with wisps of short brown hair. When she smiled, her delicate cheekbones dominated the landscape of her flawless, milky skin. She wore a gauzy top, a gossamer broom skirt, and a modest black beret, a handmade scarf hanging about her neck in a snarl of rainbow-colored wool. There was something entirely elegant about her every detail, a charm even to the simple way she sat.

The moment Ewan caught sight of her, his breath grew short.

His throat swelled with dried cotton. His heart pounded. He was dizzy, mad with love; his eyes grew nervous and his knee twitched, as if his entire right leg might give out and cave in beneath him at any moment. Never once had he suffered stage fright, but here, for the first time in his life, he was terrified. Ewan knew, even at his age, that a girl who knocked the wind out of you came along rarely, if ever.

He *couldn't* mess this up.

So he played, and he played, and he continued his awkward plunge into the depths of mediocrity. His voice cracked like a teenager bludgeoned into manhood by puberty. The music languished in the air, stillborn, tired, and repetitive. The crowd murmured, trying to ignore it, but the girl stayed tangled in the melodies. She got it; while there was not a lot there to get, she understood, felt its roots, connecting with whatever it was that it wanted to be—and never taking her eyes off him.

His set ended an unbearable twenty minutes later. He tried to keep his cool, but it was clear he was rushing through breaking down their equipment. The bassist looked down at him as Ewan unplugged from the onstage amp. "We saw her."

"Yeah," said his drummer.

Ewan looked at both of them, a bit confused. "Yeah?"

His bassist smiled. "Get down there, asshole. We'll finish up."

Ewan hopped offstage almost a hair faster than his bassist could catch his guitar. He was off, speeding to the table before realizing he had nothing at all to say, his mind suddenly blank. He swerved instead to pass by, only to see that she was no longer there. Both flustered and disappointed, he stopped dead, staring thunderstruck at her empty seat.

"Looking for someone?"

He turned and found himself towering over her. Their eyes met. She smiled, slowly raising the straw of a soft drink to her lips before taking a single, dainty sip.

Ewan stammered. His chest seized up, choking his heart, his whole body shaking with the pound of each beat. *Thumthum. Thumthum. Thumthum.* Eight heartbeats into the conversation he came to life. "Hi," he said, sticking out his hand. "I'm Ewan."

"I know," said the girl, rolling her words into a smile. "You're the lead singer of Limestone Kingdom."

"You've heard of us?" he asked, surprised.

She looked at the stage with a cool grin, amused by how rattled he was. "Um, yeah, I might have caught a show."

He turned, looking at the stage, his face now a reddish purple. "Oh, yeah."

"Yeah," she nodded. Ewan floundered for a moment more before she dove in to save him. "I'm Nora."

"Nora. Hey, I'm Ewan."

She laughed, finding him adorable. "Yes. And before you run through it again, you're in Limestone Kingdom, and yes, I've seen you perform."

He blushed redder still. "I'm blowing this, aren't I?"

"Oh no," she said reassuringly. "I haven't been insulted or called another girl's name yet, so it could get much, much worse for you. Right now, you're still in that charming, dorky, you-don't-realize-I-find-you-as-attractive-as-you-find-me territory. You're doing fine."

Ewan scuffed the floor with his feet, his hands fiddling behind his back as if he were hiding a valentine.

"Look, you want to go somewhere or something?"

"Go somewhere?" he asked. "Like where?" Then a light went on. "Oh! Yeah! Yes I would."

She flirted with a flutter of eyelashes and nodded toward the door. "Let's go."

It was cool and crisp outside, damp enough to leave dew, but not so much as to chill the bones. The club emptied right onto Sixth Street, only a light scatter of couples and cliques drunkenly wandering between each bar. Nora gracefully spun about, occasionally walking backward to maintain eye contact, quizzing Ewan on the details of his life story. She had a playful way about her, confident but effervescent, as if she was a woman already in love.

She giggled. She flirted. She shamelessly complimented him with her eyes. There was no mistaking that this girl was throwing herself at him—except, of course, for Ewan. Everything Ewan understood about girls was gleaned almost entirely from a lifetime of magazine articles and television—all of which was useless now. He was as clueless as ever.

They turned a corner and walked south, making their way across one of the wide bridges that crossed the lake, carrying them on toward south Austin.

"So, I've gotta ask," said Ewan. "Who the hell are you?"

"Excuse me?" asked Nora, cocking her head, giving him a *now you're blowing it* look.

"Who are you? How does an insanely good-looking girl end up alone at a bar, listening to a bunch of nobodies, before wandering off into the night with their *lead* nobody?"

Nora smiled, looking out over the water. "Maybe I like nobodies. Especially *lead* nobodies."

"Oh, really?"

"Sure. Do you know how hard it is to land the lead singer of a band when they're already famous? Impossible. You have to find them before they blow up, when they appreciate you as the girl who loved them when they were just a dishwasher."

"Hey, how'd you know I was a dishwasher?"

"You're a dishwasher? Oh, I can't date one of those." Nora turned back toward the bar.

"Hey!"

Nora spun back around, pointed a finger pistol at him, and

fired it with a wink and a click of her tongue. "You really think tonight is my first night in that rat hole?"

"You've never been there before," he argued.

"The hell I haven't," she said. "I've been in there a number of times. *You've* never noticed me, which explains why I was alone tonight."

"How does that explain why you were alone tonight?"

"Because maybe if you'd noticed me earlier, we could have done this weeks ago."

"I'm telling you, you've never been in my club."

"Your club? Is that why you're always helping the bartender?"

"You know what I mean. You've never been there."

"Then how do I know you like blondes?" she asked, putting one hand squarely on her hip. Slowly she ran her lithe fingers through her short brown hair.

"I don't . . . I don't like blondes," he said sheepishly.

"You do. You check out every blonde who walks in that place like you're looking for someone."

"I do not!"

"You totally do. And you're totally busted." She shook her head. "I can't believe we're on our first date and you're already lying to me."

"This isn't a . . ." He trailed off. Nora waited patiently for what he had to say next. Her reaction hinged on the very . . . next . . . word. "Wait, is this a . . ."

Nora nodded.

"So, we're . . ."

She nodded again. "You can say the word."

"On a date?"

"There it is. Yes, Romeo, you're on a date, though you're not faring as well at this point as you were just a little while ago."

"But I didn't ask you out."

"No, genius," she said, shaking her head. "I asked you. Remember? When you ditched your buddies back in the bar to stroll off with some beautiful girl into the night? Alone?"

"Beautiful, huh?" he asked slyly, trying somehow to regain the upper hand.

She stepped toward him, bringing her face close to his, slowly running her fingers up and down his chest. Ewan's eyes widened, his cotton mouth returning, his leg again twitching, tingling sensations rippling through every cell in his body. Nora leaned in close, standing on her tiptoes, whispering hot breath into his ear, almost knocking his knees out from under him. "Yes," she said. "Don't even try to pretend you're not unbelievably turned on by all of this."

Ewan swallowed hard. "Okay. Just don't stop."

Nora stopped. "Oh, too late." She turned, continuing to walk across the bridge. Ewan shook off the daze and followed her, wearing the daffy grin of a lovesick schoolboy.

"So how many times have you been to the club?"

"Enough," Nora said. She was seemingly aloof now, as if she'd lost interest in him—but only in jest. She wore a funny smile, clearly expecting him to follow, as if dangling from a string tied to her waist.

"I don't know how I've never seen you."

"Well, I might have looked different at the time."

"Really?"

"You never know."

"Well, why haven't you ever spoken to me before?"

"Because, silly," she said, wrinkling her nose. "I was waiting for *you* to notice *me*. It's no fun if it's the other way around."

"Fun?"

"Yeah. Fun."

Ewan narrowed his eyes playfully. "You're trouble."

Nora smiled big and bright, then slid her arm around his

waist, pulling herself close. "Yeah, but I'm your kind of trouble."

"You sure about that?"

"Yeah, but you'll have to trust me on that one."

They walked aglow, in silence for a moment, neither saying anything to spoil it.

Then, as if they'd never stopped talking, she looked at him. "Have you ever been in love?"

He shook his head. "No. Never."

"Really?" She crinkled her nose a bit. "Never?"

"Nope. Never met the right girl."

"The *right* girl?"

"All right, smartass. I've dated before."

"But not successfully."

He opened his mouth to speak, expecting something witty to fall out. Instead, his gaping maw sat mute, unable to form a single syllable. Then he shook it off, saying matter-of-factly, "No, I suppose not."

"I didn't think so," she said. "You have that new car smell to you."

"It's my aftershave."

"You don't wear aftershave."

"What don't you know about me?"

She smiled shyly. "Less than you think."

Ewan stopped at the end of the bridge. "Oh, really?"

"You're not all that complicated, Ewan."

"How do you know? I could be dark and mysterious. I could be a serial killer for all you know." He pointed to the swelling green park just off to the side of the bridge, along the banks of the lake. "That's why I brought you out here."

"I brought *you* here, Ewan."

"That's only what I made you think. That's how dark and mysterious I can be."

Nora took a few steps toward Ewan, shaking her head. "You're not dark, Ewan. You're not mysterious. You're cute. And you're sweet. And you would protect me from the Devil himself if he showed up right now." She tapped his breastbone with a single finger. "That's what's in that heart of yours. Inside you're just a little boy who feels that somewhere out there is a place where he belongs, but he's lost it and wants only to find it again."

Ewan peered closely into Nora's eyes. "How do you know that?"

"Because I know what that feels like. I want to find that place again too."

"Have *you* ever been in love?"

"Once," she said.

"What happened?"

"He left."

"Why?"

"He didn't have a choice. But I screwed it up. I should have known he was going to leave, but I was young and stupid and we had no idea what we'd gotten ourselves into."

"What happened to him?"

"He forgot me and went on with his life."

"And you?"

"There came a time when I realized that the only way I'd be happy was if I went out looking for happiness. So I did. That's how I found myself in Austin."

"And me?"

She looked into his eyes, smiled, and, with alarming speed, swooped in, planting a sweet butterfly kiss on his lower lip and whispering into his ear. "You're it," she said. Then she sprang away into the bushes, running headlong into the park. Ewan remained, speechless, confused both by the tingling kiss and her sudden disappearance. Then it dawned on him what she was doing. *Tag.* And he took off into the darkness after her.

She was quick. Every time Ewan thought he had her, she

would duck his tag or slip around a tree. Once she even managed to drop under a branch that Ewan failed to see, flooring him. When he rose to his feet, he caught sight of her standing a few paces away, smiling blithely, with a twinkle in her eye. "Come on," she taunted. "I know you can do better than that."

He bolted at her like a charging stallion.

She turned too late to get away, his arm wrapping around her waist as they tumbled together to the ground. They rolled around in the thick grass for a moment until he found himself on top of her, looking into her big brown eyes, his hand holding hers.

"Why do I feel like I already know you?" he asked.

"Do you believe in past lives?"

He shook his head and laughed. "No."

"Neither do I," she said. Then she kissed him deeply. Their lips met and fit together as if they had been molded as a set. He wrapped his arms around her and held her tight, one arm around her back and the other cradling her head. His body jolted to life, electric. This wasn't his first kiss, but it sure felt like it. Everything in his body tingled, his mind drifting away, floating in felicity. Ewan could feel lips and the light brushing of tongues and a thousand tiny explosions swarming over every inch of his body—but there was nothing else in the universe. Nothing at all. For the first time in his life, he felt as if he was exactly where he was supposed to be.

And then gently, lovingly, she pulled away. Together they smiled like goofy children, lost in each other's eyes. Then she whispered softly, "I have to go."

"No you don't," said Ewan. "Stay here."

"No, I really do need to go."

Ewan sat up. "Did I do something wrong?"

"No!" she said. "No, you did everything just right."

"Then why are you leaving?"

"Because I have to go."

"Where?"

"Can I tell you next time?"

"I get a next time?"

"Yes," she said with a nod. "You've earned yourself a couple of next times."

"Can I call you?"

She shook her head. "I'll find you."

"What?"

She stroked his cheek delicately with the backs of her fingers. "Trust me," she said. "I *will* find you." Then she jumped to her feet, adjusted her clothing, and took a deep breath. "Good night, Ewan." Before he could protest any further, she was gone, sprinting off into the dark. Ewan rolled onto his back and stared up at the stars.

"Nora," he said quietly. And as he thought of her, he could hear music spring from his heart and poetry spill off his tongue. Words became phrases and notes became melodies. Ewan smiled. He had to get home and write this down.

NORA RAN FULL speed through the trees. She made little noise, her tiny feet barely kicking up any fuss. Then, when she felt she'd gone far enough, she darted around a tree, arched her back against it, and smiled dreamily. Her eyes twinkled, her skin shimmering in the blackness. For years, she'd dreamt of this evening, never imagining it would actually go so well. There was always the lingering fear that she couldn't connect, that the spark that had existed before couldn't reignite. But it had. And now it was ablaze.

Nora shook her head—curly, thick blond locks spilling out in the place of short brown wisps, a deep azure washing like a wave over the brown of her eyes; her skin stretched, filling out the contours of her face into a much slimmer, more elfin, shape;

her lips puckered and swelled, becoming full and bee stung. In a few brisk shakes, Nora melted away and Mallaidh the Leanan Sidhe was all that remained. She was fully grown—a shapely, ethereal, demure woman standing naked in the shadows cast by branches in the moonlight.

Nora was an ephemeral dress she wore—woven of glamour, culled from hints of the mortals Ewan had admired at the bar. Mallaidh had probed his heart and seen what he desired most; Nora was her best approximation. After half a dozen trips, she had at long last built up the nerve to weave herself a cover. This dark, little, pixyish construct had done its job. Now it was entirely up to Mallaidh.

After fourteen years, she had finally found her hero. And she wasn't going to lose him again. No matter what.

CHAPTER TWENTY-NINE

The Cursed and the Damned

Hidden amid the bars and shops of downtown, situated in a back alley, near a particularly pungent Dumpster fed rancid scraps of fish from a nearby restaurant, there is a solid metal door that looks as if it would take a log and a dozen strong men to break down. The door sits completely unmarked, scratched, rusty, and scuffed from years of abuse. It appears to be no more than the back loading entrance of another business, though no one claims it and no truck has ever backed up to it. If you know how—if you have somehow been gifted with the secret—a simple push on the door will open it. Otherwise, it is entirely unmovable.

Beyond that door is another door—a simple wooden one—with a small, dimly lit foyer separating the two that can accommodate no more than three people snugly. The walls are dingy, poorly kept, showing their age without the slightest attempt to hide it. Above the second door is a sign, written in whatever language the reader happens to speak: ONLY THE CURSED AND THE DAMNED MAY DRINK HERE. ALL OTHERS MAY POLITELY FUCK OFF. Behind that door is a bar. And while that bar has no official name, the locals have named it for its greeting. The Cursed and the Damned.

This was a magical pocket that time forgot—a twenty-by-twenty-foot room with a shoddily assembled bar top, stray barrels and crates for seating, the walls stained, the lighting from a series of buzzing old bulbs dangling perilously from black cables and exposed wiring. There was no artwork or other decoration save for a single, cheaply framed rendition of *Dogs Playing Poker* on black velvet. Just a hollow, drab space two antidepressants shy of suicide. But the beer was cold, the whiskey Irish, and the wine a hundred years old.

On any given day a dozen or so of the same faces, all killing time, waited there for the sun to rise or set. The bar was run by Old Scraps, a wily cluricaun of indeterminate age. At twenty-three and a half inches tall, Scraps was known to challenge to a fight men three times his size and win. He wore a weathered, brown, three-cornered hat atop his wrinkled head, and a bright green waistcoat festooned with large, shiny buttons that he would unconsciously twiddle and polish while talking. When he spoke, he did so through teeth clenched tightly around a pipe, which he removed from his mouth only to wave around when making a point. His cheeks were rosy, his nose bright red, and no one could remember ever seeing him sober.

Old Scraps kept the bar stocked with the finest top-shelf liquor, borrowed as part of his tribute from an adjacent bar he kept tabs on. The wine, however, was stolen from the cellars of selfish men—regularly replaced with younger, inferior vintages, knowing the owners would rarely, if ever, discover the swap. It was said that there wasn't a wine cellar within fifty miles of Austin still possessing its own original stock. Old Scraps placed that range at closer to seventy. And on nights when the wine ran low, he would drunkenly stagger out into the street, lure a stray dog close, then ride it madly through the night in search of unmolested wine cellars. He always returned on an exhausted hound with the best wine money could buy.

Colby Stevens had become a fixture in the bar. He'd begun his stint as something of a mascot and, much like the painting of *Dogs Playing Poker,* it was a delightful irony to have him there. But over time, also like the painting of *Dogs Playing Poker,* the regulars took to him. After all, Colby Stevens hadn't been truly human since he was a child, and he was certainly more powerful than anyone else—short of Yashar—frequenting the place. So not only did they let him stay, but he had officially become one of the boys. This collection of supernatural rabble was the only crowd around whom Colby felt comfortable, and who now equally felt comfortable around him. All as lost and bitter as he, it seemed as good a place as any to let his guard down and drown his sorrows.

"I have crawled through sweltering jungles," he said one night, his voice pinched and angry from having just swallowed a shot of whiskey, and slow and slurred from the four whiskeys before that. "I have walked across arid plains. I have seen the creatures that man has created, and I, for one, don't ever want to see them again. They are not beasts of their own; they are the reflections of man cast back through a looking glass that dares not withhold a single secret or desire; they are all of man's evil and all of man's good, given material form and set loose like tiny turbulent storms to upset the delicate balance of men's lives.

There is no good that can truly come of them, only heartache, heartbreak, and agony. God doesn't hide himself away because he wants each person to come to him with only blind faith; he hides himself away because if people knew the truth, they wouldn't want to believe in him at all. It would seem that God and man have very different definitions of the word *paradise*. But so be it. I know the truth now. And all I want is to be left alone."

"Have you ever actually *seen* God?" Old Scraps asked from across the bar, his chin balanced upon folded arms.

"Shut up and pour me another drink," said Colby.

"That's what I thought." Scraps smiled and grabbed the whiskey. "I don't care how much of the world you've seen, kid. You're still twenty-two years old. Twenty-two-year-olds know two things: fuck and all. So why don't you shut the fuck up and drink this." He poured two shooters for himself and one for Colby, finishing the first before Colby could reach for his.

"I do love our chats." Colby smiled.

"Well, you better, because no one else wants to listen to your bullshit, material or otherwise."

"I don't know about that," said Yashar from farther down the bar, clearly as drunk as Colby. No longer dressed in silks and finery, he wore a simple pair of jeans, a white T-shirt, and a leather motorcycle jacket. "I've been listening to his shit for years and I'm still not tired of it." Colby leaned over and the two bumped fists as a sign of solidarity.

The patronage of the Cursed and the Damned was thin but familiar that night. Bill the Shadow, in the far corner, smoked a cigarette from beneath his fedora, casting a shadow over his portion of the room. Two older pixie men, Seamus and Walter, nursed their own small beers at a diminutive table set in the back where no one would trip over them.

Lastly, Bertrand, a fallen angel and outrageous drunk, sat at his own table mumbling to himself, his hair long, blond, greasy, and neglected, his alabaster skin having seen better days. He wore white, battered armor, a large red Gothic cross painted on its chest plate, and carried both a similarly painted shield and a helmet no one had ever seen him wear. Bertrand often conversed with himself, speaking with long-departed friends in hushed, mumbled tones sounding more like death-bed tremors than the drunken rambling it was. But every once in a while he would speak up loudly, arguing with himself, making bold declarations.

"It's not like suffering in Hell is really eternal or anything," he said through a slurred, drunken drawl. "It just feels that way."

Heads slowly turned in his direction, unsurprised but curious.

"What?" asked Old Scraps. "What the hell are you on about?" Everyone in the bar turned to Bertrand, who now held the floor.

"Hell," he said "It's not like you go there forever."

"Since when?"

"Have you ever been to Hell?" asked Bertrand.

Old Scraps shook his head. "Of course not."

"Well, it's not what you think. There are parts of Hell that are a veritable paradise. Sins of the flesh; unspeakable beauty; raw, unfiltered sensations overwhelming all five senses. It is heaven for those for whom Heaven's enlightenment holds no interest. They are patches of forever encased in immaterial amber. But the lights don't stay on by themselves, you know; they are fueled by the nightmares and torments of the imprisoned. Those perfect, dreamlike bubbles of bliss are nothing more than the coalesced memories of the punished as they beg and plead to regain their precious moments. They are stripped of them on entry and left with the anguish of their sin and the pain of their death; they are hamsters on a wheel, turning and turning until they can turn no more, just to keep the elite few undisturbed in their flawless little utopias."

Bertrand rolled his empty glass back and forth on the table, fumbling it a few times, making sure Old Scraps knew it was empty. Scraps hopped up on the bar and, grabbing the bottle, marched over to Bertrand's table.

"That doesn't make any sense," said Colby.

"What? You thought he was collecting souls for some war at the end of time? There is no end of time. There was no beginning. There just *is*. It's all just energy. Nothing is forever. One day even Hell will be gone—dried up and spent, floating through space and time as a lifeless hulk before it is consumed by whatever the next thing is. It is just another star in the universe that will one day burn itself out. That's just the way things work here. Nothing is permanent, but everything is never ending."

"So who gets to see this paradise?" asked Old Scraps, pouring the angel another glass of whiskey.

"Whoever brings in the most souls gets a garden of their own, I suppose," he said.

Colby shook his head, confused. "Wait, so the most evil men in the world get a pass?"

"What do you mean evil? What *is* evil? Do you mean sin? No, the greatest sinners don't get a pass. But the greatest persuaders do, the men who lead others into willful oblivion. They build the pyres upon which their furnace will be heated."

"Like who?" asked Colby.

"Hitler."

Old Scraps removed the lit pipe from his mouth and waved it around wildly. "Wait, wait, wait. Are you saying someone like Adolf Hitler is in this hellish paradise of yours?"

"That's exactly what I'm saying. Why wouldn't Adolf be dead center at the Devil's party? Millions upon millions of people committed atrocities and sins of all sorts in his name, at his behest, or in opposition to his influence. All of their own free will. Don't kid yourself; it's all about free will, every last bit of it. He never forced those people; he gave them the chance to become the people they always dreamt of—at a price. And that price filled the coffers of Hell for two generations. Krauts, Ruskies, Yanks, Brits, Japs, Guineas, Frogs, Polocks, Protestants, Catholics, Jews. They all did unspeakable things in the name of righteousness. More coal for the fires! But did you ever hear a whisper about Hitler pulling a trigger or flipping a switch and gassing a room full of people himself? No. You didn't. Because he always convinced someone else to do it.

"No one is born damned; you have to damn yourself. Hell's fires are fueled by the stuff of dreams and stoked with man's attempts to grasp them. Few men set out to damn their fellow man; those that do have a special place carved out in the brimstone of the underworld. The Devil loves a self-made man." Bertrand threw back the remainder of his whiskey, swallowed it hard, and with a grimace looked around the bar. "Fuck this place," he said. "Bring on the next thing."

The angel rose to his feet, stumbled toward the door, careful enough not to get his wings caught but not so much so that he didn't spill a few drinks along the way. Pushing the door open, he managed half of a polite bow before falling through, picking himself up, and making his way out into the street.

"Such sad creatures," said Old Scraps.

"Angels or drunks?" asked Colby.

"Pfff. Drunks are God's chosen few. Angels are just his messengers. Can you imagine? Being one with everything, born with a purpose, getting told everything you need to do to make the world a better place, only to have it all torn away, to be cast down, and left to experience creation alone on such limited terms? No wonder they're all drunks. This place sucks."

"Aye," mumbled the room, drinks held high, toasting misery.

"Why doesn't he drink with his own kind?" asked Colby.

"Bertrand? He does. But they have the decency to throw him out before he gets this drunk."

"And you don't?" asked Yashar.

Old Scraps laughed. "Ain't a cluricaun born that can so much as spell *decency,* let alone appreciate it." The door opened once again. "Another whiskey then, is it, Berty?" he called toward the door.

"No," said Coyote. "But I will take a beer."

The room fizzled and all fell quiet. Coyote stood at the entrance, smiling back at the looks of shock and disdain.

"*No. You. Out,*" said Old Scraps, struggling for the words, pointing angrily out the door, refusing eye contact.

"You're not going to tell me that you don't serve *my kind* here, are you?" asked Coyote.

"If by *your kind* you mean foul trickster spirits, then no, we most certainly do not."

"Oh, but I'm quite thirsty," said Coyote. "Just one drink?"

"First rule of bartending: never let a trickster speak." Old Scraps pointed a stiff finger toward the door. "Out!"

"But I've already spoken. If you kick me out now, you might be doing exactly what I want you to do."

"That's a chance I'm willing to take."

Coyote leaned back out the door and looked up at the sign. Then he leaned back in. "What if I assure you that I am quite damned?"

"Of that, I am most certain. Still won't get you a drink. Out! Out, out, and *out.*"

A moment of silence gripped the bar; a standoff, a stare down. Coyote dared not take a step farther without permission, as only a fool angered a drunk. Nevertheless, Old Scraps was equally as cautious; if Coyote wasn't there for him, there was no need to earn his ire.

"Why'd you do it?" asked Colby. All eyes fell on him.

Coyote smiled. "Whatever are you—?"

Colby interrupted him coldly, his tone bitter and calculated. "Pretend for a moment that I know exactly how smart you are. Why'd you do it?"

Coyote was caught in a lie and had the sheepish grin to show for it. "All things must be taught a lesson," he said. "Even ancient ones. *Especially* ancient ones. I am life's hard lesson."

"I know what you are," said Colby. "Why are you here?"

"Because nobody ever learns. Here we are fourteen years later and children are still slaves to their wishes. You'd think growing up would change that, but it only makes it worse."

"I think we've heard enough," said Yashar.

"Yes," smiled Coyote. "More than enough."

"Get out," said Old Scraps.

"Good night," said Coyote before fading away.

Only the overhead bulbs made noise, their stinging hum slightly less abrasive than Coyote. Yashar leaned forward onto the bar top, shaking his head. "Never, in all my years, have I met a creature who could kill a good buzz quicker than Coyote."

Old Scraps nodded. "I'll drink to that."

"Bartender," said Colby. "Why don't you hit me and my imaginary friend here with a double each? I have a feeling this is going to be a long night."

"You can s-s-s-s-say that again," Yashar slurred.

Colby eyed Yashar for a second. "Is that a new jacket?"

"Yeah," answered Yashar. "You like it?"

"Whatever happened to the robes and the sash and all the gold doodads?"

"I just wear that getup for the kids." He smiled, basking in his own cleverness. "I mean, honestly, would you make a wish to someone in this jacket?"

"I certainly wouldn't have held your hand."

"Touché." Once again, the two fist-bumped without having to make eye contact. "It's all about appearances, my friend. Sometimes it takes a bit of a con to get someone pointed in the right direction." He paused for a moment. "You know that's what Coyote was doing, don't you?"

"Yeah," Colby nodded dourly. "I know."

"But you're going to go check on Ewan anyway, aren't you?"

"Yeah, I am."

"No way I can talk you out of it?"

"You could always give me another wish."

"Forget it. You're overdrawn, my friend. You've had more than your fair share of wishes."

"Aw, but I haven't actually gotten anything I really wanted yet."

"Oh, shut up," said Yashar. "I gave you everything you asked for. Don't blame me for your taste in wishes. I could have given you a puppy and a girlfriend and you would have been the happiest eight-year-old in north-central Austin."

"And miss out on all this?" said Colby, motioning around the spartan bar.

"I could take it all back, you know. Undo the whole thing. I'd do that for you."

"Yeah, I know. But you can't take back time."

"No. No one can."

"You might as well just cut out my eyes and seal my ears in wax. I'd know what was beyond the veil, but couldn't see or protect myself from it. I'd spend my days rocking back and forth, paranoid about whatever was standing looking over my shoulder."

Yashar nodded. "I could make you forget, but . . ."

". . . then you'd have to start from scratch, yeah. New kid and all."

"Yes."

"That wouldn't work either. I'd be dead inside a week. I've made my bed, now I've got to spend the rest of my life lying in it."

Old Scraps wiped the bar top in front of them with a greasy rag, leaving more slop behind than he was picking up. "How many times are you two dillholes going to have this conversation?"

"Till we don't have to have it anymore, I suppose," said Colby. Shaking his head he threw back the double whiskey, swallowing it in a single gulp. Then he looked over at Yashar. "Finish your drink; we've got a trap to walk into."

CHAPTER THIRTY

THE RUSTLING OF THE VEIL
OR SOMETHING LIKE IT

The locals called it Crackville—an uninspired but accurate moniker for a two-block-by-two-block-radius gutter of slumlord-owned apartment complexes, sporting no less than three competing crack houses operating at any given time. It had everything a growing slum needed to blossom into a full-blown ghetto: day-labor storefronts, liquor and convenience stores, bad lighting, and a dozen places to run if the police ever bothered to do anything but drive by slowly. The only thing keeping this mess from spilling over into the rest of the city was being nestled smack in the middle of sub-suburban tract homes, guarded by well-armed soccer moms, aided by lenient laws on gun ownership. While this didn't stop the steady flow of traffic from coming in on Friday and Saturday nights to score, it did keep the transient population from lighting up their makeshift pipes too close to where the kids played. Instead, they lit up behind the overflowing brown Dumpsters sprinkled liberally throughout the area.

Ewan's apartment was on the third floor of the central-most apartment complex in the very heart of Crackville. From his front door, he could see the porches of two operating drug dens—sometimes three, as they were prone to moving around in a shell game triggered by violence or the rare narcotics bust. One had to use caution when walking through the parking lots, not only to avoid degenerates doing the junkie shuffle mumbling for a handout, but also to keep from stepping on needles or shattered glass pipes.

The apartments were cabana style, facing a pool that was a molding, slimy, still-water pond, covered in algae and a thick brown layer of leaves still lingering from the previous autumn. It gave off the sickly smell of rot residents never noticed until mentioned aloud. Swarming with mosquitos as it was, Colby liked to think of it as the birthplace of disease. There was something almost supernatural about how foul Crackville was, as if some coven of infernally aligned creatures crept through its darkest crevasses, responsible for it all. But he knew better. Only humans could invent squalor and filth like this.

Yashar stood beside the door, on the other side of the veil— out of sight from mortal eyes—vigilant for anything that might catch them off guard. Something wasn't right about Coyote's visit. There was a lingering worry in the back of his mind. *Was he missing something? By simply strolling up to Ewan's were they somehow doing exactly what they shouldn't?* While normally more cautious about such things, the bottle of whiskey he and Colby had polished off helped assuage any fears he might have.

Colby rapped on the door, half drunk, but steady enough to hold a conversation. He waited a moment before raising his fist to rap again. *KA-CHUNK*. He was interrupted by the dead bolt on the other side of the door. It opened and Ewan peered out, looking both ways as he did so.

"Colby?" he asked. "What the hell are you doing here this late?"

Colby didn't have an immediate answer.

"Is that Johnny Walker I smell?"

Colby shook his head. "No, it's far older and much harder to pronounce, especially after half a bottle."

"Get the hell in here." Ewan held the door open wide enough for Colby to step through, furrowed his brow, and then closed it behind him, dead-bolting it again.

"Sorry, man," said Colby. "I've been drinking."

"I can see that."

"You mind if I crash here tonight? I shouldn't be out in this condition." He was lying; he would have no problem getting home. But this seemed about as good an excuse as any.

"Of course," said Ewan with a wry smile. "You've done it for me."

Colby thought about that for a second. "That I have, actually."

"Let me get you a pillow and a blanket from the other room." Ewan walked into his bedroom and rooted around in his closet. Colby took a moment to soak in his surroundings. He breathed deeply through his nose, smelling nothing but stale laundry and unwashed dishes. There were no unusual shadows, nor were there any out-of-place holes. If any supernatural creatures spied on Ewan, they were doing so outside his apartment.

Ewan's place was the consummate starving artist's retreat. While no gifted painter, he was talented enough an illustrator and had lined the walls with thick sketch paper, scrawled with a series of troubling drawings. Colby had seen them before. Each was of a fairy, clearly a scene from his long-forgotten life, most depicting a little girl. Sometimes she overlooked a pond; other times she ran through fields of tall grass. Over time, Colby had pieced together some of their inspirations from his own memories. He knew the girl, but he'd rather not remember her.

On the floor was a collection of battered secondhand guitars, scattered around a warped, tin ashtray, and the clutter of shuffled notebook paper, covered front to back with hastily scribbled lyrics and sheet music. A single dim lamp lit the room, making it seem dingier than it actually was. Against the wall languished a soiled couch, no doubt reclaimed from a curb, and beside it a rickety old bookcase. Atop that bookcase—perched precariously upon a teetering pile of books and papers—was none other than Colby's old companion, Mr. Bearston.

Colby ran his fingers over one of the bear's outstretched arms. For a moment, he felt eight years old again, ignorant and innocent. He stared into Mr. Bearston's one remaining eye— cataracted with years of grime—and smiled; it was just as he remembered it. Its fur was matted from years of night sweat and frayed from as many years of play. A single round spot lingered where an eye had previously been, revealing something only a few shades off from the bear's original color. "Have you been keeping a proper eye on him, sir?" Colby asked wistfully of the bear. "I sure hope you have. You have a very important job, you know." Reaching up, he took the bear's head in one hand and made it nod. "Good. Keep up the good work, sir."

"What are you looking at?" asked Ewan from behind him.

Colby turned around. "Mr. Bearston."

"Who?"

"Your bear," he said. "Mr. Bearston."

"Oh, that? His name is Dithers. I've had him since before we met. Got me through a lot, when I was a kid, you know?"

"*Dithers?*"

"I have no idea. You know how stupid kids' names can be." Colby nodded.

Ewan handed him a stained pillow and a ragged blanket. Colby looked askance at the couch, but took a seat anyway. "What are you still doing up?" he asked.

"Writing. Working on a few songs."

"A few?"

"Yeah, I'm dizzy tonight. I don't know what it is—I mean, yeah, I know what it is—but I've got all of this music bouncing around in my head, louder than it's ever been before."

"Louder?"

"Yeah. Louder. Clearer. I've always heard music, deep down, but it's always been fuzzy, you know—out of reach. Like it was waiting for me to fill in the blanks. But it doesn't have holes anymore. I can hear the music. I'm just trying to get it right. It's still not all coming out."

"Where's it coming from?"

"Well . . ."

"Well, what?" asked Colby with a hint of concern.

"There's this girl."

"This *girl?*"

Ewan smiled, bigger and brighter than Colby had ever seen him. It was a goofy, almost embarrassing expression, like something out of a comic book or a cartoon. "Nora," he said, sighing silently after he said her name.

"Nora?"

"Nora. She was at our show tonight."

"You had a show? Why didn't you call?"

"It was last minute."

"But this dream girl somehow knew about it."

"I'm not entirely sure she was there for *our* show."

Colby's eyes lit up. "So what's her deal?" he asked. "Tell me about her."

"Her name's Nora."

"Got that. Nora what?"

Ewan's mouth hung open to answer, but his memory turned up blank. Instead: Silence.

"Okay, skipping the last name. What does she do? Is she a student?"

No answer.

Colby grew ever more frustrated with Ewan. "Can you at least describe her to me?"

"Oh! Yes! She's small. Very small. With big brown eyes and wispy short brown hair."

"Okay, that's a start."

"She's very . . . different, you know? She's got this way about her that isn't like other girls—unconventional, without trying too hard, if you know what I mean."

"I do."

"She has me writing music, man."

"I can see that."

"No, *good* music."

Colby laughed. "Are we sure this girl is even human?" He was only half joking, though Ewan wouldn't know it. "No last name, no job to speak of . . ."

"She's beautiful and her touch is like . . . fireworks."

"Jesus, man. This sounds serious."

"I know," said Ewan, a bit stunned by the idea. "You know how people talk about meeting *the one* and just knowing right then and there that they're *the one*?"

"Yeah, everyone has that. They feel it every time they meet someone they're excited about, and then when that goes south, they forget that they ever felt that way so it can feel new next time."

"Uh-huh. *Dick*. Well, that's what this feels like."

"Well, don't just stand there looking like an idiot. Play me some of this music."

"All right, but it's rough."

"I would hope so, you just met her tonight." Colby cocked a brow. "Right?"

Ewan nodded.

He sat on the ground and picked up a beat-up guitar. It was well worn, easily the most battered of the bunch—covered in stickers and nicks from years of abuse—but it had a deep, robust sound. There was something manly and rugged about it, as if it were the Charles Bronson of guitars, each chord dousing the air with the trembling bass of testosterone. If you listened closely, the guitar itself had a story to tell you. But Ewan had his story to tell first.

Colby listened to his friend lay into the guitar. The first notes were enchanting, a delicately constructed opening that drew the listener in, invited them to listen to a love story before promising to tell one, only to turn—when one least expected—into a fiery, percussive rock song with an immediate and insidious hook. Instantly, Colby was nodding along, intimately familiar with the tune, despite never before having heard it.

Or had he?

There was something peculiar about its infectiousness. It sounded like something he'd hummed a hundred times before. It wasn't the Stones or the Beatles—but it had their immortality. Their verve. Something about it wasn't right; most of the notes were there, but not enough to complete the memory it was tugging at. *What? Was? It?*

Wait, was it . . . ? It couldn't . . .

The bridge came around and, catching a break in the lyrics, Colby spoke up. "What do you call this?"

"'Pixie Moon.'"

Shit.

Colby knew what this was. Though incomplete and not enough to be considered true plagiarism, it was close enough to the original that it would draw the attention of any fairy who heard it. "The Rustling of the Veil"—a melody said to be a thousand years old that could inspire any fair maiden to dance upon hearing it. He closed his eyes and peered beyond the veil, trying to grasp the structure of the magic playing before him, but there was none—not a hint of it. It was a rollicking, foot-stomping song to be sure, but there was nothing magical about it.

Try as it might, it was no "Rustling of the Veil." But it was close enough. Ewan was beginning to remember.

"This girl inspired *this*?" asked Colby.

Ewan smiled. "Yeah. And about half a dozen others. But none of them is as close to being finished."

Colby nodded. "The song is great. A little more work—just a little—and I think you've got your first hit."

"Really?" asked Ewan excitedly. Compliments from Colby meant a great deal to him; he offered praise rarely, and only when he truly meant it. If Colby liked it, that meant it might actually be good.

"Yes, really."

Ewan smiled like a boxer having won a bout after fifteen long rounds. "I'm not sure what to say."

"Why don't you thank me by telling me more about this mystery girl?"

"She tastes like fresh-picked strawberries."

"Are you serious?" asked Colby.

"But she smells like flowers, you know, like bluebonnets in the spring. Her hair is like running your fingers through silk. And her skin—it's like a china doll's."

"Porcelain?"

"That's it, porcelain."

"So she's a cliché."

Ewan frowned. "No. She's perfect."

Colby threw his hands up in the air, defensively apologizing. "Drunk!"

"Yeah. That gets you only so far. You're lucky this girl has me in such a good mood."

"Sorry, brother."

"It's cool."

Colby swallowed hard. "Look, I have something to tell you."

"What?" asked Ewan, his hand resting flat upon the guitar strings.

Colby wavered on the edge of saying something stupid—something he couldn't take back. He had suspicions, but nothing concrete; he also still had a lot of whiskey in his system, clouding his judgment. "Don't let her break your heart," he said somberly. "Someone will always—"

"I swear, man," Ewan interrupted. "Always with the big brother thing. You're a *year* older."

"I know," he said, nodding.

"A year."

"Yes."

"One. Year," said Ewan with a single pointed finger.

"I get it," said Colby, beginning to feel frustrated.

"You know what we need to do now?"

"What?"

"We need to get you a girl."

Colby laughed. "Does Nora have a friend?"

Ewan looked on, staring off in thought. "You know . . . I don't know."

EWAN AWOKE WITH a start from a knock at the door that sat him up straight in bed. He'd been dreaming of small men again, which always made him uneasy the following morning. It took a moment to ascertain where he was. It was light out and he was in his bedroom. Everything else must have been a dream.

Staggering out of bed and into the living room, eyes bleary, hair a jungle of bed head, he looked to the couch, expecting to find a sprawled Colby, still passed out from the night before. In his place rested a neatly folded blanket with a pillow placed squarely on top. Atop that was a note.

Thanks for the couch. You can have it back now. —C.

Another knock.

"All right, all right. I'm coming."

The door was barely open before something sprang through. It leapt upon him without warning, its legs wrapping firmly around his waist, its arms wrapping tightly about his neck. "Ewan!" it exclaimed. Confused and faltering back, Ewan tried to adjust to the weight clinging to his center of gravity. As his eyes focused, he found himself staring into a pair of big, tawny brown eyes.

Nora smiled, and then kissed him square on the mouth.

"I told you I'd find you."

Ewan put both of his hands firmly on her tiny waist, and then set her down gently.

"How did you . . . ?" he began.

"Sssshhhhh," she said, putting a single, delicate finger over his lips. "I have a secret to tell you."

"What?"

She looked both ways, pretending someone might be listening. Then she leaned in close, kicking the door shut behind her with a light shove, and whispered like a schoolgirl. "I'm magic."

"You're magic, huh?" he whispered back.

She nodded.

"And what kind of magic can you do?"

"Apart from finding the boy I like?"

"Yeah, apart from that."

"I can convince that boy to carry me into the bedroom and make love to me without saying anything else." She cocked a curious brow and let his hormones do the rest. He reeled for only a moment before scooping her tightly into his arms, kissing her, and walking her into the bedroom without their lips separating once.

Ewan's bed was a frameless mattress atop a box spring on the floor, pushed into the farthest corner of the room to get the most out of the available space. He sat upright in it, his back against the wall, a worn-out old sketchbook a few pages shy of retirement in his lap. His pencil worked furiously, once again drawing the young girl.

Beside him, Nora stirred in bed, stretching out into an adorable catlike yawn that gently knocked the covers off her body. She rolled onto her side, propped her head atop her hand, and watched silently as Ewan drew. His eyes were unwavering.

"You're drawing her again?"

"Yeah," he said without looking up. "I guess I am. I wasn't thinking about it really. Just letting my hands go at it."

"Where do they come from? The images, I mean."

"Dreams, mostly. I get these faint glimmers, almost like

memories. And then they're gone. I draw them to hold on, to try to capture the feeling of those dreams, those glimmers."

"Who is she?"

"I don't know, someone from the dreams."

"Someone special?" she asked.

Ewan thought deeply for a moment, hesitating before answering. "I don't remember her. But she feels special. There's this hole in my heart every time I draw her; you know, a sick sort of feeling. Like she's someone I lost."

"Like the girl of your dreams?"

Ewan narrowed his eyes and scowled a mock frown. "She looks like she's nine."

"Love knows no bounds," she said in all seriousness. "Neither time nor space can keep two people's energies apart."

"You don't really believe that, do you?" asked Ewan, laughing a bit at the thought.

"Without question," Nora said sternly. "Love is the most primal force in the universe. It inspires us, pulling us over otherwise insurmountable obstacles. Art is created to exalt it, children are born of it, and entire lives are devoted to seeking it out in the most unlikely places." She smiled—the joy within her at the thought of it all overflowing from her upturned lips and wide, radiant eyes. "Do I believe that an emotion like love can transcend something as irrelevant as time? Yes."

"But time is a real thing. You can measure it. You can't measure love."

"That's what makes it more powerful."

Ewan laughed. "You really are into this whole idea of love, aren't you?"

"My whole life is about love."

"How can your whole life be about love?" he asked. "How many men have you been with?" The question escaped his lips before he'd been properly able to vet it, though he regretted it instantly. He didn't want to know the answer. This girl was perfection, and he knew he was about to spoil that with the sweaty, pitiless truth.

"How many men?" she asked.

He hesitated. It was too late. "Yes," he said, squinting tightly, as if that would somehow protect him from it.

"Have I been with?"

"Yes."

"You," she said.

"Yes, including me."

"Just you."

"No, how many men total?"

"Just one. *You.*"

"Wait, what? No," he protested. "Seriously."

Nora wheeled her legs around and sat up, crossing them Indian style before perching both of her elbows upon her knees, resting her head in her hands. She looked directly into Ewan's eyes and spoke very plainly. "Seriously."

"That didn't feel like a first time."

"Do you know how long I've waited to find *the guy* to do that to—to do that *with*? That wasn't experience, Ewan. That was *deeper.*"

"So that whole thing about having the power to make boys you like make love to you?"

"It only works on you."

"Whoa," he said, his mind blown. "So you're a virgin?"

"Not anymore."

Ewan looked both excited and scared at the same time. "Why me?"

"When you find a soul as pure and honest as yours—when you find someone whose arms fit perfectly around you and who chases the rest of the world away when they do—you grab on with both hands and you don't let go. If you tell me you want me, Ewan, I'll be yours until the end of your days. And when those days are through, I'll cross time and space to find you again. Time and again. And we'll be together forever, time and space be damned."

She climbed atop him, straddling him and casting aside his sketchpad. There she pressed her face to his—forehead to forehead, nose to nose, eyes locked, unblinking.

"Do you want me?" she asked.

Ewan nodded slightly, refusing to break his gaze. "Yes."

"Forever?"

"Yes."

"Then I'm yours. *Forever.*"

CHAPTER THIRTY-ONE

THE LEANAN SIDHE

An excerpt by Dr. Thaddeus Ray, Ph.D., from
his book *A Chronicle of the Dreamfolk*

Unlike the succubus (or incubus) for which it is often
mistaken, the Leanan Sidhe is a monogamous creature. Also
unlike its vampiric spiritual cousins, Leanan Sidhe are exclu-
sively female. Whether finding their beginnings in the traveling tales of the succubus, or more likely, deviations of tales
about mating with Sidhe, it is important to remember that
this particularly nasty species of Irish fairy has survived the
ages and found a fertile breeding ground in this era, with a
counterculture cover masking its activities.

Incredibly territorial, once one has chosen a mate, she will allow no other woman near him. Patient predators and capable shape changers, these fae stalk their prey, learning everything there is to know about him to craft the perfect form with which to seduce him. While they are unafraid to be seen with the men they choose, they will not make a spectacle or show of themselves. They will be quiet and demure around others, outwardly becoming whatever it is their prey desires when alone.

Leanan Sidhe feed upon two things: the sexual energy of a man, and his creative spark. If the man accepts her advances and mates with her, she is his forever; she will love no other, not so much as casting her eye at another man. The man—chosen not only for his virility, but also upon aesthetic criteria pertaining to some form of artistic endeavor—will find himself divinely inspired. He will gush creatively.

The Leanan Sidhe acts as a form of muse, triggering the creative instincts of her prey and unleashing decades of talent into singularly devastating works of genius. She will make no attempt to interfere in his work, no attempt to guide it with her own tastes. If he chooses to sit up all night composing an opera, she will not complain, she will not make any attempt to draw his attention. It is only when he has completed his work that she will once again seduce him and feed off his blend of both physical and spiritual euphoria. A man in love with a Leanan Sidhe is never more productive in his life than when she is with him.

Such is the conundrum of properly classifying this creature. She means no harm to her victim, and she will not raise a finger to hurt him in any way. In fact, she believes that she loves him, though her love is destructive. Not only does she siphon off the dreamstuff of her victim, but the bond of love is so strong between the two that her absence inflicts incredible amounts of emotional suffering upon him. While he pines for her, he creates, but soon finds that the words do not flow so freely when she is away. Deprived of his muse, the victim turns to vice, often alcohol or drugs, but self-mutilation is not unheard of. This vice often acts as the perfect cover for the Leanan Sidhe, as her feeding ultimately leads to the eventual, and inevitable, death of her suitor.

Whether this is deliberate murder has long been cause for discussion. It is entirely possible that the Leanan Sidhe has no inkling that it is her feedings that result in the death of her lover. Some argue that feelings of love and those of hunger are identical to the Leanan Sidhe, that they are indistinguishable from each other, making it impossible for her to even know which she is feeling. The act of lovemaking leaves them refreshed, invigorated and full of life. When their mates die, often midcoitus, they depart, heartbroken, and live in sadness, promising that the next man will be better, stronger, and a more capable lover, able to satisfy them without suffering an early death.

Are they seelie or unseelie? No one is sure. They could very well operate with full knowledge of their activities, entirely self-aware, outwardly expressing shock and dismay at the loss of their lover. They could just as easily be unwitting vampires, operating as muses, unaware that they cause even the slightest bit of harm. Firsthand accounts support the latter. However, considering their education, refinement, taste, and delicate, precise methodology, one has to wonder: how much of that is an act?

Conversely, if she does feel love and does not recognize hunger, then perhaps she really is a muse. After all, the men she loves leave behind some of humanity's greatest works of art: paintings, poetry, sculptures, plays. Perhaps these men contained the right spark to create these masterpieces, but needed a catalyst to bring so much of it out at once. And, as with burning several wicks in the same pot of oil, simply consumes everything he has in one, powerful, bright period of expression.

Locating and tracking Leanan Sidhe can be difficult. The first tales of them come from descriptions of the lovers of several young Irish poets. Irish poets are known for three things: their brilliance, their fondness for the drink, and the beautiful company they were said to keep. Some argue that the myth originated as a superstition surrounding the early deaths of so many of these men. Others claim that these are merely the first tales that were collected of the comings and goings of the Leanan Sidhe.

Today their presence is hard to spot. With media fixation and celebrity status often offered so early to talented artists, it is impossible to tell the fairy from your garden variety groupie. This has led to misidentifications and dead ends in a number of famous cases. During the sixties they were easily able to slip in and out of the scene, taking so many talented counterculture stars with them. Now they have to be more cunning to score a number of high-profile victims before they can slip away again. Comedians, musicians, and novelists often find themselves overdosing on heroin or mysteriously committing suicide, while the women with whom they are seen rarely turn up ever again. Once they're gone, they're gone; photographs and back stories are useless for tracking shape changers.

While Leanan Sidhe are extremely dangerous to their lovers, they are otherwise harmless. There is no known way to ward off a Leanan Sidhe short of refusing its advances or destroying it.

CHAPTER THIRTY-TWO

LOVERS IN THE AFTERNOON

"Play that song again, Ewan."

"Which one?"

"The one about your first love."

"They're all about my first love."

"You know which one I'm talking about."

"But you're my first love."

"So?"

"So are you really asking me to play a song I wrote about *you*?"

"Ewan."

"Because you know how that sounds."

"Ew-an."

"*Play that song about me.*"

"Keep it up. I can go home at any time."

"And?"

"And I'll be taking all of your favorite parts with me."

"You do have a lot of my favorite parts."

"And they'll be gone."

"In fact, I'd argue that you have all of my favorite parts."

"Play the fucking song, Ewan."

"Which one?"

Nora leaned in close, brushing the tip of her nose against his, breathing softly and deliberately. She kissed him ever so slightly on the lips and whispered, "The one about your first love."

"Oh, that one." He smiled and strummed the guitar. "The one about the most beautiful girl in the world."

Nora and Ewan nuzzled on the floor of his apartment, half dressed, passing a lit cigarette back and forth. It was raining, the air heavy with the damp chill of late winter; the sort of gray, cozy, dreary day lovers find romantic. Ewan played, the music effortlessly drifting out of him, lingering in the air. Perfect.

The song ended. Ewan cocked his head, the wheels turning inside. Nora wrinkled her nose.

"I know what's coming," she said.

"What?"

"You're about to ask me questions again."

"I was?"

"You were."

"Are you sure about that?"

"Quite certain."

He shook his head. "How the hell do you do that?"

"See? Questions." Nora stabbed out the cigarette in the ash-tray, immediately lighting up another.

"You always seem to know what I'm thinking, even before I think it. How do you *do* that?"

"I don't know. I just know what you want. I can feel it. I think it's because we were made for each other."

"You know, most men would freak out if you talked to them like that."

"Many would, I suppose."

"No, really. Everything is so permanent with you. Everything is timeless or immortal or forever or made for each other."

Nora smiled, shaking her head. "No, just us."

"See, I should be freaking out over talk like that."

"But you aren't. You love it. In a universe where you feel altogether out of place, I'm the one thing that feels just right."

"It should bother me that I'm as comfortable with this as I am."

"But it doesn't," she said, smiling. "Because we were made for each other."

"Then why can't you tell me anything?"

"I've told you everything worth knowing."

"You haven't told me anything."

Nora shrugged. "That's the point, I guess."

"I can't be the only interesting thing in your life."

Nora rolled over and looked Ewan dead in the eye. "But you are. You're the only thing."

"Who is your *best* friend?"

"You."

"No, your best *friend*."

"Ewan . . ."

"I'm serious. Before you met me, who is the person you talked to most?"

"I was never really the friend type. I mean, I spent time with people my own age, but I wasn't really close with any of them."

"Why not?"

"We have . . . the people I live with, I mean . . . different . . . values."

"What does that even *mean*?"

"It means we believe in different things. I live out in the sticks. Way out in the Hill Country. You know how folks out there can be. They put a different premium on people. Under the right circumstances some of them are very nice. Under the wrong ones they'd burn you to save their own skin. I can't live that way."

"Where do you live now?"

"I still live out there. With my uncle."

Ewan stroked Nora's hair, causing her to cuddle closer. "Not your parents?"

"No," she said. "I never knew them. My dad died before I was born. My mom left me with my uncle shortly after. I don't remember her at all."

"You don't remember your parents? At all?"

"Please, Ewan. Don't make fun of me. This is why I don't—"

"Who's making fun? You really don't remember your parents?"

"No."

Ewan shook his head. "Neither do I."

A small glimmer of a tear welled in the corner of Nora's eye. She smiled. "See," she said. "I told you we were made for each other." The two kissed.

"So you still live out there with your uncle?"

She nodded. The staccato of rain rapped loudly on the window. The storm was getting stronger.

"If this gets any worse, you'll have to spend the night."

"There are worse fates I could imagine," she said. "I have the best dreams when I sleep here."

"What do you dream about?"

"You."

"What do you dream about when you're not dreaming about me?"

"What kind of question is that?"

"The kind wondering what you dream about. What's ticking inside you, you know?"

"Well, what do you dream about?"

"It's weird."

"*Weird?*"

"You know how most people dream about things like blue puppies or showing up for school in their underwear or going strange places with people they only know from work?"

"I guess."

"Well, I don't dream about any of that. I dream about the woods. About running away from tiny men or holding hands with a little girl or monsters made out of rock. I dream about the same things over and over again. They never change. It's not like I dream about these little men chasing me through the city or the supermarket. It's always the woods. I always dream about the woods. And nothing else."

"What do you think your dreams are trying to tell you?"

"I don't know."

"Maybe they're telling you that you need to leave."

"Leave? No. I've been having them as long as I can remember."

"Well, then. Maybe that's what I'm telling you."

"That I should leave?"

"That maybe *we* should," she said.

"There's a lot you're not telling me, isn't there?"

She nodded.

"And you don't trust me enough to tell me?"

"It's not that."

"What is it then?"

"It's things you'd best not know."

"About you?"

"About where I come from."

"Why can't I know about it?"

"Because if there are things I'd rather forget, why on earth would I want someone else remembering them?"

"Sometimes weights are better carried by two."

"You read that on a greeting card, didn't you?"

Ewan smirked, busted. "It might have been a comic strip."

"You're adorable."

"You're incredible."

"Run away with me."

"What?"

Nora sat up, taking Ewan's hands in hers, staring, unblinking, into his eyes. "Run away with me. We'll take your band to L.A. and go all the way. Let's just get out of here and never look back."

"What are you afraid of?"

"Losing all this."

"No, why do you want to leave?"

"Because you're never going to be the man you want to be washing dishes in a bar. And I'm never going to be the girl you want me to be living here."

"You're serious, aren't you?"

"Very."

"Oh my God. I don't . . . I don't know what to say."

"Tell me you love me."

"Nora, I love you."

"Tell me you need me."

"Nora, I need you."

"Tell me you're gonna be a rock star."

"I'm gonna be a rock star."

"Run away with me."

"Okay. After our next show, if we tear the roof off the place, we'll talk to the boys."

Nora bounced up and down, clapping her hands. "We're going to do this?"

"*If* the show goes well."

"Then it better go well. I'll do whatever I can."

"You really want to do this?"

"More than anything."

CHAPTER THIRTY-THREE

THE PHILOSOPHER'S BREAKFAST

The sky was angry, roiling with a deep fury betraying unshackled hostility for the earth below. Flashes of light belched within the clouds, streaking from the heavens, trailed by cavernous claps of thunder drenched in a thousand tiny slaps of rain. It was a hateful storm, spiteful, brimming with malice. The sky itself fell in softball-size chunks of ice, the city buckling, breaking beneath it, windows spiderwebbed with cracks before shattering, ice and glass commingling on the ground.

Colby Stevens saw the storm for what it was, the billowing thunderhead above churning with the shadows of Hell, the air stinking of brimstone. There was nothing natural about it.

It was the witching hour and the looming threat had chased away the few remaining barflies, leaving abandoned downtown streets. The conditions were perfect for what was about to happen. Though having never before seen it in person, he was familiar with the signs. The Wild Hunt was afoot.

Colby stood in the recessed doorway of a building, barely out of hail's reach, a backpack slung over his shoulder, holding a single bottle of whiskey—a gift from Old Scraps to rush him out the door before the rare act of closing the bar up for the night. No one wanted to be out in this, even the old cluricaun.

As the hail let up, Colby hiked across the ice-strewn street to one of the city's tallest buildings and ascended its rain-slicked fire escape. The wet metal left a rusty orange itch in his palm. While spending time atop a rooftop in a storm was a terrible idea, the telltale dull roar of hooves in the distance convinced him that it was better than the alternative. So Colby took the fire escape one step at a time, trying not to think about what might happen if lightning struck its exposed, rusted metal skeleton.

Upon reaching the top, he saw that he was not alone. Sharing the rooftop, perched recklessly upon the outermost ledge, was Bertrand the angel. Suited from the neck down in his battered white suit of armor, he looked more like a lightning hazard than good company. Bertrand craned his neck over his shoulder, sniffing, his long, soaked hair flailing in the wind.

"Is that a bottle of whiskey I smell in your bag?" he called out over the rain.

Colby nodded. "You can smell that?"

"I've got the nose of a bloodhound and the thirst of his master." Bertrand sniffed the air again. "I wouldn't worry, you'll be fine up here. Doesn't smell like lightning."

Colby walked across the rooftop, pulling the bottle out of his bag. He unscrewed the top, took a long, deep pull off the bottle and passed it to Bertrand. The angel took a brief swig, gargled with the alcohol and swallowed hard.

"Shit," he said. "I figured a sorcerer would be able to conjure himself up a better brand of bourbon."

Colby shook his head. "Not in this town. There isn't enough ambient dreamstuff to put together a stiff drink of rotgut, let alone a whole bottle of the stuff." Then he took a seat beside the angel.

Bertrand took another drink, then flapped and fluttered his large white wings a bit, shaking rain from his feathers. He extended one wing over Colby, casting a heavy shadow but shielding him from the brunt of the downpour. "I've heard things about you, you know. Stories."

"I'd be surprised if you hadn't," said Colby, reaching for the bottle.

"Are any of them true?"

Colby nodded. "I'm sure there's a little something true in a bit of them all."

"Which ones are almost true?"

"Well, which one is your favorite? Just assume that one is true."

Bertrand nodded. "So what can I do for you?"

"What makes you think you can do something for me?"

"A lot of rooftops in this city," he said. "I only perch on one of 'em."

"Answers, mostly."

"You want to ask *me* questions?" asked Bertrand, genuinely surprised.

"Yeah."

Bertrand smirked. "Do I *have* to answer?"

"No. It's not that kind of night."

Bertrand and Colby had never spoken alone before, and the angel was rapidly growing impressed. "All right, I'll make you a deal," he said. "If you answer one question honestly, I'll tell you everything you want to know."

"Shoot," said Colby.

"Why won't the other angels talk to you?"

Colby looked down at the street below and watched the rain speed away from them, toward the ground. "Did you know that when you free all the dreamstuff from the body of an angel, all that's left are a few feathers and the smell of newborn babies?"

"I did not."

"One of your buddies thought he might pull the old visitation in a dream routine. I woke up as he was creeping up on me in the dark. To this day I have no idea what he was trying to tell me."

"I guess some of the stories about you *are* true."

"Like I said, there's a little truth to most of them. Everything else is perspective and window dressing." Colby took a swig from the bottle and passed it over to Bertrand. "For the descended of Heaven, your kind sure isn't fond of forgiveness."

"The unforgiven have little forgiveness to go around."

"Fair enough."

"What is it you want to know?"

"What does it take to be a good man?"

Bertrand laughed. "You want to know about goodness, so you come to someone tossed out of Heaven?"

"You fell to earth, not Hell. There's something to be said for that."

Bertrand gave Colby a surprised look, eyeing him from top to bottom. "You're far wiser than anyone gives you credit for, you know that?"

"I'll take that backhanded compliment. Now give me back my bottle."

Bertrand took a quick tug before handing the bottle back to Colby, who in turn took another long pull. "Look, I'll tell you what I know, which is the best that I can remember. How's that?"

Colby nodded, wiping whiskey from his lips with his sleeve. "That'll have to do."

"I'm guessing you're not here for the nickel advice. Love one another and treat everyone as you would have them treat you and all that?"

"No," said Colby.

"Well then, there are two types of holiness in this world: goodness and selflessness."

"They're not the same?"

"Hell no, they're not the same. They're not even close to being the same. A good man does what he's told; he follows the rules and keeps his nose clean. End of story. If he screws up, he asks for forgiveness and tries to do better next time. By the end of it all, as long as he's done his best and feels bad for all the times he's dropped the ball, we call him good.

"A truly selfless man, on the other hand, is an evil man. The most selfless thing a man can do is evil. A selfless man is one who does what he knows is wrong because he knows the outcome is ultimately for the greater good. A man who willingly commits his soul to damnation so that others don't have to? That's the ultimate selfless act. A true spiritual warrior isn't forgiven in the end—he gets no redemption—but his sacrifice enables others to live pure and chaste lives. That's the real reward. Of course, you never see that written in the fine print of the brochures." Bertrand leaned over as if sharing some trade secret. "You think the Crusaders were forgiven because the pope waved his hand and absolved them before they raped and killed and pillaged their way across the holy land? No. Heaven has no room for the self-righteous. Or the damned.

"You want the cold, hard truth? A martyr—a real martyr—isn't someone who dies for what he believes in. It's someone who gives up eternity for it. Someone who knows that they'll burn for what they've done, and does it anyway, consequences be damned."

"For someone else," said Colby, nodding.

"For someone else," agreed Bertrand. "Selflessness is only truly selfless if there is no reward but the outcome. Even in the afterlife."

"And that's what goodness is?"

"That's what holiness is."

Colby looked over with a sober, probing expression. "So, why'd you fall?"

Bertrand stared out into the rain. "You know, that's the problem with mortals—no understanding of the soul. You always assume we must have fallen, that we were all thrown out of Heaven." Then he turned and locked gazes with Colby, a hint of sadness in his eyes. "Some of us jumped."

"Do you remember why?"

Bertrand laughed. He looked away, then back at Colby, laughing again. Once more he looked away, having a hard time keeping a straight face. "You really don't spend much time around angels. We forget a lot of things—I mean, *a lot* of things—but we never forget *that*. The why is branded on our souls and stings every moment we're away. Yes. Yes, I remember why."

The dull, distant rumble of the Wild Hunt was louder now, the clamor of far-off hooves becoming more of an uproar, requiring raised voices. It wouldn't be much longer before they arrived.

"Is that whiskey I smell?" called a voice from the other side of the roof. Bertrand and Colby turned, looking over their shoulders at Bill the Shadow, rain cascading off the brim of his hat.

"Hey, Bill," the two said simultaneously.

Bill strode up, taking a seat next to Bertrand. "You got another wing?" Bertrand cast a sidelong glance at Bill, then shook the rain from his other wing, holding it over him. "Thanks," said Bill, lighting up a cigarette. He inhaled deeply. "Now, about that bottle."

Colby passed it over. The freshly opened bottle was now half empty and sloshing.

Bill drank. "I ever tell you guys about the time I saw the Wild Hunt up close and personal with my own eyes?"

"I've never heard that story," said Bertrand.

Colby shook his head silently and then reached across Bertrand's chest to signal Bill. Bill took a drink from the bottle and attempted to hand it back, but Colby waved it off and pointed to the cigarette. Nodding, Bill took another puff, and then handed it over to Colby.

Colby took a deep drag.

"It was a decade, decade and a half ago," said Bill, "out in the Hill Country. You know, deep in the Limestone Kingdom. I was living out there at the time." He looked over at Colby. "This was just before you and Yashar showed up."

"You were out there back then?" asked Colby, exhaling a puff of smoke as he spoke.

"Oh yeah. I was even there the night you went all . . ." Bill finished the sentence with a whistle, as if to signify the word *crazy*.

"Wait," said Bertrand. "You were there for that? When he disembodied a dozen fairies?"

"That's not what happened," said Colby, shaking his head.

"Yeah, I was there," said Bill. He took another drink from the bottle. "Colby's right. The legend doesn't live up to the memory."

"Thank you," said Colby.

Bill continued. "It was worse."

Colby rolled his eyes. "Oh, come on."

"Oh, you should have seen it, Bertrand," said Bill. "There we were—had to be at least a hundred of us—all standing around dumbfounded in front of the eight-year-old boy with his chest puffed out. It was surreal. First this redcap just vanishes in a fruity little explosion of flower petals and then nobody moves. A few redcaps get uppity, but Meinrad—he's the honcho out there—he waves them off because he knows better. This kid means business. Everyone, and I mean everyone, is shitting themselves. It was as if someone had walked into a crowd with a revolver—we knew that he could take out only a few of us before we tore him apart, but nobody wanted to be one of the six who would catch a bullet, you know?"

"So how many did he vaporize?" asked Bertrand with genuine interest.

"Just the one."

"Really? Because every time I hear that story, the number gets bigger."

"I told you," said Colby. "It didn't happen like that."

"But it did happen," said Bill. "That was the night that I decided to leave. I only go back for the Tithe."

Colby looked over at Bill. "Wait, they still hold the Tithe?"

"Of course they hold the Tithe," said Bill. "Why wouldn't they?"

"Because I told them not to." Colby's eyes were cold and angry.

"No, you didn't. You just came to get your little boyfriend."

Colby was genuinely baffled, drifting off into thought. He'd just assumed they'd stopped.

Bertrand tapped Bill on the chest with the back of his hand; Bill returned the bottle. "So what does that have to do with the hunt?" he asked.

Bill nodded. "The hunt came the night before Colby here showed up. It came from out of nowhere." He looked around. "Not like this. We were out enjoying the night when the roar just washed over us like a flash flood. Cut up a number of my friends right in front of me. I ducked into the shadows and watched as they took off with most everyone I knew well. After that, the Limestone Kingdom went to shit. And I've been drinking ever since."

The roar became almost deafening as the Wild Hunt rounded a corner onto the street below. While still several blocks away, the riders' gallop reverberated off buildings, rattling windows, shaking loose grit from bricks. Then the shadows of the large black goats appeared, their twisted horns flailing about in the dark, their feet igniting the earth below with horseshoe-shaped bursts that dimmed and flickered out immediately in the pouring rain. The riders whipped their steeds, pushing them hard and fast through the city, wisps of smoke trailing from their cauterized rags.

Bertrand brought a thoughtful hand up to his chin, giving a troubled look to Bill. Bill returned a firm, slow nod before the two turned their gaze back to the bedlam below. Something was very, very wrong.

The hunt from Hell galloped by without incident, without so much as looking up at the roof above. There were a dozen riders in all, their identities indistinguishable from where the trio perched. Each raced their goat as fast as it would carry them, vanishing around a street corner three blocks away, their waning thunder and smoldering hoofprints the only evidence they were still present.

"Well, that's not right," said Bertrand.

"What's not right?" asked Colby.

"The hunt," said Bill, shaking his head. "They're not *hunting* anybody."

"How can you tell?"

"No dogs," said Bertrand. "They always bring dogs. And they were traveling much too fast; you can't see anything traveling that fast in the dark, especially when you're not looking."

Bill and Bertrand both looked long and hard at Colby, their faces expressionless. Bertrand offered him back his bottle.

"You don't think . . . ," began Colby.

Bertrand nodded. "The Wild Hunt only appears where it needs or wants to be. Nowhere else."

Bertrand put a firm hand on Colby's shoulder, his caustic breath smelling as if he might ignite near an open flame. Colby wilted, his nostrils burning. "If things go as badly as I believe they will," said Bertrand, "and you end up on the right side of this, me and some of the boys will get your back. You bring the whiskey and I'll bring a pack of pissed-off angels."

Colby looked at him with confused, sincere eyes. "Why the hell would you help *me*?"

"Like I said, if you end up on the *right* side of this, we'll be there. It's kind of our thing."

Colby and Bertrand turned their eyes to Bill, who took one last drag off his cigarette before stabbing it out on the wet stone. "Most everyone I give a shit about died a long time ago. If there's a ruckus, I'm bound to want to take part. You can count me in."

"Thank you," said Colby.

Bill laughed. "Don't thank us yet, kid. There's a whole lotta hell to be had before it comes to all that. You mark my words."

With that, the rumble returned. It was like a train shrieking through the city, off its tracks, scraping and crumpling against the street below it. There was no other sound like it. And it was growing louder still.

The Wild Hunt rounded a corner back onto the street, having circled around to come back. Colby's heart jumped, skipping a few beats. His breath grew shallow; he found it hard to blink, even against the ever-increasing sting of the rain. *They were coming for him.*

The hunt stopped, all twelve riders coming to a slow trot below the three drunks. The lead rider looked up silently, its goat at a standstill. For a moment, there was a painful quiet broken only by the steady patter of rain. There came a brief, ominous rumble from distant thunder, but nothing else.

"I think they want a word with you," said Bertrand to Colby.

Colby shook his head.

"If they wanted to kill you," said Bill, "they'd ride up the side of the building and do so."

"So you guys got my back, right?"

They both laughed. "No," said Bertrand. "This ain't bad. Not yet."

"Not even close to bad," said Bill. "They's askin' nicely."

Colby sighed deeply, raising a single hand in front of his face, pinky and ring finger held down by his thumb while his index and middle fingers pointed upward as a single, joined digit. He kicked off the side of the building, descending slowly without accelerating beyond the initial drop. It took a few seconds for him to touch down, and when he did, he landed perfectly before the lead rider—a single downturned palm steadying his landing.

Colby rose to his feet, standing boldly before the hunt. He tried as best he could to look stoic, but shook like a scared kitten before the looming, flickering shadows. The goats bleated angrily, wanting to charge—but the riders steadied them. For a moment, Colby and the lead rider exchanged withering glares.

The rider—a rotten, bubbling corpse of a woman with barely any hair left upon her head, eyes nearly falling out of their sockets, and a few jagged teeth still clinging to her pus-drenched gums— swung her limp, flaccid leg over the side of her flesh-hide saddle, hopping off her goat. Grabbing her mount by the horn to stay it, she walked it forward to Colby, standing just out of arm's reach.

"What do you want of me?" asked Colby of the woman.

The creature shrieked, the wind howling her vowels for her. "Your help." She raised a single arm, placing her skeletal, rotten hand upon Colby's forehead. Colby seized up, overwhelmed with visions.

Before him he saw Ladybird Lake; he was soaring over it like a bird before descending into the waves, deep down, nearly twenty feet below its surface. The water was murky with mud, but as he sank lower, he could make out a mound of lake-bottom silt with a doorway. He moved through it, into an algae-swollen atrium with a dark recess below it into which he sank farther still. There, below the mound, was a series of dark caves leading past what looked like living areas into a sandy-floored room covered in large overturned clay pots. His gaze closed in upon a single pot, a name etched into it:

JARED THATCHER.

The woman removed her hand from Colby—shriveled, decaying bits of flesh remaining smeared upon his face. "Free him," she howled. "Free my love!"

"You want me to go down there?" asked Colby, his eyes saying *hell no.*

"His soul! Let it out! Let it out and you will not be collected!"

Colby eyed her nervously. "Do I have a choice?"

The woman nodded, smiling wickedly, patting her enormous goat on the neck. Colby understood immediately what she meant.

"All right," he said. "But only if you leave. Right now."

The woman nodded, the entire hunt bursting immediately into flames. A fierce wind kicked up, blowing each flaming rider and its steed like a bellows, incinerating them whole, carrying their ashes off into the storm. Within two breaths, they were gone, leaving Colby alone in the dwindling rain. All that remained was gentle thunder, too far away to matter anymore.

He looked up at the building behind him, Bill and Bertrand staring back, then let out a frustrated sigh, scowling at the fire escape. Then he shuffled, defeated, toward it once more. He might be doomed, but he'd be damned if he was going to let those two finish the bottle without him.

CHAPTER THIRTY-FOUR

ONE LAST STOP
BEFORE SUNSET

Austin continually ranks amongst the heaviest-drinking cities in the country, sometimes going so far as to capture the top spot from the likes of New Orleans, Las Vegas, and New York City. The epicenter of all that drinking is a single street, loaded from one end to the other with bars, clubs, tattoo parlors, and the occasional sex shop. It is Sixth Street, where college kids escape to binge drink and thirty-five-year-olds escape to feel like college kids.

Where there is drinking, there is misery. Where there is misery, there are the dark things. And Sixth Street is loaded top to bottom with the dark things.

During the day it is a vacant, lonely stretch of road with a few open pubs and restaurants serving sandwiches to the downtown day crew. But when the sun goes down and the neon kicks in, the shadows crawl out from their holes and the angels perch along the tops of buildings. As the rest of downtown closes up and rolls down their shutters, Sixth Street breathes in and exhales life into every bulb along the stretch.

Colby tried very hard to avoid Sixth Street. The things that preyed down there weren't fond of him. Few challenged him directly, knowing full well what he was capable of. But that didn't quell the dirty looks, the name calling, or the occasional spit on his shoe. Ewan worked on Sixth Street. And Ewan was just about the only reason Colby ever endured the jeers of the things that haunted it. And that's why he was here now.

After the pounding the city had taken the night before, businesses were busy installing new glass. Those that weren't had turned instead to plywood and duct tape. Ewan's bar chose the latter, punctuating their choice with an ironic sign reading: SPENT MONEY ON BEER INSTEAD.

Ewan dumped ice from a large plastic bin into the well beneath the bar. It was a half hour before opening. The bar was bright, lit by heavy, industrial lights meant only for setup and chasing out drunken barflies. In the corner, unbeknownst to Ewan, sat two demons, both mostly human in appearance, and a Boggart more shadow than man, drinking in the last lingering remnants of the previous night's anguish. They paid Ewan about as much mind as he paid them. But Colby was a different story.

"Oh, what's this piece of shit doing in our bar?" asked one demon of the other.

Colby looked up as he closed the door behind him.

"You'd think he'd have the decency to stay in his little faggot bar with all his little faggot friends," said the other.

The Boggart laughed, but dared not speak up. Of the three, he was the only one to have ever seen Colby angry before. Colby shot them a withering glare and the Boggart looked away, choosing the table in lieu of eye contact. The demons grinned wickedly.

"What the hell are you doing down here?" asked Ewan.

Colby smiled. "I've got a thing I've got to do a little later. On this side of town. So I figured I'd drop in."

"A thing?"

"Yeah, just a job. Nothing big."

"Nothing worth speaking of, or nothing you can?"

"It's a work thing."

Ewan pleaded with his arms. "Why does everyone in my life have to be so goddamned mysterious?"

"What's that supposed to mean?"

One of the demons mocked him in a pinched voice. "*What's that supposed to mean?*"

Colby peered over his shoulder, trying not to be obvious.

"You and Nora and all your secrets," said Ewan. "Doesn't anyone, you know, actually talk about their shit?"

"Nora has secrets?"

"Of course she does. I can't have anyone in my life who doesn't. Even my bandmates have their little secrets with each other."

"Well, they're brothers. What's Nora's deal?"

"Her *deal*?"

"What won't she tell you?"

"Everything. Where she's from. What she does. She's a total mystery."

"What do you know about her?"

"I know she lives with her uncle out in the Hill Country and that she was in love with some guy once, but he took off and forgot about her."

"That all sounds pretty norm . . ." Colby's eyes grew wide. "Where in the Hill Country?"

"Won't say. Just that she lives with her uncle."

"Hmmm." Colby's voice drifted off, thoughts rolling around in his head.

"She's not a redneck or anything."

"Hmmm? Wait, what?"

"It's not like she's a hick."

"What are you talking about?"

"I know what you were thinking."

"You don't have the first idea what I'm thinking."

"I need to get more ice. Hang here." Ewan picked up the large plastic tub, carrying it off into the kitchen.

Colby looked over his shoulder at the demons who in turn continued their sadistic grinning.

"What are you going to do without your djinn, wish boy?"

"Yeah, you ain't gonna do nothing."

Colby shook his head, upturning his palm. With a quick flex of his fingers he sucked every last bit of dreamstuff out of the room, every bit of lingering darkness and melancholy, exhaling it as a single ring of smoke. The puff drifted then broke apart.

The three glowered. "Oh, now you're just being a dick," said one. The Boggart gently grabbed his wrist, shaking his head.

Colby clenched his fist. "How hard do you think it would be for me to do the same to you? Find another bar."

"What?" asked Ewan from the other room.

The three stood up, angry and flustered, making their way to the door.

"I said how hard would it be to find a girl like Nora at another bar?"

Ewan returned, his back arched and the tub overflowing with ice. "Why would I want to find another girl?"

"Not you. Me, jackass. What are the odds of me finding a girl like her?"

"Why would you want to find a girl like Nora? It's not like you'd talk to her."

"That's not cool."

"No, it's not. But it's true. I've never seen you talk to a girl. Never."

"I talk to . . . okay, I don't talk to girls. But imagine for a moment that I did. What would I say? I mean, what did you say to pick up Nora?"

"She did most of the picking up, actually."

"*Reaaalllly?*"

"Wait, you don't think that a girl like that would want a guy like me?"

"That's not even close to what I was saying."

"Why is it such a big deal that she hit on me and not the other way around?"

"Because."

"Because why?"

Colby floundered for an answer that didn't have the word *fairy* in it. "Because I worry, okay?"

"What?"

"Girls like that can be trouble. She could be an emotional train wreck moving from guy to guy, leaving you heartbroken and penniless."

"You take that back."

"Ewan, Jesus. I'm not saying that's who she is, I'm saying I don't know her and I worry."

"You don't have to worry. That's not your job."

"But I do. I'm always going to worry. Sometimes I feel like you're my only connection to . . . to . . . to the real world. I'm always off in the bookstore, in my own little world, and you are what keeps me grounded, what keeps me feeling human. You're my link, and if I lose you, I feel like I'll be lost for good. So yeah. I worry."

"Is that why you always wrote me letters when we were kids? When you were off having all those adventures?"

"That's exactly why. Everyone needs one friend who makes them feel normal. Who makes them feel like not everyone in the world is out to get them. That's you. Without you, I'd go nuts. I don't think I could handle this place."

"Goddamnit, Colby."

"What?"

"I can't even be pissed off at you properly."

"That's the mark of a good friend."

Ewan nodded and dumped the remaining ice into the well. "It is. Now get the fuck out of here. My boss will be in soon."

CHAPTER THIRTY-FIVE

THE THREE LADIES OF LADYBIRD LAKE AND THE SOULS THEY KEEP BENEATH IT

The word *lake* was something of a misnomer, a polite fiction. It was actually a reservoir—a dammed-up section of the Colorado River, perfectly bisecting the city, that had at one time fallen into disuse. Only later, through civic revitalization, did it become a destination location for hikers, bikers, and joggers on the prowl. Trails lined the lake up one side and down the other, shaded by trees that ran its length both in and out of town.

Colby was given no deadline or timetable, but the weight of the task gnawed at him, demanding he be done with it. So there he was. It was night, and he stood naked at the edge of the lake at a spot a quarter mile west of the expressway, where he could still hear the traffic.

Of course, he knew of the nixie sisters by reputation, but he had never met them. There were often stories in the local news about drowned men that could be little other than the work of a nixie, and an urban legend about a woman who had drowned her husband and baby before hanging herself that local spirits often attributed to them. Hopefully, they knew as little of him as he did them, or better yet, that they had never heard of him at all.

The water was cool, a few degrees lower than the night air, tickling a bit as he slid into it. He dipped his head in the water, getting that momentary nastiness out of the way, then exhaled deeply, forcing every last bit of air out of his lungs. Then he dropped below the surface, sinking deep into the lake.

Beneath the water, Colby began his incantations. First his skin grew a thick green mucus, allowing his limbs to glide through the water as if it were air. Then his eyes grew a milky white membrane that blinked out the water, allowing him to see into the murky depths. A thick green, brown, and yellow turtle shell crept over his flesh, encasing all but his head and stubby little legs. Finally, he shrank several sizes until he was only slightly larger than a family dog. He popped his head above the water and took a deep a breath, an hour's worth of air. *There,* he thought. *Now I'm ready.*

He swam down to the bottom of the lake, paddling quickly but quietly, to the nixies' hidden lair, careful not to disturb the silt surrounding it. Swimming through the atrium, he entered a cave decorated as a sitting room. Three waterlogged couches sat positioned as if they were meant to host company. Sitting atop one of them—chained down so as to not float away—was the slowly deteriorating, bloated corpse of the nixies' most recent victim.

Colby tried not to look as he swam past it into the dining room.

As he passed through the doorway—nothing more than a large hole connecting one cave to the next—he saw one of the nixie sisters dining on a stew of things culled from the lake bottom. She looked up at him.

"What are you doing here?" she asked sweetly.

Colby grew nervous. If he spoke to explain himself, she would see through the deception; if he didn't, there was no telling what she might do.

She smiled. "Aren't you a cute little one? Don't spend too much time down here. My sisters are asleep, and if you wake them, they'll make a soup out of you." She waved him off with a flutter of her hand. "Off you go then."

Colby continued, hoping now not to see the other sisters. He passed into another cave, long and slender like a hallway. Along it adjoined several other chambers, four in all, each clearly bedrooms. At the end was the single largest cavern in the underwater den. It was huge, some sixty feet across, the floor covered with a thick layer of silt and sand.

The room was overflowing with jars, nearly 150 in all, each upturned—their necks buried six inches in the sand—upon them carved the names of the suitors they possessed. These nixies had been claiming victims here for decades. Colby eyed the names in the dark, eager to knock over the jar he was here for and be done with it. But there were so many, and he dared not loose them all; there was no telling what might happen then.

He read name after name, each carved messily into the clay with a small knife, until finally he found it: JARED THATCHER.

He nudged the pot with his turtle head, but it would not budge; he was too small and weak to knock it over. The only way he was going to overturn it was to return to normal, leaving him only a minute or so more of air to swim out. Though that left little room for error, he had no other choice. Colby closed his eyes and worked one final incantation, using the last lingering remnants of ambient dreamstuff to revert.

The water was frigid this deep down—a fact he hadn't noticed until his protective turtle flesh was gone—and the water flooded his ears, the pressure pushing in on his eardrums. He reached down with his arms, dug both feet into the sand, and tugged at the pot. It budged ever so slightly. He tugged again and gained another inch. Straining, he put every last bit of energy into pulling up the pot, finally freeing it from its moorings. A ghostly blue light slipped out from beneath, taking the form of a young man, only slightly older than Colby.

The man gazed upon him with horror, reaching out a single extended hand, his spirit drifting away in the current. "Why?" he gasped. "Why did you do this?"

Colby felt a strange sensation creeping in—a cold, dark, ominous feeling like a distant void peeking through, grasping hold of the spirit in front of him.

"Why?" Jared asked one last time, his eyes full of fear. Then Hell itself reached out from the void and dragged the spirit into nothingness.

What have I done?

Colby's lungs began to ache for air, the early stages of panic setting in. He needed to get to the surface; he needed to get to the surface *now*. Colby swam furiously, careless now of how much noise he made. *Air.* No matter how hard he thrashed, he just couldn't move swiftly enough against the current. *Need air.* Without thinking, he grabbed the wall, pulling himself along, casting himself haphazardly through the caves.

He entered the dining room and scanned for the nixie who had spoken to him. She was nowhere to be found.

Hurry! Hurry! Hurry!

He reached the threshold of the atrium, his lungs ready to burst. Then he heard them.

"Someone's here!" said a voice.

"It's just a turtle," said another.

"No. It's a man!"

Colby kicked up toward the surface, struggling to make his way to fresh air. He shot through the water like a rocket, breaking through with a loud splash. His lungs barked out stale air, and he wheezed desperately to replace it. Behind him, two small splashes.

"And just where do you think you're going?" asked one of the sisters.

A clawed hand grasped his ankle, dragging him back beneath the water. He sank toward the bottom, flailing for the surface as it drifted slowly away. The nixie grappling with him climbed his body, embraced him face-to-face. She grinned, anxious to drown the intruder for his trespass.

"Now, just who do you think you . . . ," she said, her voice stopping midsentence, trailing into worry. Her expression promptly changed. "Oh my . . . I'm so sorry!" she exclaimed, horrified at the face before her. She kicked with her fin and launched them both upward, breaking the surface, throwing him off her as far as she could. Then she swam away, terrified, as if he bore the plague.

"What are you doing?" screamed one of her sisters.

"I'm sorry! I'm so sorry! Please don't hurt us!" she pleaded.

"What are you going on about?" asked her other sister.

"Him. It's the boy. The boy sorcerer."

"Colby?" they asked together. They hadn't recognized him at first, but they'd seen him around. Everyone knew who Colby was, whether he knew them or not. And they were terrified of him. Without hesitating, the two sisters abandoned the third to the surface, disappearing beneath the waves, leaving her to stare, agape, at Colby. Colby had no idea what to make of what was going on.

"Are you going to kill me?" she asked.

Colby shook his head. "Are you going to kill me?"

"No," she said.

"Then let me swim to shore and you never have to see me again."

She nodded and Colby splashed his way back to the embankment across the lake.

He pulled himself ashore, breathless, scared out of his wits, looking back out at the water. The nixies were gone, having vanished beneath the waves. He'd done it, but he wasn't at all sure what *it* was. It was probably best not to think about it. With the favor done, the Wild Hunt should not hunt for Colby's soul, and whoever Jared Thatcher was, he was least where he most likely belonged.

CHAPTER THIRTY-SIX

ONE NIGHT ONLY

After a week of begging, pleading, and cajoling his slovenly potato of a boss into letting his band perform once more, Ewan got his chance. A local band had been hitting up the owner for more money, while Limestone Kingdom was willing to play for free. The owner came around. From then on, what time Ewan didn't spend curled up with Nora he spent in his bassist's garage, practicing their new songs.

Something was different about him. Color had returned to his skin—the pale, sickly white replaced by a fleshy, earthy pink. He smiled more. His eyes seethed with a fire, as if he'd been shown something incredible and couldn't wait to tell the world about it. There was a spring in his step, an interminable energy to his every movement. He oozed confidence; one could almost smell his charisma on the air.

Ewan Bradford was a fucking rock star. And it was time the rest of the world finally got the chance to know it.

Plugging in his amp, the place felt meager and small, almost as if it were unworthy of what he was about to unleash. He smiled, shook that feeling off, reminding himself that the magic was in the crowd, not in the rat-trap fire hazard of a club. There was a certain poetry to playing this music here first—a final *go fuck yourself* before his band made it. Something had clicked, their music finally just right. It had balls, it was layered; for the first time in his life, Ewan felt as if he had something to say. The drummer's sister stood offstage with a video camera, recording the show, the bassist's buddy, a sound technician, laying it down on tape.

All that Ewan needed now was to see Nora, to get one last playful glance from her before striking the chord that would mark the end of his old life and the beginning of the new. He glanced around, hoping she'd picked the same spot where he'd first seen her sitting, but she wasn't there. People were still pouring in, eager not to hear Limestone Kingdom, but the band following them, a local favorite. The crowd wasn't thick, but it was dense enough to make finding Nora tough. Frantically he scanned the room, looking for her.

And then he saw her. She stood at the back of the room, a foot propped up on the wall behind her, wearing exactly the same outfit as the night they'd met. She smiled and winked, noting that he'd finally found her. Then she blew him a kiss, nodding. He was ready.

BREEEEOOOOOWWWWW! The first chord resonated like a bolt of lightning striking the amp, its thunder rolling over the crowd. Everyone looked up. Everyone. Ewan paused before he touched his guitar again, letting that single, drifting note draw everyone in. An awkward anticipation hung in the air, as if the crowd had been awakened suddenly at their desks in class with no idea why everyone was staring at them.

And then he laid into his guitar like a ravenous dog on a piece of meat. There was nothing limp or mediocre about it. It was profound. It was like seeing the aurora borealis for the first time. Everything they were doing seemed wrong, but felt right. Discordant notes blended to form melodies and shockingly addictive chords. Hooks that felt as if they'd been in the audience's heads for years played to their ears for the first time. Eyes and jaws stared wide, unblinking, at the stage.

There was no stage show. No lighting. No pageantry. But their essence was palpable. Three guys pouring their hearts into a song that everyone swore they'd heard somewhere before but could not place. Everyone present would describe their experience differently, but they would all speak of it reverently, as if it were somehow religious.

The band had left a dozen T-shirts behind the bar, the same dozen shirts they'd had printed months before and brought with them just to seem legitimate. Simple and black, they had a seemingly handwritten scrawl upon them that read: "Limestone Kingdom." All twelve sold before the end of the second song.

Mallaidh, dressed as Nora, stood at the back of the crowd, beaming with pride. She knew the music well. They were fairy tunes she remembered from childhood, played originally by the master musician Dithers and duplicated with raw intensity by his ward and unknowing student. She rocked back and forth, shifting her weight from one foot to the other, nervously fidgeting with her rainbow-colored scarf, giddy as a schoolgirl.

"He's beautiful," said a woman standing next to her.

Mallaidh nodded with a love-bitten smile.

"You've chosen well."

"Excuse me?" Mallaidh gave the stranger a sidelong glance. The woman beside her was lithe, graceful and only slightly taller. She looked as if she were in her late twenties, yet at the same time ageless, with a timeless style and tattoos that looked neither fresh nor faded. Her hair was short and black, her eyes sharp and dazzling. A faded rock T-shirt clung to her body, knotted above her belly button, leaving her tight, youthful midriff exposed. Below that, she wore a pair of faded, tattered jeans, too perfectly torn to be a mistake, too ragged to be prefabricated.

The woman was the very definition of rock style. And she was eyeing Mallaidh's man.

"You've chosen very well for your first time out," said the woman.

"I'm not sure I understand what you mean," said Mallaidh.

The woman smiled. "Your first love. You can always tell when a Leanan Sidhe is looking upon her first love. There's a sort of magic to it. I wish I could go back and reexperience my first. It was incredible."

Mallaidh winced. "What are you talking about?"

"Sweetie, you knew these were my stomping grounds. Right? You had to imagine that you'd meet your mother one day. Guess which day today is?"

Mallaidh's jaw dropped and her heart with it. The thought had never crossed her mind. She'd never known her mother, never thought she'd meet her. And her pursuit of Ewan had been so single-minded that it didn't matter where he ended up—she would have followed him there. He just happened to be in Austin. Now, standing before her, was the woman who had abandoned her decades ago, looking no more along in years than an older sister.

"Wait," said the woman. "You had no idea?"

"Cassidy?" asked Mallaidh.

"Cassidy Crane."

"Mo . . . ?" Mallaidh began.

"Call me Mom and you're dead meat, kiddo." Cassidy glared facetiously, smiling at the same time. Her daughter looked just like her. She could see through the glamour—all the tricks and wiles of the Leanan Sidhe—and noted that, despite the blond locks, she was her mother's daughter. The nose, the chin, the eyes. All hers. The cheeks were her father's though, something that made Cassidy's heart swell a little as she thought back upon the days spent in his arms. Cassidy still loved that man, though were she honest with herself, most of those lingering feelings stemmed from what he'd left behind.

"I don't understand," said Mallaidh. "Where have you been?"

"Here. I've been here the whole time. Didn't Meinrad explain any of this to you?"

Mallaidh shook her head, confused. There was a quiet bitterness rising in her gut, a feeling of rejection churning behind it. At the same time, she was joyous. She'd never met her mother and here she was, on what was the third most important night of her life, when it really mattered.

"He was supposed to tell you."

"Tell me what?"

"What you are. What *we* are."

"I'm a Sidhe," said Mallaidh.

"A *Leanan* Sidhe," said Cassidy. "We're different."

"Different how?"

"You really don't know *any* of this?"

"I know that you left me with Meinrad because you thought he could care for me."

"Yeah," said Cassidy, "just as you'll choose someone to leave your child with one day. We don't raise our young. We can't."

"What?"

"We're not cut out to be mothers, you and I. We're lov-*ers*, not lov-*ing*."

Mallaidh shook her head. "That doesn't make any sense."

"That's okay. It'll come with time. You'll understand. The first few are the hardest, but you get used to it. You grow accustomed. You never forget them and you'll always love them, but it doesn't hurt the same. This one will destroy you, though." She pointed at Ewan. "He's magnificent. I couldn't have chosen better for you had I spent a year trying." Cassidy put a firm hand on her daughter's shoulder. "You've got the knack. You certainly can pick 'em. You *are* your mother's daughter."

"Cassidy, what is this all about?" asked Mallaidh.

"This is about being time that you learned who you are. And what's going to happen to the man onstage."

"Ewan?" There was fear in her voice. "What's going to happen to him?"

Cassidy looked both ways. "Look, I think I've said all I can in here." She glanced at the door. "Follow me. I have something very important to tell you."

Mallaidh looked at the stage then back at her mother.

"Come on, it will only take a few minutes. He's got at least three encores with this crowd before he can get off the stage." Cassidy walked toward the door, a lingering look over her shoulder telling Mallaidh she had no choice but to follow.

Outside the night air had a different sound to it, the music nothing but a dull bass line and drum thumping when passed through cinder-block walls and a solid metal door. The rest of the night was peaceful. They'd emerged from the atmosphere of earth into the cold, bleak space surrounding it. Cassidy walked farther still, turning a corner into the adjacent alley. She gave one last look over her shoulder before disappearing.

Mallaidh quickly followed, surprised by four hands emerging from the dark.

She was thrown up against the wall, grappled by two men half her size. Looking down upon the moist crimson sacks

draped over their heads, she knew right away what was happening. *Redcaps.* Their clawed hands dug into her flesh as she
struggled futilely against their overwhelming strength.

"You're not my mother!" she screamed at the woman.

Cassidy looked devastated, her heart breaking before her
daughter. A small tear formed in the corner of her eye. "I wish
we could have met under better circumstances," she said. "But I
love too, you know." She turned to the alley and spoke bitterly.
"We had a deal. Where is he?"

A voice cut through the shadows. "You'll find him uncon-
scious in his car on the top floor of the parking garage two
blocks north of here," it said.

Cassidy looked back at her daughter, but still spoke to the
shadows. "She doesn't get hurt."

"Were I to hurt her," said the man, "I would find myself on
the wrong side of this. As it is, I am entitled to collect the boy
as payment for the deaths for which he is responsible." The man
stepped out of the dark, his face very much like Ewan's, only
twisted, scarred, and wrinkled—like a wax sculpture left in the
sun to bake.

"Knocks?" asked Mallaidh. "What are you doing?"

"What should have been done years ago; I'm collecting on
the Devil's debt."

LIMESTONE KINGDOM HAD run out of songs. The crowd was
howling, their cigarette lighters held aloft in the air, but Ewan
had nothing left to offer them. There was no chance they were
going to play one of the old numbers, but the crowd wanted one
more song. So the band did the one thing they could think to
do—play the first song over again.

The crowd bought it. Instead of rolling their eyes they began
to sing along. This was now less of an opening song and more

of an anthem—so the second time around, they simply played it harder. The drummer pounded the devil out of his drums, the bassist played his fingers raw. Sweat poured down Ewan's chest, his drenched shirt clinging tightly to him as his lungs heaved, gulping air between bellowing notes.

Then it was over. The final guitar note faded into the air and the crowd erupted with enthusiastic applause. They were a hit. In the back of the club, the next act bickered, arguing about whether to go on at all, unwilling to follow something so overwhelming. The owner shook his head, wondering why these three had performed so poorly so many times before.

Women in half shirts, tank tops, and skintight blue jeans began lining up just offstage, their eyes expectant, waiting for Ewan, but willing to settle for anyone in the band. Ewan unplugged, walking offstage, his eyes never meeting those of a single adoring fan. He cast his gaze wide, darting past each hopeful girl, anxious to find Nora. The club was fuller than before, and as he passed, men pounded him soundly on the back, giving him knowing hipster nods of approval.

A lanky blonde with alabaster skin, a loose-fitting sundress, and a petite, unobtrusive piercing in her nose stepped in front of Ewan, nodding ever so slightly, tilting her head down, looking up at him suggestively, a slight pout to her lips. He nodded politely and tried to move past her, but she gracefully strayed farther into his path.

"Hi, Ewan," she said, her voice drifting like jasmine on a summer evening. "I'm Molly."

"Hey, Molly," he said politely but without interest. "Have you seen my girlfriend?" He raised his eyebrows, expecting the blonde to shrink away.

"Oddly enough, I have."

Ewan was skeptical. "Excuse me?"

The blonde smiled delicately, wrinkling her nose ever so slightly, as if to say *I know more than you know.* "Nora's my cousin."

"She never mentioned a cousin."

"And how much about herself has she actually told you?" she asked. Ewan began to speak but stopped himself. The blonde continued, "Has she even told you where she lives?"

"Not exactly."

"That's our Nora; way too guarded."

"Where is she?" asked Ewan.

"She's outside, with a couple of my friends." The girl stroked a stray patch of Ewan's hair back over his ear, purring a little. "She was right," she said. "You're adorable." Her fingers traced back over his ear, lingering on his lobe just a tad longer than could be mistaken as innocent. Then she reached down and took him by the hand. "Come on, let's go get her."

The two walked outside into the dead quiet of night, the open air instantly chilling his sweat-soaked T-shirt, hardening his nipples. He shivered slightly. Nora was nowhere in sight.

"Where is she?" asked Ewan with a hint of suspicion.

"Round here," said the blonde, nodding to the alley. "Hey, Molly! What the hell, girl? I've got your man."

There was no answer.

"Molly?" asked Ewan.

"I meant Nora," she said with a blushing giggle hidden behind a maidenly hand. Then she clenched that hand into a fist, clocked Ewan with a right cross, staggering him backward, sending him stumbling into the dark alley. Waiting claws caught him, immediately throwing him into a nearby wall. His body slapped into the brick, his head whipping forward, cracking on the stone. He wobbled, ever so slightly, unable to keep his balance, toppling to the ground like a sack of potatoes.

Four redcaps walked slowly out of the alley. One of them

reached with a single hand, picking Ewan up off the vomit-puddled pavement. It held him upright, clenched a clawed fist, and gave him a solid shot to the gut, knocking the wind clean out of him. Ewan flailed, gasping for air, unable to fathom what was happening.

The blonde watched Ewan coldly. She shook her head and her features fell away. Her hair shortened as if shaken off, her slight chin blunted, hardening with stubble. Her eye cocked to one side and her nose swelled until it broke. Within seconds the waif was gone and only Knocks remained.

Ewan stared, horrified, at the creature before him. It was a cruel mockery—a backwoods, inbred, swamp-baby reflection of himself, like something that had been thrown out into the street and run under a bus. His mind fractured. Images he could not understand surfaced into his thoughts. He'd seen this man before as a boy, but couldn't place where. It wasn't that they looked similar; he knew him, right down to the tilt of his eye and the patches of hair missing from his head.

A fist cracked into the back of Ewan's skull, sprawling him. Two ribs splintered beneath the force of a cast-iron boot. A claw raked down his back, cutting deep into his flesh, tearing out a chunk of his shoulder. Ewan screamed, but a hand immediately muffled him. Fists rained down. Boots kicked up. One redcap picked him entirely off the ground, raising him two and a half feet above it before throwing him farther down the alley. Ewan crashed to the ground, layers of skin scraping off as he skidded across pavement, cartwheeling into a Dumpster with a clang.

Ewan pushed himself to his feet, confused, struggling against the pain, the terror. Through the agony of his broken ribs and the dull throbbing in his cheekbone he felt sheer, unbridled terror. Never before had he been more afraid for his life.

Knocks and the four redcaps boldly strolled down the alley, savoring the fear, confident Ewan wouldn't be getting away.

Ewan looked down the alley behind him, saw only shadow. Then, glancing back, he saw Nora, a fifth redcap grabbing her behind the Dumpster. The redcap pawed at her like a drunken stepfather, smelling her hair and flicking his tongue as she wriggled against his groping.

"She betrayed you, Ewan," said Knocks, walking ever closer. "She's not who she says she is."

"What's going on?" asked Ewan with a whimper. He reached up, wiped his nose with the back of his hand, smearing blood and snot across his face.

"You are going to die for what you've done," said Knocks. "That's what's going on."

"I haven't done anything!" he cried. His voice was shrill, like a child being punished in someone else's stead. There was no *man* to his shriek, just teary, crying, terrified *boy*.

"Oh yes, you have. But the Fading has choked the memories out. Before we're done here, I'll have beaten them back into you. You'll remember. You'll remember *everything*."

Ewan fell to his knees. Images cycled, bits of someone else's childhood rattling around his brain like coins in a tin cup. He looked up at Nora. She had stopped struggling and instead looked at him with tears in her eyes. Their gazes locked and Ewan couldn't tell if she felt love or pity. "What's happening?" he mouthed to her silently.

"Tell him what's happening," said Knocks. "He wants to know."

"No," said Nora, shaking her head, warm tears streaming down her cheeks.

"Tell him, Mallaidh," said Knocks. "Tell him what you are. Tell him why he's going to die."

She shook her head harder. "No!"

"Nora?" begged Ewan. "What's he talking about? What aren't you telling me?"

"You hear that, *Nora*? He wants to know what you're not telling him."

"Shut up!" she yelled.

"Only one of us here is lying, Mallaidh," said Knocks. "Tell him who you are. Show him what you *really* are."

"No!"

"Tell him!"

The redcap holding Mallaidh twisted her arm, almost snapping it off.

She screamed, her glamour falling away.

Her hair lengthened, light blond curls sprouting from the dark roots, tumbling down to her shoulders. Her cheekbones softened; her chin narrowed; her skin became three shades more radiant. Her eyes glowed blue in the dark. Nora passed away before Ewan's eyes, the mask falling off, leaving behind something far too beautiful to be human.

"What is this?" asked Ewan. "What the hell is all this?"

"A family reunion," said Knocks. He swung his leg, kicking Ewan across the chin so hard it picked him up off his knees, knocking him on his back. "You see, this is the girl of your dreams. I know this because we are the same, you and I. In many ways. She was my dream girl, once. But you took her. And the night I lost her was the same night your mother took mine." Knocks leaned over Ewan, a bit of drool dripping onto Ewan's chin. "You owe me more than you can imagine, Ewan. I aim to collect. And this time, your boyfriend isn't here to save you."

Knocks looked up at his redcap accomplices, waving to the one holding Mallaidh. "Dietrich, let her go." The redcap nodded, loosening his grip. She elbowed him off her, bolted toward Ewan, but was halted by Knocks's outstretched hand. "Go near him and you both die. Right here, right now. Leave and you live."

"But I—," she began.

"But nothing," said Knocks, refusing eye contact. "You leave or I'll let my friends here have their way with your corpse." The words languished in the air like rotting flesh. Dietrich smiled broadly.

Mallaidh shivered, staring gravely at Ewan. His eyes were hollow, confused and loveless. She turned and ran, never once looking back, her sobs trailing into the night, flecks of glamour trickling off, leaving a brief glistening comet's tail behind as she faded into the dark. In an instant, she was gone.

"Now, how best to kill you?" Knocks stroked his chin, pacing the length of the alley. "Pick him up."

Time slowed, Ewan's mind wandering blindly through a thousand memories—things he remembered, but wasn't sure how. They were someone else's thoughts, someone else's dreams, though they swam around in his head as if they were his own. And as a redcap reached down, slinging Ewan's flopping, broken body over its arm, Ewan reached out and snatched the bloody red cap from atop his head. The redcap went limp, bowing under the weight of the grown man atop it, and the two fell to the ground.

Ewan rolled the cap around in his hand, wondering what to do with it, for what seemed like the better part of an hour. In truth, he'd raised it to his own skull before the body had hit the pavement. He didn't know why; he just did it. Strength surged through every fiber of his being. His wounds no longer ached; his shattered bones no longer stung against the inside of his flesh. He felt whole. Powerful. Invincible. Most of all, he was pissed, angrier than he'd ever been. The other redcaps scampered fleetly toward him, but it was too late. Ewan had donned the hat of a redcap.

He rose to his feet. He picked the redcap up off the ground

by the scruff of his neck, then slammed him headfirst into the brick wall beside them. His head popped like a rotten tomato, spraying the wall, catching Ewan in the back splatter. As the redcap's blood hit the cap, Ewan felt stronger still.

He spun around and swung a wild haymaker into an oncoming redcap. His fist connected with a crack of thunder, shattering the redcap's jaw, sending him backward through the alley, across the street, and, with the force of a truck, into a brick storefront.

With time moving more slowly than he'd ever known it, Ewan kicked squarely the chest of another redcap running toward him, its rib cage turning to powder. It flew backward into Dietrich, picking him up off the ground, carrying them both into the street.

Only Knocks and Otto remained standing. Redcap blood dripped off Ewan's fist; he smeared it across the bit of cap covering his brow. Ewan grew stronger still. Knocks could tell by the look in his eye that there was little chance of surviving this. Something had gone horribly wrong and once again the stolen child of Tiffany and Jared Thatcher had somehow gained the upper hand.

It was time for a strategic retreat.

"Run!" shouted Knocks as he turned the corner, scrambling for his life. The redcap followed in kind. Dietrich rose to his feet, offered his companion a meaty, taloned hand, picking him off the ground. They too ran. And before Ewan could reach the end of the alley, the final broken redcap across the street was limping away with the rest of them.

Ewan's head pounded, his heart raced, memories nearly a decade and a half old echoing in pieces through his thoughts. He still couldn't put it together; there was no way to be sure if what he was remembering were even memories at all. It was all so horrific. His nightmares of little men had been plucked from his brain and brought into the real world to beat the life out of him.

But how did he know to take their hat? And what the fuck was Nora? He looked to the sky, trying to find answers in the stars; he begged, but no answers came. Only one name stuck out. The name of a little boy he remembered once turning a redcap into rose petals; who chased off devils with a poem about lightning; who had once pulled him off an altar and walked him through the forest, away from a legion of monsters.

Colby Stevens.

CHAPTER THIRTY-SEVEN

The Truth, at Last

The text message read simply: *In trouble. Don't know what's happening. Coming over.* That's all Colby needed to know. This was a day Colby had long feared, feeling woefully unprepared for it. Though he had questions, he dreaded the answers. *What had happened? What did he remember?*

Bambambambambam! The knock came, quick and furious, screaming *open the door now!* Colby didn't hesitate; he didn't need to look through the peephole. He could feel the rush of energy rippling on the other side. Ewan was a torrent of wild emotion and raw dreamstuff. The door opened, Ewan bursting through, frazzled, uninvited.

He was a mess. His forehead was a dried, caked smear of red, his hair a greasy, blood-soaked matte. Ewan squinted, one eye swollen shut, the other merely blackened a deep purple. He paced around, his hands fidgeting nervously with the soft red cap, fingers stained red from rolling it around in them for so long. Spatters of blood crisscrossed his shirt. Fresh blood still leaked slowly out of his nose.

Ewan looked at Colby. "How long?"

"How long what?"

"How long have you known? How long have you remembered what happened to us as kids?"

"I never forgot," said Colby. "I've always known."

He double-bolted the door, closed his eyes, and mumbled to himself, barring the door with further protections.

"And you didn't tell me?"

Colby, still concentrating, didn't bother to look up. "No. I didn't."

"Well, why the fuck not?"

A pause. Then . . . "It wasn't my place," he said.

"Wasn't your place? Who made me forget?"

"You did. I mean, it just happens. What the hell happened tonight?"

"Someone tried to kill me."

"Okay, let's take this very slowly. Who tried to kill you tonight?"

Ewan shook his head. "I don't know. My brother, my cousin. I don't know who the fuck it was. He said we were family and he looked just like me. Only . . . like a fucked-up fun-house-mirror version. The monster you keep in the attic, you know?"

"What?" None of this sounded familiar.

"He had this army of little, bearded men with claws for hands and metal boots."

"And red caps, like that one?" asked Colby.

"Yeah."

"That's gotta be Knocks," said Colby.

"What?"

"Knocks. Your changeling. I mean, *a* changeling. I . . . I completely forgot about him. The changeling the fairies replaced you with when you were born. They're not supposed to live this long."

"What is that supposed to mean?"

"They typically die in childhood. Yours is still around."

"Why's he trying to kill me?"

"Hell if I know. What have you done recently to get his . . ." Colby trailed off. "Coyote." His face fell immediately into his hands. He sighed deeply, massaging his temples with his thumb and middle finger. Without looking up from his hand, he began again. "Is there anything else weird I should know about? Anything at all?"

"I have a girlfriend," Ewan stated plainly.

"*Weird,* not irregular."

"She's one of them."

Colby looked up. *Shit.*

"She was there. They made her change."

Colby's expression weakened. This was getting worse. "What does she look like?"

Ewan reached into his pocket, pulling from it a wadded-up sketch of the little girl. It was bloodstained and tattered, but still recognizable. "Like her," he said. "But all grown up."

Colby sighed deeply. "Oh, for the love of all that's holy, Ewan." He began to pace. "*Lives in the Hill Country with her uncle.*" Ewan stood in place, baffled.

"What? You act as if I should have known this." He grew angry, got mean, a caged dog barking savagely at the very end of his chain. "And frankly, I probably *should have.*"

"I didn't make you forget. It was for the best. They were never supposed to come after you. That was the deal. I left them alone, they left you alone. *That. Was. The deal.*"

"You *left* them alone? So what is your deal, anyway? You've always been weird, always kept your secrets." He straightened up and gave Colby a stern look. "What *are* you?"

Colby didn't know how to answer that. He shrugged. "I don't really know. Wizard might be a good way to explain it, I guess. That's what I wished for and this is what I got."

"Wished?" Ewan thought long and hard, trying to wrestle a memory from the tide of his thoughts. He brought one to the surface, his face mellowing. "You had a genie."

"Yeah."

"Why can't I remember this stuff? I mean, I should remember this."

"Because magic is a motherfucker."

"What?"

"The Fading," said Colby, shaking his head. "Children taken by fairies forget. It's not unheard of for the memories to return, but the brain is funny. Trying to remember something that happened to you twenty years ago is hard enough when you've had twenty years to remember and reflect upon it. When you haven't, it's like seeing images from a movie you don't remember watching but recognize anyway. You'll never remember it all. Just pieces."

"And we were . . . ?" Ewan motioned a finger back and forth between himself and Colby.

"We were friends."

"So I was taken by fairies?"

"When you were an infant, yeah."

"Why?"

"So they could turn you into a fairy and sacrifice you in place of one of their own."

"Well, how did *you* end up out there?"

Colby shrugged. "I met a djinn. I made a wish."

"For what?"

"To see the world. All the magical things there were."

"So you just wanted to see monsters?"

Colby shrugged. "I was eight. It seemed cool at the time."

Ewan grimaced. "You know, I was just a tourist until I met you.
It was saving you that drove me to make my second wish. To
become . . . what I am now."

"Why'd you do it?" asked Ewan.

"Because I promised you that I would."

"So you're saying it's my fault?"

"It's our fault. It's their fault. It's Yashar's fault. It's no one's
fault. It is what it is and now we're left to deal with it."

"So all this time, you knew."

Colby nodded. "Yeah."

"And all those times you came to visit me when I was a kid?
All the times you checked up on me at my apartment and asked
me stupid questions? You've been . . . ?"

"Looking out for you."

"Why?"

"I told you, I promised you that I would."

"I don't know whether to hug you or beat the living shit out
of you."

"When you figure it out, will you give me a few seconds'
warning, either way?"

"Yeah. I owe you that much."

"Speaking of beatings, where'd you get the cool hat?"

"Took it from one of those *things*."

"Took it?" asked Colby.

"Snatched it right off his head and then put him through a
wall."

"But he's okay, though, right? I mean, he got up?"

"Oh, hell no. His head is pulp on the pavement. The rest got
away, though."

"Oh," said Colby gravely. "Oh, this is bad."

"What, did you expect me to let him live?"

"I . . . I don't know what I expected. But killing one of them only makes this worse. Much, much worse."

Ewan jabbed his finger into Colby's chest several times, punctuating each word with it. "Hey! *They!* Came after! *Me!*"

"Doesn't matter. They'll be back for blood, in force."

"So what are we gonna do?"

"*We?*" asked Colby.

"Yeah, we. Unless you have some awesome spell that can fix this all up? You know, use your magic words and make this all go away."

"It doesn't work that way."

"Well, whatever it is you say. You do know spells, right?"

"No. Magic isn't about rituals and words. You don't just speak a phrase in Latin and then *bam!* weird shit happens."

"Then how does it work?"

"You don't really want to know."

"Yeah, I kinda do."

The two stared at each other. Colby shrugged.

"All right, the universe is energy. All of it. Everything is energy that can be altered simply by willing it to be altered. It's as if we are God's waking dream, each gifted with a small piece of his consciousness; the beauty of that arrangement is that we create the dream for him. If you can understand that, if you can wrap your mind around it, then you can conjure up anything you want from out of the ether. Provided there is material enough to do it."

"That doesn't make a lick of fucking sense. Show me."

Colby shook his head. "What? No."

"Show me something," insisted Ewan. "Show me some magic."

Colby hesitated for a second. Then it dawned on him.

He breathed deep. Then, with a bit of theatricality, he waved his hand needlessly through the air. His fingers danced whilst he exhaled slowly, deeply. He pushed a clenched fist toward Ewan—as if battling a current—placing an open hand on his chest.

Ewan felt warm. His wounds closed up; the swelling about his eyes receded, their bruising eroding with it. Blood dried, flaking off like dead skin. In a few short seconds, Ewan was whole again.

"You didn't tell me your ribs were broken," said Colby.

"You never asked."

"You walked all this way with broken ribs?"

"Yeah. You impressed?"

Colby nodded. "That's actually kind of badass." The two smiled weakly.

"Hurt like nothing else. I threw up twice."

"I can imagine." He paused. "So this girl of yours . . ."

"Nora." Ewan stopped himself. "Well, she told me her name was Nora. But they kept calling her something else. Mallaidh or something."

"Mallaidh? That *sounds* right."

"Sounds right? You don't remember?"

Colby shook his head. "Come on, she was a girl I met once when I was eight."

"You know, you really should . . ." Ewan stopped himself. He relaxed. "No, you're right. You can't recall the details of my life any better than I should be able to."

Ewan took a seat on the well-made, handcrafted leather boat of a couch that puffed slightly as he sank comfortably into it. He looked around the room—a cluttered expanse of trinkets, knickknacks, and items almost indescribable whose purpose one could only guess at—and it was at once clear to him that he didn't really know his friend very well at all. Colby walked to the fridge, pulling from it a couple of beers, popping their tops off with the bottle opener affixed to the door, and ambled back to the couch, handing a beer to Ewan before plopping down beside him. They both drank.

The two shared a moment of silence, each unsure of what to say. Ewan was the first to speak up.

"Is that a night-light?"

Colby looked over at the wall nearest the door. A small, beige piece of plastic covering a smaller lit bulb jutted from the electrical outlet. "Yep," Colby answered without missing a beat.

"All right, I'll ask the obvious question. Why do you have a night-light?"

"To scare away monsters."

"You're kidding me."

"Monsters are real, and if millions of children believe in the power of the night-light, then you can bet your ass that so do the monsters. Never underestimate the power of belief."

Ewan nodded. "Why do I get the feeling that I'll never fully be able to wrap my mind around all of this?"

"Probably because I've been trying since I was a kid and I barely understand any of it myself."

Ewan stared at his beer, swishing it around a little in its bottle. "So what the hell is my girlfriend?"

Colby sipped, shaking his head. "I've no idea. A Sidhe of some kind, if I remember correctly."

Ewan stroked his chin—thick with a sandpaper-like layer of stubble—and thought deeply. He remembered what the Sidhe were. Noble. Proud. And they had tried to kill him. It really was a strange sensation; he was reliving a life he'd forgotten through flashes of incongruous memory. He remembered snapping a man's neck, fondly, but couldn't fathom why; he recalled frolicking with monsters but being fearful of dancing with beautiful women. Everything was alien and he lacked the vocabulary to describe it properly.

"So why do they want to kill me?"

"There's no telling without asking them directly."

"You can't hazard a guess?"

"Fairies are creatures of pure emotion. When they love, they love wholeheartedly. What they hate, they hate ceaselessly. Where they are satisfied, they never leave. These are not creatures that do anything in half measures. For them it is all or it is nothing at all. Middle ground and gray areas are things of the mortal world. It is what makes people special; it is also what make fairies so hard for people to understand."

"So what now?" asked Ewan.

"Now you tell me again what happened, this time very slowly. And don't leave anything out."

CHAPTER THIRTY-EIGHT

THE FAIRY SABBATH

It was Friday, and thus Rhiamon the Gwyllion was amidst a herd of her goats, combing their beards until each was silky and straight, just as she did every Friday for as long as anyone could remember. Though it was still early in the day, she had combed quite a few goats already, humming enthusiastically to herself, blissfully engrossed in her chore. Rhiamon looked old and tired, an aged crone kneeling before an endless sea of coarse, matted fur, her tangled gray-white hair and crooked spine causing her to blend in with her goatly surroundings.

She smelled them coming before she could see them—redcaps gave off the most distasteful odor, worse even than the goats—

and where the redcaps were, Knocks was rarely far behind.

"How dare you disturb me on the Sabbath," she called out into the herd, knowing full well who they were. Her voice resonated, deep and sonorous, drowning out even the ceaseless bleating of her flock—if only for a moment.

"Sorry to disturb, mistress crone," said Reinhardt, appearing seemingly from nowhere. "But the young master desires a word with you." The redcap had one leg forward, attempting an awkward curtsy as if he were the emissary of some distant, foppish nation. There he teetered, fumbling with his hands, mangling the proper etiquette.

Rhiamon looked up at him disdainfully. "Why you insist upon running around with that absurd little creature rather than tearing him apart and soaking your caps in his blood is beyond me." She spat upon the ground.

"My lady," nodded Reinhardt, still attempting his ridiculous half bow, refusing to make eye contact. He was at once both offended and afraid, but dared not speak up; Rhiamon was a dangerous sorceress and could hex all sorts of mischief upon him with but a thought. It was in his best interests to remain polite, even when insulted—a fact Rhiamon was more than willing to exploit.

She waved him closer. "Come."

The remaining redcaps shuffled out from behind a gathering of unkempt, anxious goats. Knocks stepped forward from the gang, holding his bloody cap in his hand, showing more restraint, every bit as scared as Reinhardt. "Mistress crone?"

"Yes, young changeling?" She looked up at him, for a moment showing no emotion at all. Then she puzzled over his wounds, suddenly realizing that these fools who stood before her wanted no mere favor. Often fairies from the court came to her asking for potions or a spell—always wanting the most trivial of help— they were in love with a mortal or needed to chase off some spirit that had taken up residence in their part of the woods. This was different; she could tell by the way they stood, the way bruises crept slowly across their grim countenances. "What have you done?" she asked. "What is it you boys have gotten yourselves into?"

"Trouble, mistress," said Knocks.

The crone smiled, her wrinkles forming deep chasms of age. She set her comb down beside her. The wrinkles upon her forehead surrounding her knobby, gnarled horns began to smooth out. Rhiamon so loved misfortune that the very thought of it made her feel and become younger. Her eyes brightened and she instantly shed five years. "Go on," she prodded.

"It is the boy Ewan. He still lives."

"Of course he does," she said. "He has powerful friends."

"It was just him," said Knocks bitterly.

"Who did this to *all* of you?" She looked at them incredulously.

"Yes, mistress." The redcaps nodded in unison behind Knocks.

"And how did he accomplish such a feat?"

"He stole the cap off Karl's head and put it on."

The crone smiled broader still. Her hair began to untangle, turning from a frazzled white mess into a fine, silky, distinguished gray. The wrinkles around her eyes gave way to loose bags of skin—not yet smooth, but well on their way. "So he wears the cap?"

"Yes," said Knocks.

She cackled, alarming the goats nearest her who pattered in place.

"This isn't funny," said Knocks, his voice dripping with restrained anger.

"Oh, but were that true. If you knew what it is you've actually done, you too would be laughing."

"What have we done?" asked one of the redcaps.

"Perhaps it is best that you not know," she said with a wicked simper, the years now cascading off her a decade at a time. "Perhaps you should enjoy the pleasant surprise." Her hair shaded from gray to blond, gaining a lustrous vibrancy that shone more brightly with each passing moment; it now toppled upon her shoulders rather than nesting atop them. Her wrinkles were all but gone now, her skin becoming smooth and delicate, her eyes radiant and sparkling. Sagging flesh grew taut, firm with supple muscle. Rhiamon looked no older than thirty-five now, a very beautiful woman revealed beneath the sixty-five or so years that she'd lost—albeit one adorned with a single knobby goat horn.

"I don't understand," said Knocks. "How could not knowing be in our best interests?"

"Because you might try to stop the inevitable," she answered. "And that should not happen."

"Well, what do we do?" asked Reinhardt.

The crone, now a twenty-five-year-old knockout with curves that could stop a city bus, narrowed her eyes. "You do exactly what I tell you—step by step." She retrieved her comb from the ground and returned to working out the knots in the beard of the nearest goat.

"There are three things you must do," she said. "First you must separate the wizard from his djinn. He must not be able to simply wish his problems away this time." She reached into a bag beside her, drawing from it an ornate glass bottle, intricately carved, with fine gold inlay and words in ancient Persian: *May you rest undisturbed for one and one thousand years.* "Without the djinn, he is but a wizard. And a wizard can be bested by using his own magic and arrogance against him.

"Next you must separate the wizard from his friend. If he has done this to you alone, then I can only imagine what the two of them will be able to manage together. For this, I must teach you to use the one gift given you that you do not yet fully understand—a technique as old as the Devil himself. We must bind you together nice and tight with the hatred that makes you whole. Finally, you must use the boy's own weakness against him."

"What is that, mistress crone?" asked Knocks.

"That depends; how did you find him before?"

"The girl. The Leanan Sidhe Mallaidh; the two are in love."

Rhiamon smiled so wide that her face itself began to shed and shrink. Her curves tightened and vanished, she dwindled in size, and her eyes sat large and luminous upon her fifteen-year-old face, filled with unholy joy. "Then you must use his love for the girl. No man has ever known love that he would not foolishly walk into death for."

"How do we do that?"

"You're a changeling. You'll figure it out." She continued to smile, effervescent and now all of eight years old. "Come, if this is to work I have many things to teach you. But first, we must comb out the beard of each and every goat. Hurry, sunrise approaches."

CHAPTER THIRTY-NINE

THE DWARVEN FORGE

Colby hummed to himself, occasionally mouthing silent lyrics to a song with which Ewan was entirely unfamiliar. The two walked the streets together, heading west, Colby mumbling, taking all manner of turn and side street. At first, it felt as if the two were lost, but Colby walked with purpose, each step determined to get to the next. He knew where he was going, even if he didn't look it.

"What are you doing?" asked Ewan.

Colby stopped humming. "What?"

"What are you doing? The humming. What is it?"

"It's complicated."

"It's a long walk."

"I'm trying to remember where this place is."

"And the humming?"

Colby looked around, speaking as if from rote memory rather than really listening to what he was saying, his attention focused on finding a nearby landmark. "Space and time aren't so much expanding as they are unfolding. And if you know where the wrinkles and creases in the fabric of the universe are, you can slide down them from one thread to another. People"—he looked squarely at Ewan, paying more attention to what he was saying—"well, fairies mostly, write songs about them. If you know the words and the melody, you can find things that are otherwise hidden to the naked eye. Places like where we're going now."

"And where are we going now?" asked Ewan.

"To speak to a man about a sword."

"What?"

"So to speak," he said. "A dwarf. A kind of wood spirit. He's a *man,* and I wouldn't really call him anything else."

"I guess it would be rude to say *I'm going to see a dwarf about a sword.*"

"You'd think," said Colby, hinting otherwise.

"It's not?"

"Dwarves have it easy. They can go out into the world, live a life like anyone else, and disregard any jokes with a withering glance and a comment about insensitivity. Most people won't ask and try very hard not to stare; even when they're acting just a little peculiar, they won't notice that a dwarf's feet are bent the wrong way or that they have a few too many thumbs. It's easy to mask the magical behind a veil of politeness. The power of shame is a handy trick in this modern world."

"So we're going to see a dwarf."

"About a sword, yes."

The two turned a corner, past a thicket of trees, wandering down a long, winding gravel road seemingly leading directly into the middle of nowhere. Trees and brush grew thicker here, as did the light buzzing of cicadas in the air. They were no longer in Austin, a seeping darkness creeping in as the lights of the city faded into the faint orange glow of the clouds.

Half a mile farther up the road, a metal gate wrapped end to end in barbed wire greeted them. NO TRESPASSING. VIOLATORS WILL BE SHOT. Ewan gave Colby a cold but worried look— *Should we?* Colby nodded—*Yes, we should.*

The main house wasn't much farther; just beyond it was a blacksmith's workshop, a wood-and-steel open-air structure blackened and charred from heavy use. The air smelled thick of smelted metals, and as they walked closer, the two were blasted with blistering heat billowing out from the building. Black smoke choked the air above them, blotting out the night. But the fires were bright and the entire yard behind the house was lit as if by flickering daylight.

In the doorway stood a diminutive, stocky man, covered neck to toe in a leather apron and goat-fur leggings. His skin itself was like the apron—leathery, cauterized, cracked by constant exposure to the heat. He smoked a cigarette lazily, peering suspiciously at the visitors before stabbing out his smoke on a timber beside him. He frowned, furrowing his brow.

"Colby," said the dwarf.

"Mimring," said Colby.

"You shouldn't have brought him here," he said in a gruff, gravel-hewn voice. "Not in his condition."

"And what condition would *that* be?" asked Colby.

"Fucked." He waved the two over. "Come on in."

Inside the temperature was almost unbearable, a sweltering stream of heat pouring out of a raging furnace. Colby felt as if the sweat would sizzle from his brow, but Ewan was entirely at home, and didn't so much as glisten. Instead, he scratched the scruff of his chin, grimacing at the sandpaper he found there. He looked down at his hand, sure that he'd taken off a layer or two of skin, but he hadn't.

The oddest thing about Mimring wasn't his size; his thick, calloused skin; or his hobbies, it was that he spoke in a slow Texas drawl. While hundreds of years old and hailing originally from Germany, he'd spent the last century in and around these parts. He had grown to love it, becoming not only *acquainted* with the culture, but *one with it,* so much so that he'd become a stereotype. He took a deep breath, putting both hands on his hips, nodding with puckered displeasure.

"Whelp," he said with a sigh. "You're in for some rough times there, son. Y'all got yourselves in a heap o' trouble."

"Word travels fast," said Colby.

"I reckon it does when you're the guy everyone comes to for a good weapon."

Colby narrowed his gaze. Mimring shrugged.

"Who else were they gonna git? I'm the best smith on the plateau."

"That's why we're here."

"Well, I told the other ones that I weren't gettin' involved."

"Is that true?" asked Colby. "You're gonna sit this one out?"

Mimring spit onto the dirt floor and made a clicking noise with his tongue, thinking long and hard as he stared at Colby. "Naw," he said, drawing the syllable to its inevitable, but protracted conclusion. "Redcaps are good for business, but bad customers. The fewer there are around, the happier I'll be."

"In other words, you like them less than you like me."

"That and them redcaps wouldn't owe me a big favor if I made 'em up somethin' special." He paused. "You will."

"You got something in mind or is this more of a blank check sort of thing?"

Mimring nodded. "Blank check."

Colby traded looks with Mimring for a moment. Mimring stood like a statue, not so much as a piece of dirt or sweat moving on him. Then Colby nodded. "I'll take that deal."

"Good. I've a feeling it's the only one you're gonna git in this town 'bout now."

"A sorcerer is a good thing to have in your pocket, I suppose."

Mimring shrugged. "Yeah, you scare the shit outta me, son. And frankly, as much trouble as you are, I'd much rather have you in my debt than be the guy that wouldn't help you when you came a callin'. Now, what'ya need?"

"A sword," said Ewan.

"Will you be needin' just the one?"

Colby nodded. "Yeah."

"Sized for you or him?"

"Him," said Colby.

"You sure you won't be wantin' a pike instead? I can make a pike that'll take the head clean off an eight-point buck at ten paces."

"A pike?" asked Colby.

"Yeah, a pike." He looked at Ewan.

Colby looked over at Ewan, not understanding at all what Mimring was getting at, and watched as Ewan fiddled with a blacksmithing tool he'd found hanging on the wall. He looked him up and down, noting the red cap atop his head. Colby returned his gaze to Mimring, shaking his head. "No, he won't need a pike."

"I think he'll find it more comfortable in his condition."

"His condi . . . what the hell are you getting at?"

Mimring looked up at Ewan, who wasn't paying attention at all. "Son? Son?" He cleared his throat and spoke louder. "Son!" Ewan looked up and immediately put the tool back where he'd found it. "Would you mind stepping outside for a moment? I need to have a word with your boy here."

Ewan nodded, meandering hesitantly outside, leaving the two alone.

"You don't see what's goin' on?" asked Mimring.

"No, what is going on?"

"And here I'd heard you were the smart one, what with you traveling the world and all, writing all those books."

Colby's eyes shot wide, his expression ghostly white. "I, well, I don't—"

"Son, don't. Everybody knows you been writin' those books, just ain't nobody been able to do nothin' about it. Who the hell names themselves Thaddeus, anyway? Really?"

Colby swallowed hard. "Everyone knows?"

"Everyone that matters. Most are plenty pissed. The rest think you're just foolish and will regret the whole thing in a few years anyway. Most do."

"Most what? Most men who have seen what I have?"

Mimring smiled and laughed a bit. "Shit, ain't no one's seen half the shit you have. You're one of a kind."

"So, what? Am I supposed to stop writing them?"

"I couldn't care less. Just do me a favor and make sure I don't *ever* show up in one of them books."

"Is that your favor?"

"Hell no. That's the favor you're gonna do me for tellin' you what I'm about to tell you."

"Which is?"

"Your boy out there has done imprinted."

"Imprinted? What is that supposed to mean?"

"You ain't noticed his color? How he used to be all pale and sickly, but now he's all pink and robust? Or how he's suddenly sprouting gray stubble?"

"I . . . I didn't, actually," stuttered Colby.

"Or how he walked in here like it was a day spa? I mean, you're sweatin' off a stink so bad that you're about to stop sweatin'. That's how bad you're about to git. He didn't even notice."

"What is that supposed to mean? You don't become a redcap just by wearing their caps."

"Nope," said Mimring. "Normal people don't, anyhow."

"He's normal."

"No, he's a fairy. Got done turned into one the night of the Tithe."

"But he never fully changed."

Mimring paused, staring at Colby long enough to let the words he'd spoken sink in. "That's right. Those boys don't bother to take a child through the whole process; just get him right enough with the Devil to be able to take their place. Feed 'em on fairy milk till the point at which their body lives offa glamour and then they put 'em to the knife. Won't let 'em imprint. So your boy has been a blank slate for a decade and a half now, waitin' for someone to come along and take him down the final steps of fairyhood, and then he done takes the cap off a redcap, pops his head off like it were a melon, and gets blood on the cap. The cap he's wearing. All that pent-up glamour finally found an outlet. And he became what he's always been waiting to become. A full-on fairy."

"But he's not turned yet," said Colby.

"Oh, he's turned. He just ain't done turnin'. No going back, though. He's done for. He's gonna be a redcap for the rest of his life, however short that may be." Mimring looked over his shoulder at the forge behind him. "So I say to you again, are you sure he wouldn't be more comfortable with a pike?"

"You have something in mind?" asked Colby.

Mimring smiled, his yellow teeth glinting in the firelight. He nodded proudly. "I actually happen to have an honest-to-god John Brown pike in my possession."

"I don't know what that is."

"John Brown. The civil war abolitionist who commissioned a thousand pikes from a local blacksmith that he planned to give to a bunch of freed slaves, and as there weren't nothin' more that frightened southern slave owners like a Negro uprising, well, they sent Robert E. Lee after him and then they hanged old John Brown for treason till he was dead. Never used the pikes, but they got his blood on 'em. Spiritually, anyhow."

"And you've got one."

"And I got one. I figure I could reforge the blade with a few drops of blood squeezed from your old boy's cap—to capture his strength—and a few hairs of a sorcerer . . ." He gave a knowing glance to Colby. "And I reckon I could make something that would feel like an extension of his own arm. I mean, if you're fixin' to leave him alone at any point, and you want him to be able to hold his own, this'll do the trick just fine."

"It'll take the head off an eight-point buck at ten paces?"

Mimring nodded. "Yup. Just about." There was a brief quiet between the two. "You know you're gonna have to keep a good eye on him from here on out, don't ya?"

"Yeah," said Colby, the weight of everything sinking in.

"He's gonna become more aggressive. He'll be someone you won't wanna argue with. And once that cap starts drying out, well, animals are only gonna slake that thirst for so long."

"I figured." Colby slumped against the wall, shaking his head and staring off into the dirt floor.

"Well, it was about time that curse kicked in. We've all been waiting for that shoe to drop for an awful long time."

Colby looked up, confused. "Ewan wasn't cursed."

"No, Yashar was. Ages ago."

"Yeah, he was cursed to walk the earth or something."

Mimring gave Colby a dark, somber look that read: *you've-got-to-be-kidding-me.* "You don't even know the curse on your own genie?"

"We don't talk about it. That's his cross to bear."

"Yeah. *His cross.* All the wishes he grants are doomed to end badly, no matter how well intentioned they are. *His cross,* he says."

Colby's eyes smoldered. He didn't know whether to dismiss Mimring's dreamstuff altogether for even insinuating such a thing, or to fly into a rage looking for Yashar. The air tingled as Colby's emotions excited the ambient dreamstuff floating nearby. Mimring raised a steady hand.

"Now, now," he said. "Don't go doin' nothin' you're gonna regret. Hell, don't go doin' nothin' *I'm* gonna regret."

"I don't understand. How could . . . how could he . . . ?"

"Not tell you that making a wish would sure as shit fuck up the rest of your life?"

"Yeah," said Colby.

"How could you not tell your friend what his deal was until you had to?"

"It was in his best interest."

"His or yours?" asked Mimring.

"His."

"Are you entirely sure about that? Are you sure you didn't want to keep your little world to yourself?"

Tears began to well up in the corners of Colby's eyes. "I didn't want him to end up like me."

"Knowing more than he should?"

"Yeah."

Mimring nodded. "How'd that turn out?"

Colby took a deep breath, chasing the glass from his eyes. "How come in all these years, you're the only one to tell me the truth about any of this?"

Mimring thought hard for a moment, searching for the right answer to that question. Then he nodded knowingly. "Maybe 'cause not so many people know for sure. And maybe 'cause I'm the only one who never wanted nothin' outta ya."

Colby nodded. "What now?"

"Now you get me a few drops of blood out of that hat, a few hairs off your head, and I forge your friend a weapon that'll give him one hell of a fighting chance against those devils." Mimring smiled. "Only thing you can do at a time like this is channel all that anger into a serious ass whoopin'. That's what I'd do, at least."

"Really? That's what you'd do?"

Mimring's smile turned into a smirk. "Hell no. That's what guys like you are for."

COLBY AND EWAN milled about outside, knocking tin cans off a tree stump with stray rocks, the steady sound of a pounding hammer on metal echoing out from the workshop. They spent quite some time silently tossing pebbles at the cans, knocking them over only to set them back up again. Neither knew exactly what to say to the other, both clearly upset. Just not at each other. That, it seemed, was their only consolation.

Ewan scratched his cheek with his knuckles. "I need a shave," he said. "I could have sworn I shaved yesterday."

Colby looked closely at the stubble, now noticeably gray, aging Ewan a full ten years older than he was. "Yeah, you're looking a bit ragged there."

"So what's our next move?" Ewan leveled a cold, serious glare at Colby. "I mean, why exactly do I need a weapon?"

"Because I have places to go where you can't follow."

"What's that supposed to mean?"

"It means I have to go into fairy country to speak to the powers that be to calm this whole situation down."

Ewan nodded sarcastically, pretending for a moment that this made any sense to him. "You think you can talk those beasts out of wanting to kill me?"

"No. But I might be able to talk the rest of the court out of wanting to kill you."

"What? Why would *they* want to kill me? Didn't they let me go?"

"Yeah," said Colby. "But you killed a fairy."

"I had to!"

"Doesn't matter. You did it. Whatever truce they believed in disappeared the moment you shed fairy blood."

Ewan rose to his feet, his eyes bloodshot and blazing. "That's not fair. I was defending myself."

"Fairies care little for nuance, Ewan. To them you're a problem that won't go away until they bury you. I need to assure them otherwise."

"By telling them you'll bury ten times as many of them?"

"Not exactly."

"Not exactly?"

"No."

Ewan puckered his lips. "Pussy."

"What?"

"It sounds to me like you're pussying out. You're going to *talk* to them? All that grand wizardly power and you're just going to *talk* to them?"

"Yes. I'm going to *talk* with them. They can be reasoned with. Reason is just not what I would call their default setting. But I can get them there."

"And you're going to leave me at my place so you can talk them out of killing me?"

"My place, not yours. Yours is the first place they'll look."

"You sure about that? Last I checked they attacked me in the street outside a club that had advertised my being there. I don't think anyone knows where I live."

"Except your girlfriend," said Colby coldly.

"Well, yeah," said Ewan, not yet acknowledging the truth staring him in the face.

"Who is a fairy," continued Colby.

Ewan calmed down a bit, his eyes softening. He took a step back and then sat down. His voice went up an octave, losing its bravado, gaining sincerity. "Do you really think she's in on it?" he asked.

Colby sighed and shook his head. "I won't know that until I ask her."

"It seemed like she wanted nothing to do with it. I mean, it sure looked that way." Ewan fidgeted while he talked. The rage burning in his gut subsided, now roiling and churning with heartbreak.

"Yeah, but you never know with the fair folk."

"So you're going to see her?" asked Ewan.

"I hope so," said Colby.

"I want to stay in my own apartment. I don't care if she knows where I am. I don't care if they know."

"You'll be safer at my place."

"Will I really? Or does everything in this godforsaken town already know where you live?"

"They . . ." Colby paused. Everything did; everything he was worried about, at least. "*Shit.*"

"That's what I thought."

The hammering stopped and the heat diminished as the furnaces inside dimmed. Mimring stepped out of the workshop, his face charred and blackened with soot. In one hand, he held a long pike—a wooden shaft nearly six feet long with a blade fashioned like a Bowie knife atop it—while his other hand rubbed a greasy rag over the blade to give it a good, final polish. He stood the pike up on its end—towering over him at nearly twice his size—motioning up toward it with a nod of his head.

"This outta do you boys up real good," he said proudly.

Ewan's eyes swelled large in their sockets. "What's it do?" he asked.

"Well, the blade is so sharp that it can take a man's head off and never lose its edge. And there is no magic in the world that can heal a wound it causes—not to a fairy, at least."

"Whoa," said Colby. "You don't mess around. I heard you were good, but—"

"The best," interrupted Mimring. "You heard I was the best."

"I did," said Colby with a nod.

Mimring handed the pike to Ewan, who grasped it with a grin. He stepped back, singing it a bit to test the weight. It felt natural in his hands, as if he were born with it. Politely, he gave an enthusiastic bow to the blacksmith.

"Now," said Mimring, "let's hope for two things. One, that you'll never be needin' to use this thing."

"And two?" asked Colby.

"That I'll never be needin' to call in that favor you owe me." He smiled weakly. Colby understood the gravity of what he was saying. "Now, get the hell off my property. Our business is done here."

Colby motioned to Ewan. Their welcome had officially worn out.

CHAPTER FORTY

THE DJINN WHO CRAWLED
INTO A BOTTLE

Yashar sat in his usual seat, nestled snugly in the arms of a warm buzz as he knocked back whiskey after whiskey, faster even than Old Scraps could pour them. The Cursed and the Damned was packed, unusual for any night other than that of a fairy's death. On the rare occasion one did die, the bar filled early and emptied late, a drunken, rambling wake celebrating their passing before the memories of them faded altogether the next morning.

But this was something else.

Few ever mourned the death of a redcap. Their vile dispositions and lack of *qualities,* redeeming or otherwise, kept them from making many friends. But the death of this redcap was different; this death signified the beginning of a very long day. Everyone knew the tale of Colby Stevens the Child Sorcerer, and how he had freed his young friend from the burden of serving the Tithe. However, few knew, until that night, that this young friend still walked the streets among them. He was not off in the world living out his life; he was here, in their city. And he had killed a fairy.

This death meant a coming retribution. And if fairies were coming for that young man, there was little doubt that Colby Stevens would be standing between them and his friend. Once that happened, all bets were off. The chief reason Colby was allowed to drink in the bar was because it was better to have him as a confidant than to risk offending him. They'd grown to like him, but they had never stopped fearing him.

This night the bar was full not to mourn the passing of a dead fairy, but to mourn the coming loss of their friend Colby Stevens. Either Colby was going to die at the hands of overwhelming odds or he was going to have to do something that would put him at odds with the community once and for all. And for that, they drank all the booze Old Scraps could pour.

And no one was drinking harder than Yashar.

The door squeaked open. The bar became uncomfortably quiet. Yashar didn't bother to look up. It was the moment he'd been dreading all night; it was the moment he'd been dreading for fourteen years. While every wish he granted ended this way, there was still a surprise in the *how* and the *when* of it, and he was about to get a glimpse of both.

"Yashar," said Colby through the thick, awkward hush. "Can I have a word? Outside?"

Yashar nodded. "Yeah, but are you sure you don't want a drink first? Scraps, pour this man a shot of your finest."

Old Scraps shook his head, shrugging. "I don't think he's here to drink, Yashar."

"Well, pour him one anyway. It'll take the edge off."

"Yashar, *outside*."

Yashar stared into the murky brown of the whiskey in the glass in front of him, rolling it back and forth as if there was something floating in it. He refused to look up. "Don't get all master-of-the-lamp with me, young man. That's not how this arrangement works."

"You're drunk."

"You're perceptive."

"I don't think you want to have the conversation we're about to have in front of everyone here."

"No," said Yashar. "If it's a conversation we have to have, it's best we have it outside. There just isn't any whiskey out there."

"Here. Take the bottle," said Old Scraps, offering him half a sloshing bottle of fine brown spirits. "Now take it outside, you two."

Yashar snatched the bottle away from Old Scraps then drunkenly rose to his feet. The djinn staggered across the floor, tripping over imaginary objects, struggling with gravity like a character in a Buster Keaton routine. Friends tried to look away, but sounds of overturned chairs and breaking glass were hard to ignore in the strained silence.

The room let out a collective sigh as the door closed behind them.

Yashar stumbled out into the alley where he uncorked the bottle, taking a long drink from it.

Colby followed closely behind. "When were you going to tell me?"

Yashar finished swallowing a gulp of whiskey and wiped his mouth with the back of his sleeve. "Tell you what?"

"About the curse."

"You knew I was cursed, what kind of question . . ." He trailed off. This was new. "Who told you?"

"Does it matter?" asked Colby.

"No. But somebody *did* tell you?"

"I should have heard it from you," said Colby.

"How? What was I supposed to say?" asked Yashar. "Hey, kid, make a wish. No matter what, it'll turn out shit in the end."

"That's not too far off the mark, actually."

"It's not like that," said Yashar.

"It's exactly like that," said Colby.

"You've seen so much, yet you still understand so little."

"I had a lousy teacher."

Yashar angrily poked Colby in the chest. "You fucking take that back, you little shit."

"I won't. You betrayed me; you sold me out for your own well-being."

"Yeah?" asked Yashar.

"Yeah," said Colby, turning his back on Yashar.

Yashar took another drink from the bottle. "What do you know?"

"Quite a bit."

"No," said Yashar. "I mean about the curse. What do you know?"

"That your wishes are doomed to end badly."

"Right. Did you hear that all my granted wishes end in death?"

Colby spun around, shocked and angry. "No."

"That's because they don't. Not all of them." Yashar swayed a bit, then slumped down on the curb, bottle in his lap. He drunkenly waved Colby over, patting the curb beside him.

"No, not this time."

"Get the fuck over here. I'm drunk, I'm having trouble standing up, and this is something *you need to hear.*"

"I'm not sure that I do," said Colby.

"If you didn't need to hear it, you wouldn't be here. You'd be off getting into a fight with a bunch of fairies over a kid who should have died years ago—"

"Whoa," interrupted Colby. "*Should have* died?"

"Everyone dies, Colby. For some, it is merely what happens at the end of a life well lived. For others, it is their only purpose. Ewan was born to die. It was his destiny. You robbed him of that when you made your wish. And you've spent every day of your life working, in some small way, to push that destiny back a little further. To give him one more miserable day before his fate catches up with him." Yashar patted the cement next to him once more. "Now, sit down and let me tell you a story."

"No," said Colby. "I think I'll stand."

"Let me ask you something. When you made your first wish, what did I do?"

"You granted it."

"Did I?"

"Yeah, you did."

"Did I try to talk you out of it first?"

"Well, you . . ." Colby paused for a moment, thinking back. "I, I think we talked about it."

"*No, that's very dangerous,* I said. *I forbid it,* I said. Those were my words, were they not?"

"I honestly don't remember," said Colby, now struggling to recall the moment exactly.

"Well, I do. I remember telling you no. I remember offering you other things. And I remember you calling me on a promise and making me grant you the very wish you've spent years belly-aching about."

Colby looked down at Yashar, memories tugging at him. Yashar was telling the truth.

"Now, sit down and let me tell you a story." Colby shrugged, nodding, and silently sat down beside Yashar. "Once upon a time there was a young djinn—reckless and greedy, his heart full of wanting. He amassed a great fortune, surrounded himself with beautiful women, and lived the life of a king without bearing the responsibility of one. But he was tricked and one day found himself without his wealth, without his women, and without the life of a king, so he decided to do one good thing for the one person who showed him kindness when he hadn't a penny to offer.

"That's how the world gets you, you know. It rewards you for your wickedness and punishes you for your selflessness. That djinn gave that man everything he wanted, which, in the grand scheme of things, wasn't really a whole hell of a lot. But men can be barbarous when you take something they believe is theirs, and that young man met with a bad end."

"I know this story," said Colby. "And I know it's yours."

"But you don't know the story after, about how that young man's last wish cursed me to always bring ruin upon all those whose wishes I granted. *I wish that all your wishes would end granting all the happiness you've brought unto me,* he said. What the story leaves out is the hours he spent begging for his young wife's life as the soldiers ravaged her. How he swore revenge he would never get. How they dragged them behind their horses before finally having mercy enough to kill them."

"Well, I do now."

"Do you?" asked Yashar. "Do you know about the years I spent wandering in the desert, living out my last days as the last of the living souls who knew me passed on, to leave me starving? How I tried with all my might to make it through the last fortnight without granting a single wish to save my own life? Do you have any idea what it feels like to starve yourself half to death on principle alone? What happens to your mind and your sense of morality when all you can think about is survival and what you would give, what you would do, to keep going?

"I tried. I really intended to go through with it, but it's like holding your breath underwater and trying to drown. At some point your instincts override your own sense of self and you fight and claw your way to the surface without even thinking about it. Even if deep in your heart you don't want to, there you are, swimming and pounding and thrashing as hard and fast as you can for a single breath of air. And then it's done. You've failed. And you have to start over.

"I've gotten to that point a dozen times since then, always sure that *this* was going to be the time it would happen—the time I would finally see death through. But come sunrise of the fourteenth day, I always fail and claw my way to the surface any way I can. Your humanity isn't lost when you do something heinous for your own gain or enjoyment. On the contrary, that's distinctly human; that *is* your humanity. No, you lose your humanity when you can't think of anything *but* doing that thing, because you need to do it to survive. That's when you turn over your soul. I've granted terrible wishes, brought horrible misfortunes upon good people who had nothing to do with my curse, only to save my own life. So I did the only thing I could do."

"You tried to minimize the damage," said Colby, finally understanding.

Yashar put a finger on the tip of his nose, tapping it to signify Colby's insight. "Kids. I chose only to grant wishes to kids."

"Why? If you know it will end badly, why pick on kids?"

"Because they don't ask for anything awful. At least, they never think it's awful. With children, it's always innocent. Martha O'Malley wanted her parents to be rich, never having to work another day of their lives. She was killed by a stray crane swinging from a nearby construction site; they made millions in the settlement. Billy Williamson just wanted a puppy. A German shepherd. And when that puppy ran out into the street, a car broke Billy's back. That dog was as loyal and loving as any kid could ever want. He thanked me time and again for that dog, saying it got him through it all. He didn't know, never wondered what his life would have been like without that dog.

"Jill Matthews just wanted her parents to get back together again. She wanted things back the way they were. What Mommy never told her was how hard Daddy beat her. But she came back, because I made her. And things went back to normal. It lasted three weeks before Daddy cracked Mommy's skull open and she was gone for good. Jill never forgave me and ended up finding a man just like her father.

"I remember all of them. Every wish gone wrong. Everything I've ever done to stay alive. I've forgotten so much of this world; so many memories have become hazy and weak. The good times? They're some of the first to go. But the wishes, I never forget the wishes. Each one of them is burned irrevocably into the back of my mind."

"It's a fate you've earned," said Colby.

"The hell you say."

"You're a vampire. You prey upon the young because they don't know any better. You dress up in the silks and the gold and you put on a hell of a show. But you're a vampire, siphoning off the dreams of children and leaving them empty, dreamless husks."

Yashar's eyes glassed over with tears. He bitterly gritted his teeth, trying to contain himself. "I'm done with it," he said. "All of it. I'm gonna do it this time."

"No you won't," said Colby. "You're not strong enough."

Yashar rose to his feet and waved a belligerent finger. "I am strong enough! I'll do it!"

"Yeah, and when's that gonna happen?" called Colby, still sitting on the curb.

Yashar narrowed his eyes, speaking coldly. "Once the fairies are done with you. Fourteen days after today, I suppose."

Colby shot to his feet. "You son of a—"

"Don't you get pissed at me. This is your mess, not mine. I tried to drag you away from that boy. I tried to keep the truth from you. I tried to talk you out of intervening. This is your sin, Colby Stevens—your mess. You damned yourself the night you stuck your nose in their business, and now your precious little house of cards is collapsing, and you have the stones to come to me about what *I've* done? Sounds more like you haven't come to grips with what *you've* done."

"You're just as guilty as I am. We're both condemned men."

"No," said Yashar. "The difference between you and me is that while we're both condemned, I am intimately familiar with my sins. You, on the other hand, don't think you've sinned at all. But I'll see what I can do to follow you soon after you're gone."

Colby shook his head, stormed off, frustrated, waving his arms wildly. The two had no more to say to each other.

Yashar took a long, gulping swig of the whiskey, killing all but the last few shots of the bottle. He looked down at the remainder solemnly. "Whiskey," he said. "You're my only friend."

"Ain't that the truth," called a voice from behind him.

"If you're here to apologize," said Yashar, "I don't accept."

"Oh, we're not here to apologize," said another voice. "We're here to grant you your final wish." Yashar, now in something of a stupor, slowly turned around to look behind him. His mind was fuzzy, his reactions sluggish. Two redcaps leered at him, fondling an all-too-familiar bottle. While it had no name of its own, Yashar knew it by its inscription and the names of the djinn it had held in the past. He knew the name of every djinn that had died in that bottle. And it was only fitting now that he was going to join them.

"Well, that figures," he said. "What took you so long?"

"Traffic," joked one of the redcaps.

"Not you, asshole," said Yashar. "I was talking to the bottle."

CHAPTER FORTY-ONE

THE PROMISE OF TOMORROW

Ewan sat cross-legged on the floor of his apartment, pike by his side, grease pencil firmly in hand. Furiously, he scribbled over a torn-out sheet of artists' paper—a picture of a little girl. Of Mallaidh. He scribbled and scrawled, trying to scrape away the memory, but it held fast, lingering painfully, just out of reach—an itch he couldn't scratch. The page was a stain of black grease, small patches of white paper peering out beneath it. As he finished, he crumpled the sheet, threw it behind him into a growing pile already three dozen deep, cast out his arm, and tore another from the wall.

Ewan's eyes were growing cold, the pupils swelling, overtaking the color of each iris. His stubble sprouted into whiskers, his skin flush with color, his cheeks rosy above patches of thickening bristle.

A dull throb beat in the back of his skull. He felt feverish, but dry; restless, but fatigued. His mouth felt like it was full of sand, no amount of water slaking his thirst or chasing the leather from his tongue. Something strange paced back and forth in his gut—an ill-tempered beast clawing from inside his rib cage, raking the bars with its talons, pounding to be let loose. Harder and harder, it raked and pounded, begging Ewan to lash out, to strike the nearest thing—to break the world one piece at a time, to slit a throat, any throat, and quench his thirst on the spatter.

There came a knock at the door.

"What's the safe word?" he grumbled loudly, relieved by the distraction.

There was no answer.

"Safe word! What is it?" he called out again, rising to his feet.

"I don't know it," said a quiet voice from behind the door. He recognized it immediately. It was Nora.

He approached the door, his face inches from it. "We don't have anything to say to each other."

"You know that's not true," she said.

"Fine. I don't have anything to say to you."

"You're lying. I'll bet you can't stop thinking of things you can't wait to tell me. Or call me. Or whatever."

Ewan unlatched the door, flinging it open. Mallaidh stood meekly behind it, disguised as Nora. She appeared small, frail, and delicate, swallowed whole by the darkness surrounding her outside. She looked up at him, her eyes welling with tears, lip quivering at the very sight of him. His heart burst. He'd known that this would be tough, but had no idea that his insides would turn to jelly just seeing her. The pacing beast in his belly stayed its wrath, held back a few moments longer.

He swallowed hard. "Don't you dare look like her," he said. "That's not you. That person doesn't exist."

Mallaidh shook off the disguise like a duck would water—everything Nora falling away, replaced by lithe, tender features draped in long blond hair. She nodded. "I'm sorry. I didn't know which one of us you wanted to see."

"Neither," he said drily. The throbbing in his head had stopped, but the bitterness remained.

A swollen tear formed in the corner of her eye before plummeting down her cheek. This time his heart broke completely. He took her up in his arms, wrapping them completely around her, her head nestled squarely against his chest, her arms grappled as tightly around his waist as they could. Any semblance of composure she had hoped to maintain eroded, setting free a torrent of choked sobs. "I'm sorry," she cried. "I'm so sorry."

"Why did you lie to me?" he asked.

She looked up at him, trembling. "I've never lied to you. Never."

"Yes, you did."

"When did I ever tell you that I wasn't a fairy? When did I tell you that we've never met before? When did I tell you some bullshit story about a past that wasn't mine? Everything I told you was true; that you didn't have all the pieces to the puzzle yet speaks only to the fact that these were truths you weren't ready to know. I told you I was the little girl in your pictures. I told you that I would cross time and space to find you. I did cross time and space. And I did find you. And I have loved you, always. And I always will. So when, Ewan, when did I lie to you?"

"When you told me your name was Nora."

"What?"

"You never lied about anything except who you were."

"It's not really a lie if you want it to be true," she said. "And I've never wanted anything to be truer in my life."

"What is that supposed to mean?"

"Nora isn't just what you wanted me to be; she's what I wanted to be. I want nothing more in my life than to be the girl of your dreams."

"You didn't even know me."

"Are you kidding?" she asked, freeing a single hand from his grip and wiping a smear of tears from her cheek. "I've known you all your life. What time I didn't know you, I spent trying to find you, trying to know you again." Mallaidh looked around the apartment, for the first time noticing what a shambles it was. Pictures torn off walls, chairs knocked over, upturned ashtrays spilling filthy gray grit in swaths across dingy carpet. The place was a mess.

Then she noticed the pile, the collection of crumpled, tattered pictures of her, all smeared, scratched, and scribbled to pieces. Some were merely blotches of black, while others were mutations—little girls baring teeth and wicked claws, slobbering foam and blood into the peaceful creeks and ponds beneath them. She reeled; these nightmarish representations painted her far more redcap than Sidhe.

"No!" she cried, pushing away from Ewan, shaking her head. "That's not me! That's not what I am, that's not what we are." She walked over, picking up a particularly brutal scrawl of the little girl gripping a decapitated head, her once virginal smile carved into a raging snarl. "This isn't me." She looked Ewan dead in the eye and repeated herself. "This isn't me."

He stared back coldly, unconvinced. "There's one thing left to ask," he said.

"Anything," said Mallaidh.

"Did you know?" he asked. "That they were coming?"

She shook her head. "No!"

"I looked for you, but you were with them."

"They lured me out. I had no idea what I was walking into."

"Then who is he?"

"Who? Knocks?"

"Yeah, him."

"He's your changeling."

"I don't know what that is supposed to mean."

"You don't remember?"

"It's all fuzzy. And I don't know if I ever knew who he was."

"He's Nixie Knocks, the one they left in your place when they took you away."

"And why does he want to kill me?"

"Because he thinks you killed his mother."

"His mother?" Ewan thought deeply for a second, summoning from the depths a single, powerful memory that washed over him like a tsunami. "He's the boy," he said, his jaw slack. "The night with the goats the size of horses. He's the little boy."

Mallaidh nodded.

"And you were there," he said, pointing at her, memories piecing together like droplets pooling into a puddle.

"You saved my life," she said through a sniffle and a tear-stained smile. She wiped her cheek with the back of her hand once more.

"I did?"

"Yeah. And I fell in love with you right then and there."

Ewan gave Mallaidh a confused look. "Why?"

"It was the way you held me," she said. "The way you've held me ever since." She took Ewan by the hand. "I love you. And I'll do anything for you. *Anything.* Just say the word."

The two stared longingly, passionate confusion brewing between them. "So what now?" he asked.

She stepped forward and stroked his cheek, running her finger back to push his hair over his ear. "Now you kiss me as hard as you can," she said, "and we pretend, for as long as we can, that none of this ever happened—that none of this matters.

That none of it ever mattered. You kiss me and it all goes away."

"What if it doesn't?" he asked.

"Then you kiss me again. And again. And again, until it does."

Ewan looked at Mallaidh with great sadness, shaking his head. "They're never going to stop coming for me, you know that."

"I don't want to believe that."

"But you *know* that, don't you?" he asked. Once again, the tears welled up in her eyes. She nodded, crying, tears streaking down her cheeks, unable to say it aloud. "Then what do you imagine we should do?"

"Run away," she sobbed.

"That's what I did last time. All I did was forget. I don't want to do that again. I don't want to forget. Not now, not you." He looked at the floor, his eyes wandering to the pike beside him. "This time I need to stay and fight."

"No! No, no, no," she protested. "They'll kill you."

"I'm not so sure of that."

"I am. These are creatures that live only to kill—to kill and cause suffering. That's not who you are. That's not who you were meant to be."

"I might be more capable than you give me credit for," he said, mildly offended.

"It's not about how capable you are; it's about how far you are willing to go. These creatures will chase you to the ends of the earth to get what they want. They will kill anyone who gets between you and them. They will hunt you till they draw their last breath. Are you willing to hate that much? Can you chase them for that long?"

"You never know," he answered.

"I do. I've seen what's in your heart."

"So you want me to run?" asked Ewan.

"Not just to run, to run away with *me*," she said. "To L.A. Like we planned."

"But they'll come after us."

"I'll talk to the council. If I tell them we'll leave, never to return, they'll have to grant us passage out. They don't want trouble any more than we do."

"So they're afraid of me?"

Mallaidh shook her head. "Colby. Everyone's afraid of Colby. No one knows what he's going to do. And nobody wants to find out."

"Colby . . . ," he sighed.

"He's our best hope. As long as they're afraid of him, you and I can get out of here."

"What about him?"

"Colby? Ewan, Colby's been taking care of himself since he was eight. He's the last person in this world we need to worry about."

"When do you want to leave?"

Her eyes grew wide and, for the first time since arriving, she smiled. This conversation was really happening; she wasn't dreaming it. "Tonight."

"Then go. Do what you need to do. Buy us some time. If you're not back by dawn . . ."

"If I'm not back by dawn, what?" The ominous sound of that broke apart her smile, crumbling it before him.

He paused. "Just be back by dawn."

She grabbed him tight, kissing him, cradling his head with her hands while ruffling his hair with her fingers. "I love you, Ewan."

"I love you," he whispered back.

She turned and left without saying another word, breezing out the door—which Ewan immediately locked behind her—and disappearing into the night.

Ewan slumped onto the ground, propping his back against the door. She was gone, and with her the soothing presence that had held the beast at bay. His heart was pounding, his head was throbbing, every molecule in his body was thundering to the same, painful rhythm. Everything beat in unison. *Thumthum thumthum thumthum thumthum*. Then came the whispers— soft at first, steadily growing, a white-noise static against the background of his thoughts. He reached up to grab a fistful of his own hair and realized he wasn't wearing his cap. He needed his cap; he was suffocating without it. What at first he had confused with the weakness of his broken heart, in truth was the drying blood of his cap across the room.

There it was, draped over a chair, drying in the midnight air. He wobbled to his feet, his knees buckling, just strong enough to stand him up and stumble him across the room. His fingers swept the chair, snatched the cap off with the sharpened end of a fingernail. Ewan breathed a sigh of relief as he slipped it on, but it proved to be little comfort. Something was wrong. His cap was almost dry, only the tiniest bit of dampness remaining.

He'd only splattered it with blood; he'd never soaked it. His cap was drying out. And that meant he was losing his strength, strength he'd need if Mallaidh didn't return on time. He needed blood. But that meant he needed to kill and Ewan didn't want to kill anybody, not anyone human, at least.

His chest tightened, he swallowed hard, choking on cotton. This had gotten very bad, very quickly. He wouldn't make it to morning. The pike whispered to him from the floor. Ewan gazed at it, his mouth watering like a starving man smelling his first cheeseburger. Meat. The smell of sizzling meat and dripping juices wafting in from outside. He could smell the blood and beating hearts all around him, warm, fresh, waiting to be spilled from their sagging bags of skin.

Now he paced his apartment, clawing at the walls, knocking

over furniture, pounding his fists against his skull. The whispers had become braying voices, shouting angrily what he needed to do. It was only minutes since she had left, but it weighed upon the clock as if had been hours.

There was little choice left. He grabbed a blanket from his bedroom, wrapped it around the pike and slunk out the door into the harsh, dry darkness, chasing the smell into the city. But he couldn't bring himself to kill—not a human being. So he followed memories, scraps and fragments of stories, things said in passing; he followed unfamiliar scents across streets, through backyards, cut across alleys, until he found himself miles from home, standing on the banks of Ladybird Lake, staring out into the dark water.

He stood there, listening to the cicadas chirp along the shore, smelling hints of female flesh swimming out in the lake.

He stripped off his shirt and waited. There came the gentle sound of a *BLUMP* from the water, like a fish jumping out of it for a fly. Ewan knew it was no fish. Then two more. *BLUMP. BLUMP.* Few would have noticed the sounds, but in his sanguine state, his senses were extraordinarily oversensitive. He could hear insects mating, smell Korean food cooking at a restaurant five blocks away, knew with absolute certainty that the sounds he was hearing from the lake were those of women rising from its depths.

The first swam sluggishly toward him, lagging so her sisters could catch up. He caught sight of her taut, naked body, dog-paddling silently on the surface, her hair slicked back with lake water, tangled with sea grass, her large eyes batting at him. She was gorgeous, seraphic, looking as if she posed no threat to him at all. It was, of course, a trap, and he knew it.

Never agree to swim with a beautiful woman, that's what Dithers had always told him. *Dithers. That's where the name came from.* He missed him, and for a moment, he almost forgot his purpose. Then the two others approached, their forms hovering in the dancing reflection of a thousand stars.

"Hey, handsome," one of them called. "You here to get wet?"

"Yes," Ewan answered. "Yes I am."

"Would you like some company?" asked another.

Ewan smiled. "I think I would."

He dropped the blanket, his hand firm around the shaft of the pike. With a speed he had no idea he possessed, he tore forward. The nixies had little time to react, enough only to exchange startled looks. Ewan smiled as he sailed through the air, time standing still, their slowed expressions awash in confusion and horror.

He could taste them already. It wouldn't be much longer now.

CHAPTER FORTY-TWO

EXTRAORDINARY RENDITION

Tell us a story, storyteller," hissed the redcap through gnarly, jagged teeth. His breath smelled like a burning Dumpster, fire and soot passed over swelling rot and rancid produce. Before Yashar could answer, the redcap clenched his fat, clawed fingers into a fist, and splintered his cheekbone with a single blow.

Were he not strapped to a chair held in place by two giddy redcaps, the force of the hit would have toppled him over. Spitting through blood and broken teeth, Yashar looked up, drenched in stoic bravado. "I don't think I have any stories left worth telling," he said. He smiled a bit, attempting a laugh, but once more a plump fist connected with his chin, spun him around as far as the straps would allow. Slowly he turned his head back and, in his best Bruce Willis, said, "I can do this all night."

"We know you can," said the voice in the corner, "so cut the dimestore crap, Bottle Jockey, and tell us what we want to know."

"And just what do you want to know?" asked Yashar.

"Everything," said the voice.

"Everything?"

"Every last little relevant detail. Where they came from, where they might be going, and everyone they might turn to when this gets as bad as it is about to get."

"That's not going to happen." Yashar glimpsed the chalk outline on the floor. It was perfect—a meticulously drawn pentagram sized just right to keep him in, straps or no. They'd even sealed it with matte-finish spray so they wouldn't accidentally scuff it with a misplaced boot. He wasn't going anywhere; he'd have to continue taking hits until the redcaps had each bruised their knuckles to the point of crippling fatigue. That was how he would best them—he had to wait them out. There wasn't a person on this earth who could kill him—at least not one who would—and he couldn't think of a single thing that these cretinous little goblins could do to him to deliver anything beyond the passing shadow of pain.

"Dietrich, get the salt," said the voice.

Except that.

The redcap smiled, his malformed jaw dancing sickly in the breeze of his own breath. Redcaps were loathsome creatures, this one particularly hideous, his large eyes not quite set properly, casting an eerie, lazy-eyed leer over a thrice-broken-and-reset nose. He reached down to a small wooden table beside him, pulled from it an empty, rusted tin cup. Then, pushing aside an animal-skin tablecloth, he pulled from beneath it a wooden bucket of raw, unrefined sea salt. Dipping the cup into the bucket, Dietrich hesitated, giving Yashar one last chance to respond.

"Hmmm?" The redcap shook his head, already knowing the answer. "No."

He needn't empty the entire cup at once, but the little bastard did it anyway. Dietrich didn't just carry a grudge, he bore it on his back with pride and schlepped it like a trophy. Now, at long last, was his chance to unburden himself.

The sea salt sizzled, popping against Yashar's skin, his exposed chest bubbling like smoky bacon. Blisters swelled, erupting, raining fatty pus down into his lap. Yashar let out a cry so loud that it shook the walls, its bass deep enough to rumble a mile away, its treble shrill enough to pierce eardrums.

Knocks sat in the corner, smiling, drinking deep the agony of the man howling desperately before him. He rose from the shadows, delighted in the work of his minion.

"Wait, wait," Yashar begged, but Knocks was already buzzing off the anguish, soaking in the heroin bliss of a junkie high, shouting over the pleas.

"Hit him again!" he cried out in ecstasy. "Hit him again!"

Dietrich plunged the cup back into the bucket. The salt sailed through Yashar, carrying chunks of him with it. The floor was a thick morass of salt and sticky gobs of flesh. Yashar's screams were unbearable now to all but Knocks, redcaps recoiling from the raw power of Yashar's agony. When he howled, he howled an outrage that could level a field of trees, shaking rocks from their moorings—that the walls of the dilapidated warehouse still held at all was a miracle to the redcaps who glanced around to ensure their integrity.

Yashar writhed. He'd never felt such excruciating pain; never seen fluids leak so readily from his chest; never seen meat cleaned off the bones of his own rib cage—but there it was as his own soft tissue melted before him, down onto his stomach, off the side of his leg, onto the floor. This wouldn't kill him; he knew that. But for the first time in his long life he began to think that maybe, just maybe, there were actually things worse than death. Clenching his teeth he looked up, one eye squinting shut, his face boiling off. A gooey drip of his forehead streamed down over his brow. He looked Dietrich dead in the eye. "When I get out of this," he promised, "and I will get out of this, I will tear your arms off and feed them to you one at a time."

Dietrich glanced back at Knocks. Knocks nodded, and Dietrich smiled so wide he revealed hidden teeth even he never knew he had. "Hit him again," crowed Knocks. The cup plunged into the bucket once more. "Then put him back in his bottle and bury him at the bottom of a salt mine. I don't want any of his friends getting any bright ideas."

"Wait!" shouted Yashar. Exhausted, burnt beyond recognition, he shook his head. "I give."

"That's all you got?" Dietrich spat out.

Panting, Yashar nodded, his head wobbling at the end of his neck. "That's all. That's all I got."

Knocks smiled contently. "So you'll tell us a story?"

"Yeah, I'll tell you a fucking story." Yashar once again spat on the floor, losing two teeth with it. "It's not like I was ever going to be remembered as one of the good guys anyway. What do you want to hear?"

"Why don't you begin by telling us where we can find Ewan?"

Yashar sighed deeply.

CHAPTER FORTY-THREE

COLBY AND THE FIVE
STONE COUNCIL

Most noble council," began Colby, his tone humble, his heart heavy, his head bowed, his hands folded in front of him. "I come to you on behalf of my dearest friend."

Before him stood the Five Stone Council, the night air cool and crisp, the forest humming with crickets. Meinrad loomed large and foreboding next to his stone, his cold expression offering no comfort. Coyote leaned lazily against his—one foot propped up against it—grinning proudly, wholly aware that this mess was his doing. King Ruadhri stood rigid and stiff before his stone, glowering at Colby, disgusted. Rhiamon the

Gwyllion, however, smiled wryly, tickled by the knowledge of the havoc playing out at the hands of her redcap thralls.

Finally, at the fifth stone stood the newest member of the council, Ilsa the salgfraulein. In the absence of genuine leadership after the death of Schafer, the redcaps had no worthy representative to take their place on the council. Thus a largely ignored block of seelie had put forth Ilsa to take his place. The most charming and delightful of her kind, even outgracing the noble King Ruadhri, Ilsa was a woman of few burdens and fewer enemies. There was something very genuine about her, as if she were incapable of telling a lie; she was, quite literally, enchanting. The eldest of five sisters, she spoke not only for her kin, but for the woodwives and pixies as well. The Limestone Kingdom was not a place particularly crawling with those of the seelie court, so the few there were put their faith and voice behind Ilsa. And her presence alone offered Colby some comfort.

"We know of whom you speak, lad," said King Ruadhri. "It was not long ago that this council convened and decided upon his fate, a fate you yourself chose to circumvent."

"Yes, sir," said Colby. "I speak of Ewan."

Ruadhri nodded. "And you come to plead for his life once again?"

"Yes, sir."

"Funny," said Ruadhri, "that it is never the boy who pleads his own case, but his friend who presumes to know his will."

"I speak for him, sir."

Meinrad dismissed the statement with a wave. "And yet, this council does not recognize you as possessing such capacity."

Colby gritted his teeth, trying to hide his frustration. "Sir?" he asked.

"Ewan bears a cap, does he not?" asked Ruadhri.

Colby nodded. "He does."

"And he's worn it?"

"He has."

"And you have seen with your own eyes that the transformation has begun?"

Colby swallowed hard. "I have."

Ruadhri offered his hands outward, as if to rest his case. "Then what would make you think that, before this of all courts, a man could speak in the stead of a fairy?"

"Because he is not a fairy," said Colby.

Meinrad shook his head. "You just told us that the transformation has begun, and this is not the first we've heard of it."

"No," said Rhiamon, "it is not. I've heard it myself."

Coyote agreed. "He is a fairy, Colby. You have no place speaking for him here."

"He is not of your world," said Meinrad. "He was never meant for your world. He is of ours, a world of which you are no part, and yet you try to meddle in affairs that are none of your concern."

"They are entirely my concern," Colby retorted.

"Only because you make them so," said Meinrad. "This is neither your council nor your court. You insult us with your presence, and we must ask you to leave."

Colby clenched his fists, his blood slowly boiling from the insult and dismissal. He could lay waste to several of these fairies, powerful though they were, before a single one of them was able to retaliate. But power was one thing; numbers were another. The last thing he wanted was open war with the Limestone Kingdom.

"It appears the boy grows angry," said Rhiamon, delighted by his silent seething.

"It would appear so," said Coyote. "I wouldn't taunt him, though. There are always fairies who would love your place here on the council."

Ruadhri grimaced at Coyote. "Let the boy make his own threats so we might respond in kind."

"Oh, he's too smart for that, Ruadhri," said Coyote, winking at Colby. "He knows we need no display to know what he can do."

"Then perhaps you would like to make his case for him now," offered Ruadhri, "since he is about to be dismissed."

Coyote grinned like a satisfied cat, a mouse firmly between its paws. He pointed out to the tree line. "I believe that is what *she's* here for."

Colby turned as the council leveled their gaze at the diminutive spirit making her way across the field. She stepped into the firelight, at once instantly recognizable. *Mallaidh.*

"I speak for Ewan," she said.

"And why would you do that?" asked Rhiamon.

"Because I love him."

"That's hardly a reason to speak for someone," retorted Rhiamon. "Why, I offer that your perspective is clouded."

Mallaidh shook her head, a single tear rolling down her cheek. "I love him."

Ilsa looked upon Mallaidh with sadness. "Dear girl, I'm afraid you might not be entirely sure what that is."

"I am," said Mallaidh. "It's when your heart hurts so much you'd rather pull it from your chest than lose the one it beats for."

"What do you ask of us, child?" asked Meinrad, his demeanor more delicate than with Colby.

"Safe passage," she said. "Out of the Limestone Kingdom."

"You can leave at any time," said Ruadhri. "You are not bound here."

"Safe passage for myself and for Ewan. And you know that."

"That is much more complicated," said Rhiamon.

"It isn't, actually," said Colby, now furious. "It is quite *un*-complicated."

Ruadhri scowled, his temper barely contained behind the strain in his face. "You have no say here; this is not a matter for you."

"It is, and I will say my piece," Colby said hotly. "It was your fairies who took him from my world, your fairies who robbed him of his humanity, you yourself who put him on the sacrificial stone, and now it is your fairies again who set out to slaughter him for offenses he has not committed. You came into our world, you stole our child, and now you pretend that it is your place to judge his fate. Frankly, you can kiss my fucking ass and taste my fist as I ram it down your cocksucking throat, you uptight son of a bitch."

The wind rose up, rustling the trees as the very earth tensed beneath them. Dreamstuff was abundant out here, like water in the ocean, and Colby could feel it pulse about him with the ebb and flow of his emotions. The eyes of the council showed their alarm, even Ilsa beginning to cast an unfavorable and fearful eye upon him. They were scared, and rightly so; Colby was struggling at the very edge of fury, trying to contain himself. Only Coyote seemed relaxed, almost smiling at the outburst. No one could tell if he was enjoying himself, faking it, or merely aloof and entirely unconcerned.

"I think everyone needs to calm down," said Coyote. "There is no need to tear apart the very fabric of the universe to prove a point. We understand, Colby, you're upset."

"Don't patronize me," said Colby.

"I won't. Just promise me you won't send Schafer some friends."

Colby nodded.

"Passage for Ewan and yourself?" asked Meinrad of Mallaidh. "That's all you ask?"

She nodded.

"She doesn't know what she's asking," said Ruadhri. "He'll be dead in a week."

"She knows exactly what she's asking," said Rhiamon. "She's just not sure why she's asking."

"He killed one of the court," said Ilsa. "Would you have him go free without punishment?"

"It was self-defense," said Mallaidh.

"And how can you be so sure?" asked Ruadhri.

"I was there. They used me to lure him out to kill him."

All eyes fell upon Rhiamon, who shook her head. "I know nothing of this," said the Gwyllion. "They came to me with their story *after* his brutal attack upon them. I'm not so sure the girl is even telling the truth."

"She's telling the truth," said Meinrad. "But someone must pay the price."

Ilsa nodded to Mallaidh. "Would you be willing to suffer punishment in his stead?" she asked of Mallaidh.

Mallaidh looked around nervously, fidgeting with her delicate hands. "What kind of punishment?"

Rhiamon smiled. "The only punishment there is for killing another member of the court. Death."

Mallaidh looked around the council in shock.

"Someone must pay," said Coyote.

Colby looked on in horror.

"Do you love him enough to die in his place?" continued Coyote.

Eyes swimming in tears, expression teetering on the edge of complete breakdown, she nodded very slowly. She looked at the ground, tears spilling upon the dirt. "Yes," she said softly. "I do."

Coyote looked over at Meinrad.

Meinrad nodded. "I vote that we grant passage. For the both of them. What say the rest of the council?"

"Passage," seconded Ilsa. Mallaidh looked up, her eyes alight.

Rhiamon shook her head. "No, I vote passage only for him. She dies or he does."

Ruadhri nodded, extending a hand toward Rhiamon. "I agree with the Gwyllion. Passage must be earned with sacrifice."

Once again, all eyes fell upon Coyote. He nodded, grinning. "Passage. *For both.*"

Mallaidh hopped up and down in place, clapping excitedly. Tears flowed freely, only now streaming out of joy. "Thank you! Thank you, all of you!"

"I'd leave now," said Coyote, "before we change our minds."

There came a sudden rustle from a nearby thicket, and from the darkness stumbled a figure, staggering in the moonlight. With it came panting—pained moans chasing each unsure step. The night shrouded the figure with shadow, only at the last moment revealing her in the torchlight. A nixie, covered in blood, dripping from a gash across her stomach, took her last few steps before them, finally crashing into the dirt, exhausted.

The nixie looked up at Meinrad, extending an outstretched hand. "Please," she said softly. "The boy. The Tithe Child."

"Please what?" demanded Ruadhri, shocked at the appearance of the dying creature.

"Kill him," the nixie pleaded. "As he killed my sisters."

"What?!" cried Colby. "What is this?"

"It would appear your friend has killed again," said Coyote.

"That's impossible, I just left him," said Mallaidh, shaking her head.

"Perhaps the nixie runs far faster than you," said Rhiamon.

The nixie nodded. "It was him," she coughed. "He looked like our boy, only uglier. I would know him anywhere. He dipped his hat in our blood as I ran."

Meinrad looked sadly upon the nixie. "It would seem he has turned completely, and now dips his hat in our blood." He then looked at Mallaidh. "Passage is revoked. The boy must die."

"NO!" cried Mallaidh. "No! No! No!" She glanced around wildly, at once both frightened and furious. Then, without warning, she bolted, running as far and as fast as she could.

Ruadhri was the first to step away from his stone. "I must marshal our forces. Meinrad, grant me the right to raise an army."

Meinrad nodded. "Granted. But raise no more than fifty. Then meet here and you may lead them."

Ruadhri bowed, taking his leave. Rhiamon smiled wickedly, fading into the night. Ilsa immediately took a knee beside the dying nixie, comforting her as her spirit passed, her last breaths drawn with strained moans sounding like squeaking doors in a creaky house. Meinrad sank into the earth, becoming one with it, his presence vanishing from the circle.

Coyote turned—a satisfied smile on his lips—and walked off toward the woods. Colby rushed after him, ready to tear him limb from limb.

"I know what you did," said Colby.

Coyote came to a stop, but did not turn around. "Do you?" he asked. "Do you, *really*?"

"Yes."

"But do you know why?" asked Coyote.

"Because it is your nature."

Coyote smiled, his copper skin rippling with wrinkles. "I see you've traded your youth for wisdom."

"It's easy to spot evil."

Coyote's smile dropped into a look of disappointment, the wrinkles settling sadly upon downturned lips. He turned around. "But not so wise yet as to fully grasp the world around you."

"Wise enough to know why we're both here."

"And why are you here, Colby?"

"To kill you."

"Ah, so it's come to that, has it?" asked Coyote, a glimmer in his eye.

"Yes, it has."

Coyote shook his head. "Perhaps I was too quick to judge your wisdom, confusing it with your swelling pride."

"Give me one good reason I shouldn't kill you."

"Apart from you having to ask for a reason?"

"Yes."

"Because you know people only ask that when they don't intend to kill someone."

Colby narrowed his eyes. "You don't have one."

"Of course I don't. I'm Coyote. You've read the stories, you know my tales. I've died a thousand deaths before and I've a thousand more to die before the end of time. This is a death hardly worth telling. What I've done cannot be undone by killing me, nor will you bring an end to my mischief. You will only reset the cycle anew. Perhaps next time I will be a kinder, gentler Coyote, playing pranks on children and concerning myself with finding delicious stew. Or maybe I will come back vindictive and meddlesome, eager to set nation upon nation while reveling in the bloodbath. You never know. I don't even know who I'll be next time around. I only know who I am now, and what I intend to do. And once you figure that out, then and only then will you know whether there is reason or not to let me live."

"Or maybe," said Colby, "you're just another wily spirit, overinflating his own legend, seeding storytellers with tales of your many past lives in hopes of convincing guys like me that the devil we know is better than the devil we don't, when in truth you have but one life to give and your only defense is to convince us not to take it."

Coyote smirked, beaming with pride. "Now that'd be a trick, wouldn't it? That'd be a trick indeed."

"You're pathetic."

"Do you really think so little of me?" asked Coyote. "Do you honestly believe I did all this because I give a shit about your little friend? About a boy who cheated death only to dangle his feet over the edge every day since, waiting for nothing more than to fulfill his destiny? Dying alone and anonymous in the street? That's what the great Colby Stevens thinks of Coyote? That I spend my time putting bumblebees in jars to watch them fight?"

"Well . . . I . . . ," stammered Colby.

"You do think that of me, don't you?"

"Yes."

"You have much to understand about the nature of man."

"You're no man."

"No," said Coyote. "I am his unflattering reflection." He shook his head. "I have outlived billions of gallons of blood, and you think I somehow delight in the spilling of a few more pints. You see my hand in the affairs of a few mortals and you think that I've but wound them up so I can watch them bounce off one another in the night. Never have you asked yourself why I might do such a thing—to what end this bloodshed might serve. The trouble with human beings is that when examining the actions of others, they always apply their own ethics and point of view, hoping to understand them in the context of what *they* might do and why *they* might do such a thing. When no answer lies in that examination, they always ascribe malice. Malice, you see, is the only thing people understand without explanation. You are born with it and thus come to expect it.

"Do you know the difference between a good man and a great man? A good man looks around at his brothers, sees their ignorance, finds himself horrified by it, and sets out to educate them. A great man instead finds himself elated by realizing that his brothers will never know any better, using it to his advantage to forge an army of the ignorant, fighting to leave the world a better place. Ignorance is the only one truly unstoppable force in this world. And the only difference between a despot and a founding father is that the founding father convinces you that everything he does was your idea to begin with and that he was acting at your behest all along. Yes, people are sheep. Big deal. You need to stop trying to educate the sheep and instead just steer the herd.

"No one wants to admit that they're not smart enough to understand what's going on, so they create such elaborate fictions to convince themselves otherwise. Fairies are the construct of man and bear with them both his arrogance and his ignorance. You look at what I've done and you think this is about tormenting your friend. If I told you now that the blood about to be spilled would change the world as you know it, would you deign to stop it? Would you believe me at all?"

"No, I wouldn't," said Colby.

"Good," said Coyote. "Were you to believe me, you might not do what I need you to do."

"And all this is supposed to stop me from killing you?"

"Who cares if you kill me, Colby?" he said, rolling his eyes. "The machine is sprung. Mallaidh's run off at full speed to save the man she loves, while you've stood here threatening an old man. The events unfolding as we speak can no longer be held at bay, but a moment will come when you will be forced to make a choice about what sort of man you really want to be, and that is where my gamble lies.

"When fate finally comes for you, who will you be, Colby Stevens? *Who will you choose to be?*"

Coyote turned and walked into the thick blanket of brush, disappearing into a tangle of branches, Colby staring, standing still in stunned silence.

"This isn't over between us," called Colby into the dark wood before him.

"Nor would I want it to be," called back Coyote's distant voice.

Colby stared, bewildered, into the night, fully aware that he'd most likely just been conned. But there were worse things than finding yourself fooled by the Trickster himself. Then worse things sprang to mind. *Ewan!*

CHAPTER FORTY-FOUR

Space and Time

Ewan sat naked in the corner of his apartment, his arms tightly wrapped around his knees, covered from head to toe in blood, mud, and lake water. He was high—punch-drunk off the fresh blood soaking through his cap and dripping onto the carpet. Tingles ran along every inch of his body, his mind slowing to a crawl; he was barely lucid, unaware of the world around him. It was like floating through an electric current, each heartbeat tickling his insides like the aftershock spasms of spent love.

He drifted in and out of semiconsciousness, reliving the moment his pike struck home, spilling open the bare chest of that scaly green creature, her gape-jawed expression staring blankly at him, horrified as her innards erupted, spraying across the water—every drop remembered in crisp detail.

He liked it; he liked it a lot.

The knock at the door shook him halfway out of his daze. Something felt familiar. He looked around, saw the scraps of paper on the floor, the grease pencils scattered about, for a moment wondering if the last few hours had even happened at all. *Wasn't I just scribbling something?* he wondered. It felt as if he was drifting in and out of some dream, pieces of time folding in upon themselves and, as he began to wake, the pieces started taking shape again.

Another knock.

He rose to his feet. He saw the puddle on the carpet, felt the muck drip off his limbs; he knew this was no dream. It was taking longer to shake off the fuzzy feeling than he imagined. Slowly he wobbled, faltering, toward the door, barely able to grasp a coherent thought.

Knocks stood outside the door, taking a deep breath. *I shouldn't be doing this.* It was just nerves, but something felt very wrong. For as many years as he had dreamt of strangling the very life out of Ewan, he'd never thought it would be in a late-night ambush; yet here he stood, a sharpened piece of iron in his pocket, disguised as Mallaidh's alter ego, Nora. With the genie in a bottle and Colby distracted by the council, this might be his only opportunity, and any chance to kill Ewan was one worth taking.

Again, he rapped loudly on the door.

There came no answer.

He has to be here, he thought to himself. *Unless the genie lied.*

He rapped again.

Again no answer. *Damnit, a few seconds longer, then it was back to the warehouse for another hour of torturing the genie.*

"Who is it?" grumbled a muffled voice from behind the door.

"It's me," said Knocks. The door unlatched, swung open, the dank smell of stagnant water and body odor wafting out, almost bowling Knocks over. There stood Ewan, covered from head to toe in a moist reddish-brown layer of *god knows what,* naked as the day he was born save for the dripping red cap atop his head. He'd been hunting, and now was only a few nights shy of his transformation.

The very thought of Ewan becoming a redcap infuriated Knocks. For all the years he'd run with the redcaps, wearing a blood-soaked cap of his own, he would never be one of them; he would always be an outsider. A wannabe. All Ewan had to do was to put the cap on once; he probably didn't even want to be one. *Bullshit,* Knocks thought. *Fucking bullshit.* He wanted to stab him right then and there.

"What did I tell you?" Ewan asked gruffly. "I don't want to see her. She doesn't exist."

Knocks snapped back from his wandering thoughts. What was he thinking? Of course Ewan didn't want to see Nora; he knew she wasn't real. Hastily he formed an image of Mallaidh in his mind, running over every specific detail, from the curve of her hips to the cut of her chin. "Sorry," he said, shifting forms in front of him. He crossed his fingers behind his back, hoping that Ewan wouldn't notice any subtle differences.

Ewan motioned him in.

The place was a mess. Knocks wasn't sure what to expect, but somehow had always imagined him living in a nicely furnished, rock-star-like apartment. It's not that he thought him rich, but better than *this.* The carpet, covered in a light coat of scattered cigarette ash, like a fresh dusting of late October snow, stank of whatever it was that dripped off Ewan. This was nothing to envy; it was a tiny little shithole nestled in the armpit of a much larger shithole.

"What have you been doing?" asked Knocks.

"Nothing you'd want to know about," said Ewan, his eyes shifting nervously, as if he had some great secret to hide. He looked sick, like he'd been strung out for days on some illicit back-alley juice cut with cold medicine.

"Are you okay?"

"I am now. What did they tell you?"

Shit. Who? Who was Mallaidh talking to? "They didn't tell me anything," he said, trying to buy a little time, fishing for a hint with which to craft a believable story.

"What do you mean they didn't tell you anything?" Ewan eyed Knocks up and down.

Knocks glanced around for clues, spying a massive wooden pike, its blade smeared in fresh blood, running down and pooling in a stained circle on the floor beneath it. He looked up at Ewan, who was now piecing things together.

Ewan lunged for the pike. Knocks stepped between him and the weapon, pulling a blade from his pocket, sinking it deep into Ewan's exposed side, slipping the flat of it between two ribs.

Ewan screamed, the force of it resonating in Knocks's bones.

Knocks smiled; *finally.* "You hesitated," he gloated.

"It won't happen again," Ewan spat out. He swung, landing a blow that picked Knocks off his feet, throwing him across the room. He was as strong as a redcap now, perhaps stronger. Still rattled by Ewan's blow, Knocks slammed into the wall on the opposite side of the room.

Ewan plucked the dagger from his side, tossing it away, a spray of blood following. Gritting his teeth through the pain, he picked up the pike and charged Knocks, screaming.

Knocks shook his head, trying to clear the cobwebs from it, darting away before he was finished, the pike swinging just inches from his neck. Caught without his knife, without the element of surprise, he had no cards left to play.

I have to get out of here.

He made a break for the door, but Ewan put a stiff leg between his running feet, sending him sprawling, shattering his cheek, putting a solid knot on his forehead.

Ewan was ready to charge again.

Knocks grabbed the doorknob and turned it, flinging the door open.

Ewan brought the pike to bear once more.

Knocks dove out the door, dragging his left arm behind for balance. The blade of the pike whistled through the air, catching Knocks's exposed palm, cutting a gash across it from one side to the other. He winced in pain, losing his footing, crashing head-first into the rickety railing overlooking the fetid pool.

Like a shot, Knocks jumped to his feet, springing toward the stairs. He ran as fast as his feet would carry him, down the industrial cement walkway, silently cursing himself for blowing this so badly, praying for the miracle that would buy him time to get away. *This was all wrong,* he chastised himself; he'd gotten cocky. *I never should have tried this alone.*

His hand burned as if he'd stuck it in fire, the wound stinging like it was full of broken glass; he clenched it into a painful fist, only making it worse. Fingers throbbed, bones ached. The pain spread, setting fire to his arm all the way up to his elbow.

He reached the stairs, racing down them, desperate to reach the bottom.

MALLAIDH RAN ACROSS the parking lot, outrunning phantoms. She wasn't sure how long she had run or how fast; all she knew was that she was finally here. There were less than a hundred steps between her and Ewan; nothing was going to stop her now.

She rounded a corner, bolting up the stairs, first up one flight, then up a second. *One floor left,* she thought to herself. *Space and time.* Once again she had crossed space and time. And then she found herself beside herself, literally, running past a doppelganger bearing her own image.

They both stopped, staring, mouths agape, eyes wide in surprise. Her first instinct was to lay into the duplicate, attacking whoever it was that had stolen her face, but as her muscles tightened to throw a punch, one thought overwhelmed her. *Ewan.* She took off again, this time somehow running faster than before, scrambling up the stairs, down the derelict walkway.

Ewan stepped out from the apartment, bloody and naked, pike at the ready. Mallaidh—the sight of him still standing fluttering her heart with joy—threw her arms open wide. His eyes narrowed, his muscles clenched all at once. She smiled.

Ewan drove the pike straight through her gut.

Her eyes went cold with shock.

"Space . . . and time . . . ," she said softly, struggling for breath.

"What?" asked Ewan, confused.

He looked down at the wound. Mallaidh cupped it with her hands, desperately holding her innards in, blood pouring into them; neither of them gashed.

He looked up at the staircase, saw Knocks, still disguised as Mallaidh, standing in the shadows. Slowly, Knocks stepped smiling out into the light, raising his left hand to show his bloody palm. Ewan gasped.

"No!" he screamed.

Mallaidh toppled into his arms, the two falling slowly together to the ground. Ewan cradled her, his arm around her back, her head in the palm of his hand.

"No, no. No, no, no."

She looked up at him with a weak smile and sad eyes. "I did everything right," she said. "I did it right."

Ewan shook his head. He didn't know what to say.

"I crossed space and time for you," she continued. "I waited and I found you."

"Yes, you did," he said. Tears formed in his eyes, a slow pattern of quiet sobs overtaking him.

Mallaidh looked down at the pike, still standing upright out of her stomach. A small tear trickled down from the corner of her eye. "It was worth it," she said. "It was all worth it." The light began to fade from her eyes.

"No. You can't leave me. I won't let you," said Ewan.

"It's your turn," she said. "To cross space and time. To find me."

"No, don't leave."

"Find me," she said softly. Then she looked down at her small hand, held softly in his, quietly begging, "Don't let go. Don't ever let go."

"I won't," he said.

"I know," she said, smiling one last time. "I know."

Her body went limp in his arms.

KNOCKS LINGERED A moment; he could not have planned it better had he tried. Watching, delighted, as the two collapsed into each other's arms before his very eyes, her blood pouring out into a wide, dark puddle beneath them. Though they whispered to each other, it didn't matter what they were saying; their time was short. While this wouldn't kill Ewan, it would tear his heart clean out of his chest. There was no better way to make him suffer.

It was the greatest moment of Knocks's life. At last, he knew what true happiness was.

But Knocks knew that Ewan wouldn't hold his girlfriend forever, so he made a hasty exit down the stairs, into the empty, lamp-lit parking lot buzzing with bugs circling halogen lights. There was no need to run; Ewan wouldn't be after him for a few minutes still.

Knocks decided to take the long way home, breathing in the night. The taste of the heartbreak was intoxicating, and he relished it, replaying the moment over and over again in his head. The stars were out, the night was dark, a ridge of clouds teetering on the horizon, threatening to sweep in under the sky and soak the city with an angry Texas thunderstorm.

Two redcaps waited for him as he entered the warehouse, shifting back and forth on nervous feet, fidgeting, their caps in their hands. Each seemed about to speak, neither finding the words. Then they noticed blood like a leaking faucet from Knocks's hand, the steady drip pooling beneath him.

"Knocks," said Axel. "Your hand." He grabbed Knocks's arm and examined the wound, peering closely at the symmetrical cut. The redcap turned to his companion. "Get the mistress."

"It's nothing," said Knocks, pretending his face didn't betray otherwise.

"This is no scratch," said Axel. He dabbed a finger to his tongue, probed the wound, rubbing it along exposed muscle. The spit sizzled unnaturally. Knocks jerked his hand back. Axel shook his head. "This is bad."

Rhiamon emerged from the shadows in back. She was middle-aged, but still quite pretty, yet one look at Knocks and she aged ten years. She grabbed his hand, exposing the flat of his palm, spitting in it, mumbling a spell in an ancient dialect far older than recorded history.

Immediately the wound bubbled up, frothing red blood boiling out of his hand. Knocks cried out, falling, writhing on the floor. "Why the fuck did you do that?" he screamed. He arched his back, pounding his bloody fist on the cement.

"I had to know," said Rhiamon. "And now I do."

"Know what?" he asked, his voice cracking through the pain.

"The blade that cut you was cursed, and no magic can close it. You will die a slow and painful death from that wound, but not too slowly as to see morning." Rhiamon waved her hand, the pain in Knocks's hand diminished, the bubbles receding, the ache returning to a dull throb.

Knocks rose to his feet, cradling his hand. "What do I have to do?"

"That wound will never close," she said. "You have to re-place it with one that will."

Knocks knew immediately what she meant. He nodded silently.

Walking with purpose to a nearby pile of rubble, he pulled from it a single broken shaft of wood. From another pile he drew an oily rag, wrapping it around one end of the splintered shaft. Pulling a beaten, scuffed Zippo from his pocket, he lit the rag, handing the torch to Rhiamon.

"Hold this," he said. He knelt down to the ground and picked up a small stick, holding it tightly in his good hand. Then he whistled to the two redcaps. "Dietrich, hold my hand and don't let go. Axel!" He motioned with his eyes to his wrist. "Do it now. Don't let me lose my nerve. And for fuck's sake, don't hit Dietrich."

Dietrich grabbed Knocks's wounded hand, each gripping the other as if they were about to arm wrestle. The two locked gazes, Knocks speaking without looking away.

"Do it now," he said, before placing the stick between his teeth, biting down firmly.

Axel picked up his pike, swinging it a full 180 degrees to

sever Knocks's hand at the wrist. Knocks's scream was muffled slightly by the stick. Dietrich fell backward, the bloody hand refusing to let go. Blood spurted out of the stump.

Knocks lunged forward, jabbing his arm into the flame atop the torch.

He let out another anguished scream, the stick muffling it once more. The damp air filled with the stench of freshly broiled meat, redcaps salivating at their first whiff. Tears ran down Knocks's face, the pain just bearable enough for his anger to keep his stump in the fire. Knocks growled, fighting his better instincts to pull away. It had to cook through to stop the bleeding.

Rhiamon smiled, admiring the needless bravery. She could have healed the stump with a few words and a gob of spit, but *this* was far more entertaining. The years she'd gained worrying about the wound faded away, and she became ever younger the longer Knocks stood screaming before her.

Knocks pulled his arm out from the fire, collapsing on the ground, breathless, his stump steaming, barbecued to a charred, gruesome black. He looked up at Rhiamon.

"Like that?" he asked.

She nodded. "Something like that, yes."

He laughed—almost maniacally—finding something inexplicably funny about it. "You know what?" he said. "It was worth it. I would go through that a hundred times to see what I just saw."

"And what is it that you've seen?"

"The blade that delivered this wound run through the girl he loves."

Rhiamon lost ten more years. "He slew the Leanan Sidhe?"

"He did."

"By his own hand?"

"Both hands."

"Oh, then there is no time to lose."

"What do you mean?" he asked. "Are we moving up the plan?"

"The council has ruled," Rhiamon said through seventeen-year-old lips. "You're allowed to kill him. They're raising a war party now."

Knocks surged to his feet, forgetting the pain. "He's mine!"

"You can have him," she said, "if you're the first to claim his head."

"What the hell changed everyone's mind?"

The mood of the room dimmed, growing cold, grim. Dietrich rose to his feet, finally freeing the hand's grip from his own, wiping the blood off on his trousers. He took his cap off, held it respectfully in his hand. Axel joined him, removing his as well. Rhiamon motioned to the redcaps. "Tell him."

"What's got you two so upset?"

One of them spoke up. "We're not sure we're the right ones to tell you."

"Spit it out," said Knocks.

They shook their heads. "You're not going to like it," said the other.

"You know what?" said Knocks with a laugh. "After the night I've just had and what I've just seen, nothing could bring me down. Go ahead; tell me the genie escaped or that the boy wizard is outside looking for a fight. Nothing can kill my mood."

The two redcaps looked at each other. Without hesitating they each threw out a match of evens-and-odds. The loser grumbled and scuffed his feet.

"Just say it already," said Knocks, losing his patience.

"It's about your mothers," began the redcap.

CHAPTER FORTY-FIVE

ALL HELL

Colby walked solemnly toward Ewan, words failing him. The world was about to come down on their heads—he had to choose between standing beside his murderous friend or throwing him to the fairies to be torn apart before his eyes.

But seeing him now, all he felt was sadness.

Ewan hadn't moved since collapsing with Mallaidh. He held her, lifeless, in his arms, slowly rocking her back and forth, whispering softly as if to try to gently rouse her from a deep sleep. But she would not wake. Finally Ewan looked up at Colby, his eyes red and swollen.

"I didn't mean to," Ewan whimpered. "They made me think . . . they made me . . ."

"I know," said Colby.

"They're coming for me, aren't they?" he asked. "For what I've done?"

Colby nodded. "Yes."

"How many?"

"Most of them."

"Is that a lot?"

"Yes it is."

"How many do you suppose we could kill before they get us?"

Colby's expression hardened, entertaining the thought. "Between you and me?" he asked. "I reckon we could take out a couple dozen. Maybe more."

"I hope you're not just being optimistic."

"I'm not," said Colby.

"Do you have a problem with that?"

"I don't want to kill anyone who doesn't have it coming."

"They all have it coming," said Ewan.

"I don't think—"

"They took her from me, Colby." Ewan looked him dead in the eye. "I never got . . . I never got to show her how much I loved her. This is my chance. I'm gonna kill 'em. I'm gonna kill 'em all. And I'm asking you, will you stand beside me when I do?"

Colby nodded. "I did try talking to them."

"You did," said Ewan.

"And they did pretty much tell me to go fuck myself."

"So what does that mean?"

"It means we're probably going to have to kill them."

Ewan paused for a moment, gazing down at Mallaidh, stroking her cheek with the back of his hand. "You know what's happening to me, don't you?"

"Yes."

"I'm becoming one of them, aren't I?"

"You always were," said Colby. "We just didn't know it."

"But now?"

"You're becoming a redcap."

"I can't . . . I can't live like one of those things. I can't keep killing like this."

"I know," said Colby.

"You realize that this is probably the last chance we're going to have to talk like this, before . . ."

Colby nodded. "Yeah."

Ewan looked up. "If you had it to do over again, I mean, if you could go back, knowing what you know now, would you still do it?"

"Save you? From them?"

"Yeah."

"In a heartbeat."

"Even if you knew it would come to all this?"

"Yes," said Colby. "Even with all this."

Ewan smiled. "I used to get pretty down about having only one good friend. I always looked around at the popular kids with dozens and thought something was wrong with me. Turns out something *was* wrong with me, but one friend was all I really needed." He looked back down at Mallaidh. "What do we do? With her, I mean."

"We send her back to where she belongs."

"How do we do that?"

"Like this." Slowly, Colby knelt beside the two, putting a hand on Mallaidh. He closed his eyes. Mallaidh exploded into a beautiful puff of orchid petals, the sweet smells of summer and a glimmer of sunlight accompanying the off-white remains to the ground.

Ewan's eyes grew wide. He hadn't expected her to be gone so soon.

"Gather together the petals and bury them," said Colby.

"Do you think she would mind if I carried them around with me?" asked Ewan. "Just for tonight?"

"Mind? She spent her whole life looking for you. I think she'll take all the time with you she can get."

"So what now?"

"Now," said Colby, "we go downtown and see what sort of trouble we can get into."

IT WAS AN hour before dawn when the two swaggered into downtown. All was silent, everything bathed in a soft, orange, halogen lamplight glow, the city long since dormant, its bars locked up hours before. On the horizon, a ridge of clouds obscured the western stars, creeping over the sky toward the center of town. There wasn't a soul about; even the angels had fled to their own private roosts, trying to hurry forth the dawn with a steady flow of wine. The two were alone, walking fearlessly toward their fate, neither with a word to say to the other.

Turning a corner they found themselves walking into a thick, knee-high fog. It swirled, thinning into a wispy mist, vanishing completely around their shoulders. From within the mist emerged a dark figure, his face obscured by a large-brimmed hat, under which he smoked a thin, hand-rolled cigarette. Bill the Shadow.

Ewan breathed deeply, his eyes wide, childhood memories nearly causing him to wet his pants. For years, Ewan had suffered nightmares about this man. Now that his memories had returned—Swiss-cheesed though they were—he recognized the lingering shadow for what it was. He'd thought the fighting would begin more dramatically than this, but so be it. Cautiously, he lowered his pike, ready to strike.

"Bill," said Colby.

"Colby," said Bill.

"Good to see you."

"You too."

"Odd night for a walk," said Colby, looking around.

"Yep, I reckon it is. Heard there might be a ruckus. Haven't had me one of those in a while. Thought I might stick around and see what yours looked like."

"You're more than welcome." He motioned to Ewan. "You know Ewan."

"Kid," said Bill, tipping his hat to him.

"Bill," said Ewan, nodding back, uncertain what to make of him.

Colby leaned in toward Bill, speaking softly, "Have you seen Yashar?"

Bill shook his head. "No. No one has."

There came a stiff bark from the fog, accompanied by the dull clicking of claws on concrete. A golden retriever, his fur matted and ruffled, a small, snarling cluricaun straddling its back, appeared. It was Old Scraps. The wily cluricaun smiled, a small, homemade pike—nothing more than a long cast-iron piece of pipe with a butcher knife wedged into it—in his hand. He nodded politely, pledging his support.

"Thought I'd bring a friend," said Bill.

"We could use friends," said Ewan.

"That's the rumor. Way I hear it, Ruadhri's bringing every Sidhe on the plateau, and most of the unseelie court."

"That's a lot, isn't it?" asked Ewan.

"Oh yeah," said Colby, "that's a lot. Especially for the four of us."

"I don't know about that," said Bill. "It depends on how *bad* things are about to get."

That phrase sounded familiar. *Bertrand.* Colby smiled wryly. "Am I on the right side of this?"

"If you weren't," said Bill, "we wouldn't be here."

"Well, then," said Colby with a wry smile, "let's go get some pissed-off angels."

Fat Charlie's Archangel Lounge was only a few blocks away and extraordinarily packed for this time of night. The four stood outside—none of them welcome within—staring into the windows, waiting. After a few moments, Bertrand leaned his head out, and saw them standing there. He nodded to them, then turned around, holding the door open. With a firm whistle, he twirled his fingers in the air, rousing his fellow angels from their stupors.

Out poured eleven drunken fallen angels, each dressed in battered white armor—soiled with age and dinged from a hundred different battles—every one of them carrying a brutal claymore in one hand and a bottle of stiff liquor in the other. Bertrand was the last out the door, a nearly drained bottle of fine Irish whiskey in his hand. "My friends and I heard you might be having something of a rough morning."

Colby nodded. "It sure looks that way. You boys looking for a fight?"

"Shit," said Bertrand, "we're always looking for a fight. Especially against anything that pays the Devil's bill with innocent blood." He turned to his flock. "Boys, drink up. We're gonna kill some fairies." The angels leaned their heads back, raising bottles to their lips, drinking sloppily. Then, in unison, they pulled away their bottles, raising them into the air, sounding a boisterous yawp before smashing them on the pavement with a resounding shatter. Each angel flapped his wings, taking to the sky. Glass ricocheted off the sidewalk, whiskey splashing Rorschach patterns, feathers gently floating to the ground around them.

The night grew suddenly quiet.

Bill cocked his head, listening to the wind. "They're here."

Angels lined the buildings along both sides of the street, perching upon the ledges, swords in hand. Bill took a deep breath before exhaling a thick, sticky fog that swept briskly over the streets, snaking its way into alleys, roiling like a sea just before the storm. He breathed and he breathed until he could breathe no more, coughing out enough dewy murk to obscure several city blocks.

Old Scraps trotted his pup next to Colby and stopped, looking up at him. Colby returned the look in kind. "I like you, kid," said Scraps. "You've got bigger balls than anyone else in this town, that's for sure. I'm proud to have been your bartender."

Colby laughed. "And I, your patron. You need something to drink before we do this?"

Old Scraps grinned. "Are you kidding?" he asked. "I've been drunk for hours. HIYAH!" He spurred his dog off, disappearing into the mist.

KNOCKS MINDLESSLY FIDDLED with the blood-soaked rag tied tightly around his stump, his mind ten minutes ahead of him, in the thick of battle. They had chosen to come up from the lake, traveling alongside the river, outrunning the storm at their heels by mere minutes. Two dozen Sidhe, a handful of redcaps, and a smattering of other creatures slid quietly through the early-morning darkness. Several minutes behind them, a second contingent—nearly twice as large—made their way around the city to outflank anyone who stood with Colby and Ewan.

Knocks hoped the second wave wouldn't need to fight.

They made their way up from the banks, fleetly shuffling from building to building, the air thick and hazy, growing thicker the farther into town they pressed. *Something wasn't right.* Ruadhri sniffed deeply, wetting a finger on his tongue, raising it above his head.

He looked at Knocks, shaking his head slowly. "There shouldn't be fog in this weather," he whispered, "not before the storm."

"Sorcery?" asked Knocks.

Ruadhri nodded. "An ambush." He motioned to his Sidhe, each dressed in dark, loose-fitting clothing, bearing bows and quivers full of cursed arrows. "Fan out," he ordered quietly, "and keep your eyes sharp."

The Sidhe split up, several moving to the opposite side of the street. Two Sidhe moved to take point at the front of the group, walking slowly, soundlessly, straight up the middle along the dotted yellow median line. The fog had grown so thick that the air now buzzed with the humming of power lines overhead. There was no other sound.

There came a light whistling—like air passing through something at high speed—then a heavy thump. A shadow descended through the fog, slamming into one of the front-most Sidhe, picking him up, carrying him away into the mist.

The Sidhe let loose a volley of arrows into the sky.

Quietly they waited, listening as their arrows skittered off buildings or clacked against concrete.

Whistle; thump. The second of the front-most Sidhe vanished.

"Volley and fall back!" ordered Ruadhri. The Sidhe let loose their bowstrings again, this time retreating back toward the lake under the cover of fire.

Angels swooped in from behind, slamming into the Sidhe. Several Sidhe bounced off angelic shields, some knocked to the ground, others carried off, battered against buildings or dropped back onto the street from great heights.

Knocks and Ruadhri exchanged troubled looks. *Angels.*

Ruadhri swung his arm forward, pointing deeper into the city. "Draw your swords," he ordered, "and press on. Charge!"

The Sidhe surged forward, slinging bows over their shoulders, drawing longswords. The redcaps charged after them, vanishing into the morning.

Thunder rumbled overhead, the subtle hiss of rain a few hundred yards off. The storm was almost here; they were losing whatever advantage they had. It was time to abandon the plan and simply go all-out. Knocks reached into his pocket, pulled out his stained, dried cap. It offered him no strength, but it made a point he wanted very much to make. *Knocks belonged,* and if he died this morning, he died a part of something.

Knocks gritted his teeth—the pain in his stump far worse than he'd imagined it would be—letting his rage overtake him. He charged headlong into the city, screaming at the top of his lungs.

COLBY LISTENED INTENTLY, scattered skirmishes erupting less than a block away. The fog was so thick, he couldn't single them out, but he could hear swords unsheathed from their scabbards, the clanking of armor landing, the battle moving from the skies to the streets. He and Ewan held the line, waiting for any fairies who broke through.

"YEEEEEEEAAAAAAHHHHH!" screamed a familiar voice, its sound growing ever closer by the second.

Colby and Ewan both steadied themselves.

Shapes swelled in the fog before Ewan, but the sound grew loudest near Colby. The two traded one last glance.

Two redcaps emerged from the fog, swinging pikes at Ewan.

Ewan raised his own pike, deflecting both blows, the sudden nature of the blitz forcing him to give ground, retreating back toward an alley, bracing himself for another charge.

Colby raised an arm to react, but the screaming reached its apex. He turned in time to see Knocks tackle him, lunging headfirst out of the fog and into his chest.

Colby fell to the ground, the strength of the charge sliding them both ten feet across the pavement, tearing his shirt, scraping several layers of skin off his back. He tried to cry out, but the blow had knocked the wind clean out of him. Knocks wasted no time, pounding Colby's face with his one good fist. The blows felt like a hammer against his cheekbone, each hit simultaneously cracking the back of his skull against the ground.

Colby rolled over, kicking Knocks off, throwing a punch of his own that glanced weakly off Knocks's chin. Knocks swiftly rose to his feet, while Colby struggled to one knee, trying to regain both his footing and senses. He was stunned, wobbling on uneasy legs, unsure of what was going on. Once more, Knocks dove at him, swinging a haymaker across his jaw.

Colby spun around, punch-drunk from the hit, collapsing.

Knocks stood over Colby, fist clenched, ready to hit him again.

From the fog came the sound of scurrying. Old Scraps emerged astride his galloping golden retriever, swinging his makeshift pike, hollering an unintelligible battle cry. The blade slashed Knocks along the backside of his legs, dropping the changeling face-first to the ground. Then, as quickly as he'd appeared, Scraps disappeared, up the block.

Colby pushed himself to his feet, reaching with an outstretched hand toward Knocks. He closed his eyes and tried to feel the dreamstuff swirling within the changeling—hoping to evaporate it—but there was none. Try though he might, he could feel nothing there.

Knocks pushed himself up, rising to his feet, mindful not to exacerbate his new wounds. He smiled, proud of himself. "You can't disbelieve me," he said. "I am not held together by the stuff of dreams or the will of men. I am glued with their hate, conjured from their loss, fueled by their pain. And those are all things I know for a fact that you believe in."

The staticky hiss of rain rolled over the buildings, onto the street. Fat drops slapped the earth, the hiss becoming a roar, drowning out the distant sounds of fighting, scattering the fog, tearing it apart drop by drop. At once everyone was soaked, the streets slick. While the fog was all but chased away, the air was now bleary with rain.

Two Sidhe pushed through the last shreds of fog, emerging on either side of Knocks.

Each raised their bows, leveling their lethal arrows at Colby. Knocks smiled. "Kill him."

Both exploded into a shower of petals—the heavy *POP* of air rushing into the vacuum left behind, taking the place of any final scream they might have had. Colby pulsed with the dreamstuff he had pulled in.

"You might be nothing but hatred, Knocks," said Colby, "but they aren't." He swung both arms out to his sides, letting loose a barrage of eldritch shards—pink glowing dreamstuff hardened into serrated pieces of glass—arcing across the street, homing in on Knocks.

Knocks leapt out of the way, two shards tearing through the flesh of his stomach, another half dozen grazing layers of skin off his arms and legs.

Colby unleashed a bolt of pure kinetic force, striking Knocks square in the chest, blasting him back a full city block.

DIETRICH AND AXEL circled Ewan in opposite directions, their pikes leveled at his heart, both intending to be the first to spear him. Ewan spun about, keeping each redcap in his line of sight.

"Be mindful of his pike," said Dietrich. "Its cut cannot be healed."

"Aye," said Axel.

Ewan swung his pike at each, keeping them at bay, but they circled still. He eyed the two up and down, searching for a weak spot. Both were dressed from head to toe in greasy rags, their stance leaving their squat torsos relatively unexposed. Only Dietrich had anything different about him—an ornate, carved bottle of ancient glass dangling from a leather strap attached to his belt.

Ewan had a pretty good idea what it was.

Ewan swung his pike wildly, giving himself a wide berth. The redcaps stepped back cautiously, keeping pace with Ewan, refusing to give him any ground. Then Ewan dropped low, swinging at Dietrich's midsection. Dietrich arched his back, dodging the blow—missing entirely that the blade wasn't aimed at his flesh, but rather his belt. The pike sliced off the leather strap.

The bottle clinked to the ground, bouncing off the pavement, rolling noisily down the street.

For a moment they gaped wide eyed up the street—each comically looking back and forth at the other like players in a Three Stooges sketch, waiting for the others to react.

Ewan raced after the bottle.

Dietrich lunged for it.

The bottle stopped with a clang against the curb.

The redcap reached for it. Ewan's pike swung down. Dietrich flinched, the blade passing inches from his fingers. The pike connected with the neck of the bottle, shattering it.

Dietrich and Axel stared in stunned silence.

Ewan stepped forward toward the redcaps, his pike at the ready. Behind him, Yashar smoked up from the broken bottleneck, taking form from the head down. He grew eight feet tall, with golden, hairless skin and muscles that looked as if they could bench-press small cars. His arms were folded, his brow furrowed.

"Ewan," Yashar's voice boomed.

"Yeah?" said Ewan over his shoulder, refusing to take his eyes off Dietrich.

"I got this."

Ewan stepped away. "They're all yours." He vanished, running off into the fog.

Yashar unfolded his arms, pointing a single finger at Axel.

Axel shook his head nervously, backing away. "No!" he cried. "It wasn't me. It was him!" He pointed at Dietrich. "It wasn't me!"

"I know," said Yashar. "You get off easy." With a thought, he turned Axel inside out, the redcap's innards splattering on the pavement with a wet slap. Yashar cocked his head at Dietrich.

Dietrich eyed the pile of bone, muscle, and skin that was once his friend and then looked up at the djinn. Sneering, he spat angrily on the ground, cursing him. "Don't keep me waiting," he said. "Just do it."

Yashar flung himself at the redcap, grabbing him by his shirt with one hand, pummeling him mercilessly with the other. His huge fist pounded relentlessly into Dietrich, flesh and bone not slowing the beating for a moment. He picked him up off the ground, throwing him into a nearby brick wall, the redcap's body flopping limp as a rag doll onto the ground below.

Yashar was undeterred. He picked Dietrich up again, heaving him across the street, slamming him into another wall.

Once more Dietrich hit the ground. What few remaining bones of his that weren't completely shattered were merely broken. He tried to push himself up, but the bone in his forearm splintered, puncturing the skin. He cried out.

Yashar slowly marched across the street, picking Dietrich up, throwing him one last time, putting him through a cinder-block wall. Blocks showered inward. Dietrich writhed on the floor, trapped beneath half a dozen blocks. With a single hand, Yashar palmed a cinder block, straddling the redcap.

"You deserve far worse," said Yashar, "but I don't have the time."

The cinder block came down, bursting his head like a melon.

Yashar took a deep breath. His flesh lost its golden sheen, returning to its native olive, terrible scars marring his once smooth skin. He shrank, tufts of thick black hair growing out of his head. Within seconds he was a somewhat disfigured mockery of his old self, brutalized and scarred, but whole.

Colby stood behind him, eyeing the carnage. Yashar could feel him there but didn't turn around.

"Do you still hate me?"

Colby shook his head. "Hate that strong is only worth carrying around with you if you aim to use it to kill a man. Otherwise, what are you keeping it for?"

"And?" asked Yashar.

"I don't intend to kill you."

"I sold you out. I told them where Ewan was."

Colby nodded. "You can't hold your breath underwater forever."

"No, you can't." Yashar stood up and turned around.

Colby scrutinized him; Yashar was intact, but just barely. "Let's go find Ewan."

SEVERAL REDCAPS HUDDLED together behind an imposing stone troll, cautiously moving up the street through an ever-thickening fog, their pikes extended, their faces full of fear. The troll was massive, carved from granite, with eyes of onyx, teeth made of jagged quartz, dragging an uprooted tree for a club, the sound of grinding stone echoing off the buildings around him as he moved. The fog grew thicker still. And it began to whisper awful things.

The redcaps huddled closer, gripped their pikes tighter.

The air grew colder. The world dimmed darker.

"Just do it already," one of the redcaps growled.

The shadow materialized in the darkness. Snatched a redcap by its pike. Vanished into the murk.

The redcap screamed as if his very flesh was being torn from his body.

The troll swung its tree through the blackening mist, striking nothing. It bellowed a shrill, bitter boom that rattled windows, setting off car alarms blocks away.

The screaming stopped. The bellow echoed into the distance, the patter of rain the only nearby sound. White knuckles clasped the two remaining pikes.

A balled-up red knit cap and a pile of rent skin slopped on the pavement before them.

The shadow emerged again, dragging another of the redcaps, hollering, off into the darkness.

The last redcap flailed his pike, slashing repeatedly at the nothing surrounding him on all sides. The troll looked down at him, rockbound jaw dangling, onyx eyes wide with horror.

The redcap grew uneasy, trying to puzzle out what the troll's expression meant. Then he too was tugged away into the brume.

The troll thrashed its tree, smacking the ground around it, its trunk audibly splintering, cracking. It cried out, confused, upset. He was alone and afraid in a dark morass, both hands tightly around his maul.

Then the tree came alive, writhing, gnashing, clawing at the troll. He was wrestling a snake by its tail, fangs sinking into his stony flesh, breaking off chunks, spraying gravel.

The troll tossed away the tree, cracking it in half against the corner of a nearby building.

Bill the Shadow stepped from the fog, staring silently at the troll.

The troll took one step back, rearing up, his arms stretched wide, ready to swat Bill between his hands.

Bill slowly, politely, removed his hat, the shadows receding from his face. The troll stood in place, terrified by what he saw, eyes unable to break from Bill's gaze.

Breathing deep, Bill sucked the soul right out of his body, out through the troll's mouth, into his own. The spirit held fast, howling, phantasmal hands clinging tight. But the pull was too great, Bill swallowing the troll whole, leaving its lifeless stone husk to shatter, instantly breaking apart into ten thousand tiny pieces.

Bill looked at the carnage around him—blood and skin and stone—smiled wryly, and slowly returned his hat to his head before vanishing once more into the mists.

Old Scraps tore wildly through the streets atop Gossamer. Though the golden retriever was clearly spooked by the chaos surrounding him, he obeyed unwaveringly. Gossamer was a family dog—a good dog, Gossamer had assured Scraps—that had gotten out through a hole in the fence chasing something he'd never smelled before. He lost his way and couldn't remember his route home, so he walked the streets, hungry, for days until Old Scraps had found him. Old Scraps offered him a deal: if Gossamer would let Scraps ride him, he would show him the way home.

So the two worked in tandem, riding up and down the sidewalks, slicing the hamstrings of any Sidhe they neared. Gossamer was fast, but tired, and it would be hours before Old Scraps sobered up. Both hoped that everything would be over soon.

From the looks of it, it was.

The Sidhe had fallen back, rallying together, unleashing flight after flight of arrows into the sky. The angels had taken to the ground, but weren't as quick or lithe as the Sidhe who attacked them from afar, slicing chunks out of the weak spots in their armor. Though determined, the angels were being battered into weariness, a few dropping from too many cursed arrows, a few more dropping from too much whiskey.

Bertrand still stood, his sword dripping, his armor sprayed

with a light coating of fairy blood. A redcap charged him from behind the Sidhe ranks, his pike low, his speed incredible. The angel sidestepped, putting his sword through the chest of the creature, severing its upper body from its lower. One half of the redcap hit the ground a second after the other.

Before he could celebrate, Bertrand caught an arrow in the eye, falling to the ground, desperately trying to pull it out. The Sidhe raced to put their swords into him.

Old Scraps spurred Gossamer on, the two charging as fast as they could toward the gathering remains of the Sidhe, hoping to buy Bertrand time to get to his feet.

"One more pass, Goss," said Old Scraps, "and then we're going home to sleep this off."

The arrows missed Gossamer entirely, several catching Scraps directly in the chest. His rosy cheeks and nose went white. Gossamer sprinted around the corner of a building, finally coming to a stop. The wily old cluricaun looked down at the three arrows sticking out of him, swearing. He couldn't feel them, but he knew it was bad. His head felt fuzzy, the world tipping slightly on its side. Slowly he slid off Gossamer, slamming into the pavement. Everything grew blurry.

If I survive this, he thought, *I am going to wake up with the worst hangover of all time.* And then he died.

Gossamer sniffed him, nuzzling him with his nose, trying to rouse him. He barked sharply. Then he barked again, nuzzling him once more. Old Scraps wouldn't wake up. *Bark! Bark bark!* No response.

Gossamer licked the cluricaun's face, but still he would not wake. The dog lay down in the rain-soaked street beside him, letting out a deep sigh. *Now he would never find his way home.*

KNOCKS STAGGERED TO his feet, massaging his chest, wheezing for breath. Colby hadn't just knocked the wind out of him, he'd bruised his lungs, broken a rib. There was very little time left. The second wave of fairies would swarm over the town shortly, making easy work of the remaining angels. He needed to find Ewan before then, before someone else robbed him of the pleasure.

And then he appeared.

Ewan walked slowly, determined, toward the changeling, his pike held firmly in his hand.

Knocks smiled. *This is happening. It's really happening.*

Ewan stopped ten steps short of Knocks, propping the pike up heroically next to him. The two locked gazes. Neither man blinked.

Ewan drew breath to speak, but Knocks shook his head, waving a finger.

"I know," said Knocks. "I know. Let's not spoil this with bullshit. The time for talk is over."

The two stared at each other. Their muscles tensed, jaws clenched. Anger swelled in their guts. Ewan was the first to move, with Knocks charging him the hair of a second later.

Ewan swung his pike. Knocks ducked, the blade barely missing him.

Knocks threw an uppercut, catching Ewan directly under the chin. Ewan reeled backward, stunned. He recovered, swinging his pike wildly, trying to buy himself a little more time to clear his head.

Knocks sidestepped another swing, jabbing at Ewan, missing by inches.

Ewan kneed Knocks in the stomach, doubling him over, punched him clean in the back of the head.

Knocks reached up, grabbing the pike, punching Ewan repeatedly with his bloody stump; it hurt like hell, Knocks gritting through it, hitting him over and over—the rag beginning to swell, soaked with blood.

Ewan tried to protect his face, struggling with both hands to keep his grip of the pike. Writhing, he tried to avoid the blows, but Knocks kept landing them.

Knocks let go of the pike, and reached up, snatching the cap right off Ewan's head.

Ewan swung again, but he was too close, connecting with only the shaft, not the blade. Weakened without his cap, Ewan let go with one hand, swiping for it, missing.

Knocks tossed the cap behind him, then reached for the pike, wresting it out of Ewan's grip. He swung the blunt end into Ewan's gut, doubling him over, then, bringing the blunt end upward again, smashed him in the face.

Ewan was knocked upright. He staggered back a step, fuzzy from the hit.

The pike swung one last time, this time crossing Ewan's stomach, cutting deep into the flesh, tearing through his innards.

Ewan's jaw dropped, both hands clutching the wound. He fell to his knees, then backward, knocking his skull on the street, trapping his own feet beneath him.

Knocks held aloft his bloody-rag-wrapped stump, pointing at Ewan's stomach. "Try cutting that off to save your life." He threw down the pike as if he was spiking a football, then held both arms out to his sides. "I did it," he said, giggling. "I fucking did it. You're fucking dead." He danced around a little. "I just killed you. What are you going to do about it, Ewan? Huh?"

Ewan gurgled, leaning up, reaching a single arm out to Knocks. It was over, but he wasn't ready to concede. He rolled onto his side—one arm trying to hold in his insides while the other tried to push him to his feet. His arm gave way and he tumbled face-first onto the pavement, spilling organs into the street.

Knocks stood over him, smiling. "Look me in the face," he said. "You look death in the face and you accept it. I want to see you accept it." Ewan pushed himself up again and stumbled forward on his knees, trying now to crawl away. With a light kick, Knocks toppled him over.

Ewan lay on his back like an upended turtle, staring unblinking into the rain as the life drained from him. The sounds around him dulled; he knew Knocks was talking, but he couldn't make out anything other than the staccato of rain spattering beside his ears.

It was over.

YASHAR WIPED HIS bloody fists off. The downpour was strong and steady now, the roar of the storm drowning out all but a few distant clangs. Angels and Sidhe littered the sidewalks. Blood ran pink in the swelling rainwater. Only two angels still stood, busy holding their ground, about to be overrun by the half dozen remaining Sidhe.

In the street between them, Knocks and Ewan wrestled with a pike.

Colby screamed as the pike sliced open Ewan's stomach.

He wanted to run, but his legs wouldn't let him.

Ewan collapsed. Colby had failed.

"Motherfucker!" Colby yelled, his voice drowned out by the rain. He watched as Knocks danced around, taunting Ewan. His stomach dropped, his throat went dry. Hands became balled fists digging fingernails into flesh; teeth gritted against one another, grinding away small flakes of enamel.

Colby could feel the veil between worlds thinning, a cold, dark presence rumbling on the other side, begging to be unleashed. A voice in the back of his head demanded to be let out. The door was locked; he had but to twist the knob. *Let us in. Let us do it,* it whispered. The fabric was growing thinner by the moment. There was enough dreamstuff flowing through him to do it. Then he recognized the voice.

It was the master of the hunt.

No, he thought. *Not this way.*

Colby let loose a torrent of energy, bolts cascading across the street with whatever dreamstuff he could muster.

Knocks swept the pike in front of him, deflecting the bolts away harmlessly, as they exploded like fireworks, showering sparks across the pavement. The changeling smiled wickedly, small fragments of the energy still hopping and popping around in the puddles beneath him. There seemed nothing Colby could do to hurt him.

"Try it again, Colby. I'm sure you'll hit me eventually."

Colby reached out toward Knocks, yanking away the pike with an unseen force. It sailed past Colby, embedding itself in a brick wall behind him. Knocks stared wide eyed at the pike, smiling.

"Maybe I should have kept my mouth shut."

"Don't worry, I'll shut it for you."

Let us in. Let us do it, the voice whispered again.

Knocks laughed. "Just come here and hit me like a fucking man."

Colby ran at Knocks, fists clenched, swinging wildly.

Knocks stepped out of the way effortlessly, knocking Colby onto the ground with a single awkward kick. "Come on," he said. Colby scrambled to get to his feet, but Knocks kicked him square in the gut. "You're such a fucking pussy."

Let us in.

Knocks leapt on Colby's back, rabbit-punching him with his one good hand.

Colby bucked, tossing Knocks to the ground. The two quickly scuttled away from each other, pushing themselves to their feet.

Colby's head throbbed. His knees ached. His hands were scraped and bleeding.

Then the two ran at each other again, trading blows. The first few hits were a flurry of jabs, but the two soon settled into a groove of hitting each other, punch for punch, one after the other.

Colby swung with a haymaker, loosening Knocks's jaw.

Knocks swung at Colby, bloodying his nose.

Colby swung at Knocks. Knocks swung at Colby. Colby swung at Knocks. Knocks swung at Colby.

It had become an endurance contest, each man trying simply to outlast the other. Neither had the strength to carry on much longer. Colby swung at Knocks. Knocks swung at Colby.

Colby swung, staggering forward, exhausted. He fell to his knees.

Colby looked past Knocks, saw Ewan bleeding, crawling in the street. His frustration and rage began to bubble over.

Knocks stepped back, shaking his head with a queer little grin. "You've got nothing. You can't fight me, Colby. What are you gonna do?"

Let. Us. In.

"Something."

In that moment, he decided to let her in.

Colby closed his eyes, rewove the fabric of reality, shredding a piece of the veil, building from it a bridge between earth and Hell. The clouds rumbled their disapproval, belching out indigo streaks, lighting the world purple for three solid seconds. Everything shook and when the rumble of thunder faded, the shaking continued. The earth groaned wearily and spat out Hell.

The Wild Hunt roared out, a dozen riders strong.

Twelve massive black goats—their manes thick, shaggy, their horns long, gnarled, razor sharp—galloping ferociously toward the dying melee, a pack of howling hellhounds at their heels. Thunder now rose from the earth to the skies. Atop the lead steed was Tiffany Thatcher, more bone than flesh now, her sockets empty of eyes, replaced by the glowing embers of a hateful Hell. A few scraps of flayed, parchmentlike skin clung desperately to her jowls and rib cage, a few chunks of desiccated muscle refusing to yet break away from the bone.

Beside her, mounted on a goat of his own, was Jared Thatcher, a sad, lonely expression on his face. With them rode redcaps and nixies and the tattered remains of a single Bendith Y Mamau. Twelve creatures of Hell with hate in their eyes, bearing down on six battered Sidhe and a pair of angels.

Yashar ran to Colby. Though he couldn't yet see them, he knew what this was. "What have you done?"

"Ended this," said Colby.

"They'll kill us all, you know."

"No. We have a deal. I know what they want now. And he's standing right there." He pointed to Knocks.

The two remaining angels helped Bertrand to his feet. Bertrand turned, looking at Colby, a broken arrow sticking out of one eye. He shook his head sadly. Then the angels took to the sky, carrying Bertrand away with them like a banner fluttering in the wind. Only the Sidhe and Knocks remained in the street now, staring toward the approaching rumble.

The Sidhe scattered and the hunt split up to run them down. Few got far before axes cleft them in two, clawed hands grabbing them by their hair, dragging them through the streets. Ruadhri ran, blindly firing arrows over his shoulder, looking for some sort of cover. As he rounded a corner, he saw two beasts bearing down on him. Then he turned to see two more coming from behind.

The clawed hands each grabbed a chunk or a limb before Ruadhri was torn completely apart, his head carried off by one rider, his torso by another.

Knocks looked down at Ewan, taking a deep, relaxed breath. "You don't want to kill me yourself?"

"No," said Colby. "You've damned yourself. *They're* here for you now."

Knocks looked up at Colby, smiling. He could hear the thundering hooves rumbling toward him. The ground shook, the heavens wept. For Knocks, it was all so perfect. "I was born in the rain, you know. On a morning a lot like this."

"Enjoy dying in it, you son of a bitch," said Colby, backing away, giving the hunt a wide berth.

Knocks nodded, looking up at the sky. "The legacy of a storm is not in the measure of its rainfall or the sound of its thunder, it is in the devastation it leaves behind. I've had a good run." He cast his arms out wide, smiling broadly at Colby. "I wonder if my hand will be waiting for me in Hell." He turned his head, staring at the oncoming stampede, thinking about the last lesson his mother ever taught him.

The front-most hoof of Tiffany Thatcher's goat tore a hole in his head, splattering his brains across the pavement, each remaining hoof trampling his torso in half. The Wild Hunt roared past Colby without giving him a look, each carrying off a piece of Knocks with it. Once they all had passed, there wasn't a spot of Knocks left in this world to remember him by—not so much as a single drop of his blood staining the pavement.

The riders continued on, but their hounds came to a stop, raising their heads into the air, letting out a soul-chilling howl, turning and racing off to catch up with their masters once more. And as quickly as they had entered this world, the hunt was gone, closing the gate behind them, leaving only the waning rumble of rolling thunder to signal their departure.

Colby kneeled down beside Ewan, the red puddle beneath him grown wide, thinned by the rain. There was little life left to leak out of him. Ewan stared up at the sky, unable to focus his eyes on anything.

"Ewan," said Colby, putting his hand on his shoulder.

"You can't see me," said Ewan with a weak smile.

"Yes I can," said Colby.

"No you can't. I'm invisible."

"You're not invisi . . . ," he said, then the memory caught up with him. Tears trickled down Colby's face. Beneath him, Ewan died.

Colby could feel the swift tendrils of Hell closing in. Cold. Black. Angry.

"You can't have him," he said. Then he put a second hand on Ewan, evaporating every last bit of dreamstuff, sending it off into the city. No flower petals dropped to the ground; no smell lingered in the air; only his cap remained, staining the rainwater around it. "Go find her."

Colby looked up, the streets swollen with fairies, approaching cautiously.

He turned to Yashar. "You've been awfully quiet."

"There's little left to say."

"After a thousand cursed wishes, I guess you get used to this sort of thing, huh?"

"No," said Yashar. "You never get used to it."

"Nor should you," said Bertrand, flapping above them. He looked down upon Colby with a bitter sadness. "You unleashed Hell. You shouldn't have done that."

"We were losing," said Colby. "I had to do something."

"No," Bertrand said. "We weren't losing. We *lost*. Hell got everything it wanted today. What did you get?"

"Wait, I was just doing what you said was right."

"You were damning yourself?"

"Yeah, for all the right reasons."

"That may be," said Bertrand. "But that doesn't make us friends, compadre. The truly damned have few friends, especially among the angels. I may understand why you did it, but we're done, you and I." Bertrand raised a hand, delicately examining the shaft sticking out of his eye. He shook his head, disappointed. "You were on the right side of this for so long."

Flapping his wings harder, he flew off, drifting drunkenly into the rain.

Slowly the fairies closed in.

Colby looked up. "What?" he asked loudly of them. "What do you want?"

Amassed before him was a full half of the Limestone Kingdom, Sidhe and salgfraulein, pixie and troll. Overseeing them was the remainder of the Five Stone Council, Meinrad taking the lead.

Colby clenched his fists.

"There will be no need for that," said Meinrad, his voice deep and booming.

"Not if you turn around and leave, there won't."

"This fight is over," Meinrad continued. "The boy is dead and all offense ended. There is no more need for bloodshed."

"So why are you here?" asked Colby.

Meinrad stepped close to Colby, looming over him. "You are henceforth banned from the Limestone Kingdom. All rights of safe travel are revoked. You have until noon to gather your things and make your way out of Austin." He poked a rocky, moss-covered finger into Colby's chest. "There needed to be only one death today. You should not have interfered."

Colby nodded, the last pieces of his heart breaking. "I'm sorry." He turned, taking a step to walk slowly home.

Then he stopped.

And he turned.

"No," he said, his eyes cold, bristling with anger. "The time for me to respect the will of the fairies ended with the death of my friend."

Colby raised his arm and evaporated Meinrad where he stood.

The energy released was massive, the resulting boom echoing for miles, shattering windows, spraying limestone and leaves everywhere within a thirty-foot radius—debris embedding into surrounding walls but bouncing harmlessly off Colby, who bore neither a scratch nor a speck of dust despite his proximity to the explosion.

Colby walked slowly toward the fairies.

Once more he raised his arm, this time pointing a stiff finger at the crowd, fairy after fairy exploding into a burst of flowers and smells. The mob panicked, fanning out like a bursting dandelion.

While others scattered, Rhiamon stood still, unafraid. "What do you think you're doing?"

"I'm taking back what's mine," said Colby.

"What do you think makes this place yours?"

Colby paused for a moment, allowing the fairies a moment to take cover. "You just did; you and your ilk. I'm done playing with you; I'm done kowtowing to you. If I am to be damned, then let me be damned with purpose. Austin is off-limits. No fairy may walk here. You may have the plateau, but Austin belongs to man.

"And the Tithe—the Tithe as you know it is done. For every child taken to pay it, I will take two of yours. I will come at night and snatch your young from their cradles and I will scatter their essence to the wind. From this day forward you pay your Devil's due with your own blood—or I will see to it that the price doubles. Now, go and find yourself a new king."

The scampering stopped, fairies standing silent in the face of Colby's decree.

Colby looked around. "How many more of you need to die before you get the picture? Get. Out. Of. *My*. City."

The fairies exchanged troubled looks and, with mouths agape, began their slow, wordless retreat from Austin. Coyote smiled at Colby, winking, before making his way with the rest of them.

Rhiamon looked old, older than anyone had ever seen her. She nodded emotionlessly. "As you wish," she said. Then she turned, taking her leave with the rest of the court.

And with that, the city emptied, its magic slowly walking out with its head held low.

CHAPTER FORTY-SIX

WHERE WE ALL,
AT LAST, BELONG

Yashar stood behind the ramshackle bar top, drying glasses with a fresh rag. The Cursed and the Damned was open, but empty, much of the city's fairy population evacuating in the wake of Colby's murderous rampage. The stories grew, as did the legend, and by the time Yashar had heard tell about what he'd seen with his own eyes, they hardly seemed to be about the same morning.

The door opened, Yashar holding his breath, half hoping it was Colby walking through—for better or worse. Instead it was worse. Much worse.

Coyote.

The old man grinned, poking his head in playfully. "Truce?"

Yashar sighed deeply. "What the hell are you doing here?"

"I heard this place was under new management and I wanted to check out the specials."

"Someone had to keep the place going. For Scraps."

"Probably," said Coyote through a squint. "Though I can't imagine the wine selection being as good."

Yashar shook his head. "The man had a gift. What can I get you?"

Coyote walked in, closing the door behind him. "A few minutes of your time."

"That, it would seem, we won't run out of for a while."

"And, uh"—Coyote looked both ways, whispering—"did Scraps leave around any of that really, really good bourbon?"

Yashar smiled broadly, pulling a weathered old bottle from under the bar. "That he did."

"Line 'em up."

Yashar set down two glasses and poured three fingers in each. "So why'd you do it? Really, I mean."

"Do what?"

Yashar scowled.

"You want the truth?"

"Unvarnished," said Yashar.

"Nobody likes the truth."

"I want the truth."

Coyote nodded soberly, sipping his whiskey. "Most people can't read the writing on the wall even when it's screamed at them. They hate the truth. The truth makes them angry. The truth is heartbreak and poverty and unhappy endings. They believe there is power in numbers, no matter how dumb the numbers. They believe in one true love. They believe that living well pays off in the end. They believe in the magic of childhood. The truth is, we're all alone, even when surrounded. The truth is that someone's *one true love* ended up a thirty-euro whore in an Amsterdam brothel. The truth is that people die old, unrewarded and unloved. The truth is, children get hit by cars and don't come home. So you have to lie. They like lies. It helps them cope with the truth. And if you lie just right, you can get them to do what they have to do to find their truth."

"So, you lie."

"When it doesn't pay to tell the truth. You told Colby the truth when he asked for his wish, but it took *me* to show it to him. *You* showed him the world, but *I* showed him how the world really worked."

"And what did you get out of it?"

"Colby Stevens. It started out about ending the Tithe, but what I got was Colby Stevens. With the blood of a few I made him the man who would protect many. You're too close to him. You can't see his destiny, can you? What he could become, given the right poking and prodding? You helped make a great man. But he needed to do this first."

Yashar slammed back the bourbon, pouring himself another three fingers of it. "To watch his friend die? To become a killer?"

"A killer, pfff." He shook his head, sipping his drink. "I am life's hard lesson, Yashar. The source of man's humility. Colby needed to learn something, the fairies needed to learn something, those two kids needed to learn something. Everyone had a lesson waiting, and they learned it with blood. Sometimes that's how it goes. People learn from failure and tragedy, not success."

"Well, if you're the source of man's humility, what does that make me?"

Coyote winked from behind his glass. "His road to hell, paved with good intentions."

Deflated, Yashar quickly finished his drink and immediately poured himself his third.

Coyote continued. "You know better than anyone that nothing lasts. Nothing good. Nothing bad. Everything lives. Everything dies. Sometimes cities just fall into the sea. It's not a tragedy, that's just the way it is. People look around them and see the world and say *this is how the world is supposed to be.* Then they fight to keep it that way. They believe that this is what was intended—whether by design or cosmic accident— and that everything exists in a tenuous balance that must be preserved. But the balance is bullshit. The only thing constant in this world is the speed at which things change. Rain falls, waters rise, shorelines erode. What is one day magnificent sea-side property in ancient Greece is the next resting thirty feet below the surface. Islands rise from the sea and continents crack and part ways forever. What was once a verdant forest teeming with life is now resting one thousand feet beneath a sheet of ice in Antarctica; what was once a glorious church now rests at the bottom of a dammed-up lake in Kansas. The job of nature is to march on and keep things going; ours is to look around, appre-ciate it, and wonder *what's next?*"

"Not everything dies," said Yashar.

"Everything. One day even you."

"And you?"

Coyote nodded, a wistful, sad look in his eye. "Even me. Coyotes are not long for this earth. Within a century man will have wiped out every beast that walks that poses any sort of threat to him. One day my people will be gone and there will be no more need for me. Then I'll get to see if there is some great reward for the burden I've borne. Perhaps I will see my friends Mammoth, Dodo, and Saber Tooth again. I miss them.

"The mortals live lives so short that they hail us as timeless beings; after a while we begin to believe it. I look at you and see someone weighed down by the thought of living forever and think, *Oh, he's just a baby. He has no idea what eternity even is.* I surely don't. But I know how long fifteen hundred years can feel."

"Why are you telling me this?"

"Because your story isn't over. You've much more yet to do and none of it involves being cooped up in a bar, serving drinks to shadows. Colby has a long road ahead and he needs a guide."

"I thought you said I was the road to hell."

Coyote nodded. "I didn't say he'd like where he was going." The two shared a moment of quiet understanding, each sipping his bourbon. "You know the kids' funerals are tomorrow."

Yashar nodded. "Yeah. I do."

"And you know Colby's going to need you there."

"He doesn't want to see me right now."

"No, he doesn't. But he needs to."

CHAPTER FORTY-SEVEN

ON GHOSTS AND THINGS OF THE PAST

An essay by Dr. Thaddeus Ray, Ph.D., from his book *The Everything You Cannot See*

There are no such things as ghosts. Every place has a memory. Just as a rock may carry a scar from a scratch, so too can a field of energy. When powerful enough energies or emotions affect a field, it can warp or distort those of the surrounding area for years, even decades. If, however, those scars are fueled by dreamstuff, especially the dreamstuff of the thing that caused that scar, the result is a shadow.

This shadow is nothing more than energy reflected through warped space. It is a hologram. It can interact with other energy fields around it, but it does not think or feel. Shadows cannot be reasoned with or express themselves in any way outside of the emotions that created them. If they were born of malice, they will be cruel. If they were born of love, they will be joyful. While they can share the information stored on the scar, they cannot collect anything new or possess any memory outside of that which made them.

Haunted houses are often the result of space warped by emotion over time. Sometimes this can occur from sudden, massive damage, like a traumatic event or even a particularly joyful one, but more often than not it occurs naturally, like water eroding rock to form a riverbed. The energy left behind will often express itself by passing through the cracks and fissures in the field. Scars found in particularly dreamstuff-rich areas will often see more activity as additional energy flows through them, keeping a shadow active far longer than it ordinarily might be.

But ghosts as untethered souls unable to find rest? They don't exist. The Devil catches every crumb that spills off Heaven's plate.

CHAPTER FORTY-EIGHT

Two in a Field

The sonorous melancholy of the fairy dirge carried for miles through the woods. Even as far away as Colby and Yashar stood from the singing, the tinkling of instruments and the magic of the voices still resonated. They were in the Limestone Kingdom, standing just outside the field where Colby, Ewan, and Mallaidh had once played—just beyond the point where once they had escaped a pack of redcaps. The whole of the kingdom had gathered to say good-bye to the dozens of fairies they'd lost. Colby, Yashar, and the golden retriever Gossamer stood together to say good-bye to just two.

A pair of gray stone monuments, each one carved in the likeness of his friends, stood overlooking two small dirt mounds, beneath which lay the scant remains of Mallaidh and Ewan, a handful of flower petals under one, and a dried red cap under the other.

"Is this how I'll end up?" asked Colby, breaking a long, strained silence.

"Only if you keep making enemies," replied Yashar.

"No, I mean . . ."

"I know what you mean," said Yashar, "and I don't know. I'm not sure death would be the worst thing that could happen to you. People shun you, the fairies are scared to death of you, and even the fucking angels can't stand you anymore. The worst thing that could happen to you now is to be cursed with my life—a long one, filled with monstrous deeds that go wrong no matter how well intentioned."

"The sum of a man isn't the things he's done, it is the world he leaves behind."

"What?"

"It's something Bertrand said. One day, no matter what, you and I will both be dust and dreamstuff, and the total of our lives won't be the things we did to survive, but the things we did to change the world.

"You've spent a millennium tethered to the dreams of children and watched as those dreams grew up to face reality. In your cowardly way of playing it safe, you never offered anyone a wish that could truly change the world, and thus you've always had to sit by and watch as that unchanged world weighed down upon your dreamers, crushing them. While it's true that children rarely want anything messy, they also never want anything but that which they want for themselves. It's no wonder you hate the world you live in; you've spent the entirety of your existence feeding its most childish urges." Colby looked Yashar in the eye. "Maybe it's time you wished a little bigger."

"What are you saying?" asked Yashar.

"If we're going to be monsters, let us be monsters of purpose. Let's do something. *Something real.*"

Yashar shrugged. "Like your thing with the Tithe?"

"Exactly like that. If these things are going to fear me, let's make it count."

The two looked out into the field, tall grass waving in the wind. Two young figures emerged from the dark.

Yashar looked at Colby.

"I know they're not real," said Colby.

"Come back, Colby," shouted one of the figures, waving an arm in the air. "Come play with us!"

"Yeah, Colby," said the other. "Come and play!"

"That doesn't change anything, though, does it?" asked Yashar. "You still want to go."

"I'm not that kid anymore."

"But you're happy to see them."

"It's not really them."

Yashar looked at him incredulously. "What are you talking about? That *is* them."

"No, it's a reflection."

"A reflection of *their* energy. Energy you sent out into the wild. They just wanted to find each other and they did. You did that. This just happened to be the place their energy ran to. Don't discount that."

Colby nodded, lost in the moment. "No one chooses where or when they'll find perfection, but I want to believe everyone finds it at least once. I guess this was theirs."

"Where's yours?" asked Yashar.

"I'll know it when I find it."

"That sounds oddly hopeful."

"I've gotta believe in something. This is as good a thing as any, I suppose." Colby reached into a battered backpack, pulling from it a worn-out, faded, sweat-stained old bear. He smiled, gently placing Mr. Bearston on the ground atop Ewan's grave. Then he raised an arm to the two figures in the field and waved.

"Bye, Colby!" the two shouted.

One figure leaned in to kiss the other on the cheek, running off into the tall grass to play. The remaining figure smiled at Colby and then followed the other, vanishing into the field.

Colby looked at Yashar, nodding. "You know your job's not done yet, right?"

"Which one?"

"My wish," said Colby. "I haven't seen everything yet."

"No, you really haven't."

Colby whistled. "Come on, Gossamer. Let's go home."

Epilogue

Once upon a time there were three young fairies, a Green Man, a Lutin, and a Sidhe. One day they found themselves playing in the woods. The young Green Man ran ahead and came to a tree line at the edge of the forest. The Lutin and Sidhe ran swiftly behind him, yelling for him to stop.

"Don't step out of the woods!" yelled the Lutin.

"Why not?" asked the Green Man, about to set foot beyond the trees.

"Because past those trees is Austin," said the Sidhe.

"What's Austin?" asked the Green Man.

"Austin is where the Colbyman lives," said the Sidhe.

"Yeah," agreed the Lutin.

"What's a Colbyman?" asked the Green Man.

The Lutin and the Sidhe looked at each other and laughed. "You don't know what the Colbyman is?"

The Green Man shook his head. "No."

"He's the taker of fairy children," said the Lutin.

The Sidhe nodded. "He sneaks into your camp at night and steals fairy children out of their cradles, two at a time. Always two at a time. And any fairy who steps outside of the Limestone Kingdom and into Austin gets turned into flowers."

"Flowers?" asked the Green Man. "That's stupid."

"No, it's true," said the Lutin. "He points at you and turns you to flowers. And you never turn back. My mom saw it with her own eyes."

The Green Man didn't believe a word of it. "There's no monster called the Colbyman and there's no such place as Austin."

"There is!" said both the Sidhe and Lutin at once.

"Come on," said the Sidhe. "Let's go back to camp."

"Are you scared?" asked the Green Man.

"No," said the Sidhe, lying.

"I think you're scared," said the Green Man.

"Uh-uh!" shouted the Sidhe.

The Green Man put both hands on his hips and smiled. "Then I dare you to cross the tree line."

"Let's just go back home," said the Lutin.

"No," said the Green Man. "I dare you to go into Austin."

"Well, I double-dare *you* to go into Austin," said the Sidhe.

The Green Man stopped smiling.

"You have to accept a double dare," said the Sidhe. "Or else."

The Green Man swallowed hard. "Okay," he said. "I'll go. I don't believe he exists." The Green Man turned back around and took two steps toward the tree line, standing right on the edge. He hovered a foot over the other side. And just as he was about to put his foot down, something grabbed his arm.

The Green Man jumped, startled. He screamed.

When he looked back, he saw Coyote holding his arm.

"Don't make fun of me, Coyote!" the Green Man demanded. "I'm about to go to Austin."

"I wouldn't do that if I were you," said Coyote.

"You believe in him too?" asked the Green Man.

Coyote nodded. "Believe in him? I've seen him."

"I told you!" said the Lutin.

"You three run along now. You shouldn't be playing this close to Austin."

"Yes, Coyote," said the children in unison. Then they all ran off back to camp, none of them admitting how scared they really were.

Coyote turned, looking out over the outskirts of the city. Then he looked back at the scared children. And he laughed and he laughed and he laughed, enjoying the best joke that the great trickster had ever played.

Turn the page for an early look at the

next Colby Stevens novel from C. Robert Cargill,

Queen of the Dark Things

out in early 2014!

CHAPTER ONE

SHADOWS OF THE *BATAVIA*

October 2, 1629.

Jeronimus Cornelisz didn't believe in the devil, but the devil sure as hell believed in him.

How he, an Apothecary by trade, found himself working as an under-merchant aboard the *Batavia* in the first place was something he cared not to discuss. It was a tale of woe involving a dead child, bankruptcy and the jailing of a close confidant whose radical ideas had taken root in a few too many prominent hearts. But he did talk. A lot.

He was of fair complexion, with dark hair and darker eyes that, coupled with his charisma, made it hard to break loose of his gaze. So when he talked, you listened, whether you cared for what he had to say or not.

"God does not mock us," he said, staring off into the crystal-blue sheen of the sea. The sun was high, the sand warm across the top of his feet as he and six of his fellow sailors shuffled across the beach. The seabirds cawed in the air around him, the waves lapping the shore. It was as beautiful a day as ever there was. He nodded, squinting in the sun. "He smiles upon us. Loves us. Wants us to be happy. He demands not servitude, but experience. Gifts us with urges. Rewards us with pleasure. Satisfaction. Wholeness. Why is it that a man feels no ecstasy when he prays? There, on his knees, in congress with his maker, he feels nothing but what he pretends to. But a man on his knees, in congress with a woman, feels more alive than ever. Every inch of his body sizzles with joy, and when he explodes, he becomes one with the whole. In that moment, and only that moment, a man knows absolute peace, free of wont, free of fear.

"All the things that bring us ecstasy are banned, held captive by the new Pharisees. They put their pope on a throne of gold and silver and let him rework both history and the word that was passed down to us through their lips. And the lips of those before them. And of those before *them*. And the longer the word of God stays on earth, the longer it is corrupted to justify the illusion. Make no mistake. They hold hostage everything we hold dear to maintain their own control of it. Even the pope has his whores." He turned to look at his burly shipmate, shuffling close behind him in the sand. "Have you ever fucked a whore proper, son?" he asked him.

"What?" asked the man, looking up from the ground.

"A whore, son. A whore. Have you ever dropped a few guilders in the cup of one after dropping a few in her box?"

The man grunted, nodding, as if it was a stupid question. He was a sailor. Of course he'd been with his fair share of whores.

"When she shined your knob, who did it hurt? No one. That's the Lord's work. Pleasure for one, rent and food for another. Why would he condemn us to hell for that? The Pharisees tell us that a roll with a lady is all it takes to burn forever in a lake of fire. But if the Lord has a plan for us, really has a plan for us all, why would he plan for us to go to hell? To burn. To suffer. What God would do that? Not one that loves us. One who loves us has created an afterlife, a place where we are free from pain, free from suffering, and only know the orgiastic joy of blissful wholeness."

"So you're saying there ain't no Hell?" asked another sailor, following a little farther back.

"I'm saying that not only is there no Hell, but no Devil. He's a ghost story meant to keep the finer things in life under lock and key in our Captain's, our captor's, bedchamber. God wants only for us to do what makes us happy. He sorts out the rest."

The second sailor spoke up again, this time leaning closer. "You're saying it's okay to kill?"

"Why wouldn't it be? Killing someone only sends them to the great reward, right? And taking from someone only encourages them to take for themselves. Have you ever looked closely at the Ten Commandments?"

A third sailor spoke up. "There are no ten commandments south of the equator. Every sailor knows that." He laughed, though no one laughed with him.

"But do you *know* them?" asked Jeronimus of the third sailor, unfazed.

"I know them," said the sailor soberly. "By heart."

"We all do. But have you ever thought about them? The man in charge goes up a mountain and comes back down with ten rules that keep him and his rich friends rich and in charge. Do not steal, do not murder, obey your elders, do not covet their wives—of which they had many—do not speak ill of the Lord that passed down these laws nor dare to question or speak for him, worship no other god who might make other laws. These aren't rules to keep us free, they are rules telling you to know your place and take only what the rich deign to give to you. These are not the laws of God, they are the laws of man designed only to rule over other men. God wants us to be happy. God wants us to take what we want. God wants us to rule for ourselves. The only way to truly be free is to free yourself of your own conscience."

"That's easy to say now," said the soldier farthest in back, "but let's see what say you in a few moments' time."

Jeronimus smiled wide, his teeth speckled with bird guts, several chipped or missing from a few beatings too many. "Aye," he said. "More to the point, in a few moments' time, we'll see just how right I am after all."

The seven looked out together over the island—a flat, mile-wide coral sand wasteland, no more than three feet above sea level, devoid of bush or tree, surrounded in whole by the Indian

Ocean; its only markers three shoddy wooden gallows, constructed from the skeleton of the *Batavia*, which itself was wrecked and battered to pieces by the tide a scant half mile away. Beside the closest gallows was a barrel, and beside that a box on which sat Wiebbe Hayes, captain of the guard, his chin held high, a sly, proud smile on his lips, hammer and chisel in his hands. Behind him stood Fleet Commander Francisco Palsaert—a boorish, sweaty gnome of an East India Trading Company man who rubbed his fat little fingers together, grinning like a child molester.

"Cornelisz," he said. "You're up."

Jeronimus knelt before the barrel, placing his left hand atop it, eyes cold and expressionless. "I'll be back for these later," he said to Hayes.

Hayes nodded, placing the chisel squarely on Jeronimus's wrist. "Jeronimus Cornelisz, you have been tried and convicted of mutiny, complicit in the deaths of 120 souls. Your guilt is not in doubt. Have you anything to say before your sentence is carried out?"

"Yes. Had fortune favored me just a little more, it would be your hand up on this barrel, Hayes. Not mine."

Hayes nodded knowingly. "Though I doubt you would have granted me the courtesy of the barrel."

Jeronimus flashed the hint of a smile, concealing it as quickly as it came. "You're probably
right."

Hayes brought the hammer down.

Jeronimus neither winced nor cried out as the
chisel severed his hand from his arm; he didn't
even blink. He simply stared into the soldier's
eyes as he removed his gushing stump from the
barrel, placing his right hand directly atop the
dismembered left.

"Remove the hand," ordered Palsaert.

"No," said Jeronimus flatly. "They're a set.
They stay together."

The hammer came down again, separating the
second hand; Jeronimus once again made nary a
sound.

A soldier grabbed him by his armpits, hoisting
him back to his feet, and then led him to the gallows, where a crudely assembled ladder awaited
him. Jeronimus climbed up, step by step, the
ladder creaking beneath him, bowing his head for
the executioner to slip the noose around his neck.
Palsaert stepped forward, boisterously offering a
morsel of civility. "May God have mercy on your
soul," he said.

Jeronimus looked up, smiling, blood spurting from two dismembered stumps. "He already
has."

The executioner kicked the ladder out from under him. The mutineer dropped less than a yard; not quite far enough to kill him, just far enough to tighten the rope. There he spun, slowly choking, head swelling up like a cherry tomato, his toes stretching, scraping barely, cruelly, at the sand inches beneath his heel.

Then, one by one, Hayes took the right hand of each of the remaining sailors before they were led to their own noose, to spin and choke slowly in the sun. Each spat a curse at Jeronimus before their own ladder was kicked out from under them, and while no one would ever speak or write of it in their accounts, many thought to themselves that day that they saw Jeronimus smile each time they did, even as the life was slowly choking out of him.

And once the last man had been hanged and the life finally drained from his body, Palsaert, Hayes and the remaining soldiers each made their way to the boats one by one, leaving the conspirators behind to rot where they died.

On the shore, sitting in a boat of their own, Wouter Looes and Jan Pelgrom de Bye waited in chains, their hands cuffed to their feet. Looes was a grizzled sea dog covered in scars, a willing mutineer and right hand to Jeronimus; Pelgrom was a thin, blond, eighteen-year-old cabin boy who had only committed one murder—and that under duress. While each of the other mutineers had lied about their involvement or intent in the mutiny, these two fell upon their knees before the seaside court and begged its mercy. Palsaert granted it; though the extent of his mercy was questionable.

"You see the fate you escaped?" asked Palsaert of his captives.

Both men nodded silently.

"Let those images fester, gentlemen. For while your fate is in your hands, know that no manner of death could be as awful as that." He turned to Hayes. "Unshackle them." As Hayes did, Palsaert raised a stiff arm to the horizon and continued to speak. "Eighty odd kilometers from here is a land filled with monsters and savages. No civilized man has settled it. Maybe you'll make it; maybe you won't. Your lives are your own now. The only thing I promise you is that if I ever see your faces again, I will have you hanged before the sun sets on that day. Good-bye, gentlemen. May God have mercy on your souls."

He motioned to Hayes, who gave the boat a good, swift kick into the water. Looes and Pelgrom immediately set to rowing, knowing that what little food and water Palsaert's meager mercy had granted them would be gone before they saw anything resembling land. It would only take minutes for their small craft to vanish into the horizon and their names into legend.

And once they were gone, Palsaert gave the order and the last remnants of the crew of the *Batavia* set back out for Java, never to set eyes on these islands again.

The handless shadows hung long in the noonday sun, lifeless as their bodies, slightly twitching, swaying in the breeze. Slowly, as the boats sailed away, the shadows' twitches became more pronounced. And then they became movements. And the movements became dancing. And finally the shadows wrestled away from their bodies, loosed from the moorings of their mortal shells, free to roam and stand up on their own, no longer bound to the flat of the ground. They stood up, square faced, boxy and malformed, racing for the nearest pools of shadow before the sun could strike them down.

They hid in the dark of the barrel and of the rocks and of the shadows of the posts that held up the gallows. There they waited, watching as their old bodies swayed shadowless, birds swarming to pick them apart, tearing out their innards, pecking out their eyes. And once the day had run its course and the sun had sunk slowly behind the sea, and the boats had all sailed far, far away, the shadows crept out into the night, looking for their hands. But they were nowhere to be found, having been carried off hours before by the birds.

Disappointed, with the moon rising on the water, the shadows turned into crows—their feathers formed from darkness, their eyes a shiny black—flapping off beneath the stars toward an island thousands of miles away. Java.

Ariaen Jacobsz was strong. He'd endured torture, threats and all manner of inquiry. And as a captain and skipper of the *Batavia,* it would take more than the accusations of known mutineers, murderers and thieves to have him executed. The company needed him to confess. It was the last privilege his station would afford him. Jacobsz would never give them the satisfaction. No matter how guilty he truly was.

His cell was small and windowless, stuffy with the sweat of tropical air and body odor. No torches were lit this low beneath the castle, the dungeon always as black as night could get, even when the sun was highest in the sky. It was a miserable hole deep in the earth, but it was a damn sight better than hanging handless in the sands of an island with no name.

"Jaaaaacobszzzz," said a whisper outside his cell, waking him from a shallow sleep.

"Keep it quiet out there," he called out to his fellow cell mates farther down the hall. "I'm trying to sleep."

"Jaaaaacobszzzz."

"What is it?"

"We had a deal," said a voice from behind him. Jacobsz turned around, looking for its source. "What?" Then he heard shuffling from all sides. He wasn't alone, but as dark as it was, he couldn't make anyone, or anything, out. "Who is it?"

"Yourrrrrrr crewwwwwwww."

Hands grabbed him from the darkness, clawing his flesh, dragging him backward, choking him. Then, in unison, they upheaved him into air, and he felt the dry, chaffing burn of a rope coiling tightly around his neck.

"No! Not like this!" he cried. "Not like this!"

"Exactly like this," said Jeronimus, now a misshapen shadow of what he was. "Take his hand, boys! And spare him the courtesy of a barrel."

The next morning his jailers would find him hanged from the ceiling, his right hand severed and missing. The cell was locked when they found it and the guards swore that no one had come or left in the night. No report was made and since Jacobsz had no kin anyway, no one was ever notified about the mysterious death. And with so many of the conspirators spread out, already serving on new ships or condemned to different prisons in the region, no one took notice of just how many times this manner of death would repeat itself for an untold number of the mutineers of the *Batavia*.